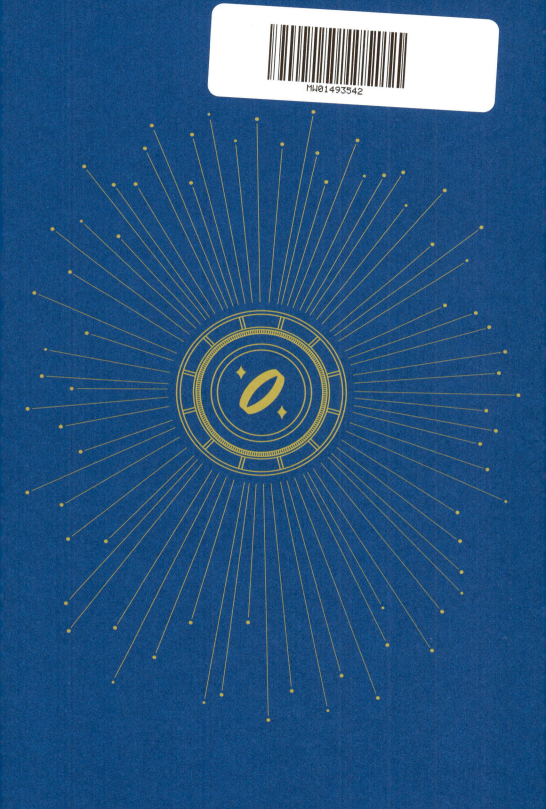

A VOW IN VENGEANCE

A VOW IN VENGEANCE

JACLYN RODRIGUEZ

SLOWBURN
A **zando** IMPRINT

NEW YORK

For every reader who was born from fire, burned too brightly, or refused to be contained.

You deserve the world. So take it. It's yours.

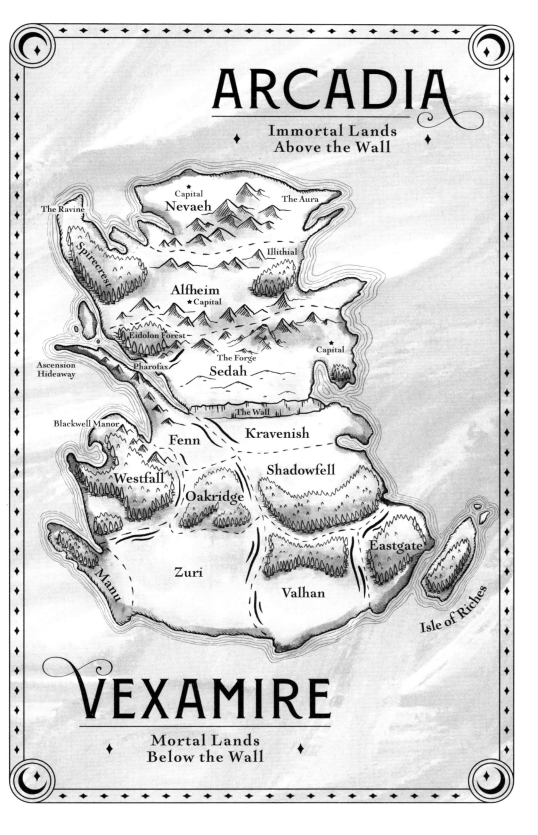

Major Arcana Powers

ARCANA	POWER
THE FOOL	*Fearlessness*
THE MAGICIAN	*Transfiguration*
THE HIGH PRIESTESS	*Mind Reading*
THE EMPRESS	*Healing*
THE EMPEROR	*Telekinesis*
THE HIEROPHANT	*Memory Walking*
THE LOVERS	*Persuasion*
THE CHARIOT	*Speed*
STRENGTH	*Strength*
THE HERMIT	*Invisibility*
WHEEL OF FORTUNE	*Luck*
JUSTICE	*Agility*
THE HANGED MAN	*Time Control*
DEATH	*Shadows*
TEMPERANCE	*Temper Others' Powers*
THE DEVIL	*Illusions*
THE TOWER	*Lightning*
THE STAR	*Warps Light*
THE MOON	*Shapeshifting*
THE SUN	*Plasma*
JUDGMENT	*Control Over Living and Dead*
THE WORLD	*All*

Dear Mortal,

A Vow in Vengeance is a heart-pounding, adult romantasy set in a college based off tarot card magic. It features elements that some readers may be sensitive to, including attempted sexual assault, nonconsensual kissing and touching, on-page suicide of an unnamed character, slavery, death, grief and loss, alcohol consumption and drug use, diaspora, forced assimilation, graphic language, violence, and explicit consensual sexual content detailed on the page. For readers sensitive to these subject matters, I hope I've handled these elements with care.

Prepare to claim your tarot . . .

Prologue

SIX YEARS AGO

RUNE DIDN'T WANT TO freeze to death in some shitty run-down cabin. She was bundled so tightly in a mound of blankets she could barely move, the air as brittle as her breaths, the unnatural cold rattling her lungs too violently for a fourteen-year-old unused to freezing temperatures. Her mother muttered to herself as she tracked a path across the wooden floors, flitting from one window to the next, looking for any signs of life. There was nothing but a blizzard beyond the frosted windowpanes, the floorboards at their feet so frozen they burned to the touch.

But they couldn't risk a fire. The patrols would know someone was home, and they should've left for the Selection with the rest of their village three days before. As newcomers, they just had to pray their absence would go unnoticed.

The immortals had already taken Rune's father the year before, when she was thirteen.

And her twin brother when she was six.

No more.

Rune ran a thumb along a broken toy of a king, the last remnant she had of her brother. Her mother had buried the rest of his belongings and hadn't been whole since he was ripped from her arms. And from her father, Rune had only the small bone pendant attached to a necklace she'd never taken off. It was carved like a fishhook, could even be used as one, something he'd learned from his own parents. But he was stolen from her before he ever passed the lesson on. Her thumb traced its curves again and again, as if winding that path would bring him back.

Rune coughed lightly, wrapping the blankets more tightly around herself, missing the warmth of the Isle of Riches more than ever. Her mother shot her a look, reminding her to be silent. Sometimes it felt as if every time her mother looked at her, she only saw the twin that was missing.

Then a knock sounded at the door, stopping Rune's heart and silencing her breaths.

It could only be immortals patrolling the area. *Druids.*

Terror flooded her veins. She didn't fully know what the punishment was for not taking part in the Selection. Anyone caught was never heard from again. They'd be killed or taken, and in the end, she wasn't sure which was worse.

Rune's mother crossed to her, shoving a supply bag into her arms full of her tinctures and tonics; she'd always had a talent for creating remedies for colds and salves for wounds. Rune tried to stop the tears from spilling over as her mother kissed her forehead—just once—then pushed away from her as if she couldn't bear Rune's skin on hers a moment longer and pointed toward the small, hollowed crawl space beneath the floorboards.

"The druids are the worst of the three kinds," her mother had told her earlier that day. "They have the most deadly magic."

But even if they could sense someone in the house, they wouldn't be able to tell how *many* people would be inside. Something her mother was relying on.

Rune shook her head. She didn't want to hide—this was all she had left. The door pounded, rattling.

Druid magic wouldn't allow them to enter a human dwelling without permission first, a piece of protection left over from the Great War. But they could still break down the door. Which meant they had precious minutes . . . less.

Rune, her mom mouthed. It was a plea, her lower lip trembling as though she couldn't bear to do this. They'd been strained for so long that this one betrayal of emotion broke Rune. She nodded, moving as quietly as she could, vision blurred with tears, and slipped into the hiding place.

Her mother cupped her cheek as she crawled inside, wiping a tear away before placing her forehead against hers, and leaned in closely to Rune's ear to repeat an old phrase from the War, one she liked to say often in the quiet nights when the absence of their family was the loudest. Her breath tickled Rune's ear.

"They may steal my freedom, my love, my very breath, but so long as I do not fear them, they hold no power over me."

"They hold no power over me," Rune repeated quietly, her voice shaking.

That knock on the door became more insistent. Her mother nodded and stood tall, proudly in their tiny, one-room cottage as if she were crowned and draped in gilt instead of worn, patched clothing.

Already hating herself, Rune pulled the boards back into place over her head, staring up through the joints where the wood didn't lie flush. The wooden planks nailed over the door groaned. Rune clenched her jaw, tears freezing on her cheeks.

"Open the door!" a voice growled.

The crawl space led outside. She should go but she was frozen in fear—

The front door crashed open. Rune struggled to look through the slats. A shadow fell over the space. She peered through the slats, trying to silence her breathing, and saw . . . wings. Enormous wings darkened the doorway, the sunlight behind them leeching all their other features. The floorboards creaked loudly, and Rune resisted the urge to close her eyes.

"No need to make a mess of my home." Her mother's voice was firm. "You've found me, so I'll come willingly."

No, no, no please.

There was a light tread on the ground as her mother moved quietly past their towering forms out the door. Rune held her breath.

"Should we check the house for others? Leave a post on her door?" a guard asked.

"Burn it down," another growled. "Sends a better message."

"There's no need—no!" Her mother's protests were drowned in the rush of flames.

Fire licked across the floors with unnatural speed, devouring everything in sight, curdling books and furniture to molten ash. The heat was growing as Rune backed away in terror as thick black smoke coiled in clouds, crowding the small space, and her eyes dried out as the darkness spread.

The instinct to run was overwhelming, and her hands clawed at the dirt under the house desperately until they reached ice and snow. She kept crawling, then staggering, away from the heat and ash. Only then did she turn to see the flames engulf her home.

There was no sign of the druids and her mother. They were simply *gone.*

The wood groaned as the cottage collapsed. Her heaving breaths were distant even to her own ears.

There was nobody to run to, no one she knew who could help.

So she turned her back on the flames, her mother's last words growing in her mind, taking root like a weed, until it was all she could hear. *There's nothing to fear.*

But fear was one of the only things Rune had left, except for the darkness seeded beneath it.

Hate.

She would get her mother back. Along with her father and brother.

But first she'd have to survive and kill the fear eviscerating her senses.

So, she ran.

And she never stopped.

Royal Decree

FIFTEEN YEARS AGO, a royal decree was signed by the three immortal kings in response to the mortal uprising. It reads as follows:

> Henceforth on this day, the first of Ninth Month, mortals will undergo the Selection each year, a reaping of one hundred souls as penance for their cursed uprising. Each of the nine remaining mortal territories will submit to the Selection process at random, and without defiance, or summon our fury.
>
> Failure to appear at the Selection will result in forfeiture of life and/or property.
>
> These souls will never see the mortal lands again.
>
> Pray for our mercy.
>
> —Signed,
King Altair of the Seraphs,
King Silas of the Druids,
and King Eldarion of the Elves

1

The Selection

The Fool represents infinite potentials in the cycle of tarot, beginnings, new paths, and adventures to the unknown. There is great risk, yes, but also the potential for great reward.

M Y BOUNTY POSTER stares back at me from the craggy remaining walls of this ruinous city. Rune Ryker, wanted dead or alive. It's a good bounty, I'm worth a lot—especially if I'm brought in still breathing. All because the Lord of Westfall would like to make the punishment for my defection hurt. Fair enough, since I left him in a pool of his own blood among the burning wreckage of his manor.

He deserved worse.

I push through the crowd of huddled families gathered in the shadow of the monstrous Immortal Wall, ignoring their hushed, last-minute prayers. It's a day where no one wants to be noticed, let alone draw any attention to themselves. But I'm not just anyone, and this isn't just any day. If even one scared person in this crowd looks up and recognizes me, I'm fucked.

It's the Selection, and I *need* to be chosen.

Not arrested.

Selection day is always filled with the stench of terror in a selected, mortal territory. Every human dragged across miles and mountains to reach what remains of the capital dreads this day more than any other. A day their families will either be spared or torn apart.

At least I have no one left to lose.

A dark hopelessness weighs the people of Westfall's movements, from their downturned eyes to the hunch of their shoulders. I both pity and envy them, those families who don't know what it's like to be victims of the Selection yet. I slip through little pockets of whispering as they huddle away from the Reapers who patrol this razed city.

The capital is barely more than heaps of ruins now. It used to be the jewel of the mortal kingdom of Vexamire. But it was in Kravenish, the territory closest to the immortal realm, so it had been the first to fall. The wreckage of a courtyard is still visible where the seraphs brought down their power. White streaks of lightning burned across the broken tiles. Tattooed into the dirty façade.

Thousands were said to have died in seconds. The mortal uprising never stood a chance.

Still, my bounty is plastered to the few standing walls, unavoidable. My moon-white hair, light brown skin. I have to hand it to the artist, they got my scowl right. They even captured the gold in my eyes with nothing but parchment and ink.

I need to get the hells out of here.

I hike up my hood and tuck back my voluminous curls, weaving through the masses. The last thing I need is some antsy asshole looking to make a fast coin by turning me over to the Reapers. I'm not looking to waste out my days in a human prison, or worse . . . be returned to the Lord of Westfall after my hasty escape. But luckily most of the people here look exhausted from the travel, hunching against each other, avoiding eye contact with any passersby. Their worried whispers snag my attention.

"The druids are the worst of them," a young man whispers to another, eyes red. "Sorcerers, all of them."

It's true. The seraphs have their brute strength, the elves their persuasion, but the druids' magic is the most daunting.

"Rune?"

The sound of my name halts me in my steps, but it's just a street merchant, peddling runic talismans, a scar across his lip. "Spare you from the Selection? The druids can't stand them."

I roll my eyes as he tries to shove one into my hand, expecting gold for it, and pull my hood up.

"I doubt that." Humans can't do magic, not without dying, everyone knows it. Whatever he's carved into those polished stones is nonsense.

"You sure? Who knows what the druids will do to an innocent girl like you." The vendor tries to leer past my hood.

I shove by him before he can get a look on my face. "Try your tricks on someone else," I grumble. "You'll get no luck here."

He mumbles something before shuffling off to prey on a new pocket of trembling humans.

I brush by a young woman asking her group, "I heard they always pick people our age. Do you think that's true?" She gnaws her nails as she clutches her cloak tighter around her.

They take anyone they damn well please. I've witnessed their wrath myself.

Then spent six years struggling to survive the ramifications, stumbling into the service of the Lord of Westfall. A fate worse than death. I experienced hell to prepare for this moment, to have a chance at being strong enough for whatever is beyond that Wall. For them to finally hold no power over me.

I ran that day. I won't run again. But my hands still sweat as I shoulder my way toward the front. Screw this, I'm done hiding.

The crowd thins as I move forward. A hundred people will be chosen from this mass of thousands, like every other year, and taken to one of the three immortal realms on the other side of the Wall, as penance for the uprising that happened nearly fifteen years ago. I was only five then and barely remember the Great War. Not that it would matter if I did—we're forbidden to speak of it. But the only way to cross into their kingdom is the Selection. It's a weakness they don't even know they have— and I am about to exploit the hell out of it.

I take in the Wall. It's enormous. The immortals guard their precious magic behind its swirling granite stone, hoarding it like a dragon with gold. Crimson sands gather halfway between us and it, containing magic in every grain that no mortal can cross.

I know, I've tried, but it only left me unconscious, and I woke hours later with a terrible headache and a nosebleed. No, the only way over that Wall is by getting Selected. Which is exactly what I'm here to do.

A memory filters back, a rhyme my father taught me. We were walking along the beach on the Isle of Riches. I was maybe five years old, and he'd handed me a bright bloom from a flame tree, the red petals framed around one white lick of fire that flared inside them. He recited the words: "*Beware the druids of fire, who use humans in their games, their magic devours desires, mortal souls they seek to claim.*"

I clench my fists at the memory, my gaze narrowing at that insufferable Wall. They have him on the other side of it.

The immortals take turns deciding who gets to Select each year, like some twisted game, and this year it's the same druids who stole my mother for refusing to play. I'm done letting the Selection toy with my life, my fate.

I've lied, cheated, turned myself into a weapon to survive. The girl who ran from the cottage died when she put herself in the service of the formidable Lord of Westfall. I first met him when I was fifteen, a year after my mom was taken, snow bitten and scared, and he'd promised the one thing I desperately needed: safety. Then the one thing I wanted: strength to overcome my fear of immortals. But it had a price—everything always has a price. And each act of service demanded more of my soul.

I'd started small—collecting secrets, blackmail on certain lords or ladies. With each passed whisper I'd climb another rung, until I earned the title of Wraith, the Lord of Westfall's supreme spy. But sometimes he had me do worse things, too. I never enjoyed hurting others though, no matter how guilty. I hated obeying him and then eventually loathed myself, too.

So, I burned every bridge by setting fire to the Lord of Westfall's precious manor. Without his protection, I'm no one. Worse . . . I have the biggest bounty on my head that the mortal kingdom of Vexamire has ever seen.

No backing out now.

Laughter, so out of place in this grim setting, reaches my ears. I note a group of noblemen and courtiers to my left—I've seen some of them at the Lord of Westfall's manor, mingling in his raucous, sinful parties, or around the castle in drug dens and brothels. He keeps blackmail files on all of them, not that any of them know. They're the only ones smiling, not bothering to keep their voices lowered, knowing their status means they're unlikely to be Selected. Pricks. They're also the exact people I need to avoid. If I recognize them, there's a chance they'll do the same. One of them looks up, attention perking, eyes narrowing my way. I tuck my hair beneath my deep hood, turning away from them, and push my way to the front.

My breaths quicken, legs trembling as I straighten out the new tunic I purchased with every last dreadpenny I owned. The eggplant coloring isn't as rich as druid crimson, or black, but it's the best I could afford. Human tailors can't replicate the finery of the immortals' garments. My new emerald cloak hangs loosely around my neck, matching my scuffed boots. They're the only part of my ensemble I've had for years. My mother embroidered the boots with golden thread, sewing moons and stars into their velvet sides. They're worn but clean, and perhaps the druids won't notice. Though I've watched the elves turn their pointed noses up at dirty humans before.

The elves take the artistic and pure, while the seraphs select the strong and beautiful.

I'm neither of those things. But the druids? Maybe they'll want someone who's become nothing more than rage—someone more like them.

"Hells, moon-cursed," a woman nearby mumbles, and sidesteps away from me, steering her child as if I'm a bad omen. My chest frosts, my heart closing off into something small and shriveled. Most don't care about such things. I tuck my luminous hair behind my ears in frustration, the tell that some generations back someone in my bloodline mixed with an immortal, a seraph, judging by my curls' snow-white color. Being "moon-cursed" was common on the Isle of Riches, but that's a thousand miles from here.

Five people down from me, I catch the eye of a boy with deep crimson hair, cut close on the sides but longer on the top. He meets my gaze, eyes rolling at the woman who commented, a wry smile on his lips. He's lava-cursed, druid-mixed, so I'm sure he gets as many stares as I do. I wonder if they'll be more likely to choose him because of it.

I glance over my shoulder at the nobles, now quietly grumbling, some nodding toward me. Shit. Someone shuffles beside me and I jump. A young man with hair so blond it's nearly silver. His features are uncommon for Westfall, so he's not with the noblemen. He must be from somewhere farther east, someplace even colder. His crystal blue eyes narrow at the red sands ahead, flicking to the top of the Wall.

He searches for a nervous conversation starter, glancing at my skin tone, and blurts, "Where are you from? Near the equator?"

Classy.

"My father was from the Isle of Riches," I say with a sigh. I take in his light tunic and poorly fitting patchwork cloak, yet his hands show no sign of working farms or lumberyards, not a callus to be seen. It's suspicious.

"Your poster is quite memorable, Wraith of Westfall." He says it so calmly, like there isn't a massive bounty on my head. My nails bite into my palms hard enough to leave marks. The stranger scoffs, a sneer on his coy lips. "I heard the Lord of Westfall's palace was left in ruins. His face so marred he's barely recognizable. His Wraith was spotted fleeing the scene."

"That's too bad." That he lived, anyway. I'd hoped Thane Blackwell would have died a slow, painful death by now.

The stranger rolls his eyes as I glare up at him. "Don't worry, I'm not here for your bounty. Though I'm sure some here would be interested."

This guy. I didn't bring any weapons today, but I wouldn't need one to knock him down a peg. But I can't afford a fight, so I give him a tight smile.

"Let me guess, you're from Eastgate? Shadowfell?" The second guess brings a slight tick to his jaw, a tell that I'm on the right track. I edge my words, a subtle knife readying to strike should he be a threat. "You wear the coat of a poor man but have the hands of a rich boy. You running away from something, little lord?"

I glance knowingly toward the nearest pillar of bounties and his smile falters. He growls, "Something like that." There's an edge of darkness in his eyes. A pain laced there that I recognize. "Most don't run toward the immortals." His cutting gaze scours me. "But looks like we both are."

"Why don't you tell me your name? Save me a walk to see what you're worth."

He raises a brow at me. "Kasper. You?"

I tug on a strand of my spider's web, and the information bought or blackmailed clicks into place. He was truthful, as that's the name of the adopted son of the Lord of Shadowfell. Was he running from home and got caught in Westfall's Selection? Or does he want to be Selected, same as me? I lull him with a bite of the truth, to see if it might cause a drop in his guard. "Well, I'm not a Wraith anymore. My name is just Rune."

He chuffs at that, and I can't blame him for it. The name isn't a common one.

The audience releases a collective gasp, and my attention jerks back to the front, to the red sands a hundred feet away. Darkness has spread like ink spilled in water, right at the line between our realm and theirs, warping the air around it, like a mirage on desert sands. But it's only grown colder. Kasper no longer matters. I move him to the back of my mind. I've never been to a Selection where the druids were in charge, only the seraphs who appeared in streaks of light and thunder, and the elves who opened a tunnel draped in diamonds from the grounds at our feet.

Neither of them made my legs shake the way druids do, stepping out of shadows.

They remind me of the dark that lies in wait between the stars.

Powerful and mysterious, but in my world, that usually means dangerous.

They unfold from the shadows like liquid death. Every one of them filled with the confidence of killers, wolves on the hunt. They're clad head to toe in intricate iron armor. Most have wings and horns of some kind, the only features that differentiate them from their militaristic uniforms and identical, expressionless masks. Some march with strange animal familiars trotting at their sides. Jackals and corvids. Serpents and jaguars. I've heard rumors they keep more magical varieties of creatures but despite my searching don't see any with them. Do the druids speak to the beasts? What keeps the familiars tethered to their masters?

"Here we go." Kasper shifts on his feet as if readying for a fight.

"Just stay out of my way," I hiss back, letting a frightened elder slip between us.

My heart batters against my ribs as the reality of what I'm about to do seeps in. My father once told me druids were born from seraphs and demons, and that the pits of hells could be seen from their palace windows. I grit my teeth. It was just a fable, a bedtime story meant to warn of their danger, like a line of acid green on a venomous snake.

My spine remains rigid, and I don't flee.

But other mortals do. There's a ripple of screams and the crowd jostles. The druids spread out, infiltrating and surrounding the crowd. Their palms glow, energy snaking up my legs and pulling until my knees hit the ground.

Around me, everyone is now kneeling, forced to by magic.

A stillness settles. The druids stop stalking the crowd and straighten, looking to the Wall. I take a moment to assess them—their ears are pointed like the rest of the immortals, but beyond that, I cannot tell much of their features, not with those bare, simplistic masks covering their faces, just like the glimpse I caught that day they took my mother. Their armor barely allows a glimmer of skin to be seen. Maybe they *are* demons.

A flash of light blinds us, and a druid appears from the flame, his movements as smooth as a lynx. A crown of stag-like antlers rests on his brow; his brilliant silver eyes glow beneath it. The wings across his back are twice the size of those of his troops. He must be the Chooser for this Selection. Their unholy king.

A druid woman, draped in gossamer spiderwebs, stands at his side.

A young man trails them, wearing all black, his clothes regal yet militaristic, the golden accents setting him apart from the rest of the troops, his long dark hair parting around spiraling black horns. His cunning indigo eyes are visible from here, though his wings are not sinewy like theirs but instead feathered like a raven's, the color shifting in the light.

Lastly stands a child who cannot be much older than eight. His onyx hair rests on his shoulders, face masked like the rest of his family, the horns around his head small and stunted.

They look out over the sea of kneeling figures. If I'm to be Selected, I must be seen. It's why I saved every copper snail and silver spider to pay the clothier to spin me a cloak designed to shine, to catch the light, with dyes uncommon of humans so the colors would force me to stand out. I pull my hood back and let my hair fly behind me like a wild banner.

See me, notice me, look at me, I demand, sending the thoughts out like a prayer. A curse.

My focus catches on the older of the two princes. The break of clouds highlights his sleek, shining black hair as his gaze settles on me. My heart startles as his eyes hew closer to purple. Is it a trick of the light? Or some druid feature? His head tilts, eyes trailing me up and down, his attention unwavering despite the fury in my gaze—until I moisten my dry lips, and then they seem to be all he can look at.

Well . . . *he* certainly notices me.

"Hail to King Silas, Queen Vesta, Prince Draven, and Prince Ansel of the Vos Dynasty," a vizier announces. He wears rich robes of mauve, standing out among the druid crimson, blacks, and gold, and trails the king like a shadow, always hovering, attention locked to him.

"Prince Draven and Prince Ansel will be performing the Selection as is the rite of passage for our people," the king states, his voice deep and hoarse like a shovel scraped over a shallow grave. He lays a gentle hand on his youngest son's shoulder, his fingers limned in bone-scaled armor, and the absence across my shoulder burns like fire.

As if the phantom trail of my father's hand traces the same path.

Prince Ansel takes a couple of hesitant steps away from his parents, round eyes scanning my side of the crowd beneath that sinister satyr's mask. His steps are as faltering as a newborn deer's, a child performing a ritual he doesn't understand the consequences of. I think of my brother, younger than this boy when he was Selected. Steel laces up my spine.

I will *make* him choose me if I must.

Yet Prince Draven stops him from heading my way, turning little Ansel around and whispering something in his small, pointed ear. Prince Ansel nods up at his older brother, grasping his hand, and Prince Draven tugs him toward the other side.

They'll make this Selection together. My hopes sink. What if they've made all their Selections before they reach me? The young prince would have been easier to guile, willing and eager to submit.

Prince Draven seems . . . more difficult.

I cannot tell his age, but he doesn't seem much older than my twenty years. But the effortless grace of his movements sends a warning firing through my chest. It whispers he's something other, something magic, a dangerous predator to watch and not turn my back upon. His eyes are the only visible bit of him beyond his tall, muscled form and long dark hair, wearing a mask like all the others. Yet, that gaze lingers on me again and again, a crinkle visible in the corners as if he finds me amusing. My lip curls, yet I can't stop staring right back.

This prick has probably had everything handed to him his whole life. I focus on his narrow waist, his muscular arms, and shoulders. Even his damn legs are powerful beneath the dark cloth. Damn it, he must have a weakness somewhere. I force my gaze from lingering too long anywhere else, and his eyes flit back to me again. I swear there's some smugness there, as if he can read exactly how I just drank in his strapping body.

What an asshole.

While others duck their heads, I keep my eyes on Prince Draven. He whispers instructions to his brother, allowing the boy to make guided choices. At first, Prince Ansel wavers, but then he grows more confident with each Selection. When one girl cries, Ansel freezes, head swiveling back to his parents with worry. The Queen nods, encouraging his wickedness, so he continues, Draven a hissing serpent at his side.

The Selection speeds up, and the choices come faster. Prince Draven never deigns to pick, though his whispers in his brother's ear make me wonder if he's secretly chosen them all. They Select as many in the back and middle as the front.

They're only a few steps away. My heart races when Prince Ansel stops, and my breaths halt with him. He counts on his fingers, then turns to his brother.

"How many more?"

"Four," Prince Draven supplies. His words ghost across the nape of my neck despite him standing several paces away. My lungs don't catch enough air. I can't risk waiting another year to be Selected. It must be now.

"Oh, good. Only four," Prince Ansel huffs, relieved. As if this is harder on them than the families here. He walks a few more steps, choosing the lava-cursed guy even though he kept his head lowered. Then, a ginger-haired girl my age, chin held high, throat bobbing, tears streaking down her freckled face. Prince Ansel walks nearer. So small up close.

He stands inches from my face. I thrum with anticipation. *Me, choose me.* He takes me in, then my hair. He points to Kasper instead, his small, soft hand lifting and Kasper's shoulders sag in respite. Now, there's only one to go.

My stomach churns, readying to flip.

He's confusing my snowy hair for age. He probably doesn't know what *moon-cursed* even means, as it's only an affliction of mortals. My face heats, temple sweating as my window closes, hopes shuttering.

The young prince's fine-boned shoulders slump, eyes glazing over the crowd beyond me, but it's clear he's exhausted, and the rest around me are actual elders, rarely chosen. I glower at Draven, who holds my gaze as if he enjoys seeing me on my knees, but he doesn't whisper anything more to his brother, letting him choose. Or be persuaded. I see my opportunity.

"Pick me," I whisper in a rush. Those beside me lean away sharply. Prince Ansel's steady sapphire eyes snap to mine, and I'm surprised at how commanding they are for a child. But then he startles and steps back into his brother. I wince. We're not allowed to speak to the immortal royals. It's strictly forbidden, worthy of execution. My gaze slowly travels upright, meeting Prince Draven's burning indigo stare at well over six feet tall.

The color shifts, turning purple before my eyes. Definitely not a trick, then, but some magic I don't recognize. There's a light in them that shouldn't be there, a daring playfulness, like a wolf toying with a hare before it sinks its teeth in.

His head tilts to the side, and then suddenly he kneels, still taller than his young brother, but now closer to my eye level. Draven's hand supports the small of his brother's back to keep his spine straight, undaunted.

"She isn't supposed to speak to me," Prince Ansel whispers worriedly, looking to him.

Prince Draven appraises me in that same steady way, devouring me. His tone is mischievous as he utters, "Well, I guess we'll just have to keep that a secret between the three of us, won't we?"

Prince Ansel gives a small giggle, as jarring as if it were released during a funeral. Yet he nods.

His small hand lifts and points square at my chest.

2

The Wall

The Magician card is the next step in the Fool's journey, a claiming of agency and manifestation. But in
its reverse, it represents the loss of autonomy and
being tricked by an illusion.

I FORCE THE SMIRK off my face as Prince Draven observes
me. It's not joy that burns beneath my skin but righteous,
blinding vengeance. Draven's gaze lingers a moment longer
before he saunters back to his parents, a hand on his young
brother's shoulder.

With the one hundred chosen, the Selection is at its end.

For once, I am among the unlucky few.

The noblemen who were watching me before glare outright
now, but I only grin smugly back at them. I'm sure they hate knowing one of their "untouchable" buddies was laid out by a peasant
girl like me, and now they'll never get their retribution. I rub my
eyebrow with my middle finger and chuckle as they glower, but
I'm done kowtowing to them, done minding my tongue.

Guards separate the Selected from the crowd, hands on their
swords. This is it. Dread dances with anticipation in my chest
as I look up to that Wall. The answers all finally within reach.

I haven't prayed in years, but I say one now since there's no one left to do it for me.

Let me find them. And if not, let me live long enough to make these immortal bastards pay.

Druid guards file around us, our group stumbling into a column, organized only by its fear as we begin our walk toward the Wall. Prince Ansel returns to his mother and father's sides, the former sweeping him into an embrace. Proud of his wickedness.

The king takes note of my glare. He whispers something to his eldest son, and Prince Draven releases a scoff angled in my direction. My eyes narrow.

His mother's hand rises, and a card follows the movement, floating at her fingertips. It levitates on its own, darkness branching around it. I've rarely seen magic so closely, outside the few moments when immortals parade their powers at their Selections. I don't know its rules, its limitations, or whether it even has any—let alone if it compares to godly might. Surely it *must* come with some price?

I watch as that darkness seeps out. A billowing shadow grows, obscuring my vision and engulfing the king and small prince. It spreads like a gathering storm, and I throw my arm up, stepping back. My heel catches on something—

A rush of wind flows past me, moving my hair, and a hand grasps me under my arm before I can fall. Prince Draven looks down at me, righting me on my feet. Oh great, this asshole. He smells like the expensive colognes of noblemen. There isn't a speck of dirt on his finely crafted onyx suit and every inch of him screams of entitlement. Yet he holds me as if I weigh nothing and helped me when I would've let him fall flat on his masked face.

"Thank you," I grit out. His family is gone, vanished in that casual display of might. The sand shifts at my feet, becoming soft and making it harder to tread through, crimson as clay. We've crossed the Red Line.

"You know . . ." His voice is low as he looks me over, his eyes as dark as forgotten, haunted places. "Most would address me as Your Royal Highness."

I clench my jaw, annoyed to find him falling into step at my side. His eyes focus on my face with rapt attention, as though I'm a fascinating creature that has not been named or a new toy for him to play with.

"Apologies, Royal Princeling, for not groveling more. I am but a weak human girl being marched to her death, and this is all the humanity I can spare you."

A dark, low chuckle sounds from him, like a growl caught in his chest. "Wow, well, I was going to offer to spare you the climb." He looks meaningfully at the Wall looming in front of us. "As a thank-you for helping my brother make an easy choice that I imagine I'll one day pay for."

"I don't need your pity, Princeling." I'll be sure they regret choosing me. I side-eye him, but he steps away, where shadows rumble darker than storm clouds, a tarot card curling at his fingers.

"Enjoy the climb, then." His eyes sweep over me and the heavy darkness swallows him up.

The wind howls as we near the Wall. Druid guards usher us along, growling orders, forcing the Selected into compliance. The back of my head nearly touches my shoulders as I crane my neck, searching for the top. It's unnaturally tall, built and broken into the mountainside, swaths of granite swirling throughout it, smoothed by magic, enforced by curses. My breaths draw short as a cold breeze wends around me.

I don't know what awaits me on the other side, only that my family are lost in those lands somewhere. The uncertainty of what happens next has haunted my every nightmare since I was six. That was the year the elves took my twin brother, at the first official Selection. When I'd curl up in our room each night after, I wouldn't look for monsters hiding beneath my bed, but immortals.

This close, I can see that stairs have been built within the Wall. The granite whorls confuse the eye, obscuring them until we're at its first steps. The switchbacks are tight and narrow, and there's no time to swallow my fear as I reach the precipice. The druids will not slow for anyone, shouting and shoving us along.

After the first six flights, my thighs are burning. As the Wraith, I might be able to scurry up buildings, scrunch myself into the opening of a window as rain pelts my skin, or perch in a tree for hours in the dead of winter, but these steps are not standard or even, and it's like hiking the face of a mountain. Magic fills the space between breaths, an intoxicating sweetness coating my senses, my tongue. A little pulse radiates from the stone as if the Wall holds a heartbeat.

We trudge on, our breaths becoming shallower as an hour passes, then two. The stairwell darkens. A vein of blue light traces a pattern across the rich stone in the walls, as if the night sky skipped scattered stars across its surface.

I wish I'd brought my blades to carve some gouges into it.

Prince Draven is probably at the top of this cursed stairwell laughing his privileged ass off. That annoyance spurs me onward, frustration mounting with each step. I'll be damned if I show how tired I am when I reach the top.

Vexamire stretches out the higher we climb, beautiful but desolate. I thought I would see bereavement lanterns flickering across the kingdom, but the nearest towns are little specks of light far below, barely closer than the stars above. It looks . . . small. Insignificant.

I've traveled its mountains and valleys, but I can't say it was ever really home.

I've been to the cities of Valhan, the last mortal library in Manu, and even the southern savannas of Zuri. My parents moved us constantly, hoping to prevent us from being in a territory that would be Selected. When I was little, we spent a full year on the Isle of Riches off the coast where my father was born, and I can still hear the coqui frogs croaking when I fall asleep each night. It might've been the one place I felt at ease, where my looks didn't make me stand out but blend in.

The southern part of the continent was like that, too, but the north was harder—the people with it. I glare at the dark lands below. I'd bet everything I own that this diminished vision is an enchantment, reducing our might.

What's power and magic without someone weaker to trample on?

Crying comes from up ahead, persistent as the noon bell tolls in the clock tower of Westfall. The child sounds too young. I increase my pace and find him on the next landing. He's beautiful, hair as golden as sunflower petals, tear-rimmed eyes round. Every bit of him is tiny: his limbs, height, and waist. He must be two, at most three. Those ahead of me walk by him, all looking but doing nothing.

Someone must've carried him to this point. Someone must've given up on him.

But I won't.

I scoop him into my arms. His wet face burrows into my nape, pale skin pressed against the bronze tones of mine, cries bleeding my eardrums. I hear a scoff behind me and look over my shoulder. Kasper. He pants, "You should've left him. Maybe they'd have returned him to his family."

The nearest soldier stands resolutely against the sidewalls of the landing, watching the child disparagingly. Bastard. All of them heartless.

"They're as likely to throw him over the Wall as they are to return him to his parents."

My pace slows from the extra weight, yet I force myself onward. Through will, sheer spite, pure hatred. The boy's sopping cries calm as I huff out a melody my mother once sang.

"Sing of the child, both restless and wild, sing of a land without fear."

He must recognize the tune even through my tired wheezing. After another landing, he stops sobbing, slumping against my neck as he drifts to sleep.

"Shade, you are not. The immortals are lost. Even walls can fall with each year."

The irony is not lost on me. These steps are sturdy, unnaturally perfect. So long as the seraphs, druids, and elves continue living, this Wall is going nowhere.

All at once, we turn a corner unlike the others, the top of the Wall. This could be my first look at the Immortal Realms. My heart thrums. But the stairs end, and we're on an open terrace, a green lawn stretching to an unclimbable section of cliffs, and a tunnel leads into the heart of the mountain, lit by torches, the Wall stretching off into the darkness on either side. A large, sprawling willow tree, the mightiest I've seen, spirals above the tunnel on a little outcrop, fireflies floating between the branches, like fallen stars trapped in its limbs.

The druids all stand before the tunnel entrance, waiting for us to gather on the grass spread at their feet. Flags of each nation hang behind them. I remember them from the previous

Selections, though I've never seen them hung side by side before. Wands of red fire for the druids, silver swords on royal purple for the airy seraphs, and coins in gold for the emerald flag of the earthen elves. The fourth flag is cobalt, the colors of the mortal kingdom of Vexamire, a white, intricately carved goblet at its center. It's the most worn, and a line splinters down its center leaving it in tatters, as though it will tear completely apart with the next breeze.

Every rumor, legend, and tall tale runs through my mind about what comes next.

Soon, I'll know what happened to my family when they reached the top of the Wall.

A wild, horrible thought flies through me. Perhaps we're all about to be slaughtered. Or beaten. Or eaten.

It's not as though anyone has ever returned to tell the story.

The guards hiss at us to move, and I trace my way through the others, trying not to wake the child as I kneel beside the lava-cursed guy on the neatly trimmed lawn, directly before the prince. A light of interest sparks in his gaze as he notices where I've placed myself. My chin lifts defiantly—I expect him to look away, but he holds my glower in an unspoken contest. Gods, he is aggravating. The king watches us all, silent, until we are all supplicated before him.

There's uncomfortable shifting among the quiet, everyone wondering where the hells we are and what happens next. The king stands as immovable as if captured in stone.

Finally, he deigns to speak. "The children of this Selection will be taken to our Royal Court whilst the rest of you will remain here. Those of you under the age of eighteen, come forward." His eyes are like scythes catching the silver moon. "Now."

Children stagger forward, a few of them gangly teenagers. A druid guard enters my line of sight, gloved hands held out for the child in my arms. He has cold copper eyes but grasps the child with surprising gentleness. I only clutch the boy harder.

"No." I pull back, the child jostling, stirring.

The guard glances over his shoulder at his king, whose attention has swiveled our way at the commotion. Behind him Prince Draven watches me closely, those unsettling eyes lingering on me and the child. He shifts his feet, head tilted, and for a moment I get a view of the golden skin at his throat and intricate tattoos peeking out of his armor.

The guard presses, "The boy goes to the Court with the other children."

"Take us together. I'm underage," I lie.

Kasper scoffs at my gall. The guard hesitates and turns to King Silas, holding two fingers up. I meet the druid king's gaze. Surely, I look young enough despite my snowy curls to slip among the youth. But his eyes narrow as he reads my face, like a passage from a book he dislikes—one that's glanced over but fails to sink into the bones, bind the soul, or steal a breath. The king holds up one singular finger. The message is clear: take the boy, leave me.

I wince in pain and beg the guard, "Please, take us both."

The guard shakes his head, so I let the boy go, swallowing my worry. He barely stirs as the guard picks him up and lets him lean into his chest before he lopes off to herd the children into a separated group. A moment later, a dark shadow blooms, and the druid guards shepherd the children through it. Fire burns within me, like a fanned flame. I can't find the words. More children, lost.

I turn to pick up my glaring game with the prince and jump, hand flying to my chest.

King Silas stands before me, a cruel sharpness in his gaze. "How old are you really, girl?"

How did he appear so fast? So silent? If I had my daggers with me, I'd slice those ankle tendons and plunge one through his chest. I tremble in rage, a mantra repeating in my mind, *All immortals must die.* The king just moved to the top of my list. I bite down my fury, knowing I need to play nice until I find my family.

Finally, I grit out, "Does it matter?"

His head tilts to the side, waiting.

I swallow, hating the submission, but add, "Your Majesty?"

A hungry darkness flits across his face. "Good, you *are* capable of learning."

His words are begging for an equally cutting answer. I glance at Draven, still watching me with arrogant eyes. Apparently *prick* is a passed down trait.

The king prompts, "Well?"

"Twenty," I answer honestly. If the rumors about their powers are true, he might be able to rip the answer from my lips. Trying my hand at treason twice in one day is stupid, even for me.

"Hmm." He steps away, scrutinizing those left in his care.

The ground trails with burn marks wherever King Silas passes, a little flare of fire sparking as his boots graze a blade of grass. He takes us all in. Not a single person here is a child, nor is anyone old or frail. Prince Draven stands mutely, yet I swear there's a glimmer of pride in those hooded eyes. Is this part of his design?

"You have all been Selected to join the druid kingdom of Sedah." King Silas's voice is sharp as a blade.

My heart startles. Join?

"Princes Draven and Ansel did a fair job, though I would not have chosen some of you. Count yourselves lucky." He blatantly looks to me.

I can't stop the simmering scowl I return. I don't know how my training would hold against an immortal, but I want to find out. My attention flickers again to Prince Draven, drawn into his orbit. His hands are clasped behind his back, watching the king with undiluted attention. He doesn't seem to take his words about his choices as a slight. Perhaps his anger is eclipsed beneath that mask. Or maybe I'm just trying to humanize a demon. Maybe it's the Wraith in me, but I want to unravel him, piece him apart, find out all his dirty secrets.

King Silas continues, "Before any of you can be allowed into my kingdom, you must take the Oath. This looks different in each kingdom, but the rites are the same. You will pledge your undying loyalty to my realm."

My head jerks up—*this* is why no one has come back. This forced allegiance, daunting as it is, kept my family from returning. Some of them might still be alive. That hope robs me of any misgivings.

"The alternative option," he adds, "lies off to your right."

Like dominoes, our heads all flicker to the place he gestures, where a plank has been affixed to the Wall, stretching out over the expanse of nothingness, a thousand-foot plummet to the flat, ungiving grounds below. The idea of it churns my stomach.

King Silas says, "Not many have chosen that path. Though you mortals do like your flair for dramatics." What a hypocrite. "When you make your pledge to me, I promise all the lies you were fed about my kingdom, and the immortal lands of Arcadia, will be mere phantoms to the reality that lies ahead of you. You will be given chances you could only dream of in your small towns and villages. But you must choose this greater destiny for yourselves."

Druid soldiers step forward, flanking his sides, their masks creating the illusion they are all the same in the torchlight. Their familiars slink in the shadows behind them.

The fireflies that flicker above blink out.

I cannot see beyond the druids, not even to the parapet along the wall.

Then Prince Draven strides over to me, holding a small silver bowl in his hands.

"Choose." His voice is a grating hiss. The wood plank stretches off the side of the Wall, hauntingly illuminated in the dark. It's cruel magic, has to be. Tempting us with the freedom of death.

Drink or die.

It's not much of a choice.

I search the bowl tilted my way. Whatever viscous fluid lays within is tinted crimson. It looks an awful lot like—

"It's not blood," Prince Draven whispers.

My heart skips in a dangerous pattern, relief coursing through me, mixed with panic. I reach for the bowl, but he doesn't release it. He holds it firm, both our hands around it, his fingers surprisingly warm and unsurprisingly strong. Some part of me wants to fling its contents to the grass. Maybe that's why he holds it so resolutely. I'm forced to bring my face to the rim, lips parting as I take one last free breath.

Prince Draven hisses, "Or maybe it is . . . maybe I'm just a liar."

I glare at him, half masked in shadows in the fiery light. The only way to find out what happened to my family is by drinking this. The only way back is forward.

So, I drink.

3

$- \cdot \rangle \! * \! \langle \cdot -$

Arcana

The druids are said to be the only group of immortals to worship the darkness, their gods reigning from below, their magic most wicked. They are acolytes of chaos and revelry, their tarot cards capable of stripping life like sandpaper wearing varnish off wood.

—Ascension pamphlet signed A.C.

FOR ALL THE PRINCE'S WORDS, I can't discern what I'm tasting. I nearly pull away as the liquid slides onto my tongue. The taste of copper makes me think the bastard did slip me blood before I realize that's the metallic bowl. The drink is thick and coats my tongue with something sweet as jelly. It's a strange flavor, leaving me warm and tingly, the taste addictive, and when I look up into Prince Draven's eyes there's a spark of amusement there.

He tugs it from my mouth. It takes me a full minute to realize I'm still licking my lips. I might've drunk the entire bowl if they'd let me.

He leans close, voice lowering. "I know you're thirsty, but try to leave some for everyone."

Oh, fuck right off. My face heats as Prince Draven passes the same bowl to a guard, who takes it to the next person. He reenters the seamless line of druids, and his father grasps his hand, something gold glinting in his palm.

"I thought she'd have chucked herself off the Wall for certain," his father says quietly.

I glare openly now as Prince Draven accepts the coin smoothly, his indigo gaze passing over me once more, a spark of pride firing through his eyes.

As if he has any say over my fate.

He cocks his head to the side, that long black hair tilting, as though he just heard my thoughts.

I turn my head and watch the others all accepting the drink willingly.

It has done nothing to me, no side effects aside from the want for more. Kasper hesitates, watching me as if waiting to see if I might keel over. Still, he allows it to be tipped into his mouth. I swear he holds it there as if he might spit it into the face of the druid who offered it. A moment later, his eyes roll back, hypnotized by the flavor. He swallows, panting with want, eyes wholly black. I blink, and the image is gone, his eyes piercing blue and bright again.

Once the bowl has passed through the lips of every soul, it simply disappears.

Now what? I turn back to the king, confused, and he lifts a hand, silver fire traces the fingers he stretches toward us.

There's a beat, all of us holding our breaths.

Then my gut twists in horrific pain, and I gag.

Words tumble from my mouth, "*I bind my soul to serve your kingdom forevermore.*"

The same words pull from everyone here, and I'm left gasping. I hadn't been ready, the Oath drawn from me with such little warning.

A tingling, like tiny needles, begins prickling all over my body. I curl over, bracing myself against the grass. I can't focus on anything or anyone else as the pain grows, burning through me.

Stop, please stop, I think desperately as my body cramps and squirms under the pressure of that magical binding. I drop, mouth opening in a silent scream, and taste dirt as I kick and scrape against the ground. My eyes and ears burn as if heated raw beneath the sun, my skull aches as if my teeth are being pulled, fingernails stinging like splinters have shot up between the nails and tender flesh.

Others scream, crying out around me, but I don't join them. I'm too stubborn, though the pain at the back of my skull dazes me.

I'll do anything, just stop. I can't help the thoughts blaring through, but then I hear a voice within me, too close for comfort, as if someone whispers directly into my ear.

Yield, it demands.

I hate myself the moment I hear the words because I know I will. After a few more excruciating seconds, I do. I allow whatever that voice is to grasp hold of my mind and squeeze out bits of me, like pulp from the rind. When it's satisfied, I clench my fists into the earth below, and my hands tear up dirt.

But it's over. I survived. The pain is gone as quickly as it came.

The king's hand draws back, and his silver eyes flicker among us all, writhing and panting on the ground. I force myself up to my knees, wiping soil from my face. My jaw hurts, and my tongue runs over sharpened canines. What's happened to me? As I look at my fingernails, they morph from pointed immortal talons to normal nails again. I wonder if even my eyes hold a glow like the druids'. Tears spring forth before I blink them back. I place shaking palms over my ears and find they're pointed.

Trembling with rage, I glare at the king. I want to call him a bastard, to curse him for doing this to me, but however hard I try, I can't. He is *my* king now. I had sworn I would serve no one again but myself when I burned the Lord of Westfall's manor, but now . . . I belong to them.

Prince Draven watches me from his father's side. He's inscrutable, merely observing me as if he's waiting for something.

My body is hollow-boned and unfamiliar. The air doesn't sit right in my lungs. Sound warps around me, and my vision tunnels. The skin across my face prickles as though spiders crawl under the surface.

Someone gets up and runs, a woman older than most of the others here, and she doesn't hesitate as she reaches the plank affixed to the wall. The guards don't stop her. The ginger-haired girl who cried at the Selection whispers, "No." One moment, the woman's there. The next, she's gone. We continue to kneel in silence, and it takes a long time to hear the thud that follows her flight, my shoulders jolting from the sound. I shouldn't be able to hear that, but my sense of sound is enhanced along with everything else. Even the silence afterward is loud, my senses in overload with this newly transformed body.

The king continues as if there were no interruption.

"You are now all members of *my* domain," King Silas announces. "You will never be welcomed back to the mortal world. Even your loved ones would hunt you and hate you. So, bury those lives, those dreams, those names if you must. Your transformations are not complete, but this will help you survive beyond this Wall. You are still very much mortal. You are changelings until you prove yourselves worthy and complete the Descent at the end of the coming spring. Then you will become immortals. Let this be the first day of the rest of your lives. You are meant for so much more than dust and will serve me and my people well."

He flourishes his hand to his hip, drawing a deck of cards from his belt, and they shuffle themselves as if peeled apart by invisible hands before lying motionless in his palm. He gestures to us to rise, and we do, my legs stumbling, unused to my new form. I brush the dirt off my skin, eyes watering in outrage over the nonconsensual transformation of my body.

"These are tarot cards, each steeped in their own magical history, containing the ability to act as a conduit to whatever magical gift, or Arcana, calls to you," King Silas explains. He puts his spidery hand over the stack of cards and, without touching them, draws his hand upright, palm toward the audience. A card from the top of the deck follows, floating in the space between us and himself. Its black and gold foil design glows in effervescent light, beams shining out of it like the crowning of the sun.

Despite my rage, I find myself leaning forward, noting the card displays a genderless crowned figure sitting atop a throne, a sword in one hand, scales dangling from the other.

"Tarot are used to help channel the twenty-two types of magical gifts discovered by druids, each called a Major Arcana, gifted to us by our holiest god, Azazel, Lord of Death." With a flick, the other cards in the deck fly upright, orbiting around him. "Every druid, whether they be born as Azazel's Children or come to our borders as changelings, have a calling to one of these gifts and can use tarot like siphons to control their magic, to tame that power to their fingertips."

I've heard of tarot before. Charlatans would parade decks of cards through Westfall each year, claiming they were ancient relics that could channel magic in the mortal realms. They were all fakes, of course. Even if they'd somehow gotten their hands on a real deck, mortals couldn't channel magic—everyone knew it was a death sentence.

Magic needed a place to feed from—energy or life, it always came with a price. Mortal lifespans would burn up like lit tinder against the power of it.

The king brings his hands together, catching the cards in a golden web strung between his fingers. He settles the deck between his hands and holds it out toward us collectively. He's offering my heart's desire, drawing my attention like a moth to a flame, even knowing I'll likely get burned. No one offers power without cost. "Power in Sedah is granted to those with the most talent, not by blood, history, or coin but by what is offered. You want power? Prove it. You want magic? Take it. Now, changelings still come at a disadvantage. This will be corrected with training and time at our Forge, where you will learn and be rebuilt into something new. Step forward in turn and put your hand over the cards. Show me your potential."

Every eye in that space darts to the king's open hand, holding that deck. None of the others dare move forward, to grasp greedily at such a promise in case it's some trick.

But Kasper takes a hesitant step, then another, until he's before the king. His hand quakes as he holds it over the pile of cards.

A single card floats from the king's palm into Kasper's hand. Kasper clumsily plucks it from the air. I've never seen a human perform magic. It's impossible. Except Kasper isn't merely a human anymore.

Neither am I.

We're now something in between. The whispers of excitement surround me, as if this is all some gift and not a horrible bargain. Why change us at all? Why give us power?

Kasper allows the vizier to take it, jotting notes on a roll of parchment. Kasper's eyes widen and search them as he waits. I can nearly feel his impatience brimming in his taut shoulders. He's barely breathing.

"The High Priestess." The vizier explains, "She represents intuition, divine wisdom, instincts. An incredibly useful Arcana, and one I share."

"Thank you," Kasper says blankly, mouth a taut line as they fold the card back into the deck and reshuffle.

He bows his head and walks back to the others, and soon, a woman from the crowd eagerly takes his place. The excitement grows around me as the throng surges toward the front. They accept all this so easily. I let the newly minted half-druids stream forward to find out how much power and possible riches await them and linger at the back instead.

I put my hands on my knees and breathe, but my senses are too heightened. I can smell the citrusy grass mixing with the dew at my feet. The charged scent of cedarwood and vetiver trailing Prince Draven, the clean linen and iron of the guards, the smoke and cinnamon clinging to King Silas. I break away and stumble toward a small fountain, hands stretching for the water. Splashing some on my face might reset my sensory over-load, yet I only stare in horror at my reflection when I reach it.

It's not my face anymore . . . it's the enemy's.

My eyes glow with gold, my ears are pointed, and my hair . . . it's horrifically tamed. The curls have given way to something silky and straightened. It's sleek and shines so brightly it looks infused by the moon hanging above, a clear contrast to my skin.

The courtiers of Westfall might say it's beautiful now, yet to me, it feels like a betrayal of who I am. A forced assimilation, a stripping of my heritage and my history. Nearly everyone on the Isle of Riches had the same wild curls, and now . . . they're gone.

I open my mouth, and hot tears well as I see the fangs bared back at me. My pointed, immortal ears, the brightness in my eyes like freshly minted gold. My breaths are ragged and uncontrolled as I gape at the hateful image of myself. I can't risk showing weakness here. I can't even remember the last time I let myself shed tears. This will not break me. The immortals will not have the last laugh. Slowly, the fangs recede as my breath steadies.

"It's going to take some getting used to," a soft voice says at my side. It's the red-haired girl, her ears and fangs pointed like mine, her acidic-green eyes glowing. I quickly wipe my face as she stares at her reflection over my shoulder. Somehow this transformation nearly suits her. Her freckled skin glows golden, whereas it was pale, almost translucent before. Her hair is fuller, the orangish coloring infused with gold streaks. But she doesn't look any happier than me. "I didn't think this is what became of the Selected. We really are dead, aren't we?"

"In every way that matters," I reply, turning to watch as someone else eagerly steps forward, placing their hand over the king's deck.

The line before the king is dwindling. Those who've received their Arcana seem trapped between joy and confusion. The druids are giving us magic, turning us into them, but this was supposed to be a punishment, a damnation. Of all the fucking scenarios that have plagued me leading to this moment, being handed power was not on my list. "Why would they give us power? Wasn't the Selection designed to hurt us?"

"I . . . don't know." The girl's brows come together. She turns, staring over her shoulder at the others. "I didn't think about it like that. I assumed taking us from our lives was the punishment."

I mull over her answer.

"What's your name?" I ask, needing all the information I can gather. Between the Oath and now the offering of magic, I don't know what will come next. Maybe she'll have gleaned more information or maybe become an ally in a den of vipers.

"Ember."

"I'm Rune," I reply.

Her head quirks as though she wasn't expecting that. She smiles, though, nodding to me, and I return it.

"You better get up there," she says. "Don't want to get into trouble."

"Oh, but I am trouble." I don't know what makes me say it, but she giggles and the tension of everything that's happened lessens. Looking to the shrinking line I ask, "What was it like? Doing magic?"

"Well, trouble, it was an odd sensation. Like a vibration from my wrist to my palm."

"What chose you?" I don't know what the options are beyond Kasper's draw.

"The Star." She shrugs her svelte shoulders. "No idea what it means yet."

I walk to the meager line in front of the king, waiting my turn.

What would the world beyond the Wall, in my small territory and others, think of the knowledge we could *become* immortals? Would they vie for the opportunity to become elves and seraphs? Would they beg for places among druids?

I stand in line dead last, and when my turn comes, the king's eyes change from a tired sort of boredom to a flaring interest. I don't understand him or what kind of game he's playing. But I put my hand out over the deck of cards he cradles nonetheless, wondering how stupid I look. Even in this altered body, there's no obvious tingling of magic, nothing unexpected.

I feel absolutely nothing.

Then everything.

If the king wasn't watching me so interestedly, I'd have gasped from the pull of the cards on my hand. An invisible weight is tied to my small hand as it hovers, and it takes everything to hold it back from slapping down against the deck, as though an anchor weighs down my palm. My body tilts forward . . .

I force my fingers upward as that pull grows stronger, and the cards begin to part, shifting. There's a tremor—I don't know if this is normal. Kasper's drawing seemed much smoother. I should've watched the others . . .

The wrenching becomes unbearable, and I grasp my wrist with my spare hand and force it upright. I gasp, and a card fires out of the deck. The king catches it from the air as if a dagger had been hurled at him.

I'm breathless, sweating, and cold as I stare at the back of the card, bearing the same golden symbols as the rest of the deck. The king holds it up, his mouth a tight line, nostrils flared, and for a moment I think he's angry. But then he passes it to the vizier as if it's nothing, spoiled by the fact the vizier gulps when he touches it.

I watch them carefully, waiting for whatever news will break. Is it bad? My hands curl to fists at my sides as I quickly count the guards surrounding the king, the exits of this place. Could I run, fight them if it came to it? Or would the Oath force me to endure whatever punishment they see fit?

The vizier starts hissing into the king's ear and I catch the word *impossible*. My eyes flash toward Prince Draven as he peers over his father's shoulder, a strange battle waging in that look. Surprise, certainly, as he blinks it back, but when his gaze finds me again, he looks at me more critically, his eyes assessing every inch of me.

"That good, huh?" I ask the prince with a wink. Let them think I'm at ease as I strategize my options.

Prince Draven shakes his head at me, rolling his eyes, and he releases a huff.

"Mistakes do happen." There's a certain challenge in his voice, as though he's daring me to prove him wrong.

The king doesn't explain, merely takes the card back from the vizier and folds it back into the deck with deft hands, shuffling it with ease. He tells me, "Draw it again."

"I don't understand. Did I do it wrong?"

"Do it again," King Silas orders.

Prince Draven's eyes flicker between his father and me. I clench a fist in anger before laying my palm flat again, hovering above the tarot deck. This time, the king's eyes are on me, intent. King Silas passes his spare hand between the air, dividing me from it, as if to be sure I did not somehow trick him before cupping the deck again. A strange thought occurs, more feeling than word, that I have somehow unsettled the king of druids.

The pull calls again. It's like lightning striking the base of my skull—emotions spin out within me.

My hand shakes worse than before.

"What are you feeling?" the king asks quietly.

I take a moment to answer, my hand resisting the pull of gravity. "Unimaginable weight."

"Are any of your other family members moon-blessed?"

So interesting that they see being mixed as a blessing, whilst mortals view it as a curse. I eye him uncertainly, but the truth spills out.

"My mother was lava-cursed; my brother . . . we weren't sure, his hair was brown but, in the light, sometimes emerald. But he was Selected too young to fully tell," I confess, nearly gagging as the words tumble out. Like I couldn't resist it or his questions. Maybe I can't now that I've sworn the Oath, and that thought unsettles me.

"He wasn't the only one Selected from your line . . . was he?"

"No—" But I cut myself off before I can elaborate this time. The enchantment presses in, broiling around me, growing hot enough to make my hair curl again. The pulse of magic claws at my throat. I see a flicker of annoyance cross his face.

"Stop resisting."

"He was Selected when we were six." I gasp, "My father when I was thirteen."

"That would've been the elves, and the seraphs . . . yes?" King Silas demands.

"Yes."

He looks me over as if he's searching for lies. "Where's your mother?"

"Your people took her the year after." I grit my teeth. Glaring into those dominating silver eyes. I'm not sure I've hated anyone so strongly.

"I don't remember any lava-cursed being chosen then." It's Prince Draven, breaking my staring contest with his father.

"That's because she avoided it, and your people came and broke down our door."

Draven's gaze narrows beneath that mask, and I realize in a jolt of fear that I've revealed I was also avoiding Selection, and if I saw what happened to her, then surely I was with her.

"So, everyone in your family was taken then?" Draven asks but I don't feel compelled to answer him and I realize a flaw in the Oath. I think only the king can force the truth from me.

"You came here with hatred in your heart. I felt it the moment I saw you," King Silas interrupts. It's not a question. "Choose."

My fingers attempt to pull upward, but they bend down against my will. Like they'll snap if I move them back. He looks at my hand, and his sharp silver eyes take in my face again, judging every inch. "Pull."

With all I have, I yank my hand back, nearly cracking my wrist in two. A card rips out again, flipping in the air, and this time I see it. Spinning in golden foil glory, our world is held like a womb by a woman with flowing, perfect curls. The king snaps it up again, spinning it around so he can see it.

The World.

"Interesting." He shows the vizier, whose eyes are just as wide as before.

I'm certain I drew the same card by the king's measured reaction. Why did he force me to draw it twice? Then, the entire deck is gone in a flash of quick movements.

"Is it bad?" I ask.

The vizier's wide-eyed look seems to say so.

"Magic is never bad. Only people are." King Silas looks me up and down, as if he's trying to see through me. "Take her with the others for now." He turns and addresses a druid with deep gray wings whose dark hair is streaked with silver, but his body is strong, his posture incredible. "Commander Soto, the Selected are now released to you."

Several soldiers branch off to the king's side. One of them snaps his fingers and magically draws out a card with a flourish, darkness gathering again like smoke, just as it did at the Wall, creating a portal. The king gives me one more curious glance before he and his kingsguard disappear through the darkness, the vizier falling in at his side like a shadow.

There are still plenty of guards left for us changelings though. I watch Kasper's reservations grow, Ember crossing her arms and holding herself tightly, the lava-cursed man eyeing the guards closest to us.

"What's your name?" I hiss at the guy beside me. I don't know what's to happen next, but I want to have as much information as I can get.

"Morgan." The name seems so plain for him. He's handsome enough, built strong, and toned like a blacksmith. His hair is more crimson than the natural orangish gold of Ember's, but it complements the bronze of his skin. He asks, "You?"

"Rune," I say.

He nods like it fits me, giving me a lingering smile.

Prince Draven's dark feathered wings shuffle irritably, bumping Morgan's shoulder hard as he steps to Commander Soto's side. It draws my wrath, as he doesn't so much as deign to apologize.

I follow his wake just as Commander Soto calls to us, "Everyone gather up. You don't want to be left in the darkness, I promise you."

I stop near the prince, the retort on my tongue dying as I realize something is about to happen. Ember steps up beside me, her expression nervous as the changelings all gather closer. I give her a tight-lipped smile as the guards encircle us.

Draven says nothing, his eyes closed. Intent. Then blackness gathers around his shoulders like a cloak made of night.

A moment later, the shadows twist, becoming a mighty storm that envelops the entirety of our group. My hair whips around me in the gale, and Ember clutches my elbow like a lifeline. The ground sifts immaterial beneath my feet, and everything smells and tastes like ash. I cough, stumbling in the dark, and collide with something solid. Someone. Draven grips hold of me, to stop me falling over him. The swirling winds don't shift his feet; he's as immovable as a mountain. I nearly push him away, but his strong hand steadies me. I'd cry out if I could, but I'm choking on the panic pulsating through my body.

All at once, the darkness relents, flaring wide. I gasp and quickly straighten up, getting my bearings. I'm standing between Draven and Ember in a mighty canyon. Ahead of us, across a wide obsidian bridge set over a lake of lava, rises an enormous castle, its blackened peaks like blades pointed toward the sky. Magma oozes around it. A volcano far off to the right provides a stark backdrop to the imperious spires and turrets. The air is so dry it burns the skin, and though it's night and the skies shimmer with starlight, it's muted from the light below us.

A screech rends out from our right, and I instinctively duck down as a mighty beast flaps over us. A dragon . . . no, a wyvern with scales of onyx, its horns as spiraled and twisted as Draven's. My heart leaps into my throat—I've read about beasts like these in the Lord of Westfall's library. He even had one of their skeletons displayed in his grand hall, but some part of me doubted any still lived today. But this one is very much real, stealing the breath from my lungs. It glares at us with a mighty golden eye before it soars to the walls of the massive canyon we're settled in, roosting along the rim. Beside me, Ember's mouth hangs open.

"Holy shit," she mutters, stealing the words right out of my mouth.

Commander Soto addresses our group, his salt-and-pepper hair catching the wild light of the lava pools. "Welcome to the Forge. I am Commander Soto, protector of this institution, trainer of the Wyvern Aerial Legion, royal guardian of Prince Draven, and second in command to only His Majesty, the king." His voice is deep and authoritative. "This academy will become your home for the next year. After that point, you'll be either given the chance to stay and continue your development into an immortal or relegated to a trade school or labor camp you're best suited for. If you complete your classes, you will undergo the final transformation. Only those with the strongest wills survive the Descent process."

I feel the bodies of the others tense around me.

"These walls are no haven, and you will face many challenges that test your limitations. That is why it's called the Forge. You are here to be built into something more. Brittle metals break under the duress of too much heat, but the greatest grow stronger."

Commander Soto nods to us, leading the way forward, and the guards take up their place at our sides. But where would we go? I don't even know where we are and couldn't even find this place on a map, let alone imagine a way to reach the Wall or escape beyond it with the Oath in place.

I take a deep breath and try to calm my nerves. I don't intend to be here longer than absolutely necessary. My mother is in this kingdom somewhere, maybe even within the walls of this place, my father and brother in the lands beyond. My best chance at finding them is to stay here and see what I can discover before I act. At least for now. Maybe they'll even give me the tools of escaping this glorified prison.

I remind myself of this as Prince Draven leans close, whispering in my ear, "Welcome home."

4

Sedah

A Wraith is held in highest regard among spies and lowest among courtiers. They are the shadows in murky alleys who hear your every secret, the darkness lying in wait where lovers cheat beneath the moonlight, and the whispers that follow at your back should you offend their masters. The crueler their lord, the more deadly the Wraith.

PRINCE DRAVEN SAUNTERS forward before I can retort, leading the way with Commander Soto. I realize the prince is taller than the other druids, muscular but not bulky. My fists clench as I watch him, and he glances at me over his shoulder, eyes crinkling in the corners like he's laughing at me. Unrelenting prick.

"He sure seems interested." Ember falls in line with me.

"Not sure why I'm so lucky," I grumble.

"I don't know, but whatever you're up to . . . keep it up," she says.

As if getting Draven's attention is something I want.

She must see the outrage in my eyes because she shrugs her nimble shoulders. "It could be a good thing to have the prince's interest. He could be an ally or a tool." She tucks her fiery hair behind her newly pointed ears. Those emerald eyes are wide, stark against all the lava casting orange and red over this place, and she seems mesmerized by the grounds.

"I hadn't thought of it like that," I confess. She has the mindset of a Wraith. Our language is secrets, blackmail, anything to survive. My gaze travels to Draven and I realize she's right. I hate the immortals so much that the thought of charming one to be of use never even occurred to me. I take in the jutting spires and daggered points of the castle as we cross the onyx bridge. "So, what the hells is this place? They're really going to train us in tarot magic?"

"Well, it's not like we can use it against them." Ember bites her lip, bright eyes taking in everything. "Not with that oath in place. We can't run."

Morgan sidles up beside us. "Makes sense they want us to be useful."

"Yeah, at what fucking cost?" Kasper snarls, and I look back at him, watching this place as if demons will crawl out of the lava river below us.

The wyvern on the rim of the canyon roars, and I eye it, my breath a stunted thing in my chest as the beast takes flight and lands somewhere within the castle. I ask, "Did that commander guy say he headed a wyvern legion? They actually fly on those things? Most have wings themselves—why do they need them?"

"I don't know. Maybe they breathe fire?" Ember wonders, flinching as the volcano rumbles in the distance.

I've never seen a map of Arcadia—they've been banned from the mortal lands. I need to get my bearings, learn more. Hopefully, this Forge has answers.

As we cross the onyx bridge, I crane to take in the sheer breadth of the dark castle. I look around at the nervous expressions of the others. It'll be a miracle for them to survive this place. Even with allies. Even with friends.

I'm not sure my odds are much better.

The magnificent arched doors open on their own at our approach. The entry hall has sleek obsidian walls—the floor is black marble with gold and white veins. A stunning twin staircase with crimson carpet curls up to the second floor. A set of double doors are propped open to a courtyard beneath them. Large ruby banners with fiery golden crossed daggers . . . no . . . wands, four stars printed above and below them, the symbol of the kingdom, hang on the walls, nearly floor to ceiling. Tables line the hallway, with neatly folded clothes stacked in piles upon them. Unmasked druids, all of them more refined than average mortals, await us in a line, clearly expecting us. Even their plainest are pleasantly attractive. My steps falter as I notice large bins for rubbish behind the line of druids.

"To be part of this institution, you all need to dress appropriately, ready for training, sparring, and integration into your new kingdom." Commander Soto holds the attention of every person with the slightest raise of his voice. "Any items you've carried this far from your old lives will be destroyed, cast into the fires as an offering to our holiest god, Azazel. For today, you start a new life. You may keep the shoes on your feet unless you do not have a decent pair, in which case you will be provided one standard issue."

Everyone waits and he looks around at us expectantly.

"The sooner you change into your new attire, the sooner you will be able to turn in to warm beds and full bellies."

I stare in disbelief, but I'm one of the only ones. Many here are poorly clothed and hungry. Commander Soto turns to Prince Draven, not paying attention to the rest of us.

"You heard the commander. Get moving!" one guard shouts, so close it feels like a needle in my ear canal.

I shuffle forward, panicking as I grip the little figurine of the broken king in my pocket. I received it when I was five, from Four Kings Day on the Isle of Riches, a celebration of the time the four great kings of old, three immortals and one mortal, sailed across the Great Sea and divided the continent.

We'd dress up as the kings, leave out boxes of hay for their mounts to eat, to be replaced at night with sweets and toys. I was so happy to find the little figure of the mortal king in my crate the next day, but my brother Remus wanted a closer look and his arm snapped away. It was our biggest fight. Now it's my only token of him. I have so few of my family.

I didn't bring much, and I'm sure they want us to strip to be sure no one's brought any weapons. But I'm not ready to cast my old life into the fires of some immortal's god. Subtly I pull it from my pocket, and as I take off my boots to change clothes, I slip it inside, carrying them along.

Morgan branches away from us, asking for new boots, his own ragged and the soles worn. Kasper follows him hesitantly, lining up at the men's attire, and he looks down at the selection with his nose up, even though the craftsmanship is so fine that the gold pins on the collars look as if they're the real thing.

"I think the women's clothes are this way." Ember leads me past the men's and gender-neutral fits to ones catered to female bodies.

As I make it to the front of the queue, a druid guard demands I strip down. Everyone else is doing so, but still, it's violating. I check, but Draven isn't watching—no one truly is. Begrudgingly I set my boots on the table, undress, and slip on black, form-hugging leggings. The crimson tunic has a herringbone pattern up the front and a collar that hugs halfway up my throat. The front clinches my chest tight, the fabric stiff. I wonder if armor is secretly hidden inside. I pull my trapped hair out, my necklace emerging. When I search for my old clothes they're already in the rubbish bins.

"Those are my boots." I point to them and the guard begrudgingly hands them back, but the little broken king is gone. My face scrunches up as I try to hold back my fury at the violation, the outright theft. I jerk them from his hands and turn away.

"Wait a minute." The guard points to my throat. "Give it here."

Shit.

"It's just a necklace—" Hells, I should've hidden it, but I'm so used to it against my skin I didn't even think about it.

"It's not allowed. No jewelry is," the guard growls.

I freeze up. This necklace is all I have of my father. I've worn it every day for seven years. They already took the only thing I had of my brother's . . . my culture.

"It . . . can I just—" I hate that this druid can hear emotion in my voice. I will not break down in front of this asshole—I won't let them win like that.

"Give it over. Now!" The barked order draws eyes, but I stay frozen, fists clenched. I don't want to make a scene. They could kill me for this so far as I know. But I don't want to lose the necklace either.

"What's going on here?" Prince Draven sidles next to the counter, gaze imperious.

"She won't hand over a personal item," the guard tattles. "Tried to sneak in another one in her boot."

"Wow, I bet you're fun at parties," I snarl before turning to Draven. "It's just a necklace."

"Then why won't you give it up?"

"It . . ." My face heats as I chew my lip, searching for the right words. "My father gave this to me. I will keep it out of sight. I won't wear it if that's the issue."

"Your attachment is the issue." He says it so matter-of-factly. Silence stretches but I can't bear to take it off. "What's your name?"

"What do you care?" I spit back. *Monster.*

He chuckles, and I simmer in anger. "I'm not a monster." Draven's head tilts as I startle, uncertain if he just read my thoughts or can assume them from my glowering. "And we don't need these here, now that the Selection is over." The prince reaches up slowly, unclasping his mask. I can't look at anything else as he lifts it off.

He's too symmetrical, too pretty, and my attention doesn't know where to focus first. On those eyes that have shifted once more, sparking violet, or that coy mouth that curls nearly cat-like in the corners, his smile just a little sharp. Edged with danger. My cheeks heat as I take in those full lips, his straight nose, the perfect chisel of his chin.

The more I stare at him the broader his grin becomes. He doesn't have any tattoos on his face, but I can see them peeking along his neck around that armor. I wouldn't be surprised if he was covered in them.

He's gorgeous.

But he's an immortal, I remind myself.

I force my gaze to the slight point of his ears, the black horns that spiral toward the heavens from his full head of dark silken hair, and the wings that tighten a bit closer on his back.

The most beautiful flowers are usually the most poisonous.

"Maybe not a monster. Still an entitled princeling," I manage, though my voice is embarrassingly quieter than moments ago.

His eyes alight, but otherwise, he remains nonplussed. "Your name?"

I swallow, trying not to be ensnared by his cursed beauty. "Rune."

"Rune." His deep voice tastes my name with something like relish, as if by repeating it he's drawn us unbearably closer, until he's the only thing in focus. "Give me the necklace."

Prince Draven's gaze traps me, forcing blood to rush to my head, leaving me stupid and embarrassed. He holds his hand out for it. Somehow it feels easier to give him something I love so deeply, instead of the soldier.

I shove it into Draven's palm. Smoke coils around the curves until it's swallowed by darkness, leaving only my rage.

"Good girl. Now, that wasn't so hard, was it?" With all the arrogance in the world he turns on his heel, slipping a shining tarot card back into a little box clipped at his hip. Did he just enchant me into giving that up?

I glare as his powerful form cuts back to Commander Soto's side. The two lead the way out of the entrance hall, out into the open grounds beyond.

"What just happened?" Ember asks me, looking between the prince and me.

"Nothing I can't handle." However long it takes, I will make that prick pay for this.

"Come on, Rune." Morgan snaps me out of my haze as he and Kasper trail the other changelings after the commander and prince. Ember lightly touches my shoulder and my wrath rebels at the sympathy in her eyes, but I follow.

The entrance hall opens onto a large oval lawn divided by a walking path and surrounded by beautiful houses, each with a grand sculpture at its front. Expansive stone and brick buildings rise behind the homes, likely containing classrooms. My feet falter at the sight of hundreds of other druids already standing at attention along the crossed path dividing the open space, all maskless, all of them beautiful terrors.

We are ushered toward an empty quadrant on the field.

My breaths are shallow, my lungs hollow in my chest as I take in the furious stares at the front of the crowd. The druid guards move us into disorganized columns. Beside the others, we're undisciplined. The druid students glare at us like they want to skin us alive.

Draven falls into a phalanx of initiates that have left a space for him. I notice a blond male and female druid lean over to him, whispering his way as if they're all old friends, bright smiles on their faces. He brushes them off, facing forward. I follow his attention to where Commander Soto stands at the center of the open space, finally removing his mask and clipping it at his hip.

He has the appearance of a man in his forties, though I wonder how many centuries he truly is. He's got light brown skin, sweeping salt-and-pepper hair tied in an intricate bun, dark cat-like eyes, and a neatly trimmed beard around his jaw. Like so many of the druids born of Sedah, tattoos creep up his neck, swirling in waves, complex patterns connecting each line with symbols I don't recognize.

"Welcome to another year in the Forge, this one marked by a large joining of Selected," Commander Soto says.

The tension of those around me is a palpable thing, thick enough in the air to choke on.

"It's my duty to remind immortals to refrain from harming changeling members of your class. We understand that time-bound traditions established by our ancestors allowed for competition at the Forge of the highest levels."

Commander Soto turns in place to take in every Sedah-born druid, and a ripple moves through the audience at the warning in his glare. "However, changelings still have significant disadvantages to those fully druid. It is against conduct, as it always has been, to attack any student in their bedrooms, classrooms, or anywhere outside sparring and training sessions. With the development of the Selection, know that you are expected to grant respect to your peers and recognize one another's contributions to our sacred kingdom of Sedah. We need each other, especially as tensions rise to the North. The success of one is the success of all. So, I ask you to remember your true enemy."

My skin prickles, sweat beading my forehead. Fuck. Against conduct? Judging by some of the looks blazing our way around this audience, I don't think that will deter them.

Draven and his friends look comfortable, as if they've already been here a year or more. I notice all of them wear pendants at the high-collared necks on their uniforms. Draven has two, though others have three or four of those daggered wands, the handles spindled. There's only one on my own collar, so they must indicate year.

But even those Sedah-born druids in our column with only one pin at their collars look more than capable of breaking us with ease. And like they want to. Commander Soto's limitations of keeping attacks to training sessions don't exactly ease my mind.

"Tonight, you will claim your beds in your appointed chambers, called Hearths, alongside those with the same Major Arcana," Commander Soto informs us. "Your assigned classes will be posted in your Hearths in the morning." He looks around the Oval at all of us, and my back straightens beneath his unimpressed gaze.

Good, underestimate me. Better men have made the same mistake, not realized it until far too late. So long as I get what I came here for. My family, and if not them, my vengeance. There must be some kind of trace or record of the other Selected that have come to Arcadia before in this place. Colleges have libraries, knowledge. It could even be possible my mother is here, or maybe in a town close by. I look around the space with renewed interest at the labyrinth of buildings, with their vaulted arches and gargoyle sentinels.

"Find your Hearths. Get some rest, you'll need it," Commander Soto orders.

All at once, everyone's moving, and I fall into line beside Ember and Morgan. I hiss, "How are we supposed to know which ones we go to?"

"I don't know, but I don't think they trust everyone to settle in for the night." Ember watches the druids over her shoulder, the guards still lingering in the crowd. She scrunches her eyes closed, then forces them back open, looking as tired and overstimulated as I feel. It's odd to see the Selected with such changes, and I notice a young man take off his glasses, look them over, and then discard them. Being a changeling will have advantages, but beyond surviving using magic, I don't know what else yet, and no one's bothered to explain.

They haven't even told us any details about learning their magic.

Druid guards shout orders directing us, as the Sedah-born druids walk by us with little sympathy to how lost we all are. I hear one guard growl to someone, "Higher-powered Arcana are at the top of the Oval. Lower ones like yours are toward the entrance hall."

"How do we know if they're high or low?" Morgan asks us quietly.

"Mine had a number, did you notice one on yours?" Ember chews her lip.

I barely glimpsed my card.

"Just look to the giant stone statues." Kasper's gaze narrows on a house on the right near the entrance hall. A marble statue of a holy woman with her hands raised to the sky stands outside it. The house beyond, or Hearth, doesn't look particularly imposing, yet Kasper hesitates to go to it.

Huge castle walls extend beyond this open central space and the buildings for classrooms, cradling the campus up to the sides of the mountains and volcano. They'd be impossible to scale, and the only apparent exit is the bridge we walked in on. I trail Ember as Kasper takes off toward his Hearth, Morgan and I searching for our own. The king acted as if mine is rare, so I'm betting it's at the higher end of the Oval, where the house is smallest.

Prince Draven lingers at the back of the column with a cabal of older students. Few druids have wings or horns, but he and his friends all do. None of them have familiars like the guards, though. Are those something earned? His gaze lightens as we lock eyes, coy lips curling, his stride so utterly, annoyingly confident. I turn away, seeking out a statue that matches that tarot card I drew, the World card.

"Oh, this is me, I drew the Star." Ember points to a tall golden star statue with four long points, smaller rays radiating between them. Carved in finely printed letters above the door are the words *The Star's Hearth*. She turns to me. "Maybe we'll have classes together tomorrow?"

"I hope so." I'm hesitant to put too much optimism into the thought. I like her. She gives off a calming, friendly energy, but I haven't had a friend in years, not since Kiana, and she wasn't merely a friend. The thought of her is like a weight sinking, a reminder of pain. I push the memory of her away. I can't think of her, or the Lord of Westfall, and what he did to her when he sensed how close we'd become. She's the one person I can no longer search for. I turn away from Ember quickly.

"Shit, I think I'm over there." Morgan stands beside me, craning his neck across the Oval. My eyes sweep over the Hearths as he points at one of the statues. "Does that look like the Moon to you?"

"Definitely a crescent moon." It glimmers, made of a pearlescent opal.

"What did you draw?" he asks.

"The World," I reveal, but he shrugs.

"I suppose we'll learn what they each mean at some point, and how they choose."

I don't answer. I remember the pull of the deck, as though the World and I were inexorably drawn to each other. As if it'd reached into my soul and unspooled the two desires fighting for control within me. Reunification and revenge, so opposite but pouring from the same wound.

Few people are in our column now, spaced out as we walk. Draven's still surrounded by his group of friends, though he stops with them at the penultimate house.

"Finally." I reach the house opposite of the entrance hall. An enormous globe stands outside the doors, a woman holding it like a womb, all of it made of gold. It's the smallest house, confirming just how rare it is among the host of others. I hesitate at the short row of steps leading up to its front door. I turn to Morgan. "The druids don't seem to be happy we're here. Watch your back."

"Don't worry about me." He winks, but then his look turns serious, and he leans too close. "Tomorrow we should all find each other. Stick together."

But I don't want to make anyone any promises. People can be allies or anchors, and I'm already fighting to keep my head above water in these uncharted seas.

"See you tomorrow, Morgan."

The doors to the World's Hearth are open, but I don't hear anyone inside, and no one approaches. A large circular window sits above the main door, like a great glass eye.

The rest of the Hearths seemed to be full. Why is no one else here?

I cautiously enter. The floors are made of wood laid like herringbone; the ceilings are seamless granite blocks. The walls remind me of forests—varying textures from woods to calming green stalks edge the space. A clean, modern kitchen is tucked into the entry, opposite a water closet, and I pass it by to the main living room. Comfortable furniture takes over the central area, holding a fluffy couch facing a lit fireplace. There's a fountain of stone and glass against the opposite wall, the tinkling water the only sound in the space.

"Hello?" I step farther in. A spiral staircase leads up to a second floor lined with bookshelves, a balcony overlooking the central space.

There are only two open bedrooms. I spot a jacket draped over a chair beside a small chess table in one of them. So, someone else does live here. Little knickknacks and personal effects dot the shelves. I branch off to the empty room on the right. An enormous bed takes up the two-story space, a loft reading area above, a library ladder leaned against one wall. I resist a smile—at least one whole wall and another in the loft are filled floor to ceiling with books; too many to read in one lifetime, though there's space for more. This many books in one room in the mortal realms would've invited a raid from the Reapers, the immortals preferring to keep us ignorant. I relished the Lord of

Westfall's collection, one of the rarest and largest, he'd told me, but it didn't hold a candle to this.

Here, the books shine like jewels. Maybe they'll have answers for me.

Warmth emanates from the lit fireplace against one wall.

An enormous arched window provides a clear view of the volcano in the distance, lava burbling at its top. More druid robes hang in the closet, a single wand pendant affixed to each in militaristic placement, demarking the lowly rank of my first-year status. A bathroom branches between the two rooms, a joint space, but at least it seems I'll have only one roommate.

But for all the charm of this place, it feels like a trap, coiling as it readies to spring.

My gaze searches every shadow, but I'm alone.

The skin of my neck feels bare without the bone fishhook pendant my father left me, my pockets empty without the little broken king I usually run my thumb over like a worry stone. But aside from possibly poisoning the arrogant prince, I'm not sure there's anything I can do about it.

They hold no power over me, I repeat beneath my breath, letting out a tight sigh as I sit on the mattress, the exhaustion of the day settling into my bones.

My gaze falls upon the hearth of my room, the merry fire cracking a log and sending sparks across the wood. I think of embers trailing behind King Silas. There were tales that the druids' power was tied to fire, that they could listen in at every candle and flame . . . perhaps the legends were right.

My life has been marked by fire, too.

I think of the Lord of Westfall cursing my name as his manor burned around him. The scent of flames still clings to my hair.

Then something far worse—the smell of ash in the air as I ran across the snow . . .

Footsteps snap me from the nightmarish memory. Someone's here.

I brace myself, walk over, and throw open the door.

Sprawled on the couch—as if he owns the place—is Prince Draven.

"Don't worry, darling," he says in that huskily sweet voice, eyes settled back on indigo. "I don't want you here either."

5

Roommates

The Knight of Wands is ruled by fire and cannot be tamed, and though charismatic and alluring, his impulsiveness can lead to dangerous desires.

OF ALL THE PEOPLE, demons, whatever he is, to be stuck in close proximity with, he's the last I'd choose. All I see when I look at him is my father's necklace disappearing into the shadows. The weight of the day snaps something in me.

I bend down, yank my boot off, and chuck it straight at his stupid head.

It's something I never would have dared do to the Lord of Westfall. But I'm done scraping and bowing and kowtowing. I left that version of me behind to burn.

Clearly, Prince Draven wasn't expecting it, but he's on his feet impossibly fast. I barely register the blaze of golden light in the air, a tarot card of a skull-faced grim reaper flashing, and my boot disappears into shadows. My fury doubles, my vision reddens as I realize I've just thrown the last thing my mother gave me away.

I grasp a glass vase off a sideboard just as a portal opens above my head, the boot colliding into my temple. I stagger, clutching the wound in shock.

"You demonic little asshole!" I growl.

He warns, "Don't!"

I hurl the vase at him anyway. He merely twists his hips, the glass launching past him and shattering in the fireplace. He turns to me with a snarl on his full lips, his mouth open in outrage, as if he hasn't earned a lick of this fury. He's earned the whole damn platter.

I grab the next thing I see, a penknife, and this time, when I throw it, he doesn't try to avoid it. A flash of a card and it turns into a salamander. He brushes it off, where it skitters across the wood floors and jumps happily into the fire.

"I liked that pen knife," he says humorlessly.

"Then go fetch your new pet," I snarl.

"That's not how magic works," he mocks.

As my fangs slide down, his come out to match, wings spreading high. He truly looks like a beast now. I back into the sideboard, a second vase toppling into my hand.

Draven grits his teeth. "Oh, come on."

I chuck it at his head, but the vase pauses as if trapped in time. He moves around it, yanking it from thin air, and bears down on me. I'm frozen like a fossil in amber glass. *He* did this to me. I try to break from it, throwing my might behind each movement but I'm stuck in place; panic rises.

He thuds the vase back onto the buffet, his hands moving in constant, furious motions, drawing a combination of cards I can't make out. My body jerks into motion as if on strings, walking forward like some puppet, plopping into an armchair, a blanket unraveling into ropes that strap me down.

He levels a glare at me. "First rule of starting a fight in another kingdom: don't start shit until you understand how things work." He holds up a tarot card of a man hanging upside down, his hand glowing crimson red before he flicks the back of the card. The color dissipates and movement slowly returns to my body. I jerk forward, as if everything I've tried to do catches up at the same time.

But he doesn't release the ropes. He holds up another card, this one of a grim reaper. "Second rule of instigating: use your head." Shadows open above me. I flinch as my boot drops into my lap.

He stops walking, dropping back onto the couch, his hair less perfect than moments ago, his face a little red. "Then maybe you'd have thought to . . . I don't know? Learn how to use the magic we've promised to teach you *before* attempting to murder me for no gods damned reason."

"No reason? You stole something from me!" I slam against the bonds, but they won't budge.

"What're you . . . oh. Is this all because of that trinket?" Draven's clearly flummoxed, his head rolling back. He twists his hand, and the shadows reappear, the pendant along with it, cord looped around his deft fingers. "Is this what you want?"

My mouth curls as I look him over, his smug face half cast in shadow, lips lifting in a daring smirk. He's not in the armor he wore to the Selection, but instead wears a black buttoned shirt, the top undone. Hints of tattoos peek out, including two entangled serpents, one white, one dark.

"That's mine," I growl.

He stands, coming around my back. Every part of me seizes, preparing to fight as he leans over me. My necklace is strung between his hands, his breaths coiling at my nape, a caress against my ear. "All you have to say is please."

I turn to take more of him in, but we're too close, our breaths sharing the same space.

"Please give it to me." I meet his eyes. "And I won't break your pretty fucking nose."

Draven scoffs, tongue tracing a sharp canine, and I can tell he's caught between amusement and annoyance. Chewing his lip and whatever retort he looks primed to fling at me, he laces the necklace back in place, drawing it flush against my skin. He crosses to the couch, scooping up his tarot cards he left on the coffee table.

He huffs out a sigh, lazing confidently, arm resting across the back. My glower fades—but only slightly.

"Why didn't you just let me have it back there?" I ask, eyes narrowed.

"Because you're not allowed to keep . . ." He looks me over, and I swear I hear the amendment in whatever he was going to say, his tone adjusting. I'm sure to him a bone pendant necklace is the epitome of peasantry—the very threads along his collar and every button tracing his chest shine in molten gold. He clears his throat. "You can't hold on to anything that ties you to your past. Whoever you were before means nothing now."

It means everything, whatever lands I'm in.

He tsks and a suspicion raises in the back of my mind once more that he heard that thought. But Prince Draven just leans forward, elbows on his knees, strong hands shuffling his deck of cards, the paper black as pitch, the gold foil patterns shimmering in the hypnotic movement.

"What about the other items I brought . . . is there any chance—"

"Your clothes likely have met the incinerator by now."

His gaze travels the length of me as I fall against the ropes. I don't care about the clothes . . . well I do, but not the way I do losing that piece of my brother.

"Were they dreadfully important—"

"Why are we the only ones in this house?" If I'm stuck with him, at least I can get information out of him. I'm certainly not going to open up to him about something so personal.

"It's a Hearth," he corrects. His eyes avoid mine as easily as he did that question.

"Can you untie me so we can have a civilized conversation?"

"That depends. Are you going to behave?"

"So long as you give me some answers."

We stare at each other for a moment, and I recognize something in him that I see in myself every time I look in the mirror. Resolution. Stubbornness. We might sit in these chairs glowering at each other until our bones grow brittle and our hair gathers dust. He rolls his eyes at me finally, impatience winning even if trust is too fragile to lace between us, and my ties drop. I rub my arms where they squeezed too tightly.

"You and I are the only ones to be chosen for this Arcana in half a millennium."

I knew it must be rare by the lack of rooms available, but . . . I didn't expect it to be that extraordinary. "Why is that?"

He shrugs, wetting those lips as he avoids my eyes, wrists coaxing, fingers twisting as he shuffles those cards over and over. "I've no idea. It's . . . an extremely coveted Arcana. I'm just as confused as everyone else as to why it'd choose someone who so clearly doesn't want anything to do with us."

I force my expression into neutrality.

"Is it coveted because people want to be closer to *the prince*"—I gesture in his direction—"or for its rareness?"

Draven's smile spreads like a wildfire. "Both." He examines his nails, and hair rises on my arms as I wait for the talons to appear that I know he can summon in a moment. But he keeps them at bay. "The World as your Arcana means you have immense magical capabilities."

"Oh, like that little magic show you just put on?" I prod, pointing blatantly at his cards now. "Seemed an awful lot like you were trying to impress me."

He ignores my jab. "It also gives you immense political influence. You could be . . . useful." *Or dangerous*, is what he doesn't say. "But perhaps the Arcana won't stick. Maybe it'll decide you're not worthy of it."

"Well, fuck you, too." I grasp my necklace, clutching it tightly until it digs into my palm. He said that last sentence as if it was on his mind from the moment the World chose me. "So . . . me being chosen means your special Arcana is a little less rare . . . am I a threat to you?"

He meets my gaze, incredibly steady. I don't look away.

"Only if you stand in my way." His coldness is far more chilling than his fire ever was. "I'm up at four thirty every morning, gone by five. Stay out of my sight, and I'll stay out of yours. Don't try to kill me in my sleep. It'll go very poorly for you."

He moves toward his room, all preternatural grace. I stand, nearly tripping on the loose ropes of the blanket, stepping out of them awkwardly. My anger has mostly subsided, but I'm still frustrated, nerves burning through me so hard that I shake like a lightning-struck tree. I'm not done with this conversation.

"Are you going to tell me what the hells the World Arcana's magical power is?" The heat from the fire doesn't reach me. For all the warmth this room inspired when I first entered, I feel nothing but cold and alone now. "What's the big secret?"

Draven doesn't look back at me, only stares ahead into his room, a refuge my questions hold him back from. I think about what Ember said, *He could be an ally, or a tool.*

Finally, he turns to look at me, the shade in those eyes brightening again, resting in indigo.

"It's all of them. Everything." Those full lips quirk up in the corner. "If you're strong enough."

His eyes flick away dismissively, but I'm not done.

"I don't understand this place."

He stops, blinking nonplussed. "Weren't you paying attention?"

"Why are you training *us*? We're enemies. I thought we were going to . . . I don't know, be enslaved or something?"

"And you volunteered for that?" His head tilts, and it strikes me with painful awareness that he's not a man at all, but something more. Something worse. He has the beauty of a god and is nearly as dangerous. He grins wickedly. "Let me guess. You thought if you got Selected, you'd be let over the Wall and then just . . . find a way to elude us? To find your missing family in a totally foreign land? You really don't think much of immortals if you thought it'd be that easy."

"What choice did you leave me?" I hiss through my teeth, "Everyone I loved was taken by you people."

He wears the epitome of boredom on his features. Ignoring the emotion blazing in my eyes, he straightens his wrinkleless shirt. "You seem to enjoy lumping us all together. But your scent isn't anything I recognize. So, tell me, Rune, did the *druids* ever choose someone you love?"

"The elves and the seraphs—"

"Are not druids," he finishes for me. He shakes his head. "Humans like to pretend the Selection is random. It makes it easier. But the truth is we all have our own qualifications for who we take. With druids? We pick people with no one in the mortal realm left to mourn them."

Blood rushes out of my face, leaving me shifting on my feet.

"And those who avoid the Selection? Would they be put here, too?"

"Your mother isn't here." His lip curls. "Selection deserters are considered undesirable, untrainable." His gaze travels my face meticulously. "Be glad no one seemed to realize you deserted, too."

"Is that a threat?" I don't take those lightly.

"Observational skills." The prince releases the door handle, wings spreading wider at his back. "If I were threatening you, there wouldn't be a question."

"Where is she?" The words blurt from me in the face of his cold disdain. I want answers. "She avoided Selection, and you took her—"

"*I* took? I recall doing no such thing."

I hate the spark that brightens those eyes. He enjoys this, fucking with me. He's jealous I was chosen for this stupid card, too, I can see it written all over his privileged face, and although I'd bet that he hates me, it's nowhere close to how I feel about him.

"I spared your brother from another choice on his little conscience. All I ask is where she is. Give me that much." I clench my jaw in the face of my nemesis and his eyes narrow, lip curling.

"Well, you provided my brother a traitorous kindness, and I did the same for you and your little . . . trinket. So, I'd say we're even." Yet he doesn't retreat to his room, nor use his magic. Instead, he lingers, gripping that handle, like he can't quite make himself go.

I push. "Tell me, and you won't have to watch over your shoulder for more flying vases." I don't know what makes me think he'd even listen. Maybe it's his hesitation.

"Is that a promise?"

"It's a deal."

His gaze travels the length of me. Chewing his lip, he comments, "All those who avoid the Selection are sent to the Destarion, the prison of No Realms. Last I'd heard any who survived that abstention were sold to the elves."

My heart drops. Clenching my eyes and jaw tight, I force myself to take a deep breath and then ask, "What becomes of them?"

The last dregs of hope shred in my chest as he shrugs. He picks at his cuticles with his thumb. "Usually nothing pleasant. But I'll remind you that you're bound to this realm; you can't just leave." He chews his lip but then adds, "You'd be better off applying yourself to this new life. A better one, surely, than whatever you left behind."

"You have no idea what I've left behind," I growl.

"Enough to beg for something that could've been far worse." His gaze narrows as he looks me over head to toe. "Stop carrying them with you."

He wouldn't understand. I can't believe I came all this way and chose to be Selected . . . on a fool's dream. None of them are here, and now I'm stuck in this realm for eternity.

My nails bite into my palms as I search for any lie, any trick in his words. "You said only those unmissed were Selected. What about that child?"

"An orphan. They all were." He yanks open his door, and I watch, my wretched heart drowning in hopelessness, as he enters but he halts, turning back to me. "Gone by five. Don't try to kill me," he reminds me viciously, and *snicks* the door shut in my face.

I march over to my own, slamming it and locking it tightly. Not that it'll matter. With all that magic, I doubt a door would stop him. But it eases me a little. I cross over to the shared bathroom and lock it, too. I change into a simple silk set of pajamas and crawl into bed. A lamp takes up most of the space on the bedside table, not lit by oil or candlelight. It's bright and warm, lighting cascades from a strange, orb-like object inside it. More magic.

It's comforting, even if it's the only thing that is.

So, I leave the light on, hoping it keeps out the darkness and the prince who commands it.

TRUE TO HIS WORD, Prince Draven is already gone by the time I wake up, my overwhelmed body sleeping heavily until the sun peeks through the curtains. I get ready quickly, annoyed by the frizz-free hair, its silkiness that feels so unfamiliar. When I return to the living room it's to find my schedule pinned to the noticeboard.

Beneath a copy of my bounty poster.

I rip it down, clutching the note clipped to it in tight, neat writing.

I didn't know I was in the presence of a celebrity.

What a fucking prick. I crumple Draven's words and toss them and the bounty against his open door. Clasping the schedule, I take a hard look at it, wondering what the hells I've gotten myself into.

8–9 . . . . Introduction to Tarot and Culture

9:30–11 . . . . Major Arcana

11:30–1 . . . . Minor Arcana

1:30–3 . . . . History of Arcadia

3:30–5 . . . . Divination and Readings

5:30 . . . . Sparring

I notice sparring doesn't have an end, but I have little time to focus on what it will entail, as my first class will start soon. The classes have general building and room numbers beside them, and a small, printed map pinned to the back. Packing a plain black side bag with a notebook and pen, I swing it over my shoulder and head off to the first class, swearing about Prince Draven under my breath.

The map takes me a bit to understand but the Hearths and the grassy Oval are a good reference point, and I'm soon headed the right way. Introduction to Tarot is in a large stone tower with a circular roofline. My pace has been dragging this morning, weighed down by Draven's assurance my mother isn't here. I've learned a lot of tells in my time as a Wraith, and he didn't seem to be lying. But now I feel directionless, knowing only that I need to survive long enough to figure out my next steps.

The lecture hall is bustling with changelings, the sound of shuffling and whispered conversations overwhelming. I stand in awe at the precipice. Balconies ascend above me; the domed ceiling is made up entirely of windows, and light shines through it, illuminating the grand space. I've seen marvels designed by mortal hands, but nothing like this. Carvings of the same tarot card figures and imagery I've seen outside each of the Hearths are chiseled into the columns around the room. Living trees line the edges, their branches holding small reading lamps with live bats and birds roosting in the limbs and leaves. It's too magnificent of a scale for mortal engineering, and I back against the sidewall, clutching my note bag tightly.

"Oh, thank gods, you're here!" Ember's warm smile envelops me, and I relax a fraction. Scooping her hand around my arm, she leads me up into the audience, decidedly aiming for an empty section of seats beside Morgan. Everyone here appears to be from the Selection. She sits, and I take the seat beside her.

Morgan leans over her to talk to me. "I heard it's just you and the prince in that last Hearth. You don't have to . . . sleep in the same room, do you?" His hands grip his notebook, knuckles whitening.

"No. It's a big house."

"I don't trust him," Morgan hisses.

I don't trust anyone. I shift the subject. "Do you have to share rooms?"

Morgan shakes his head and Ember whispers, "No, but I overheard that anyone in a house lower than Justice has at least one roommate."

"Lower?"

"In power. The Fool I guess is the lowest on the might scale, whereas the World is considered the highest." Ember looks to me meaningfully, but I don't feel any more powerful than I did last night. This body might have changed to something stronger, built faster, but no sudden gifts like what Draven showcased sift in my veins. Ember rattles off, "The lower on the scale, the more common the Arcana, too, which is why most are put in those categories, druid-born or changeling."

"How'd you find out all this?" I raise a brow, and she laughs.

"Turns out the Star Arcana are a pretty chatty group."

An older druid steps onto a platform in front of the black chalkboard. Despite his silver hair, and the gentle twinkle to his eyes, he's built lithe and strong, his movements not stiff but swift enough that I believe he could hold his own in a fight. He slides one chalkboard over, revealing another with prewritten notes beneath it.

He announces, "I am Professor Atum, and this is the only class in which all of you, my students, are changelings. I, myself, was once one, too."

The auditorium quiets, shock coiling within my chest at the casual statement of that. He seems both whole and content, and I don't know what to make of the idea that there are those of us who would find happiness here, in the home of our tormentors.

He tells us, "The first set of tarot cards was found in the forest of Eidolon in the North, thought to be a gift from the druids' mightiest god, Azazel, to help a nearby village survive a harsh winter. Since then, every set of cards has been made from a tree within that forest, which is why keeping your set together, keeping that tree and its magic intact, is so necessary. I'm sure you all have many questions—"

"What use are the lower of the Major Arcana?" a young man with messy hair asks from the front row. "I was only given the Emperor."

Professor Atum casually sets a large spherical marble on a desk between the board and us. He places his tarot deck beside it, opening and casually shuffling them out. With a motion like he's pulling a marionette upright, a card slips out, suspended in the air on invisible strings. It floats until it hovers before his outstretched palm, a twinkling golden glow surrounding it.

"The Magician. This card is nearly the lowest of Major Arcana, found on the might scale just above the Fool, and three spaces below the Emperor."

His spare hand parts the air over the orb, and as he does, it transforms, its material turning to pure gold before our eyes. I cannot fathom how much money it would fetch, the problems it would solve in the mortal realm.

"Yet it still can transform materials. Even change lives, through the power of alchemy." There's a moment of silence as Professor Atum assesses us. "Every single one of you holds the potential to enrich our world through your efforts—but first, you must understand how we use magic for the greater good. The Major Arcana, which direct what forms of magic we are attuned to. The Minor Arcana, which enhance the Major Arcana. And the deck's storytelling ability, what each card represents in metaphor, offering guidance and even divination when used altogether. Tarot cards, like the druid community, are strongest when kept together."

He steps out from behind his desk, arms crossed. "In this class you will learn what each does and how that contributes to the kingdom of Sedah. You will learn to understand our cultures and customs and how we use magic to support every aspect of them. Write this down."

I GLANCE AT A CLOCK over Professor Atum's head almost an hour later, my hand cramping from vigorous note-taking. Somehow, there are still five minutes left before this class ends, and I force myself to break, rubbing my right hand to work out the stiffness. I've made a column with the Major Arcana and their powers, but they don't all make sense to me. The Tower wields lightning, the Emperor uses telekinesis, and Death controls shadows. They don't fit quite right. Not like Strength, whose power is an enhanced version of its name, or the Lovers' ability to draw out the truth in relationships and improve fated mating bonds.

Whatever the hells those are.

I don't know how I'll ever keep it all in line. Reading the list and knowing I'll eventually be able to wield all these powers leaves me in disbelief. If there's one thing in this world I'm sure of, it's my ability to distrust anything that seems too good to be true.

Better that than to prove myself a fool.

A bell rings, and I'm pulled out of my thoughts as everyone packs up. I gather my things and we scoot along the lecture hall's row to the stairs, slipping out of the room into the hallway.

"Did any of that make sense to you two?" I ask.

Morgan chuckles.

Ember looks through her notebook. Somehow, she's managed to adorn each page with neat little drawings. Her penmanship is beautiful, everything tidy and thorough. Meanwhile, there's still ink smeared up the side of my hand.

"I think so, but I'm not sure what the ability to wield light and fire means as a life skill," she says thoughtfully, reflecting on her own powers of the Star.

"Just think of it this way—we'll never need a torch again," Morgan teases.

"I don't think we'll need torches or lanterns." Ember points to the magical lights in the sconces of the hallway as we walk along. "Pretty sure they got that covered."

"Star Arcana work in the forges to create our weapons," someone snarks, bumping hard into Ember's shoulder as they pass by. The druid girl bares her teeth at the indignation on my face. Her eyes are upswept, pretty freckles dot her cheeks like constellations, and her hair is long and straight, tied up in a black wave down her back. "If you weren't a bunch of scabs, you'd know that."

And I thought she was pretty until she had to go and say that.

"Scabs?" My lip curls, though sweat beads my temple at the confrontation. "Is that the best you can come up with? Immortal lifespans, but *scab* is the most original you got? It's a wonder you're not all extinct."

She stops abruptly. "What did you just say?"

The tone in the hallway shifts, and it dawns on me that most of the druids around me are Sedah-born, their tattoos and nicer gear setting them distinctly apart. My fists clench, talons sliding from the beds of my fingernails, but I don't want whoever this druid is to realize she's getting to me with so little effort. I force a relaxed smile to my lips.

"Should I have said it slower?"

"How did Prince Draven wind up Selecting someone as wit-less as you?" She looks me up and down as if it's impossible based on whatever she sees of me. "You don't belong here. Only *pureborns* do. And if this were twenty years ago, I'd have your head on a spike. You and your worthless, dirty-blooded mortal friends."

I step forward, my boots nearly pressing against hers. She's taller than me, but I won't let her make me feel small. She's the least of what I've faced.

"You really underestimate my level of spite." Calm laces my voice, though I'm sure there's fire in my eyes. "Just for this, I think I'm gonna give it my all. If for nothing else than to see you so threatened by us."

Her long lashes flutter, and then she's lunging. I reach for a knife that's not there, remembering too late I left my weapons in Vexamire, and she grabs me by the throat, lifting me off my feet. *How did she move so fast?* I'm slammed into the stone wall behind us. My head cracks, lightning shooting through it. The hallway erupts. Changelings and druids brawling throughout it. I even catch Kasper throw an unblocked punch into a druid's jaw, felling him in an instant.

My focus swivels onto the girl in front of me. For someone so slight, she shouldn't be able to pin me here with one hand. Her grasp tightens, and some gurgle comes from my throat, but it certainly isn't the *Fuck you* I planned on saying. I scrabble for the pen in my bag, trying to slide it out. It's not a knife, but it can still be a weapon.

"Get off her!" I hear Ember scream.

Two druids, likely my assailant's friends, block Ember from reaching me. My fingertips can't get purchase on the pen.

Fangs bared, the girl snarls, "You mortals are so weak. Just playthings to us. And if there were a way to reverse the Curse, we'd have wiped your lot out during your pathetic uprising."

"What . . . Curse?" I cough.

Her eyes widen as if she's let something slip.

"Mira!" a voice hollers over the crowd, the tone so chastising that everyone stops, and Mira drops me to the floor, where I steady myself against the wall.

There's a ripple in the hall as the crowd's attention shifts to a furious professor. He looks as if he could be her father, though I keep that observation to myself. He gestures to an open lecture hall behind him, speaking to everyone, "I am Professor Vexus, and I teach practical magic with Major Arcana. You're all late."

6

Practical Magic

The last act of the mortals during the Great War appears to be . . . permanent. I'm afraid it is best to go forward with the proposal of the Selection, though we will continue to seek out a cure.

—Magical Division of Alchemy to King Silas

W E SHUFFLE INSIDE, quickly finding our seats, and the class settles beneath the gaze of Professor Vexus, his annoyance smothering the room. He stands with his arms folded at the front of the class: lithe, pale, and livid. Brushing his dark hair back with a couple of descended nails curved to points, he addresses all of us, his tone as cutting as broken glass.

"What started it?"

He looks around expectantly, but I keep my mouth shut. I don't know what it's like here in Sedah, but in Westfall, there was a general saying about not snitching that really sticks with me now. I lean back in my seat, waiting for someone to say anything, massaging the back of my scalp. Miraculously, there's no blood.

It stays quiet. Apparently, druids abide by a similar code.

"Fine," he growls. "I'll go ahead and make some assumptions then. The first thing I'd like to remind you of is that *none* of you fought in the Great War, as you were all children. You may have had to live with the fallout, but you can all stop pretending it was your damned fight."

Across the room, I see Mira scoff lightly.

"Secondly, although the changelings are admittedly replaceable, killing them over minor slights causes a great detriment to all our futures."

Beside me, Kasper scowls. I wonder why they'd care if we were killed.

"You're here to prove your worth, not to bring down others around you." His gaze holds mine briefly before sliding to Mira's, softening. His hands clasp behind his back, perhaps to hide those extended talons and create a pretense of calm. "Now, for those new to our lifestyles, druids cannot channel their magic until age twenty, at earliest, which is when they enter their first year at the Forge. They may know more from seeing others wielding it and growing up within our customs, but they have as much practical use with it as you all do. Here, you're all at the same level."

I glance at Mira, feeling considerably less intimidated by her, and notice the druids seem muted.

"So, the first thing we are going to do is give you the equipment you will need to siphon and cast magic," Professor Vexus explains in a clipped tone.

Everyone straightens at that, the room tense as a piano wire. He gestures to two teaching assistants at the edge of the room, and they move through the class, placing a small black box on each desk. When mine is set down, I take in the fine foil details of the wooden case. A humming fills my ears, my thoughts clearing as if the world has washed away and the only thing in existence is me and the deck of cards encased in this box.

Professor Vexus snaps me back into focus. "The first rule of using tarot is do not let others handle your cards. Your personal energy signature will become part of your deck, and letting others touch them will transfer their energy into them. If someone does tamper with your cards, you must clear the energy, and we'll go over that later. The second rule of tarot is to know your intention before you cast. This can prevent mistakes from an accidental draw if it does not align with your purpose, effectively stopping you from making a poor choice in judgment. The third rule . . . try not to get into a fight with someone with a higher Arcana than you."

It takes all my effort to clamp down the smug smile that wants to spring to my lips.

Professor Vexus continues, "Additionally, always keep your cards together with you. Once you make your Descent at the end of the year, the magic will be a part of you, and you'll be able to perform some limited magic *without* your deck and have your Major Arcana inked across your dominant hand."

He holds up a hand and I can plainly see a thick rectangular tarot card tattooed across the back of it. My own flexes, and I wonder how badly it'll hurt.

"However, for most of us, our magic will always be strongest *with* them to siphon our intentions and prevent burnout.

"The last thing to remember is you have physical limitations, and channeling too much energy can cause you to burn alive from the inside out."

My heart stutters in my chest, and everyone glances around. That's a possibility?

"Your changeling or immortal bodies can protect you only so much. So, you will start small and build up your tolerance over time. Now . . . pick up your decks and take the cards into your hands."

I flip the hinge on my black box, and the cards slide into my palm. There's a familiar texture to them, though they're a little larger than playing cards, and when I rub my thumb along their surface, the slightest vibration tingles up my hand. Their smooth faces are dappled with raised gold foil set against deep black, making each one intoxicating to look at. The art is symmetrical, delicate—I've never seen any crafted thing so beautiful.

"Hold them as much as you can over the next few weeks, sitting with them for at least ten minutes each night," Professor Vexus says. "For now, to practice, you will be split into even groups, your Arcana sorted as follows . . ."

He slides a chalkboard to the side, having already written out the groups. There are more people in the lower Arcanas, so they'll have more people to practice with and learn from. I check for the World, but the list ends at the next highest Arcana, Judgment. Tentatively I raise my hand.

Professor Vexus looks me over, lip curling. "Yes?"

"The World isn't up there."

"That's because only Prince Draven has been blessed with that Arcana."

"Prince Draven and me."

The rest of the druids break into a flurry of whispers, like wind buffeting through the leaves of a mighty forest. The desire to add something snarky to this reveal itches my skull, but I manage to keep my jaw clenched tight as one of his teaching assistants joins him on stage, whispering in his ear. Professor Vexus's eyes go wide, and he stares at me as if I've turned from lamb to lion before his very eyes, his gaze tearing me apart. He clenches a piece of chalk, walking to *Judgment* on the board, and hastily scribbles *The World* beside it. Tossing the chalk in the tray beneath the board as if it personally wronged him, he turns, addressing the rest of the room.

"Quiet down. Now, beyond the classroom, you're welcome to practice your magic with consenting partners, but do not use them against your classmates without their knowledge, unless you want to spend a night in the Boiler. It's the building that rests closest to the volcano, Mount Hestia. That place is the anvil to which your misdeeds will be struck from you," Professor Vexus warns.

My jaw clenches; of course there would be a place to deliver punishment here.

"The more you put into your cards, the more you will get out of them, so I recommend you spend your free time wisely. You'll have practical exams at the end of term, as well as midsemester exams. Until then, we're focusing on getting you to learn your Major Arcana. Today, we will practice summoning your magic and getting your cards to respond."

DRAWING THE WORLD wasn't easy when it chose me, but today, I've failed to get it to respond to me even once. The curious eyes around the hall have turned to disappointed grumblings and unimpressed once-overs by now. Although everyone is practicing the movements Professor Vexus showed us to draw out our power from the cards, my face still heats from all the flickering attention. As he passes me, sweat beads down my temple, my hand shaking from the attempt, and the professor stops, standing just within sight.

How incredibly annoying.

"Some find flicking the top deck in their card helpful in summoning the one they desire," he comments loudly over my shoulder, using me as an example of failure. "Though a flow of your wrist, with your middle finger pointing down to flashing upward, is the *correct* way of drawing your card out. As if you were tracing a clock from six to twelve. True masters do not need to physically touch their cards at all." He looks down his nose at me.

I'm doing every movement just as he says but still nothing happens.

"Of course," he sneers, "those with the higher of the Major Arcana may soon find themselves unworthy of it. Perhaps yours will settle lower, somewhere more fitting."

I give him a measured smile, though all I can think is I have a middle-finger movement I'd love to share with him. The bell rings and everyone stops, most looking relieved, but probably none more than me. Half the class or more are still staring. I'm not used to having all eyes on me. As the Wraith of Westfall, I specialized in staying unseen. Now I'm the center of unwanted attention.

As I go to gather up my cards and place them inside their container, my fumbling hands slip, and they spill across the ground around me. Everyone sees, but no one stops to help. Professor Vexus scoops up his own bag and strolls out without a backward glance, adding to my embarrassment. I track down every card on my own and the others shuffle off, Ember getting swept up in the crowd.

I count the cards as I gather them, realizing I'm one shy of seventy-eight.

"Shit-damn-piss," I grumble, getting more frantic as I search beneath the neighboring desks. Someone passes in front of me and moves to hand me something. The Knight of Wands reflects the light, catching my eye as he holds it out. I reach for it quickly, slowing as I glance up and find a handsome druid before me, his hair jet-black, skin bronze, smile roguishly charming, eyes a cutting silver.

"Fuck, I forgot I'm not supposed to touch them, right?" He flinches a little at his lack of decorum. "Sorry about that."

"It's fine." I wave off the worry forming between his brows, and his face relaxes. Trembling like a gods damned fool, I slip the card in with the rest of the deck. Professor Vexus had mentioned briefly that the cards could be cleansed by keeping the deck in its box for thirteen hours. It means I can't practice tonight, but I have a feeling I'll be too tired anyway. They should at least be recharged by morning.

I'm surprised he's still standing here. The rest of the class has already gone, and I realize the friendly ones likely didn't want to impede my studying by gathering up my deck for me.

"I'm Wynter." He holds out his hand, and we clasp arms in a very human greeting. My gaze is drawn to the vascularity of his forearms, like he's been hewn from magnificent marble. He doesn't have horns or wings, but there are druid tattoos lurking under his sleeve, though his clothes are standard-issue. "I drew Judgment. I was trying to figure out how to approach you with that."

"Oh . . . we're partners." I'm not sure what to think. He's a little too pretty to be studying with, as likely to distract me as help me, second only maybe to Draven. Factoring in Wynter's personality and he's much more appealing than the prince. "I'm Rune, by the way." To my surprise, he doesn't react, but maybe he'd already heard it. "You have any luck drawing your card today?"

"Um, yes." Those silver eyes scan my face. "Well, once anyway."

Relief eases the disappointment that's been rankling me. Maybe I'm not so far behind. I smile softly, and he returns a dazzling one of his own.

"I better head to Minor Arcana," I say.

"Me too." Wynter's gaze traces from my eyes to my lips. He blinks and then gestures for me to lead the way. I'm surprised at the easy candor between us.

"Sorry if you were drawn into the fight before class."

Wynter frowns, shoulders jumping in a slight shrug. "I was late. I think I just missed it." I'm not sure if he's lying or not. Though I don't know why he'd bother to spare my feelings.

"Apparently, we all were." I tuck my hair behind my ear. The silence between us longs to be filled, so I find myself adding, "What does the Judgment Hearth look like?"

"Not very crowded." He rubs the back of his neck. "But honestly, a little creepy. Feels like Hollow Festival, but . . . all year round."

"Hollow Festival?"

"It's a day where we dress in costume to honor Azazel, god of death. Though most just use it to party." Wynter grins when I raise a brow. "There's more to it, of course. Some dress like tarot cards, or skeletons, or the monsters Azazel uses to guard the Underworld."

"Interesting." I look him up and down. "What's the power that comes with Judgment?"

He grimaces, running his tongue along a pointed canine. "Power over the living . . . and the dead. Mind control and necromancy, including the ability to summon spirits. King Silas has the same ability." Wynter adds tentatively, "What about you? The World is as powerful as it gets."

"So I've been told." Disappointment seeps into my words. No one seems to think I deserve it or that I'll manage to keep it. What happens if I don't? Will I have to redraw? It makes me want to prove them all wrong, to shove it down their throats. *Lost* doesn't quite cover how I'm feeling. I'm stuck in this realm, the Oath makes sure of it, and even if I find out where my family is, I'll never be able to reach them. There must be a solution I'm not seeing. Maybe one in the magic they're foolishly teaching us. My wrist prickles painfully beside my tarot cards, now clipped to my hip. Looking Wynter over I say, "Prince Draven mentioned that with higher Arcana comes more power. King Silas said power is what decides things here. Have you found that to be true?"

"Power is the only thing that matters in Sedah. I'm sure the mortal lands aren't different."

"Ours stems mostly from riches." I think back to that orb turning gold. "But that doesn't seem to be as valued here."

"Magical power translates to social power within the Court— it can elevate you nearly to royalty." Wynter leads the way out of the building and into an adjacent one.

With enough power, could I have my family brought here? If the immortals can transfer mortals to other realms, maybe I can buy their freedom.

We stop on the threshold of another classroom, just as big as the last one.

His gaze flits over me. "Where are you sitting?"

I spot Ember and Morgan and invite Wynter to join me, slipping beside them. Kasper is on Ember's other side, looking sullen, his lip busted from the fighting. Maybe it's not just my family on the line. Perhaps it's the cancerous idea of vengeance that makes me want to put my all into these cards, feeding off every cell within my traitorous body.

If I become powerful, I can change things.

If I can change things, I can bring it all down.

7

) ✳ *(•*

The Prince

The High Priestess represents intuition, knowing,
and listening to one's heart, but in reverse there is
ignorance, secrets, and an untrustworthy person in
our midst.

I RUB MY TEMPLE to ward off the coming migraine brought
on from sitting through Minor Arcana. This class concentrates on the fifty-six cards of lesser magic in each tarot deck
that all of us use to enhance our Major Arcana. It's overwhelming. The Minor Arcana are made up of four suites, representing
the four kingdoms. The wands of fire represent the druids: cre-
ativity, attraction, and new beginnings. The airy swords represent the seraphs: clarity, strife, communication. The gold coins
of the earth represent the elves: money, promise, stability. And
last, the cups of water represent the mortals: emotions, relationships, openness.

"Weakness," Mira whispers under her breath from a row
behind me.

I clench my fist around my pen and continue my notes.

I learn the other kingdoms don't use tarot magic, they have
their own. Seraphs can manipulate air and storms, their mighty

bodies rivaling the Strength Arcana among our druids. The elves manipulate the earth, drawing gold and jewels from the ground, and though not as strong, they're typically faster and more agile than other immortals. Their abilities are akin to our Justice Arcana, and they can apparently craft amazing machinations and weaponry. But tarot cards were a gift from Azazel, focusing druids' magic into an ability and recognizing that each druid is naturally more attuned to one type or another. Essentially tarot became the siphons that give them greater range than the other immortals and arguably more power.

I raise my hand, and petite, olive-skinned Professor Fenrys calls on me. "Yes, Rune?"

"I still don't understand why we would use aces or twos in the Minor Arcana to enhance our powers. Why not just use the higher-ranking cards like pages, knights, queens, and kings?"

She nods eagerly, seemingly happy to know anyone is listening.

"Let us imagine you have the Magician Arcana, and you wish to change an object to a different form. Perhaps something that has a fragile starting form like a glass dish into a slightly stronger crystal one. If you were to use a higher numbered Minor card, you could fracture the dish before you even begin to change its form, effectively taking a battering ram when all that is required is a gentle touch." Professor Fenrys smiles at the class, and I'm glad to see I'm not the only one whose brows have relaxed into a state of understanding.

Others like Mira roll their eyes at me. I don't care if I embarrass myself by asking questions. I'm more interested in making sure I understand it all. Anything I can learn here will be useful.

"Or perhaps you're a Moon Arcana, and you need to shift your form in a small way, let's say change your hair color. It might need only a Seven of Cups to boost it along, whereas the King of Cups might cover you head to toe in fur."

The class laughs at that.

After that I attend a class on the history of Arcadia, from its founding by the first druids of the Eidolon Forest to the ruling line of the Vos Dynasty, who have lorded over the realm for at least four centuries.

Then a class on tarot card readings, using what each card represents and how they speak to each other to create a reading. My attention slips as the professor goes over several ways of drawing and laying our cards in different spreads to help us reflect on what may be happening around us. The most common arrangement is three cards representing the past, present, and future, though some are as complicated as ten-card spreads. Its accuracy seems murky, and I'm too pent-up to focus.

When we're done, it's time for sparring, and after a day of writing notes and being overloaded by facts, I relish a chance to hit something. Or someone.

Apparently, every druid of Sedah is required to learn sparring and weaponry, even with the ability to wield magic. There's a likelihood, the instructor tells us, that we could lose our cards or be faced with enemies that could overcome our magic.

The entire student body, including Draven, share in this all-years open space, filled with changeling and druids in various form of fight practice. Hand-to-hand combat, sword fighting, and a hall for archery. Some, like many of the druid-born, have a natural, lethal approach. The changelings have almost no combat training among them. It's one area where I have a distinct advantage.

I'm hardly listening as our instructor focuses on teaching us first-year changelings basics like how not to break our thumbs when punching or how to hold our arms and shoulders to protect ourselves. How to step, move our hips, and throw our power around.

I know how to fight.

Curiosity strikes. How does Draven handle himself on the mat? The answer: with brutal grace.

Draven ends each fight with speed and efficiency, as if he refuses to yield an inch of time, not toying with his challengers but instead putting them down with haste. Like he has somewhere better to be. Most are hesitant against him, and I cannot tell if it's his title or ability that causes their steps to falter. He shows mercy to none of them, and even after facing half a dozen opponents, he still looks as if he's barely broken a sweat.

But when I square off with a druid across the mat, the first punch I'm unable to block has me seeing stars. Mira laughs unkindly from where she stands on the sidelines.

My attention shoots immediately to Draven, watching me across the gym, lips curved down. Is that disappointment? Or just distaste? I stand and throw my whole power behind an uppercut, and the druid girl I face goes sprawling, knocked out cold.

I think I've fractured something, and my hand trembles with agony. I sit, plunging my fist into a bucket of ice. Mira broods in a corner. Subtly I glance Draven's way. He's not looking at me, not directly. But I swear to the stars a coy smirk lifts the corner of those luscious lips.

HOURS LATER, I walk back to my Hearth, sore and aching.

My Wraith training means I can climb any surface I encounter and use knives and a bow masterfully. Yet the rigor of the drills our druid trainer subjected us to left me limping, my hand healed by an Empress Arcana. I spotted Draven a few more times throughout the session, working across the room with other second-year students like himself. He handled every hit with battle-worn refinement, never hesitating.

Each step leading to the World Hearth takes a small toll, and when I open the door, I'm grateful Draven isn't here, at least not yet. I move to the kitchen and open a cold box, ice magically kept frozen inside, the kind of thing only the rich would have prototypes for in Westfall. Here, it looks commonplace, masked to match the white oak cabinetry. Food lines the shelves, and I spitefully grab a sandwich wrapped in brown paper with Draven's name on it.

I move to the couch, kicking my boots off on the rug, leaving soil everywhere. Setting my tarot deck down on the coffee table, I unwrap the sandwich and give it a sniff. My senses have been in overdrive all day, leaving me exhausted. It hits harder, in the quiet of the house, just how irritated I've been from this bodily transformation. My sight is sharper, my sense of smell stronger, my hearing so robust that the slightest sounds can be grating. The taste of ordinary things is either intoxicating or repulsive, and touch—well . . . even the smallest graze of a hand against my own sends goose bumps down my arm, as if I'm constantly balancing on a knife's edge.

Draven's sandwich seems to contain spinach, a cheese too rich for me to name, some form of heavily seasoned poultry, a slathering of mayo, and something unfamiliar with a reddish-orange coloring. The bread is flaked with green seasoning, spongy and buttery beneath my fingers. I take a hesitant bite, afraid I'll find something unsavory, like a human toe, but it's . . . delicious? Within a few moments, I'm cramming the last bits of crust into my mouth, relishing every bit, staring into the fire with tired eyes.

"Did you enjoy that?"

I jump, turning to find Draven leaning against the sideboard, arms crossed with a dark warning in his gaze. I lick my fingers, not bothering to answer him. That was more comment than question and I don't feel the Oath's forceful need to comply. I'm growing increasingly certain I'd only have to if the king demanded an answer, but he's just the prince. I didn't realize he was back. The only sound I've heard is the wood popping in the fireplace. I stretch, scooping up my tarot deck, my toes wiggling on the coffee table. He stares at them, full mouth turning down as if I've disgusted him.

"You have any more of those sandwiches?" I ask.

"I don't think I should share imported aioli with barbarians," he says.

"Where's it from?"

"Idyll."

"Never heard of it."

Draven sighs through his nose, eyes rolling.

"I'm not surprised, the Reapers keep you mortals in such ignorance. So many great libraries burned. It's a miracle any of you can read. But for your limited information, it's a kingdom across the great Emerald Sea."

Something invisible brushes my feet, and I jerk them from the table. I fold my legs around me, glancing at his hand hovering over his deck, and wonder what ghostly magic he used to pull that trick. I think the Emperor is responsible for telekinesis. This is only the second time I've seen him today, and already he's annoying me.

His eyes narrow. "You owe me for stealing my dinner."

"Be grateful I didn't steal anything of greater value," I warn with a pointed grin. I'm still angry with him, and I want his spoiled ass to know it.

"What else should I expect from a Wraith?" He watches me with amusement as I look sharply at him. His smile only spreads at my wariness. "Maybe that's what I should call you. *Wraith* fits you better than *Rune*. Yours is such an odd name for a human."

"Well, your name sounds like your father fucked a bird, Princeling." To my surprise, he scoffs out a laugh at that, and I wonder if no one has teased him about it before. "I thought what we were before didn't matter?"

"Not in any way that would halt you from seizing your power." His gaze devours me, too intense. Yet I can't look away. "But if you think my guards wouldn't have researched anyone sleeping under my roof? Well, I had your poster before you were asleep."

"And how do you know when I fell asleep?" My gaze narrows.

"You snore like a bear." The reply is so quick it leaves me blinking like an idiot. He glances at my cards on the couch. "Shouldn't you be practicing?"

"Apparently, I can't. Someone else handled a card of mine, and I need to let the energy reset." I shrug a sore shoulder. Training with their tarot cards is the best chance I have of getting the kind of leverage only power can buy, to find out where my family is, and find a way to secure their releases. I don't understand Sedah and all of its rules yet, but power is a universal language. I sigh. I'm so tired maybe it's better I can't try tonight.

"But you want to. So desperately." His eyes narrow on my face.

I return the hardened stare, lifting my chin. So he *can* read my thoughts.

Draven smirks as though he's figured me out, not a complex puzzle, but one meant for a small child. "You resent your father for being Selected. You think he could've avoided it, but his pride caught their attention. You loved your brother, but after his loss, your mother never saw you the way she saw him. And her? Part of you is relieved she's not here so you aren't burdened with saving her after how she treated you. Glad she's left you free to claim the power you've always lacked—"

"Stop that!" I launch to my feet, all my insecurities unraveled and thrown back in my face. My eyes burn, my hands tremble. There's no way he should know any of that. No way he could. He must be reading beyond my current thoughts to my entire catalog of memories, resentments, and pain as easily as a left-open diary. A window looking straight into my darkest shame.

His indigo eyes are like the bottomless ocean and his voice is soft as he says, "It's nothing to be ashamed of. I would hate my family, too."

"I don't hate them. I've never hated them!" I shout at Draven's arrogant face. *You're hiding an awful lot of ugliness behind all those refined features, Princeling.*

He flinches, as if I spoke the words aloud. His fingers coax over his pack of cards, a golden glow lining them.

My eyes slit, and my fangs extend. *Stop projecting your daddy issues onto me.* I shout the thoughts as if flinging them across a canyon.

The golden light blinks to nothing at Draven's hip, and his eyes burn crimson.

I glower right back, snarling, "I love my family. But apparently the only chance I have of seeing them is to play your little games." He scoffs as I scoop up my cards. "Am I not your prisoner?"

"You have access to immortality and power beyond measure whilst those in your homeland starve and crawl over each other

like rats for an ounce of the access you've attained in a night."
His head cocks to the side, jaw clenching shut. "*Prisoner* isn't
the word I'd use."

"But am I allowed to leave this place? Travel the immortal
lands without guard or chaperone?" I clench my jaw. *Power
beyond measure.* What good is it if I can't get my family back? I
came here wanting answers, but I feel more lost than ever. How
many years will it take to earn enough power to find them? He
doesn't answer and I scoff. "So, I can't leave. Probably ever." My
lip curls. "As I thought . . . a prisoner."

"Even if you had permission from my father to leave these
lands, you would find the elves are not so generous and the seraphs less than holy." Draven folds his arms, fingers curling. His
tone turns casually dismissive, a challenge weaved within as if
my ignorance is bottomless. "A few years of learning to wield
what's called to you, so you're not a danger to yourself or others, isn't a large ask considering the exchange in magic."

"If I could snap my fingers and have my family back at the
cost of burning these cards and all their power, I would."

"Whatever you say, Wraith." Hands in his pockets, his nose
twitches, face curling to a snarl. "You *asked* to be here, if I
recall."

I stand up, growling, "I wanted to find my family, not be stuck
here with some entitled asshole who's half pigeon."

"Two avian jokes in one evening. Real clever." He rolls his
eyes until he notices me marching to my room. I'm done with
him and his attitude toward me.

Shadows swarm around the door, slamming it closed before I
can reach it. I turn to face him, ready to start shouting, but he's
closer than I thought, and I careen back into the wall.

"Ow! You idiot!" I shove him in the chest, and despite finding nothing but hard muscle, he winces, the Death card glowing

and hovering at his side. We learned about its power today—he uses it to transport through shadows and manipulate them to grab things, so I snatch at the card. If I can imbue my energy on his deck, I can stop him—

I gasp, the card morphing from gold to red, burning my hand as if I've grabbed a hot poker. Death's skeletal face brands my palm, bubbling my skin.

Draven yanks the card back and grasps my bloodied hand, turning it over. "What were you thinking?" He groans, "Everyone knows not to touch someone else's cards in the middle of a spell!"

"It's only my second day here, asshole!" I roar back.

He flings my door open, marching me through the room and to the bathroom. Within seconds, we're inside, and he shoves my hand under running water. It cools the burn, but the card imprint is seared into my skin.

"Great, now I get to live with this forever."

He huffs, but his tone is calmer when he says, "Well, you can say you've brushed hands with death quite literally. It'll be quite an icebreaker."

His eyes flick over me, checking my reaction. It was . . . almost funny. But my hand still hurts like hells, my scowl becoming more of a grimace.

His glare softens with each moment as he spills his cards out across the bathroom counter, searching them. "Where is it? Here."

He summons the Empress, and the pain begins to subside slowly. He cups my hand, his other keeping the card held as close as he can to my palm without soaking it. I glance at him, his shoulder pressed into mine, dark brows furrowed together as he concentrates, some of his silken black hair nearly tickling my shoulder. His clothes are better than the standard-issue

garments the other changelings and I wear, finer than any druid's, embroidered with symbols of his family's empire in shining onyx thread raised across the dark tunic. Draven smells
like spiced rum and sandalwood, and when he bends closer,
his hair brushes my arm, smelling of vetiver. It makes me want
to lean in.

"There. I think . . . I mean, the rest should fade in time." He
releases me as though I'm made up of fire, and I lurch away
from him, cradling my hand with the other. A skull's still visible
on the heel of my palm. The rest of the imprint has thankfully
dulled.

"Shouldn't you be better at this, Princeling?"

His heated gaze edges to violet once more. "I think the words
you're searching for are *thank you*."

I flex my hand. At least it no longer scalds. "Thank you for
burning me."

"That's not—" He cuts himself short, mouth pinching as he
shakes his head, raking a hand through his long hair. An angry
smile slashes against his lips, and his eyes roll to the ceiling.
Draven's tone drips with matched sarcasm. "Try not to touch
any more active Arcana. Or the sparkly part of a lit torch. Or,
you know . . . stick your hand inside a dragon's mouth."

"Got it," I snip right back, walking back toward my bedroom, the only other door leading to his own. Before leaving, I
turn back, his words rankling the fire within me. He looks very
human, gathering all the tarot cards up. He *did* just help me, I
suppose. I clench my teeth but manage to grit, "Thanks."

His gaze cuts to mine, a softness in them now. "You're
welcome."

"Are you going to have to let them reenergize?"

"Yes. I probably shouldn't have healed you, but I thought
making you walk to the healer's ward would leave things rather

permanent." He says it casually, as if understanding healing and touching Arcana cards while in use is something one learned as a child.

I suddenly hate how behind I am in this world.

He chuckles, and I shoot him a glare. "Sorry, just . . . I don't get you. Stuck between all these things you want. Unlikely to give yourself any of it."

"That's because you're a man." My growl has his eyes flaring, charging red. I step into my room and hiss back, "Stay the fuck out of my head."

His face drops as I slam the door on him, locking it for the night. My shoulders slump. That wasn't as satisfying as I wanted it to be. I cross over to the built-in window seat, curl against the glass, and stare off at the volcano. It's dangerously close, the lava burbling at its top and bleeding down its sides casting an orange glow that cascades through the window and the stained glass around the panes in a symphony of color. It feels as if the magma could reach us, yet the magic of this place holds it at bay.

My thoughts stray to Draven, the way he smelled, the feel of his hands cupping mine . . . wait. He can probably hear these very thoughts. I curse myself, not wanting to give him the satisfaction. Who knows how far that kind of power can span. The violation stirs within me. Like a drop of black paint mixed into a gallon of white, that feeling of safety within my mind is gone, never the same shade again.

I choke down my anger, staring out the window at the pulsing volcano, hypnotized by the oozing lava, its path leaving brilliant hues through its river channels. It burns all. Is stopped by nothing.

Stuck between all these things you want. Unlikely to give yourself any of it. That's a privilege I've never had. A moon-cursed peasant woman with brown skin? Never.

But I'm so over playing by others' rules.

Why should I allow anything or anyone to get in my way?

I came here to reunite my family, whatever the cost. So, I will, even if it means mastering this power and taking down any immortal that stands in my path. The prick princeling included.

That thought has my fury cooling like the bubbled black rock where the lava ceases to travel. But something worse fills its void, seeping into my chest.

Staring at that volcano, I feel small, alone, unloved, and unseen.

Tears swell like the high tide, releasing with shaking breaths as I stare into the fiery sea.

I remember raging about the immortals to my father once, when my mother was too depressed to climb out of bed, too hurt by the loss of my brother to even eat. I loathed every immortal with all that I was, but my father held me close and said hatred was a poison. A cancer that would eventually infect every bit of one's soul, eating me alive. It would not harm the immortals who hurt us. Only action could. But neither poison nor blade would heal my pain or correct our loss.

Healing was a gift only I could give myself.

Yet sometimes healing is not *enough*. Sometimes things first must burn.

Eventually, I exhaust myself to sleep.

I SIT IN THE BACK of a chaotic classroom the following day with Ember, Morgan, Kasper, Wynter, a girl from Death's Hearth named Amaya, and a boy from the Fool's Hearth named Felix. The purpose of this class on divination and readings is to draw out cards and interpret them, letting the storytelling side of tarot explore our futures, pasts, and what is happening around us. Professor Anstead described how we would feel a slight vibration in the air as we ran our hands over the cards' surface, to tell us which was the right one to pull. It's like picking a lock; the slightest bump something only the cleverest fingers could sense, and I happen to be pretty good at that. It requires a closer connection with our Major Arcana though, so we're given time at the end of the lesson to practice drawing those out.

Mine stubbornly stays put.

Amaya pulls Death with ease, darkness reflecting in her large brown eyes, her hair straighter than if it was ironed, and jet-black. Ember draws the Star nearly as often and even adds a neat trick of snapping her fingers beforehand. It glints with opulent light, spinning in the air. Felix watches her in awe, his smile charming but crooked, brown hair hanging in his face as he leans in, watching her work reverently, his own Arcana laying loose across the top of his deck. I bite back a smirk, wondering if Ember sees the obvious worship in his eyes.

I glance down at his stack of cards and find myself drawn in with a question.

"So, the Fool card is which number exactly? It's a Major Arcana, but I've heard professors reference its numbering differently," I comment.

Felix sits up, brushing his hair with his hand, smiling wide as though he's just happy to be included. "That's the fun thing; it's both the lowest and highest Arcana." His grin broadens at my surprise. "Yep, even higher than the World. But the power is fearlessness in its upright position and inducing fear in its reverse. How it manifests all depends on the user, I guess. Obviously, it rarely topples the World, if ever."

"It's typically a card used by royal guards and officers, allowing those capable of mastering it to rise quickly in the ranks,"

Amaya says. She and Wynter are the only druid-born in our group. Neither seem to mind.

"Yeah? How does the High Priestess translate to a job?" Kasper asks, struggling to summon his card from the stack, almost as if he doesn't want it.

"The ability to read minds is a useful one for sure." Amaya shrugs her lithe shoulders, voice dry.

My heart skips a beat—somehow, I missed connecting that ability with Kasper's Arcana. "Lots of lords and ladies want a spy in their midst, someone to keep them informed of people's thoughts and intentions."

"Great, like a pet," Kasper grumbles, his hand curling over his own stack of cards as he attempts to draw. After a moment, the High Priestess flips upright, the top lifting slightly from the pile before lying flat again. "Gods-fucking-damn-it."

Morgan swallows at his side, running a hand through his dark crimson hair before asking, "Is that what we're here for? To get trained and sold off to the rich as workers? Amusements?"

"No—well, some will." Amaya sits up straighter, fingers swimming over her stack like they're competing in a race as she summons again. "The Court controls Sedah, with the king and his family ruling at the top. The ancient houses and families are vast, and many of us have specific roles in the kingdom. For example, I'll likely be brought on as an assassin or a spy, once I can manipulate shadows and eventually use them to travel. If lucky, I might be brought in as a courtier to one of these ancient families, should they ever need to travel with discretion. Shadows can be used to cloak oneself to near invisibility, or travel by portal, even move things. It's not as useful in spying as the Hermit's invisibility, or the High Priestess's mind reading but . . . I'd rather be a spy or a courtier than a killer."

I swallow hard, shifting in my seat. As a Wraith, I was all three.

The Lord of Westfall's prodigy. I glance at Kasper, but he's not able to control his cards *yet*. My thoughts are safe for now, but how many others like Draven can read them when I'm merely existing in the world?

"But you won't get a choice either way?" Morgan pushes, and I clench my jaw.

"We'll be lucky to be chosen by a wealthy family." Wynter shuffles his cards but avoids our uncertain stares.

"What happens if we aren't?" Kasper asks.

"Some are dropped into the infantry. Glory can still be found there." The distasteful look in Amaya's gaze makes me think it's a death sentence. "Some may find a financier. Open a business of their own, that sort of thing." She looks between us all doubtfully, though not unkindly. "I've never seen one run by a changeling, though. There are also less sought-after jobs, all necessary to keep the kingdom running. Not earned or honored."

"Like manual labor?" Morgan guesses, his stack of cards shifting under the silvery power in his palm.

My leg bounces. I hate being the last in our small group to draw my card.

"Yes. Mining, building, infrastructure, scullery, housemaids, gardening, that sort of thing," Amaya tells us.

I stop, thinking of a life stuck scrubbing floors, powerless and surrounded by the powerful. I'd rather die than spend my life serving these bastards.

"Great, I'm guessing that changeling scabs get chosen for those unfavorable jobs over the cushy ones," Kasper groans. Silence settles over the group as we wait for Amaya's response.

"No, actually, changelings are usually chosen first by wealthy families because—"

"Amaya Penderghast." Professor Anstead's stern voice causes me to jump, resounding right behind my ear, and the others jolt, too. I notice a thin scar marring her face like a split in a river, crooking its way from above one eye to the hollow of her cheekbone. Her gaze does not sway from Amaya, who shrinks in her seat, shoulders hunching. "Show me your draw."

Amaya's hand quivers as she lets it linger over her stack. After a moment, the Death card floats unsteadily from within the pack into her palm.

Professor Anstead narrows her stunning emerald eyes. "Now summon a shadow."

"I . . . don't know how yet." Amaya's eyes dip to the floor.

"I guess you don't know everything, then," Professor Anstead says icily.

I glare at her tone as she turns on her heel and marches away. Amaya stares at the cards stacked before her, hands trembling over shining gold-leaf surfaces. My curiosity grips me, and I lean forward.

"What were you going to say? Why would the rich prefer changelings?" I wait, but Amaya only shakes her head, focusing on her work. "Is this something to do with the Curse?"

Wynter clears his throat, looking away. Ember, Kasper, and Morgan all meet my eye, suspicion gathering there.

What the hells are they keeping secret that involves changelings?

8

Training

I wonder what the full extent of druid might is, with their arcane magic. Is it something our scientists can ever replicate? Or do they stand shoulder to shoulder with the gods? I can only foresee one way of stopping them permanently. We must match their magic with that of our own. By whatever means necessary.

—Personal diary of uprising leader Kieran Ceres

DAYS LATER, I stand across from Amaya in the sparring ring, still curious about what she almost let slip. The focus in these first weeks of brawling seems to lie solely on training our new bodies to withstand physical combat. Though none of the druids have been exactly accommodating to us changelings, at least Amaya hasn't tried to kill or pin me to the mat in an embarrassingly fast way, like Mira. It's more than I can say for Ember, who is currently being looked over by an Empress Arcana, healing a collar bone a druid has broken. Over the last few days, I've had both my femur and elbow snapped, the first courtesy of Mira, the second a freak accident when facing Felix, who hasn't stopped apologizing since.

Thank the gods for healers.

Although I was trained in fighting by the Blades of Westfall and know most of the introductory material, my new body is stronger and faster than my mortal form and I feel as if my muscles have forgotten their former skill. Amaya swings at me, and I dart my head to the side, dodging her blow. Watching over us is a third-year student with a Strength Arcana that allows him to channel precisely that. His body is muscled in a way anyone would envy, his skin flawlessly toned mahogany, and he's one of few druids at the Forge with wings. When he *thwap*s the back of my knee with a staff, I adjust, stalking farther into the ring.

"Watch your footwork," he barks. "You nearly stepped out of the circle."

"Yes, because I'll be seeking thinly drawn circles for all the fights I plan to get into—" A cracking pain hits the back of my head before I can finish.

"Environment is as much an obstacle as your enemy. Use it to your advantage, or be humbled by it." He leans on the staff now. His hazel eyes flick to something behind me, and I duck, turning and smashing my fist into Amaya's ribs. She stumbles back, cupping her left side, hunched over, teeth grit in pain.

"Oh shit, I'm sorry." I grimace, taking a tentative step closer.

Amaya slinks into a spinning kick, sweeping my feet from under me. I collapse to the mat, my body marred in stinging pain. I'm still wrapping my aching head around the maneuver as she helps me up. She smiles and teases, "I'm surprised you fell for that one."

"You sold it well."

"Maybe you're just gullible?" She bumps me with her shoulder.

A minor weight releases from my chest, as if I've had a belt cinched around my ribs, and a grin curls my expression before I can stop it.

She points to my lips, her amusement growing like a shadow spreading across the earth. "Ahhhh, so she can smile."

My gut churns as if I've been caught doing something cruel, and it drops from my face. When was the last time I allowed for that? Something as small as a smile shared with a friend. Kiana. But she was more than just that. My gaze for some reason snaps to Draven across the room, currently using his forearm to choke a third-year student into submission. His eyes flash to mine, both of us appraising the other—

"Attention! Seraphs on the premises." Commander Soto walks into the room, and a moment later, seraph guards stalk in. I remember the seraphs from my father's Selection, their unmatched beauty, purple robes, silver armor, and most of all, their wings, ranging from snowy whites to tawny tans to rich earth browns. Some guards even boast colors that remind me of the tropical birds from the Isle of Riches, with vibrant blues and greens. All of their wings are feathered, unlike the druids', where such wings are a rarity.

One, with wings like winter, pure as snow but lined with gold, wears a crown woven in her platinum locks. This seraph princess marches straight for Draven. Her expression is cold, her large and achingly blue eyes holding only scorn as she sweeps the room. But when she reaches Draven, they shimmer with emotion.

The grit of his teeth and the haste in which he pulls on his shirt tells me he's not happy to see her. Is a seraph visit a regular occurrence? From the held breaths around the room and the tension stiffening my instructors' spines, I'm guessing not.

But soon I cannot focus on the princess and her crown of starlight, nor Draven and the taut lines of his shoulders, because trailing behind her is someone I never thought I'd see again.

My father.

My mother and I were always closely knit, like patches of a quilt—sometimes clashing but sharing the weight of the same hardships. But my father and I were cut from the same cloth. I'd never felt more understood than when sitting beside him in silence, or when feeling the warmth of his hand on my shoulder. He was the one who taught me to hold my head high, to treat any obstacle as if it were no more than an anthill, even if it was a mountain.

Before I know it, I'm running to him.

"Rune?" Ember calls, but I ignore her, parting through the sea of onlookers. Their suspicion keeps them rooted in place, and I move around them like a river over rocks. I can't take in whatever sniping words Draven has for the seraph princess, nor the stony propriety of her too-perfect posture. When I reach the front of the crowd I stop, boots squeaking on the tiles.

My father doesn't look a day older than when he left, but there are other changes that nearly make him unrecognizable. Mainly the wings across his back, both large and downy and perfectly golden. His skin is the same oak, darker than my bronze, while his eyes are radiant gold like mine, more so now that he's been transformed. His hair is shorn and black, his beard well-groomed, cleaner than any day I spent at his side.

"Dad?" I can barely breathe the words, and his attention snaps to me, eyes blinking in confusion, then panic, aghast as he looks me over. There's a slight upturn in his ears, a smoothness to his features where they were once rough-hewn. But he's not chained or shackled, and I can't stop staring at the wings. Accusations rise in the back of my throat. His hands tremble, and my eyes water at the sight of him. What has stopped him from returning to us?

He was likely sworn to fealty. Same as me.

I bury the pain of why and rush into his arms. He holds me tightly and all at once I'm small again. The years of suffering, of breaking myself over and over to survive this world shed from me like a snake from its skin. His arms are a shield that both protects and disarms, scented with his familiar aroma of vanilla mixed with petrichor, as if he flew through the rain to get here.

"Captain Riordan? Who is this?"

The imposing tone of the seraph princess has me straightening, and I take a step back from my father, suddenly remembering myself. Draven watches my every movement closely, his cunning eyes tracing the echoes of my father's features in my own. But the princess wears a frown, brows drawn together.

"My apologies, Princess Reva. This is my daughter, Rune." He introduces me with all the pride in the world, his voice quavering with emotion, chin up as he looks to her.

A captain? The other guards watch him warily, but they don't bark orders at him.

My father clears his throat. "I know you are here to discuss your betrothal"—Draven and I lock eyes and I've never seen him so cagey, hands flexing at his sides, leg bouncing. I look at Reva. She's beautiful, yet the ice in those eyes looks unlikely to thaw—"but would you allow me a moment with my daughter? I haven't seen her since she was thirteen."

Reva looks me up and down, scrutinizing every sweaty inch of me.

"I need you at my side. But she can stay." Reva turns to Draven, his eyes darker than the bottom of the sea on a moonless night. "I'm growing tired of these games. Your schooling hardly matters when you are to be ruling at my *side*. Your delays grow boring."

"This forced betrothal more so." Draven pulls out a small tin, taking out wrapped paper that he puts between his lips and lights, a flame flashing in his palm. It doesn't smell like tobacco; it's sweet, intoxicating. I wonder what it tastes like as he breathes in deeply, smoke pluming like some great dragon. "I am not content to sit docile at anyone's side, nor to leave my great country for one as morally constrictive as your own."

The other changelings and druids watch on, rapt, pulled into the drama of it. Instructors shoo their attentions away, ordering more drills, but I catch many watching over their shoulders. Draven's guards form a wall of bodies around us, separating us from others' curious stares.

"It doesn't matter what you desire. Our fathers set this into play years ago, or have you forgotten your oaths?" Reva's brow rises severely, her lips full but pursed tighter than a coin bag. There is no humor on her face, just cold, rule-abiding pitilessness.

"Those are our fathers' oaths. We've made none to each other." Draven lets that smoke spool, coiling up the sides of that coy mouth of his. I've never liked smoking, and certainly never found it sexy before, not to mention how very rude it is to do indoors, in a sparring gym no less. So why can't I stop staring at his mouth? His gaze shifts my way, delight forming there, and I clear out my thoughts, like beating dirt from an old rug. He seems loath to shift his attention but finally he looks dismissively to Reva. "At the very least would you consider ruling from here?"

"My father desires your people's loyalty, not these lands. So, unless you have something better to offer, I will tell my father to set the dates." Reva turns on her heel, flipping her long hair over a shoulder. Draven glares daggers at the back of her head, fangs peeking the next time he puffs more of that heady smoke. I turn to my father, clutching his hand tighter in mine, my eyes threatening to water. No—he can't leave. My heart pounds offbeat, drowning out everything else. I just got him back, we've barely spoken, and it's all happening too fast. My father hesitates, looking between Reva and Draven before blurting after her.

"Your Majesty. Please. Your father reassured me that if my daughter should ever be Selected that he would pay for her transfer into Nevaeh. Allow me to take her with us."

He grips my hand, his own warm in mine, and my hope flares bright. Every moment of pain and uncertainty from the last seven years might be worth it if I can just leave with my dad right here and now.

Reva looks me over, gaze narrowing slightly. Finally, she nods, a softness there I haven't seen, like she would do this for him, and only him. She turns to Draven, waving her hand dismissively in my direction.

"What do you want for the girl?"

As if I'm property to be bought and sold. My seller the one who hates me the most. But however deep the insult of my worth burns, I'll endure it to be with my father. Hesitantly I meet Draven's gaze and to my surprise his fangs have slid down completely, crowding his mouth. His nostrils flare, back straightening, those eyes of his brightening as he looks me up and down. Why does he seem so angry? This should be a win for him. Stomping out whatever delicious thing he was smoking, he walks to my side.

"Rune has been chosen by the World. The only one besides myself blessed with this power." A muscle feathers in Draven's jaw as he looks down on Princess Reva, her eyes hardening. What is he doing? "Her cost is too steep for even your deep pockets, princess."

Are you kidding me?

"Stop your games. Just name your price." She rolls her eyes.

My father squeezes my shoulder more tightly and my breaths fall short. Draven's eyes linger on me, and time stands still.

Let me go.

"A life for a life. You want her? You'll have to take your claws out of me. End our betrothal. It's the only price worthy of such a loss for our people." His eyes are as dark as the bottom of a coal shaft, and he won't look at me any longer.

I cannot believe he's leveraging my return to my father, possibly my only surviving family member, all for his own greed. *Pretentious, privileged prick.* Tension charges between us. I swear I want to slip poison into his little imported aioli.

Arrogantly he lifts his chin, running a tongue along those canines as he adds, "Take the terms to your father. He has until Autumn Equinox to decide if he cares more about this betrothal neither of us wants or keeping his promise to his second-in-command."

"You're truly a cruel bastard." Reva's lip curls.

"It's a win for both of us." Draven folds his arms, strong muscles bulging beneath the thin shirt he wears. Reva stomps away, and my father squeezes my arm once, pulling me close.

"I will fix this. Hold on, baby girl."

My heart shatters at the nickname. He kisses me on the forehead and trails after the seraph princess, the other guards following his lead like a pack of wolves.

The rest of the hall picks up in volume at the seraphs' disappearance, and it's only Draven and me in this pocket of the sparring hall, though his guards still linger, separating us from the rest of the space.

I turn on Draven, the corner of his lip curling at the livid look on my face. I want to shove him into the wall at his back, but I know that doing so would land me a night in the Boiler. Instead I step toe to toe with him, my finger nearly in his face. From this vantage point, I have a glorious view of the vulnerable slope of his neck, and the smell of vetiver and cedarwood washes over me. His long, silken black hair begs to be grasped, and when his eyes find mine, they spark in violent joy at my fury, slowly churning as if a fire lies in the depths of that indigo.

Commander Soto clears his throat and steps closer to us, but Draven just holds up a hand to halt his interference. "It's fine—"

"No, it isn't. Why didn't you let me go! I'm worth nothing to you," I whisper furiously.

"I meant what I said. You hold unmatched value in this kingdom. And there is no way in Hells Below my father would ever allow *both* users of the World to leave this kingdom for theirs. The only way *he* would approve it is if I leveraged you in my stead. And your oath of loyalty lies with him, so you will need his approval anyway." He leans forward, voice curling against the nape of my neck, coiling in my ear, and making me heady. "Curse me if you want, but I just guaranteed you getting what you desire, whether you or your father are capable of seeing that. After all, if there's one thing the seraph princess despises, it's being told no. She'll argue on your behalf, and your father will be even more convincing, wanting to save you from me."

"You are such an arrogant—"

A sickening crack snatches our attention, and the hall goes silent. Draven pushes through his guards and I slip out after him. Four mats over, a changeling boy with emerald, forest-cursed hair twitches across the ground. My heart catches in my throat as he goes still. Mira stands, dusting off her fighting leggings, blood staining her hands, and she looks around the hall, taking in all the eyes on her.

"Sorry." She looks to Draven, clearly for approval. From the nonchalant shrug of her shoulders there's not an apologetic bone in her body. "He was weak. It just happened."

I can't stare at his lifeless body anymore or take in the absence of emotion in those pale, open eyes. Prince Draven leaves my side and marches across the room toward Mira, the only movement in the vast hall. She goes white, stepping aside. Draven reaches her, face curled into furious anger, and he swoops down, wings hunched on his back as his hand hovers over the body. His other palm cups the tarot cards holstered to his thigh, and several rise, a golden, spider-webbed orb spanning all around him, Mira, and the dead changeling.

The entire hall holds its breath. I find myself following the path he created, feet soft on the marble floor as if it's the frozen pond near our old house, my boots soundless like the skates I once wore. Draven continues to pull on the magic of more cards as I draw nearer. I'm mesmerized as the Four of Swords moves to the forefront, the Empress behind it, then Judgment reversed, and finally the World, controlling the rest. His eyes sparkle like the night sky, a wash of deep purples and blacks and golden flecks like stars. The air warps around him, crackling with energy.

The Four of Swords drops to the floor, the outline of the card burning and smoking, and a moment later, the Empress follows, the fiery silhouette of the healer card seared into my eyes. All that's left is a green acidic smog around them.

The boy's head turns, and he whispers something to Draven. Chills lace up my spine, sending goose bumps across my skin at his lifeless eyes. This must be dark, twisted magic. A few gasp, relieved, but this close I can tell something's wrong. He moves like a puppet on strings, not naturally. I cringe when I notice his neck still bulges with a break. Draven nods, and the boy drops his head back, motionless again. Draven scoops up his cards, his hands flexing at his sides as he stands over the changeling.

Then Draven turns on Mira, growling something into her ear that makes her eyes water. Now, regret seems to be the foundation of her bones. His attention no longer desired. She starts begging, but he just holds up a hand to silence her and leaves.

I'm left in momentary shock, my fists clenching tight enough to leave half-moon cuts along my palms. Action flows into me. I follow Draven out, ignoring the stunned crowd of onlookers.

"Hey! I said hey!" I shout at his muscular back as he throws the doors open wide, exiting into a small courtyard between the sparring gym and dining hall.

The sun is close to setting, and smoke from the volcano casts it in red hues, the sky a wash of amethysts and tangerines. He turns, his brows knitting together as I march right at him.

"What the hells happened? Why didn't you heal him?"

"He was already dead." His voice is toneless, and I'm unsure if there's a lack of emotion or if he's merely exhausted. Draven's expression turns dismissive as he walks back toward our Hearth, saying only, "I did all I could."

It's not good enough. "No. You need to try again—"

"I'm not a god, Rune." His glare pierces me like daggers, spilling me open.

I choke on a grief I don't understand. After all, I didn't know that boy. "But he was moving. You were so close, and you just gave up—"

"His soul was trapped in his body, confused by what happened." Draven's eyes pale in the last flare of sunlight. He's so still, so quiet, that I want to shake him. "He couldn't come back, only be helped in leaving his body behind, safe in knowing

I'd pass some information along to someone he cares for. Now, if you're done with your tantrum, I'm tired."

He glances over my shoulder, and I turn. On the other side of the doorway, several druids and changelings linger beyond the inlaid glass, quite obviously pretending they weren't listening in on our argument. My face scorches from my hollow cheeks to my ears as if I have a gloriously raw sunburn. Shadows linger around Draven, and I know what he's about to do. He'll disappear into that space between spaces, the same one that brought us all to the Forge.

I grasp his wrist, and his eyes flare a dangerous shade of scarlet that has me shrinking.

But I don't let go.

Behind us, the doors fling open. A changeling girl named Fallon bursts through. I watch as a few I don't know follow her, including a murderous-looking guy who I think goes by Ward. At the very back of the ten-person throng are Kasper and Morgan.

Fallon points an accusatory finger at Draven and screeches, "You get back in there and fix him!"

"I can't," Draven repeats, looking less resigned and more on edge than he did with just me. "Go back to your training."

"I've been telling you, they're all liars." Ward shakes with anger. "They only use the Selection as a way to continue their lines, to breed us like pigs!"

My heart jolts at his words, confusion tumbling through me with an edge of suspicion.

The knife tucked up Ward's sleeve is visible for only a moment, the silver glinting in the light, and then Ward curls his arm up and hurls it—straight at Draven.

In an instant, my Wraith instincts take over. I throw myself into Draven, slamming us into the walkway. The heels of my palms ache nearly as bad as my scraped knees, yet I remain crouched over him, protecting the prince with my body. Draven's hand curls around the back of his head, teeth gritted in pain. He stares at me in confusion before we both notice Ward and a couple of others rushing toward us. Draven uses his strength to roll us, flipping me below him, our hips pinned together before he pushes back to his feet, yanking me with him.

Draven pushes me behind him and his shadow magic rears up, the swirling edges sharpening into spikes. It blasts outward, pinning the students by their clothes to the walls of the sparring gym, and Ward cries out as a spear of darkness pierces through his shoulder into the bricks.

Plumes of black smoke ignite across the scene, armed soldiers barreling out of them, tackling everyone who followed me out.

The guards pull the pinned attackers down, one slamming Ward into the pavers, blood and teeth flying from what I assume must be a broken jaw. My meager lunch rises up, choking me at the sight of his tongue lolling, eyes widened with pain, a guttural scream unleashing from his throat. Draven's glaring at everyone, hand still clawed around my forearm.

"Your Majesty, what would you like us to do with them?" a guard asks.

"They need to calm down. Let them sweat out a night in the Boiler." Draven looks between the attacker and a wall behind us where the knife is stuck to the mortar between bricks. He points to Ward and the sparring hall. "Give this one the same punishment as that idiot Mira." He turns to me, eyes sparking. "As for you . . ."

He summons Death's sweet shadows and steps back, allowing the darkness to engulf him, and jerks me to his side. A heavy blackness hums and pulsates all around us, billowing as if we're in the midst of a violent hurricane. A scream catches in my throat as he glides us through the shadows. Light is a flickering, muted thing above us, and I swear there's something feral in the darkness's movements, as if the black smoke may devour me if he lets me go. My body shivers, my grasp weakening, but he says nothing, only tugging me tighter against him. I burrow my face against his chest, clenching my eyes shut to block out the wild visions of dragonish wings and the outlines of demons.

There's a ripping sound, like a match struck in a cave, and then mercifully, light.

9

The Curse

The Seven of Swords is the liar's card, a tell that you've been deceived or manipulated until now. It's time for the truth.

WE'RE IN A BEDROOM that's a mirror to my own. Draven's room. I brush my windswept hair back, disoriented from the sudden change, my eyes quickly taking in every detail as fast as I can process. Books fill every inch of space along the shelved walls, stacked in corners and teetering in wild piles throughout the room. The three Immortal Realms of Arcadia are rendered in great detail on a mural across one wall, riddled with pins as though he's been studying it. Tracking something. His richly tailored clothes are strewn carelessly across the floor in places, his bed halfway made. I finally notice an older woman tucking in one side of the sheets, a laundry basket at her feet, staring at us both in shock.

"Your Majesty, I did not think you'd be back before your classes finished—"

"My plans changed, Magda." Draven doesn't bother looking at her, his eyes wholly alit on mine. "Rune requires my fullest attention."

I don't break the magnetic draw of his eyes as I hear the maid tsk and hurry out, closing the door gently behind her. Has she been the one cleaning my room? I'd naively assumed it'd been done by some magic enchantment in this place, like how the lights turn on without a source to heat them, or how my clothes fit perfectly without visiting the tailor. But perhaps they have a different energy source than mortals. Perhaps someone took note of the size of clothes I chose for myself. Draven holds me too close, his exhalations ghosting against my neck, our breathing matching and heavy. Finally, I press my hands against his powerful forearms, and he releases me.

I pace away from him, nearly tumbling over a pile of books, the topmost with the title *Ancient Weapons: A History of Arcadia's Finest Forge.*

"You should've let Magda stay. This place is a gods damned mess." I lean against a wall of books, one of the only clear spaces. He stands as still as a statue until something in my stare breaks the mirage, his hands curling and fisting at his sides.

"Why did you save me?" From the harshness in his tone, you'd think *I* was the one who'd flung a knife at him.

"I don't know." It's the truth, and it's not. I can't begin to unravel the complexities of what I've just done. Ward had done what I fantasized about doing to immortals so many times before, and yet . . . the best answer I can probably form is *it felt right.* Instead, I spit out, "I need you alive to trade me to Nevaeh."

A piece of the truth if not the whole of it. The way he observes me is as piercing as a collector pinning a butterfly to a board. He chews his lip, tilting his head back, and reads my body language like an open book, arrogance lining that cocky smile. We keep staring at each other, and finally, he runs his hand through his dark hair, those raven wings tucking tightly to his shoulders, flickering from black to blue to purple, an oil spill of colors. He turns from me, crossing to his bed, ripping the pillows off, hands flattening along the space between mattress and headboard, his wings ruffling irritably.

I finally ask, "What're you doing?"

"Dearest Magda . . ." he mutters, and suddenly pulls out a small crystal, holding it up in the light. He calls his cards forth, the World channeling Temperance, and a moment later, a crack fissures through the object. It turns dark, no longer opaque. Temperance stops magical powers, and I guess it works on enchanted objects, too. He chucks it into his fireplace, which lets out a flaming *whoosh*. Then levels another look at me. "She's a spy for the king. That crystal can be used to listen in. I usually find a new one in my chambers once a week."

"Your father doesn't trust you?" My arms fold across my chest as I examine his room. There are walking paths between the book piles, and he has a second-story sitting area, like me, with even more books. There's far more personality tucked into his space than mine. Knickknacks and charms, baubles and jars of various plants, metals, and mushrooms that strike at my curiosity. All I can think is that the librarian might have a conniption if she saw all these books strewn about.

"I'm sure he has his reasons." Draven crosses his arms, too, still standing near the bed as if he needs to keep it between us. "Now, didn't you have some more shouting you wanted to do without everyone watching? I'd rather get it out of the way so I don't have to hear you stewing all night."

"Maybe stay out of my head, and you wouldn't lose sleep over my thoughts," I snarl, drawn back into the fight with frustrating ease. I've never met anyone so unrelentingly aggravating.

"We both know why you think that." A daring smirk curls the edge of his lips, sending an unwanted heat rushing through me. He undresses me in a glance. "I don't even have to read your thoughts. I can scent the desire all over you."

"I said—stay out of my head!" I move around the bed at the same time as him, the two of us nearly chest to chest in a few strides.

"Then stop shouting thoughts like you're flinging them across the lava river!"

"I don't even know what that means!"

"Blessed with every power in the world, given the gift of holding power equal to mine, maybe even stronger, but you're not letting yourself take hold of it!" He throws his arms up, his wings flaring wide across his back until they blot the light from the window beyond. Each feather is impossibly detailed. The colors shift in the light between onyx and indigo and some kind of blue I can't name. Yet he seems so large with them extended, as if the room is too small for the both of us. He blinks, mastering himself again, and the wings fold tightly. "Not that it matters; you'll soon be out of my hair. Off to the seraphs."

"I thought you didn't want me here!" My finger points right into his stupid, pretty-boy face. But he does want me here, doesn't he? Why else encourage training? Maybe I'm not a mind reader—

"You're right! I mean, you're right that you're not a mind reader," he snarls, correcting himself mid-sentence, his face tingeing pink from the exertion of shouting at me. "And no, I don't fucking want you here. Not when you leaving means I might be able to get out of this stupid betrothal to the Nevaeh princess. The last thing I need is another chain around my wrist."

"Oh, like being betrothed to some gorgeous seraph princess was such a death sentence!" I spit, voice dripping with sarcasm. "So happy I can buy your way out of the only inconvenience imposed on your absolutely privileged life."

He steps forward, and I back into one of the bookshelves, the singular bony claws at the end of his wings digging into the wood above my head hard enough it splinters. His hands clench the shelves behind me, and I'm trapped between his powerful arms. The way his muscular chest rises and bluntly falls makes it clear he's barely tethering himself, and his eyes bore into mine until I can see nothing else.

"It hasn't been a privileged life. It hasn't even been a good one," he snarls, and his fangs slide forth. "Every ounce of power I possess, I've earned. Nothing has been given to me. Nothing."

"Says the prince," I say quietly.

He smirks, but there's no joy in those darkening eyes. "I wasn't born one," he growls.

I'm braced against the bookshelf as his eyes scan my face. All I can do is blink. Inside, a tidal wave of emotions rises to choke the breath from my lungs.

His throat bobs, swallowing hard as though he hadn't meant to reveal that, but he continues anyway. "I was Selected. Just like you, but far younger. I navigated all this on my own." His eyes graze mine with all the command in the world. "That's not common knowledge among students. You're forbidden to share it."

Yet there's no invisible power laced in that command. The Oath's orders are limited to direct questioning and commands by the king. Not that I would share the information without it. It seems . . . personal.

"So, the king isn't your father? Why would he choose you as his heir?" Why not just make his own? Adoption among royals is rare, at least for humans.

His eyes narrow slightly. "You really don't know about the War?"

I stare at him, lost in those words. "The records of the Great War were wiped from the history books, along with every rebel caught in the fight. Speaking of the rebellion is an act of treason." But my parents would whisper about it in the dark of night. The way they spoke of the uprising leader Kieran Ceres, you'd think he'd been a god, not a mere mortal from a broken royal line.

Draven winces. "The mortals were losing the War. Desperate, the uprising leader, Kieran Ceres, sold his soul to an immortal goddess in exchange for the ability to conjure dark arts. It still required blood magic, but only a drop of his blood, and wouldn't consume him the way magic had with other mortals who'd tried it."

I had heard whispers about the mortals figuring out some magic, but never more than rumors.

Draven continues, "Still, even with all this new power, it wasn't enough to win. So, he and his top alchemist created something that would hurt the immortals for the rest of time—a curse that would allow them to kill the immortals' legacy. By the end there was only one answer for immortals: the Selection. Mortals forced the Selection to exist, just to survive."

I breathe, "What Curse?"

"That no immortal could ever produce heirs again," he reveals. My stomach begins to churn, my mouth sweating as bile rises. "Every immortal born in Arcadia was cursed. The only way for lines to continue, for our numbers to ever expand, is through the Selection. It's why changelings are made. Why else did you think they'd take children?"

"To be cruel."

He looks disappointed in my answer. As if I see the world too black-and-white.

"Immortals have never been kind to their mortal neighbors. But humans took away an ability many hold dear, even beyond the games of succession. In turn, our forebears cursed me and you to this life." He stands taller, his wings releasing from the wood of the shelf with a groan, fangs sliding back up into his skull, his arms dropping to his sides. I stay against the wood, eyes burning as they threaten to water.

My head spins, but what other response could the mortals have expected, enacting a curse like that? The immortals take and take every year with the Selection, but I didn't think this was why. Elders are rarely chosen. Only the young and strong are sought after, especially children. To continue immortal lineage.

"Why do they even need a lineage if they live forever?" I growl.

"Immortals can still die, Rune. Not from old age or sickness, but they can succumb to accidents and bloodshed, even if we can withstand more than mortals. We also want to expand our populations, our army. Many died in the War; our numbers were already less than the mortals by half before the War, so of course it was on everyone's minds," Draven says, his gaze tracing every detail of my face. "Immortals aren't gods."

"This is why changelings are chosen by the elite families? Not because they earned it, or for their power, but . . . to continue their lines?" Sweat slickens my spine, and I stay frozen against the wall as he turns back to me.

"Yes. Though the two go hand in hand. Changelings get more power and security, and the royal lines survive. At least . . . in a way. They share no blood with their heirs, but they get to choose them. Train them."

My thoughts spiral and I ask, "The druid-born here . . . are they all changelings like you? Picked as children and raised in the Court?"

"Not many. Druids are still . . . *selective* in taking children. Only orphans." He fiddles with a ring. "Most of our classmates are the last of the druid-born. Mere children when they were cursed. Like Mira and some of her little sycophants; it's likely why they hate changelings so much."

Because we will have what they never will. Whether we want it or not. Immortals don't just want to expand their ranks by bringing in mortals they can transform into changelings, but to breed *fertile* ones, untouched by the Curse, and therefore able to sire the next generation of druids, circumnavigating the Curse altogether. Disgust fills me. The Curse is cruel, but so is the Selection the immortals made to combat it. Though the Selection is not the punishment I thought it was . . . it's worse. The mortals' twisted self-preservation robs me of making the decision of bringing a child into this twisted world and forces the choice onto me instead. It guarantees mortals' survival, at the cost of our freedom. This is what Ward and Amaya were talking about. How long did the druid-born think they could keep it a secret . . .

"Why the secrecy?" I try to swallow, but my throat's too dry.

Draven's head tilts, and he runs his tongue along his teeth. "I guess they realized changelings tended to perform better and had a higher survival rate through the Descent when they thought the magic came without a price."

"Everything has a price." Nothing is free. My anger toward the immortals grows again. My choice to have children or not should rest in my hands, no one else's. I want to scream it at him, but he's a changeling, too, stuck in a similar position. "So . . . your betrothed . . . the seraph princess . . . she's a changeling?"

"Yes. Let's just say our king owes a debt to Nevaeh, and they demanded that payment be made by blood." Draven stalks to his bed again, collapsing atop it, running his hands through his hair as he lays on his back. His wings dissipate in smoke, his horns, too, the Moon Arcana shining at his side, channeled by the World. I didn't know he could take those immortal markers away, but the Moon is the shapeshifting card.

What's left is someone very human, very raw. So, this is what he looked like before the Selection: a beautiful disaster. Draven speaks to the coffered ceiling, "Ansel will lead the druids when it's time. But my father resents this because Ansel's Arcana is Judgment, like his. Only you and I have drawn the World in centuries. He wants my power to lead our people, but he's stuck with this betrothal as much as I am."

"Why is that?"

Despite the rest of him appearing so mortal, the color of his gaze still sifts, a ruby hidden beneath sapphire sands. "When Kieran Ceres was captured, the seraph king wanted him executed along with all the other rebels and their children. My 'father' stayed his hand, insisted on a trial."

He pauses, taking a breath. "Their plan was to kill Ceres but villainize him enough to prevent martyrdom among the mortals. But they failed to realize that his alchemist had already given Ceres the Curse and the trial provided a perfect audience for an assassination of royal immortals. Its power killed hundreds of gathered immortals, including the seraph king's first wife, and spread from sea to sea, affecting every immortal in Arcadia. The seraph king has blamed my father and his mercy for it ever since. He demanded blood in return, and they settled on this stupid fucking betrothal."

My head spins at the information and Draven's surprising candor. A deep-seated distrust slithers out—he could be lying, but to what end?

"I'm not lying, Wraith. If you don't believe me, you can check the history text wedged beside where you hid that little trinket on your bookshelf. The answer's been there the whole time." Draven smirks as my heart jolts in my chest. Ever since he returned my father's necklace, I've kept it hidden away, not wanting to get caught with a personal item. Despondently I think of the little broken king of my brother's that was taken from me.

"I'll invite you to stay out of my head, and my room."

"Only my magic has entered either, and only the latter because my father's also been spying on you, but if you'd like him to listen in, I'm happy to stop collecting them." He slides me a sarcastic smile, and I just roll my eyes.

Of course I don't want that. I fidget. I didn't know what to look for, or that such magic existed, but my room feels less safe than before.

"And I'd be out of your head if your thoughts weren't so damn loud."

"Did you want me to know? About the Curse?" I don't know why he would.

"I think everyone should know. It's your body. Your fate." He runs a hand through his hair. "I wish I'd known sooner."

I release a breath. There's nothing about his behavior that reads as a lie. "So . . . your father can't just break the betrothal?"

"We're already on the verge of war. The druid king knows the seraph king wants to eradicate the Curse and annihilate the mortals in vengeance, but our kingdom is situated between them." Draven clenches his jaw, and I wonder if it's rage cracking between his teeth. "The druids lost more than the other immortal nations the last time around. Our power makes us useful in a fight, but the seraphs found us expendable. With the Curse still in place, my father knows it'd be foolish to attack the mortals, as they're our only source of growing our numbers. He will avoid it at all costs."

"And if the Curse was no longer an issue?" I fold my arms, hugging myself a bit.

"Let's hope we never find out. But . . . I shouldn't say more."

His eyes fall on me and I can hear the accusation in the loud silence. I'm about to be transferred to the seraphs. Soon we could be on opposite sides of a new war. The words *be careful what you wish for* ring through my mind. But it's my father in the seraph realm. I must try to be reunited with him.

"Be glad you have a father who loves you so deeply. I honestly think mine would rather slit my throat himself than risk me spilling any secrets of our country to the seraphs. Not that I ever would." He reveals this dark confession to the ceiling, his gaze as black as his contemplations.

"Is he not like a true father to you?" The Lord of Westfall's cruel face enters my mind and I force it away, back into the recessed shadows of my nightmares. I expect Draven to snap at me. We're veering dangerously close to the personal. I'm surprised when he laughs humorlessly.

"He . . . adopted me as a weapon. One he honed to his level of perfection, no matter the method." Draven's lashes flutter a little and my stomach turns. "I think he learned to care for me. The seraph king saw that weakness and that's why he demanded me as recompense. My 'father' has held me at arm's length since." Draven's jaw clenches, bones stressing under flesh.

My heart sits at the back of my throat, choking me. "Do you think you just sparked the war?" If I get transferred to Nevaeh, will I have to turn right back around and fight the very people I escaped? I'm sure I'd be forced to swear a loyalty oath to the seraph king, which would mean no running, and as the king's royal advisor, there's no way my father would be freed to just go. But when I think about Ember, Amaya, Wynter, and Felix, I can't see them as my enemy.

"I admit I've listened in to the princess's thoughts. The seraphs' halos are meant to block that gift, but she doesn't wear it every hour of the day." His gaze skims my knowing glance, a dangerous smile coiling his lips, before he amends, "Don't be jealous. Getting that close didn't involve anything too scandalous."

I roll my eyes, why would I care, but my face heats.

"However, as much as she might desire me, she wants to be revered by her people. Marrying a 'heathen prince' would tarnish her image. She cares about how she's perceived more than anything in this world. The seraphs see us as occultist, nature-worshipping monsters, who revere the 'wrong' gods. If you're still feeling sorry for her, know that she doesn't want this either."

I wasn't. Or at least pity didn't quite soothe the serrated edges of my thoughts around her. I hated the way she looked to my father as though he'd poured his love into her in my absence. Even her sense of entitlement around Draven. As if she owned a bit of him. I cut those thoughts off as a smirk edges his mouth, his eyes sparkling to life again.

"If your father agrees to give me to Nevaeh, what happens to me then?" I ask quietly. My father had a rhyme about being chosen by the seraphs, too, one I stewed on long after he was Selected: *Beware the seraphs of the skies, obsessed with truth from on high, they judge and punish every lie, atone your sins lest you die.*

"Cute." Draven's tone drips in sarcasm, and I shift on my feet, face flaming.

"Just tell me what it means for me." He seems honest right now. Even as I try to pause my thoughts, wondering how he might use them to his advantage.

"You'll probably be entered into their military academy, the Aura. Separated into clerics and scribes, soldiers and politicians.

It's a mirror of things here, but more severe. Perfection is the only allowable thing in that kingdom." His eyes roll to the coffered ceiling, his tone dripping with disgust. "But after that, you'd be placed with whatever seraph was most worthy to be your marital partner. It's all arranged. You'd have less choice than here, where you have great potential, and therefore power and say. Here, you could choose anyone you wanted."

I wonder if that truly means *anyone*.

"But there, perhaps you'd be able to see your father more. He must have considerable sway over the seraph king, although I've heard he's not wholly trusted, as a former mortal."

A jolt of concern seizes me.

"Still, if the king allows him to watch over the princess, he must be able to bend his ear. But Nevaeh is a difficult place. I'd be glad to never live there. They judge people based on their intent and inherent goodness. You're sorted and placed depending on it. Not just who you want to be but who you are beneath it. Along with any parts that might be deemed flawed."

Pass.

"My thoughts exactly," he adds, and I glower at him.

"How do I stop you from doing that?" I hate the ease with which he reads my mind. It makes me feel exposed, as though every moment he's gathering more leverage against me. I force my thoughts onto a field near my old home, the way the winter stripped the trees bare, the snow silencing the grass and the animals into cold, hushed whiteness. Try to hear my thoughts when they're buried beneath ice, *Princeling.*

His head tilts, brows twitching, but I keep my thoughts quiet.

"Train. Learn to block your thoughts, but you'd have only a couple weeks to dedicate to it. This High Priestess Arcana is the one responsible for the ability to read minds." He gives me an arrogant look that grows darker. "Those of us attuned to the High Priestess can guard our thoughts, persuade others. Seraphs can't hide their lies or thoughts. Their halos change color when they speak even a small falsehood. They value honesty and goodness above all."

"You could teach me to build some walls, ones that could help." I chew my lip, nerves fraying. He looks me over from head to toe as if to silently ask why he would bother, and I tack on, "Maybe it'll work there, but if not, it'll help while I'm here. So you don't have to hear my voice, if for no other reason."

"Well . . . that alone might be worth suffering your presence." He sits up, grimacing as if he's mulling it over. "I suppose it'll give me some quiet, and if you're really set on being reunited with your father and living your life in Nevaeh, I'll get to break this betrothal and continue working toward my reign here." A hunger grows in the far-off look of those eyes, as if they search through something unseen, a feast of every opportunity he thought was denied him. He leans forward, elbows on his knees, suddenly the prince again, even without the wings and horns.

It occurs to me the command he holds may not just lie within his immortality. Looking at him now, I see how ambitious he is—his desire to lead, to command, annoyingly entices me.

His voice is hesitant in anticipation. "I don't know if this training will help you there, but it might give you some leeway at least . . . to survive. Are you sure that you want this?" His narrowing eyes suggest he can't imagine a life where he'd give up certain power for another person.

"I want to go," I say, and he slides me a look. I emphasize, "I *will* go."

"Good." The apple in his throat bobs. "Then let's move to the living room."

He stands and walks by me, and his heady scent washes over me. I hesitate a moment. I don't know why his agreement bothers me the way it does. What did I think? That he'd try to convince me to stay?

When we enter the comforting space, he summons the World to channel magic through his other Arcana cards. He summons the Moon first. His wings and horns reappear in smoke, as if he's worried about eyes on us even here in this private space. He summons another card with such ease, golden magic dancing from his fingers, leaping to all the curtains until every window is veiled.

Draven comes to stand at my side and shows me the Emperor shuffled to the forefront of his summoned cards. Spying crystals draw into his spare hand, one flying out of my room, the other from a potted plant. He mentions casually, "The Emperor represents security, discipline, stability. And he grants the ability to move things with our very minds."

Once again, he switches to Temperance.

"And Temperance removes magic?" I confirm, curious.

"You *are* paying attention." He grins slowly. I bite my cheek and avoid answering.

I allow myself to imagine, just briefly, being that powerful—using the World to summon all the cards with ease, outmatching all other Arcana . . . I toy with these thoughts as he breaks and destroys each crystal just like he did the first, more slowly, so I can watch them turn from bright glowing crystal to dim rock, and then he casts them all into the fireplace. When the sizzling sound stops, he sits on the sofa, gesturing for me to join him.

Draven places his tarot deck on the coffee table, and I copy the motion with mine. He shuffles his cards, spreading them in one hand and with the other picks out a card. His deft fingers flip it until I can see the High Priestess clearly.

"In her upright form, the High Priestess allows the wielder to read the minds of others. But every Arcana can be read upright or in reverse, and it can also be summoned that way. So, in the reverse form"—he flips the card until it hangs upside down between us—"she can be used to manipulate and exert influence over others. The most successful druids with this Arcana can use it to fan an individual's fears, desires, or corrupt their thoughts. Though it's a low-ranking Arcana, many courtiers keep them around—often in roles as handmaidens, butlers, or perhaps even in their inner circles—for their influence."

"You make the summoning look easy." I chew my lip.

"You can snap your fingers—it helps. Or flick the top card. Training wheels for summoning." Draven gestures to my cards.

I've tried flicking the card to no avail, so I snap my fingers in a flourish over my deck only for nothing to happen.

"It's not show tunes, Rune."

I shoot him a glare. "I'm trying." I straighten up, his words stoking my anger. To calm myself, I focus my thoughts again on that field of snow, the repressive silence of it. The heavy weight of the world my singular, quiet companion.

"Like this." His hand envelops my wrist, slowly guiding it. Again, he shows me his own, the command in that firm snap, as if he's giving the order to a wayward hound.

I try again, putting my anger behind it, and am surprised when the World floats upright, summoned by my demand. My mouth drops open. I did it.

He bites back a smug grin, no praise, just pride shimmering in those eyes—of himself or me, I'm not sure. He flashes his hand to me, the one with the World card tattooed across the back. "If you were to elevate to a full druid, you could channel some limited magic without a deck. This little technicality is why you're constantly on my mind unless I'm actively shutting you out."

"You sound a little obsessed," I say.

"You're not the only one I have to endure, just the only one louder than my own thoughts." He smirks as my lips curl and continues as if I haven't interrupted him. "You don't need access to tarot to mentally shield, only to look into others, so there's a chance it'll help you in Nevaeh. With both our hands on the reins, I'm hopeful we can shut it down completely. I think we'd both prefer that?"

"Just fucking teach me," I growl, and his full lips curl.

"Earlier . . . you were imagining a snowy field. I couldn't hear anything for once, but I could see that as clearly as if I stood there myself. Where was that?"

"A place in Westfall, near my old house," I say, hands fidgeting in my lap.

"Why there?" His stare and question are innocent. The answer is something else.

"It was safe," I manage.

"That's all?" His gaze narrows, tinging sapphire, as if he can sense the omission but cannot decipher it.

"Why do your eyes change color?" A truth for a truth. I doubt his is as layered as my own. "None of the other druids have changing eyes."

He blanches and glances away, running a hand through his long black hair, thumbnail grating one of his horns in the movement. "That hasn't happened since I was young."

"Seriously? I noticed it the first day—"

"Let's just stay focused on you. Back to your snowfield. If it's safe, we can use it. Now close your eyes. I want to try something."

His reservations have fallen away, and in their place he wears a disarming smile. If I didn't know I was looking into the soul of a wolf, I might have thought we were sharing a laugh. I'm not sure about closing my eyes around him. His eyes slowly narrow the longer I wait. I lean closer, as though I'm sticking my neck through a noose, and clench my eyes shut.

"Good. Now breathe. Slower. In. Out. I want you to remember that image, but I want you to pull back from it a bit. Imagine that snowy field as a painting. Now picture the wall it's affixed to. It can be anything . . . but I want you to envision the most impenetrable barrier you can, thick enough that even a dragon with all its might could not shake it."

It feels a bit stupid, but as I listen to his deep voice, I allow myself to breathe slower, my mind sinking into my body, getting lost in the command of his words. I imagine the field of white, and as my focus steadies, I can pick out the brushstrokes in the canvas, then the gilded frame, made of pure gold. It sits on a wall of plain concrete, lit by torches.

"Focus on that wall, make it real." His sweet-smelling breath ghosts my face. "Keep it steady. No matter what."

I sit, imagining the painting behind my closed lids.

And then suddenly, I hear a thud. The picture moves, swinging a bit before clacking against the wall again.

Draven sighs loudly through his nose, distracting me.

"Did you just try to break down my wall?" I ask coyly.

"Yes. You should see what I'm seeing. It's not going to hold." Draven shifts his weight on the sofa. I keep focusing on that wall in my mind, a headache forming at my temples.

"It'll hold," I growl.

He huffs a laugh, and as I'm staring at that wall, it shakes again, hard. The painting falls to a concrete floor, and I can *hear* something breaking through as if it's real. The wall dissolves, chunks dropping to the ground as it caves inward. On the other side talons rip and tear, scales glisten, a great glowing purple eye stares back.

My eyes snap open, and the vision fades, but the chill remains, my heart hammering in my chest.

"You sure about that?" His brow rises.

I roll my eyes and say, "Again."

10

The Invitation

King Altair of the Seraphs confirms he is willing to consider altering the arrangements of the betrothal between Princess Reva and Prince Draven, in exchange for the safe return of my daughter, Rune Ryker. The Council of Archseraphs is hopeful this will present our nations with a path toward peace at long last.

—Riordan Ryker, Hand of the King

T HE NEXT WEEKS PASS in a blur. Between the constant training of my mental wards, classes, and sparring, I barely notice fall creep its way into Sedah. The volcano cools, no longer streaming an ever-flowing tide of lava, and the rivers begin to slow. The air clears from smoke and debris, and chill breezes snake through the mountainside on autumn winds. The days fill with colors as if doused in paint, the grassy Oval turns gold, and the trees curl in crimson, amber, and brightest orange, their bases surrounded by beds of brilliant leaves.

I wish I was less exhausted to fully appreciate it.

I sit with Ember, Kasper, and Wynter. Amaya, Morgan, and Felix are grouped into the table right beside ours, both groups chatting in the Atrium where we all eat and study. The two-story space has a domed glass ceiling, a running fountain that wends like a river through the lower floor, and various living trees dotted down its center. My favorite spot is upstairs where I can see the fountain in the open space below and look out on the birds who've nested in the trees to keep from the coming cold. Most of the first- and second-years sit in the dining hall for meals, but we find it too stuffy.

I cram a blueberry muffin into my mouth, trying to draw on my last dregs of energy for the day as I practice summoning the World card. It's coming easier now, usually stalling only briefly before it rises. I'm not sure if I'll be able to bring my tarot deck with me into Nevaeh. Draven confessed he doesn't know either—if I would remain a changeling forever or become a seraph one day instead. But I push myself to learn as much as I can just in case, especially the High Priestess, which might shield my thoughts from being an open book. And there's also a part of me that just hates the idea of falling behind.

So, I continue to draw, to give in to learning about my very special Arcana, one that I hate to admit I'll be sorry to abandon should I have to leave it behind. But despite the World's massive potential, it needs to siphon magic from the other Arcana to truly do anything, and I still struggle to draw up a second card. Everyone else only needs their Major Arcana card and maybe a Minor Arcana card to enhance their magic, but I need two Major Arcana cards to do anything.

Master of none, but at least I'm not limited to only one.

My attention snags on Mira in a group of other druids across the Atrium. Her arms shake as she helps hang a large golden paper banner announcing the Autumn Equinox Ball. The day after she murdered the changeling boy, she was taken to a post outside the refectory and whipped for all to see. The changeling who'd attacked Draven, Ward, was flogged beside her, though given surprisingly fewer lashings. His jaw was mended by a healer, the rest left to heal naturally. It's been weeks, but Mira still struggles to do basic physical tasks. I've also seen Ward limping during sparring, slower than his partners now.

Amaya leans forward. "The Autumn Equinox will be your first introduction to the Sedah Court, and thus your first chances to make a good impression. Most druids have already been intro-duced, as families pay a tithe for such a privilege when we come of age at sixteen. Though some coming from less distinguished families may be making first impressions, too."

"Me, for example," Wynter says, his Judgment Arcana spin-ning magically on the tip of his finger. Now he's just showing off.

"Ah, so this is the time the Court gets to make dibs, right?" Kasper barely looks up. He's managed to progress to not only drawing his Arcana but *using* it, and I note that he glances up at Ember, who looks suddenly away, cheeks rosy. My gaze snaps back and forth between them, before I check my own mental shields. He leans in and whispers something in her ear and she covers her mouth with her hand, giggling about something.

"These two," Morgan mutters to the rest of us, copying Amaya's notes.

I look around, and a curious feeling seizes my chest as I sud-denly realize how much I would miss them when I go to Nevaeh. Even sitting in this place, studying this magic. Draven's taunting face flashes across my vision for a moment. I certainly will not miss *all* of Sedah. I keep my voice low, choosing just one of them to share the news with.

"Hey, Em. I just wanted to say . . ." I clear my throat. Why is this so hard? My hands fidget in my lap. When was the last time I had a friend? Kiana started out that way . . . but we quickly became much more than that. Two young women forced to survive horrors untold, finding light only in each other. But with Ember, she's like a sister. Or maybe she could've been if I stayed. "At the Equinox Ball, I'm hopefully going to be sent to the seraphs. With my father."

Ember's emerald gaze widens. "That's who that seraph was? I saw him put his hand on your shoulder but . . . I figured if you wanted to tell me . . . you would in time." I see her dart a quick look at Kasper and realize the group must have been speculating, but her voice stays blessedly low. Her eyes flit between mine, as if she's reading the vulnerability I'm trying to tamp down. "I'm so happy for you."

"Yeah, I just . . . wanted someone to know. In case I didn't return." I can barely swallow for the optimism lining my throat like razors. Hope is more dangerous than fear. Her warm hand squeezes mine, warmth spreading through me, chasing the darkness.

"I'll let the others know after you're gone. But . . . I'll miss you, trouble." Her grin is dazzling enough for me to smile right back. Her eyes shine, making my own threaten to water. But the moment breaks.

"What're you two whispering about?" Morgan demands, leaning over from the other table, his smile faltering when neither of us answers him.

"Maybe Rune's finally confessing her little secret." Kasper runs a hand through his platinum hair.

Wariness courses through me—what does he know?

His brow raises to prompt me, and I check my mental wards, confirming they're still in place. When I don't reply, he scoffs. "About your little bounty posters? You all know she was a Wraith in her home territory, right? Collecting secrets for a living."

The rest of the table stares at me. An awkward silence descends upon our group, broken only by the reverberating sounds of others in the Atrium enjoying a meal, studying together, or walking around us. Do immortals have Wraiths in their courts? Do they know what it means? Draven did, but he seems well-versed in mortal affairs. Amaya and Wynter look lost, but Felix, Morgan, and Ember all look at me more critically. Shame unexpectedly slinks through me. My life as a Wraith forced me into choices I wish I'd never had to make. I think of the sweet young man who fled across borders because of the blackmail I gathered, the affair that shattered a family, and the time I was caught spying on a man twice my size, leaving me with so many broken bones I couldn't move for months. All of it done under the Lord of Westfall's orders. But I'm the one who has to live with it. And there were people I helped in secret . . . but Wraiths aren't known for the ones they spare, like that mother and her children running from an abusive lord. She would not have made it into hiding if not for me, but a few good deeds don't balance my scales.

Still, my jaw clenches, ready to defend myself.

Felix blurts, "That's really cool. I worked at a bookshop, reading about adventures, but you were having them." His grin is a fascinated, intrigued thing. "Do you have a copy of your bounty poster? I'd frame one if I had one."

"Outlaw Felix?" Ember prompts, half laughing, and relief hits me.

Kasper sneers—this is clearly not the reaction he wanted. His arms fold so tightly they become pretzel-like.

"Oh, we can come up with a cooler name than that," Amaya says with a grin.

"Fugitive Felix?" I suggest, and he smiles broadly, the light in those brown eyes sparkling as he opens his mouth to reply, but then Morgan loudly clears his throat. His brows crease along with his forehead, and his accusatory stare is hot as a brand.

"When were you going to mention this to any of us?"

I cringe at his tone. It wasn't exactly anyone's business.

"Our lives from over the Wall don't matter, right?" I say quietly. That was the selling point anyway. "I don't know much about any of you either."

He frowns, his eyes searching my face as if he sees me in a new light. "We should change that."

"You're right, we all should." I give the table a tight-lipped smile, some part of me wishing I could be held to it. Only Ember sees through my empty offer.

"So, Rune, I hear we're allowed to bring a date to the ball. Are you going with anyone?" Wynter's smile is soft as snow and melts me like sun glancing upon it.

I'm so surprised at the question I nearly tip my coffee all over my notes. I manage to get my grip back on it, only a few splashes hitting the pages, which I dab up with a napkin.

I can't pretend I hadn't noticed how he sometimes makes excuses to walk me to my Hearth even though it's out of his way. Or that he always saves me a seat beside him. Morgan's eyes flicker between me and Wynter, narrowing, before holding to me.

I reply, "No, I'm not." Not much point when I'll be leaving. Wynter's lips quirk as I switch the subject. "So . . . are we expected to perform anything at the ball? I know we will be meeting people from Court and the different Hearths."

"I hadn't thought of that." Felix pulls a face.

A druid girl with flawless, deep brown skin and long sweeping black braids walks past our table and Amaya leans out to her, waving. "Cleona, do you know if we need to be able to perform anything at the Equinox?"

Cleona looks around our mismatched group, her enchanting hazel eyes lingering on me a moment before she turns back to

Amaya. "I really hope not, I've barely managed to draw the Sun once a day let alone in front of an audience."

A speedy messenger approaches the table, likely a second-year Chariot Arcana judging by his unnatural speed and the double wand pendants pinned onto his high collar. He lays a bouquet of black roses on the table in front of me, each petal limned with crimson. He smiles at my confusion, then races away. Morgan reaches forward and hands me an ebony card tied around their stems with my name on it.

I open the envelope, and my eyes immediately flick to the bottom where it's signed *Princeling*. My blood heating, the expansive room turns hot and cramped as I snap the card closed. I would rather not read this in front of everyone.

Cleona nods to the roses over my shoulder. "You should ask Prince Draven—he would know."

"I will." I cringe to suppress my smile. Everyone looks between me and the flowers.

"What's it say?" Ember leans over, looking at the jet-dyed paper, the golden ink gleaming.

Resignation wins, so I open it to read:

Wraith,

With the Autumn Equinox in only a week's time I am in
desperate need of a date. Luckily for me . . . you owe me one.
I think you can guess the favor?

—Princeling

Ember leans over my shoulder, mouth agape. She grasps the card and shows it to Amaya and Kasper, the latter of whom looks supremely uninterested.

"What's the favor he's talking about?" Wynter asks curiously.

"Nothing. I ate his sandwich, he wasn't impressed." I tuck the card away in my pocket. Draven's invitation to the ball must be his cover for introducing me to the seraph king, nothing more. Of course, he's also been teaching me to block mental attacks each night, but that feels like a favor for both of us. Mortified by the stares, I add flippantly, "He just likes to mess with me."

I half expect to see him around some corner laughing at my flushed face. But I don't, of course. In fact, I've never seen him here. My brows draw together as I realize I've not seen him outside our Hearth and the sparring gym. Where does he go all day? I've seen other years, and it's not like I haven't caught myself looking for him.

Ember grins. "Imagine the dress you'll get to wear going to the ball with the prince."

"Don't remind me." My shoulders slump. I'm sure it'll be something embarrassing or ridiculous. The thought of all that attention makes me want to curl inside myself like a turtle.

"Well, we may not get much say in how things run here," Morgan growls quietly, leaning in close enough that I take in his salted caramel scent. His gaze locks on my lips and I'm suddenly aware of my body, the way his knee leans heavily against mine, the distance of our chests as they rise and fall. "But it doesn't mean you have to dance with him."

"Yeah . . . you could dance with me." Wynter's gaze snaps up and I suppress a grin, squashing my smile, but traitorously my lips inch upward in the corners anyway. I manage a jilting little shrug and can't help but notice a hint of darkness crossing Morgan's face, like a shadow flitting between rooms.

But he doesn't own me.

I tell Wynter, "I don't see why not."

II

The Equinox Ball

The Three of Coins suggests that working together is vital for success, especially when striving toward the same goal.

T HE WEEK OF the Equinox Ball brings additional decorum. Draven takes a personal interest in my aptitude for putting my foot in my mouth. So, while my friends are learning basic etiquette, I'm stuck spending the time with him instead, working right up until the ball. He sits in the armchair of our shared living room, feet propped on the coffee table, eating another of his delicious sandwiches that he refuses to share.

"Again," he demands, gaze flicking up and down with scrutiny. "I don't understand how you can bow angrily, but you're managing it." His wings drape off the sides of the chair, dusting the floor. I've never been so tempted to pluck him like a chicken. Tone dripping with pure boredom he adds, "That wouldn't go the way you think. And shields up."

I shake my head, clenching my jaw and fists as I rebuild my mental barriers. Taking a deep breath, I shudder out the tension and try again. I curtsy, imagining Draven as King Altair of the seraphs instead, evoking my desperation to impress him.

"How were you not executed every week in Westfall?" Draven rolls his eyes, taking another large bite of his sandwich.

I growl, pacing the room. I stomp over to the waterfall in the corner, letting the soothing tinkling calm my nerves.

After a moment he comments, "At least you didn't drop your shields that time. Not that anyone would need to mind-read to see that you want us all dead."

"Not all of you." I think about the changelings, and even the druid friends I've made in this kingdom. A stone sinks in my chest. "I'll admit the reasons behind the Selection weren't what I thought. Mortals carry responsibility for it, too, and some immortals aren't responsible for it at all, especially changelings . . ."

"No . . . they weren't." Draven's tone is measured, as if building a bomb between syllables.

I round on him. "But *you* participated. All the royals do. Hells, you're the one responsible for every changeling this year." I stare him down, but his reaction isn't the fire I expect.

He holds my gaze, and though he doesn't observe me with any pride, there's no humility either. "What do you think would've happened to me and Ansel if we refused?" His counterpoint comes with a snarl, wings folding tighter, and he crosses his arms. "But you're right. I made the choices so he wouldn't have to carry the burden of it. He's too young to understand, and I'd like to keep his innocence intact as long as possible."

"Will you hide behind that excuse when you're king? 'There was nothing more I could do'? 'This is the way it's always been done'?" I can't decide if he's just like them. Or worse because he was Selected himself. "I'd like to sleep at night knowing that at least one royal doesn't deserve to die for complicity."

"Then leave Ansel off your list." Draven stands and my back straightens.

He and I are on far better terms than when I arrived, but my body still screams *predator* when he moves too suddenly. My heart pounds, my skin heating.

He holds his hands up, letting out a sigh that releases from his shoulders. "You're not the only one with a vendetta. Trust that I don't intend on running my kingdom the way it was ruled before. But as your desire is to go to Nevaeh, I can't say anymore. You'll just have to trust me."

"Trust you?" I take him in. Not the curled horns that part through his hair, the hunched feathered wings with a bony claw at their arches. Not even the changing eyes that mark him as something *other*. Just what I've seen of him, what I know, even what he's told me. I haven't shared the revelations about the Selection or Curse with anyone. It felt like betraying the twisted truce we've established.

He holds out half his sandwich, the oddest olive branch I've been offered. But I take it. I eat a bite, savoring the rich flavors.

"As far as I can throw you."

"I can work with that." Draven, spread out so casually dominating in that chair, looks me over, his gaze lingering on my training gear, and I know what he'll say before he speaks. "But you can't go in this. What kind of host would I be if I shipped you off to the seraphs wearing that."

I roll my eyes to the ceiling but a little part of me sparks with interest. It's been a long time since anyone cared about me, even if his reasons are selfish.

"Wouldn't want to make you look bad." Snark slides into my tone like a knife into a sheath.

"Impossible. I could go with literal garbage, and they'd still give it compliments." He grins smugly and I blow out my lips, stunned by his arrogance.

"Do your worst then." I give a mocking smile to battle his haughty one.

"And have you call me a prick? Again? No, love, I think I'd rather see what you choose." He gestures toward my room, walking ahead of me, hands in his pockets. Why does him calling me *love* feel like a finger traced along my jaw? I grip the necklace at my throat, toying the pendant along the cord. He leans against the doorframe, waiting for me to catch up.

"You're actually letting me choose?"

"With me, you always get to choose."

I nearly argue him on that before remembering I was the only Selected he did not choose. I lift my chin as I bypass him, but when I enter, I don't see anything laid out, nothing changed from the ordinary. I turn back to him. "Well?"

"I figured I'd make you something myself." His eyes shift from indigo to smoldering violet, daring me to play.

His clothes are always beautiful. Even when he wears the same uniform as the rest of us, his outfit still stands apart, accented with extra gold or silver that shines as if made with the real thing, framing his collar and lapels. I wasn't expecting this, but I'm not sure exactly what I was anticipating. Something bought . . . I suppose.

I demand, "Are you just going to stand there?"

He laughs, rocking on his feet. "Is that supposed to be an invitation?"

I want to snap, but I just give my best sarcastic curtsy. "Do you need one? What are you, some kind of vampyr?" I laugh but he doesn't, and it suddenly hits me that those beasts of nightmares may actually exist on this side of the Wall. I swallow, hand scratching my neck.

"Don't insult me, Rune. I'm far prettier than most of their kind."

"I'll reserve my judgment." I make sure my mental shields are as strong as steel as he pushes off the doorframe, an indignant grin on those full lips, eyes bright with challenge. I think to myself, in my little mental fortress, that I'm not sure I've ever seen anyone as *pretty* as him.

His gaze caresses me, as if he wants to tear down those shields to know exactly what I'm thinking, and from the tense lines of his shoulders, fists in his pockets, I think it's taking his full restraint. Finally, he releases an ungraceful snort and moves toward me, taking in the room nearly identical to his own, though I haven't adorned it with anything. Not much point in knickknacks and baubles when I'm supposed to be leaving tonight.

He lingers beside a freestanding mirror, its arch decorated with swirled golden accents and hand-painted filigree. I join him, and he eyes me head to toe, drawing on the World, and through it the Hierophant, a memory projecting in front of us, everything filtered with a golden sheen.

Before me, three styles of dresses appear, displayed on mannequins, pulled from Draven's memory. Ball gowns of black lace, crimson silk, and some gold ethereal shining material too lavish to name. I cannot imagine any of them belonging to me—not just because of their sheer worth and beauty, but also their impracticality. They're itchy and restrictive with giant bell-shaped skirts. My Wraith training won't allow me to enjoy them without wondering whether I could even fight in one. As I stare indecisively, a woman appears in the memory, and the way she devours Draven with her eyes starts an ugly coil slithering through my gut.

"Your Majesty, all these styles are fashionable, but this one is cutting-edge if you'd be interested—"

"Not that one," Draven's deep voice replies, and suddenly the imagery reverses, the woman and her hungry gaze stepping back out of frame, but I get a glimpse of the dress. A dangerously low-cut gown that's far out of my comfort zone. But it's nonrestrictive . . . and . . . maybe just for one night, I should let myself be draped in something beautifully feminine.

"Why not that one?" I ask Draven over my shoulder. His eyes lock on to mine, the pupils spreading like the dawning of night.

He runs a strong hand through his hair, chewing his lip before his voice rumbles out like thunder wrapped in midnight. "If you were to wear that one . . . I wouldn't be able to think straight for the evening."

I read him over: his lips parted, his position behind me drawing closer, nose near enough to be breathing in my scent, his hand flexing at his side, knuckles turning white. He may not like me . . . but he wants me. There's a power in that, but it's quickly seceded as my gaze is drawn to the lines of his neck as he swallows, the arc of those perfect cheekbones. Whatever this blossoming attraction, it's one we're both feeding. Well, shit. The memory attendant reappears as she holds it against herself, meant to entice him, and a devilish urge seizes me.

"Then I want that one," I tell him. What am I doing? I'm meant to be a shadow and here I am embracing his spotlight. The space grows hotter than the volcano-warped air outside, sucking the breath out of the room. "Don't want you scheming too much."

He bites his bottom lip, eyes shifting firmly into violet.

"One distracting dress, coming up." With that Draven summons the Magician.

He steps forward, his free hand hovering beside me, moving up and down without ever grazing my skin, before lifting to the golden-threaded collar of my tunic. I freeze. A vibrating tingle races along my body wherever the fabric touches, shifting and expanding. The material unfurls around me, tightening or elongating in places until I'm clad in a silver ball gown of smoke rendered solid, laced with spider silk. It drapes across my form, leaving little to the imagination. The color fades as it rises, as if I'm a storm cloud, the hem darkest gray. The dress hugs my waist and chest, while sheer sleeves puff at the shoulders, tapering into tight silver cuffs around the wrists that shimmer in the light as if woven from metal blades. My hands rove across my chest, tracing the neckline that plunges nearly to my navel, and around to my bare lower back. The gown flows to my ankles but slits reach nearly up to my hips, where the fabric pulls tight. There is too much of me exposed to the world.

"You said do my worst," he reminds me, eyes taking in too much.

"Prick," I hiss, but I cannot hide the desire written all over me, my breaths too short, my chest too flushed. Our gazes explore the other, leaving me heady. I don't know when things changed between us—whether it was during those long nights of training or if it's been subtly building ever since he mentioned he was a changeling, too. When I stopped seeing him as just my captor and instead as someone I want to conquer.

Draven's lips are inches from mine. His finger crooks under my chin, tilting my head up. This is it. His mouth parts, and I swear I see a glimpse of those fangs, his breaths ragged.

But then my hair is righting itself, the frizz of the day smoothing away, straightening to a silken waterfall down my back, draping well past my shoulders. His fingertips rub against my earlobes and dangling diamonds weigh from them. The lightest touch of his thumb against my collarbone and a choker appears at my neck, and there adorning the center is the pendant my father gave me, somehow elevated by the rest of the riches I wear. When my hand moves against it, my fingers trip over jewels that could've bought my kingdom and everyone in it.

"It's too much." I feel silly. The woman staring back at me in the mirror is nearly beautiful and dressed like royalty.

"It's not even close to matching all you deserve." His breaths caress my neck, his words curling in my ear. "But it'll have to do."

"What is this game?"

"I want to remember this. You. Right now. Anytime Nevaeh threatens my people or tries to start a war. I need to know not everyone there deserves my wrath when I'm left to rule." Draven's gaze keeps settling on my lips, as though my mouth holds all the answers nestled on my tongue.

"That required all this?" I gesture at the dress, the jewels.

"It certainly helps." He grins coyly, gaze taking in every inch of me. "My father insisted I bring a worthy date, and it is your last night here." His shoulders drop as he looks me over. Is it regret lining his ever-changing eyes?

My heart plunges into ice as I wonder if the riches are some sort of misplaced pity.

But then he shakes his head, his voice low. "When I allow my father to hand you to them, I want them to know you hold value, so they don't try to discard you."

"And what do you get out of it?" I ask, trying to swallow down the thirst he's left me with.

"A solid night's sleep." His words don't hold any sarcasm. Instead, his gaze is too full, too wanting, that it snatches my every errant thought. His eyes dart away. "And freedom from my betrothal, of course. There's one more thing." He flips the Moon into his hand, and his face transforms to a mask of kohl and bone-white paint that makes him look like a skeleton king. His tone turns soft. "It's part of the history of the Equinox, the acceptance of the changing seasons, harvests, our own beginnings and endings."

My hand lingers over his softly now as he traces it up one half of my face, using the Moon to make up mine, too. Split vertically, one half is me, the other his painted match.

He promises, "Just until I let you go."

I observe myself in the mirror. I look a bit terrifying but for the first time feel as if the intimidating armor I've tried to build these last years is finally in place. The shell finally matches the tempest gathering inside.

"It's time to go. We're more than fashionably late for the ball." He holds a hand out to me, darkness wafting off his shoulders, and a portal opens behind him. I gather my dress in my hand, hurrying his way. His arm loops around my waist, his glance stealing the breath from my lungs, like a bellows gathering all the available air.

"Why didn't you say so sooner?"

"It's good to make an impact." He passes me an arrogant smile. "First-years are always premiered later in the evening, brought in like treats for the Court to devour."

My lungs grow tight, and the reality of being transferred into another kingdom weighs on me. I hiss through my teeth, "If anyone touches me, am I allowed to stab them?"

"No, but I can."

WE ARRIVE IN a palace that could fit the Lord of Westfall's manor within its entry alone. I run a thumb along my father's pendant to ground me. My nerves fray as I'm drawn between knowing I will miss Sedah and the anticipation of seeing my dad again. I've missed him every single day, and out of everyone in my family, he and I were always the closest. For so much of my life, his voice has been the one guiding me toward the moral path, the *right* way. A compass always pointing north. I worry my lip when I think about all the morally gray paths I've walked to get here.

What if he no longer sees me as the sweet daughter he left behind?

Draven's gaze travels over me and I clear my expression, asking, "Where are we?"

"The capital of Sedah. This is the Court, one part of the Royal Palace." He's scanning me, and I'm unsure if he's going to ask about the momentary emotion that flits over me. I dance our conversation away from that intimacy.

"You grew up here, Princeling?" It's opulent to the extreme, the walls black marble, the carpet at our feet plush and crimson, and every accent is made of gold.

"Not in this wing," he whispers, his eyes bright at the indignation on my face. Entitled, privileged, pampered—"Shields up, love."

Draven leads me down an enormous flight of steps. Every head lingering in the ebony and ruby-painted hall turns my way, noting my diamond-lined slippers, my plunging neckline, the lace of my sleeves covering as little as leaves in a pool. I am smoke, a ghost, a rippling fog, and he is the darkness, the unforgiving night, his suit so onyx it seems to warp the eye, never catching the light, only the glints of gold accents along it showing like stars in the midnight sky.

We pass druids dressed in resplendent gowns and rich suits. They wear either makeup as a veneer or dainty skeletal domino masks, and most are tattooed up to the neckline, yet every one of them takes note of Prince Draven and then, belatedly, me. It's difficult to not shy from their obvious stares and the way so many seem to dissect every inch of this gown and my light brown skin beneath it. I've never had as many eyes on me in my life as when I came to Sedah.

"Stop craning, start preening." He whispers, "You look gorgeous."

Draven turns away, as if he didn't just utter that riling commentary into the curve of my ear, causing my toes to curl. Now he nods to every passerby, as if they're all just as interesting as I am. I glare at him, silently daring him to look back at me, so I can search those ever-changing eyes for a hint of honesty. He doesn't meet my gaze but his arm crooks around my lower back, pulling me against his heat, bathing me in his heady scent. Why does he have to vex me like this? The warmth he gives ebbs and flows. Quick as the summer tide that first leaves me burning and then cold as the shortest day of winter. I lift my chin and look ahead, trying to blur those bright-eyed gazes to the background, but they graze me all the same, like hounds nipping at my heels.

Passing them by, we enter a room that's a little of everything I imagined and yet so much more. Four thrones are placed at the end of the hall, black and gilded in gold, the backs arched and pointed toward the ceiling. The king's sits highest, and all are already occupied except for the one left for my date.

The room itself is decorated as though we've sunk into the bottommost pits of the deepest sea. It's a show of sheer power, staggering in its brilliance. The walls are jet-black, with great columns of onyx crystals puncturing the space here and there, electricity undulating inside each, like bottled storms that flash and ripple within their glass. It illuminates the hall in unfiltered pulses of whites and blues, like the heartbeat of a great slumbering beast. Druids linger in pockets, eating or talking, or both, but all consumed by conversations, or else gyrating to the ethereal music echoing through the throne room, invigorated by the atmosphere.

Like dominoes ticking over, the crowd heaves and their eyes find him, then me.

There's a flurry of curtsying, and bowing, and some glaring. Then the music softens to nothing, revealing the whispers underneath.

Prince Draven walks forward as if he doesn't notice any of it. I wish I didn't. I long for whenever their eyes will quit piercing through me like needles. I hate that my mind tries to diagnose what each of them is thinking, sorting through the cancer of their cruel looks.

Draven whispers to me again, but this time his eyes slide to mine and stick. "Just look at me."

I nod, swallowing down my fear and worry.

We stay together, and my gaze doesn't leave his face. Even if he glances forward, his attention always floats back to me. I try to keep a smile hitched to the corners of my mouth, challenging myself to look at every angle of his cheeks, his chin, the fine bones around his brow and eyes as if I will need to recreate it to perfection later, but truly I'm looking for a single flaw.

Something to make this feel easier. It *should* be easy. Any good daughter would think it was. I finally get to be reunited with my father, I just never thought it would feel like leaving something else behind, too. Every beat of unease in my heart feels traitorous.

My hand twitches, and I'm unsure if it's the tarot deck I want to reach for, or those gloved hands of Draven's. His shoulders flex near imperceptibly, given away only by his black velvet jacket scrunching over muscles, a slight shift of those wings. He lifts his chin, fingering the gilt buttons at his chest.

"Watch your step," he tells me in a hushed breath, and I look forward, realizing we've reached the thrones.

King Silas is the only one in attendance without a mask or makeup, and I swallow a gasp before it can sustain any air. I study him closely—he is as beautiful as any of them, his skin pale, but his angular features strangely alluring. The edges of his face bear a few stylistic tattoos in black, symmetrically matched against his cheekbones, an upward-sweeping crescent moon across his forehead like a set crown. Parting his hair, those antlers are bone white and ridged. Wisps of night float off his back, eddying swirls that line the space between those dragon wings.

The king is handsome, compelling, yet I can finally tell he and Draven share no blood.

For the prince is staggering in his beauty, more striking than any other I've seen.

King Silas looks down on us, eyes flitting between us as if he can sense something growing there, but I'm unsure if it gives him pause or makes him eager to be rid of me. Prince Draven smiles, bowing his head, though I know more is expected of me, so I copy the curtsy we practiced. The corner of the king's lips pulls up in a smirk at my clumsy movements, but he doesn't seem dismissive, thank the gods.

"She learns quicker than you," King Silas tells Prince Draven.

I watch only his feet, noticing the intricacies of the throne, scales chiseled into its sidings like a great black python. For all my spite, I'd love to glare him down, but the love for my father keeps me in a perfect pose of submission. For now.

"She'd have made a better heir to be sure," Draven responds facetiously. "Unfortunately for our kingdom, she has some-where holier to be. When will our guests arrive?"

Draven's so casual, thumbs looping into his pockets. With that strange electric energy highlighting his suit, the crushed velvet pattern of little skulls mixing into the ivy and thorny roses stands out more starkly.

"They're already here." King Silas looks behind us.

I turn, my breath catching desperately in my chest as I spot the seraph king entering the hall, my father at his side.

12

The Halo

When the Seven of Wands represents a person, it is someone who is dynamic, a born fighter, one who will defend others' honor, and rise to the challenge.

THE SERAPH ROYALS are an imperious, humorless lot. There's the king with his golden eyes, hair, and wings that match as if he were dipped in molten gilt. He'd be handsome if it weren't for the sour look he wore, the symmetrical features of his face darkened by the thunderous temper in his stare. Gazing upon everything as if it spoiled his day. He makes King Silas seem temperate by comparison.

Then there's Princess Reva at his side, full lips pursed to a thinning line as she tries to catch Draven's attention, but he only watches me.

Despite what he said, I'd bet my life she still wants him.

Behind her comes my father, and my heart lodges in my throat at the sight of him. He looks unharmed, but harried, his jaw clenching when he notices Draven's arm looped around mine. I squirm a bit beneath the judgment in his eyes.

King Altair is not my king—not yet—but the druid people bow their heads as the seraphs pass, showing deference to them, and so I take their lead. When Altair and Silas face one another, the entire hall stills, watching.

King Altair approaches the dais, drawing his daughter to his side, and my father hovers at his other shoulder, apart from the seraph guards. His eyes flick between where Draven and I stand off to the right and back to his king.

King Silas rises, so much higher up on that dais, imposing as if he were cut from a twisted tree, looking down on us all like a dark god of old. He addresses the seraph king, but there's not a trace of warmth in his features, like a fire frozen over.

"King Altair, I'm glad you've come in good faith to discuss this trade and the ending of our children's betrothal. As much as my Court is dying to eat the feast of our exchanged words"— he looks around the hall with a smirk, and announces—"I think it best such important discussions occur between family." King Silas steps down from the dais, and Draven's mother and little brother, Ansel, follow.

Draven's jaw clenches, his eyes on the seraph king as if a viper has slipped among our ranks. I've never seen a hint of fear on his features before, but I see tinges of it in his loathing.

As King Silas passes, Ansel tugs Draven's other hand. I hear him whisper quietly to his brother, "Is everything going to be okay?"

He's smaller than I remembered at the Selection, his wide sapphire eyes brimming with worry. As he anxiously bites his lip, I can see he's missing a canine. Guilt pools inside me, thinking of how I wanted to manipulate him at the Selection.

Draven blinks the fury off his face, hitching on a genuine smile as he puts a hand on his brother's shoulder, and whispers back, "Of course it is. I'm here."

"Does this mean you get to stay?"

The hope in the boy's voice breaks my heart. Draven doesn't speak about his little brother with me, but seeing the soft way he interacts with Ansel, the way he always bends closer, his wing wrapping around the boy's small form, shifts an icy blockage wedged in my heart.

Draven nods and Ansel grins, exhaling shakily.

"Is that your girlfriend?" Ansel whispers, but he's a small child so his voice is loud.

"Quiet," King Silas snaps, gesturing for the band to continue, to drown our words, the audience still silently watching us.

I notice a few druids whispering behind their hands, eyes on me.

Princess Reva shoots a look at Ansel, but I realize the young prince is referring to me, not her. Draven quickly mumbles something to his brother, who giggles behind his little hand. The princeling wets his lips when he meets my gaze, a smile that softens and then heats.

King Silas walks toward a small private seating room off the main ballroom and the rest of us trail after. The music fades as the door closes behind us. This dim space contains blackened wallpapers and furniture, sconces chiseled into skeletal hands, and stone gargoyles in every corner, perched as if they hold up the very ceiling. Druid guards fill in every shadow, standing still as statues. King Altair bristles at their presence, despite his own guards falling in around him.

At my side Prince Draven barely breathes, his hands fisted, eyes glued to King Altair's movements, as if the seraph might just try to incinerate us all at the smallest insult. Draven's mother, Queen Vesta, and little Ansel sit upon a rich velvet sectional, large enough for all of us. King Silas offers Altair a seat, but to his clear annoyance, Altair stands, so the rest of us follow suit.

I can't help but notice the way Draven subtly puts his body between his family and the seraph king. His hand hovers against the middle of my back, his wing gently curling around me.

Across the room, my father and I glance at each other quickly. Years of waiting for this. Hope struggles to flare in my chest, and I hate that my fate lies in the hands of all these immortal men. The invisible strands of diplomacy stretching across the room fray with every razor-edged glower between King Altair and Draven. The tension between our two groups only grows within the silence, as if the wrong uttered word might lead to war.

"So . . . let's settle our affairs. Prince Draven's offer was not one I was privy to before he made it, but ultimately I agree with his logic." King Silas glances at me, his hand out, and hesitantly I step away from Draven, the cold air causing me to shiver, until I'm at the king's side. "If you will call off the forced betrothal between my son and your daughter, even for the high price of Rune Ryker, the only other World Arcana in centuries, we are ready to accept it."

King Altair doesn't bother to look at me, he only holds King Silas's stare, until finally his expression breaks into something like a sneer. "I never said I was willing to break the betrothal. Merely consider delaying it."

My gaze flicks to Draven first, his eyes liquid hot, a burning orange that glows in the dim light. Dread fills me as I glance to King Silas next, his face still as stone, clearly unamused. Princess Reva shifts on her feet, cheeks heated. King Silas scoffs, his head cocks, and I note a crease forming between his brows as they furrow together.

"You expect to take a Selected as valuable and as rare as Rune for *nothing* in return?" A deadly glint fills King Silas's eyes.

My father meets my gaze, the warm gold the only comfort he can give me, and eyes widen as if a knife has slid into his gut. He was clearly not expecting this either. I force my eyes to remain dry, telling myself they did not give me this hope only to snatch it away in an instant.

"My consideration is something most would *die* for." King Altair finally turns his heated gaze toward me, though his tone doesn't soften, even an inch. "Let me look at her, let us see if she's as valuable as you pretend."

King Altair reaches his hand for mine in such an entitled way I nearly draw back just to spite him. But my father's jaw clenches and his eyes bulge as he watches his king lean toward me, and I think better of it, stepping forward and taking Altair's proffered hand. He holds it in that stupid frail way men always try to take my hand in theirs, as if we're about to engage in some dance. His bright golden eyes burn like liquid flame as he commands, "Kneel."

I go to obey, despite the venom limning my body, but something stops me, some magic I don't understand. It hits me like a lightning bolt, the Oath.

I turn to King Silas, and he waits a beat before nodding to me, as if he needed to prove that he still controls me. My body overcompensates, and my knees bend so fast and hard they thump against the black marble floor beneath us. I fume at the indignity. I'm sure I'm supposed to look at King Altair's knees, or the ground, but I raise my eyes and look at him full-on.

King Altair holds his halo in his hands, a strange humming sound emanating from it, growing louder as he moves the ring of light toward me. I watch as it expands. He loops it over my head, where the bright firelight hums around my neck. My immediate reaction is to tear it off, to pull that heat away from my flesh, but Draven flinches so hard when my hand rises that I stop, fighting the instinct. A strand of white hair brushes the halo engulfing my collar like a ring blade, parting it into two snowy filaments that float to my feet, having danced too close to the edge. It takes everything not to show my fear. My eyes swivel to my father for assurance, but he's frozen.

"Look me in the eye," King Altair demands.

I do.

"This halo is designed to show me if you are worthy of Nevaeh. Show me who you are, girl."

Holding his stare, I think of my wall, my snowy field. His eyes narrow as the image takes over my mind.

I think of Draven's warning. *The seraph king wants to eradicate the Curse and annihilate the mortals.* I try to fight the rage that burns through me. I can swallow it down to be with my father. Even if it'll feel like a wildfire rages through my chest. Draven said there was no hiding anything within Nevaeh, not from the seraphs and certainly not their king. I lock that snowy image in place, the impenetrable fortress, the endless white field, and focus on one thought. *I am good.*

The halo makes a metallic noise, a *shickt* sound that raises the hair across my body, and it closes tighter around my neck. I lift my head, terrified to let it touch my skin. The fear laces anger through me, entwining through my marrow. I don't know if I can keep it from burning through my eyes.

"There you are." King Altair sneers as he looks down at me on my knees, trapped.

I realize too late how intense my gaze is, my nostrils flared, my mouth a snarl. Fuck.

He glowers at me. "Now let's see if you're capable of honesty. Where is the rest of your family?"

My father looks only at the ground. Eyes never lifting. He's never been a coward . . . why the hells won't he look at me? I focus on King Altair, confused why he's even asking.

"My brother was taken by the elves. You have my father."

"And your mother? Where is she?" King Altair presses.

My father meets my stare now. His head shakes ever so slightly. A warning maybe, not to lie. I don't know for sure. Suddenly, he feels like a stranger, where once he was more familiar to me than my own face.

"The druids took her six years ago," I reply honestly. "For avoiding Selection."

The color blazing around my throat changes from white to gold. King Altair's gaze goes a little slack.

So the halo gauges my ability to tell the truth.

"Where is she now?" King Altair's question is not for me, but King Silas.

Silas's brows narrow, clearly lost. "I've no idea."

"She was sent to the Destarion." Draven's fists shake at his sides.

I'm too terrified to think straight, but even if I wasn't, I doubt I could figure a way out of this noose of star fire.

Draven's nostrils flare, veins straining. "Try that little trick on me if you don't believe me."

"The halo would likely burst into flame," Altair snarls.

"Watch yourself when you speak to my son." The back of Silas's hand glows emerald along a tattoo of the Judgment Arcana. The ability to control both the living and the dead. He flexes it, silver eyes glinting with acidic green. "And let's move past these dramatics. Do you agree to this trade or not? We won't accept a delay."

I lift my chin to look at Altair, trembling to my core. He sees too much, this halo knows every lie, sees straight through to the righteous anger woven in the fiber of my being. But I *can* let this fury go . . . for my father.

The halo's light turns red and another *shickt* sounds, my throat so dry I want to swallow, but the warmth of the halo halts me. If I breathe too deeply, I won't have a head on my shoulders. It knew I was sitting here, lying to myself. My eyes flutter as the heat burns, but I force my expression to be neutral even though rage devours my heart, bile rising in my throat. An anger that's built from the Selection, starting with the one when I was six, when I lost my brother, and realized the severity of what it was. Then when I lost my father and mother, slashing scars across my soul. Amping to this last one, burning it all up from the inside out.

Altair's jaw tightens, as if he's biting back his full judgment.

"What is your destiny, Rune Ryker?" King Altair's light eyes draw up that field locked in my mind. But there's something new in the image I've never seen, glinting gold. For a moment it overlays what's in front of me, like a window into the past.

After the druids burned down our home and took my mother from me, I ran. Desperate and alone and terrified I sprinted as hard as I could. Until the breath stopped holding in my lungs, the winter winds no longer pushed at my back, and my legs simply gave out. I collapsed at the edge of that snow-strewn field. The tears ceased spilling down my face. It was then I left behind the soft girl I was. Like a serpent shedding its old skin, the former life went with it. I begged any mortal god listening to help me survive. I vowed that if they did that, one day I would make the immortals pay for their Selection. That I would not stop until I'd found my family and reunited us. It'd take years until I'd remember my promise, until I would snap at the Lord of Westfall's side and come back to myself.

But now I see something in that memory that had not been there that day.

I dig at the object, a golden peak visible under the deep wet slush that burns my injured hands. It's heavy, metallic, and its cold touch bites as I pull it from its half-buried spot. I lift it up in my mind, the sharp ridges of the crown both familiar and not. While I turn it around, inspecting it fully, I realize why. It's mended, smoothly, with pieces from every immortal king's crown.

Then I know something undeniable. Unexplained but certain all the same.

It is mine.

It belongs only to me.

The image vanishes as quickly as it came. I don't know if it was a vision, a prophecy, or a hallucination. My hands are held out in front of me still, and the phantom outline of what I'd envisioned shimmers in my palms. From the looks on everyone's faces, they see it, too.

Understanding what it foretells.

I can't focus on the intense stares of those around me, only King Altair's simmering fury. He's going to kill me.

And I know in an instant why—he sees me as a threat to Arcadia. How could he not after what we'd all seen? My breath catches as the mechanical hum begins again.

"Father—no!" Princess Reva tries, grabbing for his hand.

Then shadows erupt around me. I drop as if the floor has shattered beneath me, plummeting into the darkness at the same moment I hear one last *shickt*. I'm yanked through the shadows—the sound of a fast-riding chariot blaring in my ears one moment, gone the next—and then I'm colliding into Draven.

He thrusts me behind him as King Altair suddenly closes the distance between us too fast, wings spanning out so wide they engulf us. A heavenly, golden sword appears in his hand at the same moment Draven calls a black sword crackling with fiery red energy along its blade. I've never seen it before. It's glorious.

He slams it against the glowing edge of Altair's sword to keep him back, his own burning like lava, sparks flying. His mother and Prince Ansel scream, but I can't see beyond the two males in front of me. One protecting me with his blade and body, the other intent to annihilate me. My gaze shoots to Altair's halo, only large enough for maybe a wrist to slip through, but certainly not a neck.

"She is an abomination. You saw the truth of her. Give her to me," Altair growls.

Thunder crackles through the room and lightning sparks off Draven's blade, the burning energy cutting into the seraph king's sword. "Touch her and I'll end you."

"STAND DOWN!" Silas hollers, and a green energy sluices into the two of them. Altair and Draven break apart, as if puppeteered to do so, their eyes glinting emerald for a moment. The strange coloring dissipates.

The seraph king lifts his sword, looking at the notched split Draven's blade carved from it. Altair's mends itself, light weaving to fill the spot until it is unblemished once more. I watch as Draven's blade transforms, too, bending and coiling and shrinking until it is a ring along his finger, glowing fiery red before cooling out again.

Princess Reva breathes heavily, reaching for her father's arm, but he jerks away.

Prince Ansel slips his mother's grasp and collides into Draven's other side, arms wrapped around his waist. I've never seen the princeling so absolutely feral. He bares his fangs, protecting both me and his brother before his mother scoops up the child and sweeps out with a couple of guards. The tension in the room is more tightly drawn than a nocked bowstring.

"You dare use your magic on me?" Altair demands of Silas.

"You forget that I, too, am king," Silas growls. He strides forward until he stands between them, a poisonous jade light filling his irises, and I realize he did not use his Judgment Arcana just against Altair, but on the seraph guards, too. Their eyes glow green, swords drawn, standing ready to bring their own king to his knees. "I tire of your demands, Altair. I know what the others say of my kingdom. The elves refer to us as 'night elves.' Mortals call us heathens, worshippers of chaos. And you seraphs call us demons. But we are druids, not some weakened version of your peoples, but our *own*. You forget our strength with every slight, and I am so very tired of pretending I am remotely in fear of you."

My father's hand inches toward the hilt of his sword, and he looks to me with a mirrored desperation and devastation in his amber eyes. I want to run to him, cling to him while we have the chance.

"Your debt to me still stands, Silas Vos." Altair is as immovable as a mountain and yet Silas does not look any more tamable than the sea. "Give me this girl. I will handle her as I see fit. Then we can call off this false truce. My daughter Reva deserves better than this leftover uprising scab anyway."

His daughter folds her arms, her gaze shifting between Draven and me. At least she attempted to stop her father from beheading me. I swallow, panic firing through every synapse at how close I came to death, a position I'm still in but at least now I'm on my feet. Draven and his father exchange a look. Judging by the way they hold themselves, prepared for a fight, I realize we're inches from catastrophe.

My hand slowly moves to hover over my deck. I realize how badly I should've been mastering more powerful Arcana, ones that could aid in a duel. I don't know if I can help in a fight of this scale, even though it's all I want at this moment.

My father holds no green glow in his warm eyes. Yet he hasn't moved. Not to stop his king from executing me, not to beg for my life, not to *do* anything.

"If you insult my son, then you insult me. I will do what I should've done from the start of this arrangement. Prince Draven." Silas gestures to his son. "Do you want to end this betrothal? You know what it will cost."

Me, I realize, *it will cost my life.*

My breath catches. I don't think there's anything I or anyone here will do to stop the seraph king should Draven hand me over. My father can't. And Draven could guarantee he isn't stuck with these horrific people for an eternity. I hate how my knees quake. How powerless I am.

"You would allow *him* to decide this?" Altair's face curls into a scowl. "She is a danger to all of us, Silas. You included, and I've never known you to back down from a threat."

Silas ignores the sheer fury drifting off the seraph king, still waiting on Draven's answer. I've never seen the prince so still. Desperately I open a small sliver in my mental shield, binding a thought up and spearing it to him. A promise and an offer. All I have left.

Save me and I will give you anything.

Draven's head tilts toward me, recognition in his eyes, along with something hungry.

Anything? His dangerously soft hiss fills my head like an empty cup. The wall I've opened allows his dark smoke to pour inside, but I don't stop it. I let him see I mean it.

His eyes flutter for a heartbeat, then harden as he turns to the kings.

"Rune is not livestock for you to slaughter. She is a druid of the highest Arcana, the only one besides me chosen for such holy power in over half a millennium." Draven's fangs grow increasingly prevalent. "You saw her holding a crown because *we* are fated. She is clearly meant to be my queen."

His words ring like the tolling of the bells, my destiny sealed inside them.

13

⸱⸱ ☽ ✳ ☾ ⸱⸱

Fated

Can something made still have a fate? It cannot be
said with certainty whether changelings can have
mates, as they were created not by divine hands,
but by our own.

S HIT. SHIT. SHIT.
I stand frozen as Draven draws that over-brimming arrogance onto his shoulders like slipping on a new jacket. I envy his
careless ease. I swear on the gods themselves King Silas smirks
at his son's audacity before turning to King Altair.

The two leaders stare each other down and energy crackles
through the room as the kings of light and dark square off.

"You're going to break your word to me?" King Altair
demands, light burning around his halo as he places it back
where it belongs, the blinding aura a deadly crown encircling
the golden one in his hair. Silas clenches his jaw as he takes in
his son with a calculating look.

Draven links my hand in his. My palm is sweaty, and I wonder how he can bear to touch me, but his grip only tightens.

Finally, my father rushes to whisper in Altair's ear.

"Please, my king. She is my daughter, and I promise it will never come to pass. She's only wanted a simple life, never glory, never power." My father's gaze flashes back and forth between me and his king, tears lining his eyes, a desperation there I haven't seen since my brother was Selected.

My heart clenches in my chest when I realize he believes the words he's swearing to Altair.

But they're not true.

That simple, sweet girl isn't me, not anymore. He doesn't know what I've become.

Altair puts up a hand to stop his rushed words, but then the princess moves forward, graceful as a gazelle, her words quiet, as if in the presence of mourners.

"Father—let them deal with the girl. Spare Draven. He could still be an ally."

Altair silences her with a look and then tells Silas, "This is not over."

Light slams from the ceiling, warping the very air. It flashes out, and all the seraphs are gone, leaving streaks of white painted across my vision.

He's gone. My father's gone.

I blink several times, shoulders slumping, and then find King Silas bearing down on Draven, all his calm thrown out the window. Instantly I go tense, moving forward, but my Oath stops me from doing anything as he grasps Draven by the front of his regal suit.

"Don't you ever surprise me with shit like that again," he snarls. "I'd have thought you of all people would've known better than to pull a weapon in front of Altair."

He releases Draven and turns to me. It takes everything to hold my ground. "I don't know what you are, or what you will be, but know that if I think you're a threat to this kingdom, I will not hesitate to end you myself. Now as far as your future, you've successfully burned the bridge to Nevaeh, and seraphs do not forget even the smallest of slights." His voice is a hiss. "Draven may be willing to risk his life and our future to vouch for you, but I am not. You're lazy, insolent, and so far, talentless."

His words sink like stones, but I lift my chin, spite the very makeup of my being. Silas turns his attention back to Draven, shaking his head, wearing an angry smile. "I need to go sell this mess you've made to the rest of Court. I sure hope you know what the fuck you're doing, boy. You're stuck with her now."

He leaves us, the untenable tension in the room lifting with his departure. A few guards linger and Draven trembles at my side, his fists clenched, jaw equally so, eyes burning crimson. He clamps them shut and when he opens them again, they shift drastically to indigo. I don't complain or move my hand away as he squeezes it so tightly my knuckles burn. His other hand draws the World and Death and then we're back in that transportive darkness, the wind howling like wolves around us.

The next moment we're in his room. Outside the massive arched window, night has fallen, the sky moonless, the volcano gone cold. I've never seen it so dark here. The stars are spectacular. Thank the gods, since they'll be the ones I'm looking at for the next four years at the Forge, and then an eternity more at Draven's side.

What does this mean for finding my family? Is there any chance of seeing my father again? I claw my hand through my hair, more lost than ever.

Draven shirks off his overcoat, casting it over an armchair before slinking into its cushions, staring into the fire. Another chair sits across from his, a small table with a chessboard halfway through play between them. I throw myself into the velvet of the empty seat.

"What the hells was that?" I demand, and his eyes flick to mine, but they're not indigo so much now as a bright, tempestuous violet.

"You said *anything*."

"Yes, because I thought you were clever!" Anger grows with every syllable and my hands shudder on the armrests.

"I told you if you wore that dress it'd be distracting." His grin is a wild wicked thing, as if the oppressive heat between us is a welcome diversion from the shitfest we just escaped.

I can't look at him without shivers running across my skin. I bury my face into an accent pillow. "Become your queen? Marry you? Fuck off, Draven."

"Don't flatter yourself. I'd marry a broom handle if it secured me my kingdom—"

I drop the pillow. "It'd be more likely to fuck you than me."

His gaze snaps up, incitement visible in his clenched jaw. "You should be thanking me. Most people would beg for the power that chose you, the might and ambition I'm offering you—"

"I'm sure you'd love for me to beg."

"Want me to fetch King Altair? I'm sure he'd be happy to execute you instead."

I force myself to take a breath. To calm. I need to think my next words through carefully.

"I just . . . I don't understand how that went so sideways!" I can't get a firm breath in my lungs. My heart's beating so wildly I feel its pulsations in my fingertips, my neck, even my toes. It's rocking my entire body, yet he sits there so calmly. "Why aren't you upset?"

"Why should I be?"

"You just traded one shackle for another."

He should be livid, berating me about how much I've cost him.

"But this one owes me her life." His lips twitch and his nostrils flare as he watches me closely. "And at least this manacle comes with much prettier packaging."

My cheeks heat at the arrogant smile curling the edges of his lips like paper held to flame. He's just saying that to mess with me. To get a rise. Obviously, I'm not comparable in beauty to the seraph princess Reva, who I'd have thought was a goddess if I didn't know any better. Maybe he's just trying to stop me from yelling, but I'm in too pissy of a mood.

"Like the princess was anything to scoff at."

"Well . . . you've seen what her dad's like."

He looks to the chessboard in front of us, making to move one of my white pieces for me. I swat his hand away, taking it for myself. Annoyingly, I realize it was the right play and put the rook down in the spot he'd been angling toward.

My mind whirls as I attempt to figure out my next steps. I'm tied to Draven. I need to know what he needs, what he desires most, so I can barter it for what I want. My family returned to me, a place of power here. As of right now I don't have another option, as my plan just got chucked through the window. There will be no going to Nevaeh. No reunification with my father, maybe ever. I clench my eyes shut, forming my words carefully.

"You're out of your betrothal. Free to rule here as the heir now." I watch his performance of self-satisfied prince critically. There's a deeper motivation he's hiding behind the carefully curated mask. "What do you want from *me*?"

He smirks, moving to the black pieces and grasping a bishop, and his throat bobs before he says, "I need a partner." His gaze locks on mine, and the firmness of his stare emphasizes his words are oddly true. No jokes, no games. "My father may want me to rule, but I defied his trust tonight. Put us on the edge of a war he very much does not want. I'm not wholly sure what my actions tonight mean for me. But I intend to rule with what's best for all people. I need someone I can rely on. Without question."

I lean forward. "Where do mortals fit into *your* vision?"

His smile falters. Soberly he says, "I want to end the Selection."

"End it?" My heart skips a beat. Of all the things I thought he'd say, it wasn't that. Now he has my attention.

"I don't believe in the Selection. I know how contrary it sounds, as I got here through being chosen. But I think people should be given the choice to join, not treated like cattle."

Those wings on his back shift. They're likely a constant weight and reminder of the ways in which he's been changed. Unwillingly, like me, at least at first.

"Many would choose to join us on their own. But forcing this assimilation, tearing families apart, the elves enslaving many of their Selected. It breeds resentment, uprisings, hatred. It cannot go on."

"Do you intend to find a cure for the Curse?"

"There is no cure," he says so firmly I wonder what he knows.

He unbuttons the top button of his shirt, adjusting in his seat, giving me a view of his curved collarbone, patterned with tattoos. Two serpents, one white, one dark, intertwine at the bow of it. I wonder what the rest looks like, how mapped out his skin is in ink.

"At least we have to assume there isn't. They've been searching for one since the start of this. No one's ever found another way to undo it now that Kieran Ceres is dead. Nor locate Kieran Ceres's alchemist and inventor of his weapons. So we instead offer mortals the chance to enter our kingdoms. Instead of taking tithes, we offer incentives. People will hesitate, but eventually they'll come. We have forever to wait. The immortals will ultimately realize that seizing people against their will has to bring our downfall. I think I can convince them; it's the mortals I worry about."

"I doubt they'll come with the Wall in place." The great mammoth of stone is formidable, and people won't trust it, not in the next lifetime. "What if you destroyed it?"

His head tilts. "The Wall is what keeps magic here. To destroy it would release it across the lands." He swallows, his jaw ticking. "The reason you and the others were made into changelings is because a mortal body cannot hold magic long. It devours their life force, and without something eternal to feed on . . . it's an ugly business. It could eviscerate all of them, razing the lands. And us? We might lose our immortality with it unleashed."

I shift uncomfortably at the horror of that thought.

"But I'll need to become king first," Draven says, his voice firm. "By any means necessary."

I weigh his words in my mind, knowing full well he likely sees the possibilities of what he's asking, spinning webs and cutting threads. The politics of the immortals' kingdoms are complex, but it's not my first time thrown into a messy court. I just need to know the players to try to manipulate the pieces. But I'm not offering up that kind of assistance without reassurances. My family's protection first and foremost, and I want to know how far he'll go to secure his crown, and if it will satisfy the revenge I so desperately crave.

Meeting his unbreaking gaze again, I realize he knows being this up-front with me risks his life, too. He's trusted me with that much of him. Joining forces might be the worst thing I ever do or my best chance at getting everything I came here for.

"And how do you plan to do all that as king of Sedah?" I shuffle my queen, frustrated by his sudden silence. His gaze shifts, unfocused, as though mulling something. His black bishop slowly takes a pawn off the board.

"Come on. Try me, *partner*." I'm exhausted by this cat-and-mouse game.

I use a knight to take one of his pawns, the little figures creating a line along the edges of our board. Tit for tat.

Draven sighs, deflated in the safety of this room. "I never thought I'd meet another World wielder . . . until you. You changed everything. Together, we could do what I feared was impossible. Arcadia is broken. We could heal it."

I almost laugh. But for the first time since I've known him, he looks vulnerable. I've seen him coy, cunning, and charming, but this is something more. How old was he when he was Selected?

His eyes catch the flickering light of the fire as he tells me, "The War might be a distant memory one day, but for immortals it's fresh. For Altair more than most, and I fear things for mortals are about to become even worse. My father has stood between Altair and all-out war, but without our tentative alliance, Altair may decide to test my father's resolve. I'm not convinced my father would stop him from grinding mortals to dust, even if he didn't join him. Then the seraphs will finish the war they started."

"Because of me," I finish, my leg bouncing beneath the table.

"And *me*," he adds. "But if you help me get my crown . . . I can forge a path to peace."

After a short pause, he continues, "I know you don't wish to be here, Rune. You wanted to be with your father, and perhaps kill a few of us along the way." He smiles at my blunt stare. "But perhaps telling the world we're fated will help your goals of seeing your family again."

"And how is that?" I ask, arms crossed.

"It grants you protection as my intended. And royal power can stretch beyond borders. We could find your family, negotiate for them. People would be willing to do a lot for someone fated to the future king. They'd see it as a personal favor to me, one they could call in." His middle and forefinger hover above his black king and queen for emphasis. Seize power. Reunite my family.

"But I have to marry you first?"

"Yes. Two World Arcana would command the respect of the entire Court, and we need them." His gaze falters, skirting from mine as though we are caught in some dance. His fingers caress a rib, as if he's tucking his heart back into place. "There's so much you don't know, Rune."

"Oh, well, I wonder why," I spit sarcastically.

"But I will tell you everything. And as for marriage, once you've helped me take the throne, you have my word you can just walk away."

"You'll let me?" I narrow my eyes, but from the way he takes me in, I can tell he's not anything like the Lord of Westfall. There's strength in his humility, even if he rarely shows it.

"Yes. And I doubt anyone could stop you from doing whatever you wanted once you've harnessed the full potential of the World." He smirks and gestures at the board. "It's your turn."

I realize it's not just him who could win, but me. If I take the chance.

"Our fated status would be to convince the Court, and our marriage political only . . . if you wish."

I study him a moment, slouched in that chair, head back, throat exposed and vulnerable.

I believe him. All of it. Maybe it's stupid, but my instincts are usually right. I square my shoulders and lean over the board, quickly moving a piece closer to his king.

"You keep using that word. What the hells does *fated* mean?" I ask.

He seems relieved that I'm still willing to listen. "For druids it's like soulmates. That we're bound to each other by fate," he says, moving an onyx piece from the chessboard, the bishop again, to capture my white marble rook. "The Court can't deny that kind of claim without evidence; it surmounts anything: love, arranged betrothals." He grins, a clever fox. "It's important for it to be believable. That guise would allow you certain privileges, and me an incomparable ally, so that I can do what must be done."

He levels a look at me, and I know that being with him will mean far more than a ceremony and our names written side by side. "I don't demand a small price, Rune. But a steep one. I need your help to make Arcadia safe for everyone. That means taking the throne. All of them."

The vision reemerges in my mind. Bloody hands and that crown of four kingdoms welded together over that snowy field, silent as a graveyard.

His gloved hands steeple, teeth clamping hard enough his jaw muscles flex. He really wants this. I doubt he's even dared to voice it aloud, as it sounds awfully close to treason.

"You want to rule all of Arcadia? The druid kingdom isn't enough?"

"You think I'm greedy?" There's a slight scoff to his voice, as if he assumed that would be my reaction. Yet he speaks as if he sees a future that I can't, one he believes in as much as if it were right before him. Every time I make a move now in our chess game, his is instant. Too far ahead.

"I don't want their lands or power. Only safety for my people. For all people. King Altair has positioned himself above my father and the elven king, readying himself to become an emperor, a tyrant. But *why should he lead*? So long as he's in power, we're all at risk, and the elven king may as well be his lapdog. Altair will oppress the mortals and eventually other immortals, too. Someone is going to rule all lands in this game of kings, so why not me? Why not a queen, too?"

I pause, looking at the chessboard, lost in thought. King Altair was terrifying, powerful. I don't think I've looked into eyes that held so much disdain before. But I didn't ask for this, fighting to save the very immortal kingdom I've hated all my life. Though, I'd be saving the mortal realm with it.

"Fixing the world is a nice dream, Draven. But practically?" Even girls untouched by the Selection were faced with the kinds of limited options I was. The stark differences between haves and have-nots was smothering. A world so dark any sparks of light that entered it were quickly snuffed out. I try to not think of Kiana's beautiful smile, swallowing hard. "Where would you even start?"

A smile blossoms on Draven's lips, the first genuine one since we retreated here. He can see my openness, that I'm willing to at least hear him out. Running a hand through his silken dark hair makes me wish I could comb through it myself. I look at the board and realize he's already won but never announced it.

"There was a prophecy once . . . that someone would draw the World as their Arcana and gather four fabled artifacts to save us from ourselves. The Arcadian Artifacts. I've seen the prophecy myself. My father called the Arcadian Artifacts a fairy tale." His eyes glimmer in the darkness. "But after seeing that crown in your hands, I believe they exist. You're the key to helping me find them."

14

The Deal

The Eight of Swords represents confinement, restriction, and potential self-sabotage. But in its *reverse* form, it is representative of possibilities and freedom from one's problems.

AIR SIZZLES BETWEEN US, heated by his unbreaking attention, before it trails down my face, settling on my lips. He thinks I'm the key to this impossible dream? Or a tool to be used? He tilts his head as though he heard that, but my mental wards feel secure, and he moves a rook piece, oddly lining himself up for me to take it.

"These objects are considered legends, fables, stories to inspire." He gestures vaguely to the tomes stacked on his desk. "But there are hints of them throughout history if you know where to look."

I sit back surveying him. "So, go get them, Prince. You *also* have a World Arcana, if I recall."

"And if I recall, *you* held the crown in the vision. That vision, Rune . . . peace between druids, seraphs, and elves must be won. King Altair won't be the one to bring it to Arcadia. But I could. With you." Draven's eyes hook mine. "These objects are how I get power and you get your family. How we both get vengeance against the immortals who've held it all for too long. This is the only chance I have of becoming king of Arcadia, and that you have of getting your family back."

I slouch back in the chair, scoffing. Four legendary items and a pretend betrothal, but my family returned to me. He dangles power wrapped in promises, and I can't help but reach for them. But I need to be cautious. If it sounds too good to be true, it probably is. Folding my hands in my lap, I meet his indigo eyes and concede a nod.

"What objects could bring all four kingdoms to heel?" I ask, finally.

A grin flashes across his face before he turns earnest. "In the mortal lands, there's an enchanted grail. It's said that a drink from this cup will reveal your truest self and break all bonds. Oathbreaker, cleaver of spells. Presumably made to spare mortals from immortal bonds and ties."

"Any pledges?" I ask, heart racing.

"You'd no longer be sworn to my father. You could find your family, break their bonds, too. They can possibly be transformed, returned to their mortal forms." The light from the fire reflects in his eyes, bright and brilliant and hellish, the blue all but waned away.

"Why would *you* want such a power?" My wants for it are simple, plain as he outlined, but this is an item he already desires for himself.

"We can serve no one but ourselves if we're to succeed." That includes his own father. Would he strike against King Silas if it came to it? Is that guilt gathering in his eyes? Or am I assuming too much of someone who longs for power?

"And the other items?"

"In the seraph kingdom, there's a sword," he says. "Lightbringer. The blade is considered cursed, but it disappeared during the Great War and is rumored to be hidden in a temple across their borders. I can't say it's there for certain, but it's said to contain the trapped soul of a fallen god. Whoever wields it will control a power that could bring all of Arcadia to heel. One that could kill even Altair, who is not just a seraph but a demigod."

The fact Draven protected me from that kind of danger at all leaves me stunned. I refocus on the mysterious sword, possibly the best tool in our arsenal. "What kind of power does it contain?"

"I don't know. But it's killed a demigod before." Draven rolls his shoulder, fiddling with that magic ring of his, and I wonder if it burns. "Somewhere in Sedah there's also a wand that could summon an army of hells' finest, splitting open the world, capable of portaling entire armies. As for the elves . . . they have a ring so powerful that it can be used to bend others' wills. Imagine being able to erase hatred from every mind. Or at least make them lay down their swords?"

"Cup, sword, wand, ring. Those are the suites of the Minor Arcana."

"Truth masking as legend. They're also the symbols on our flags." Draven points to his map. "Our ancestors have been crying out for the items to be found, brought together. But we'd rather pretend they're fairy tales than try for peace."

"They *could* be fairy tales, Draven. A hope sprung from your own ambition. I'd rather *not* partake in a useless treasure hunt." Pass. Hard fucking pass on this whole childish endeavor.

His eyes narrow.

"I am not one for flights of fancy, Rune. There's proof of each of them, and plenty of it—volumes documenting their presence in every major event since the birth of Arcadia." Draven grabs a book, flipping it open to a marked page before thrusting it in front of me. In the beautifully illustrated plate of a great battle, a seraph is depicted riding a winged lion and holding a sword rendered entirely in gold foil. "Lightbringer at the Battle of the Bastion, a seraph civil war not even five centuries ago, where Altair's grandfather came into power." He searches another pile and spreads another open book atop the first, pointing at a detailed rendering of a ring, the mechanics of it theorized, showing it changing sizes on its own. "This book is only three centuries old, and it specifically says these drawings are from a visual inspection of the ring. There is evidence."

"Why would immortals even allow these items to exist?" It seems too dangerous. If one person were to gather all of it, they'd be equal to a god.

"Once created, well . . . who destroys weapons like that?" He smirks, eyes sparking with desire. "They were created when the lines were drawn on each map. The how and where are up for speculation, but the why is clear. Power."

"And no one else has looked?"

"They've tried. But few have my resources." He gestures to the vast collection of books, some seemingly from the seraph, elven, and mortal lands, judging from their titles. "None would test our might with such items. My people would be freed of fear and tyranny. The mortals spared of the Selections. We'd be united territories—we'd be rid of the boundaries that have us fighting over dirt. Use those very tools to unite the land again. Who better to lead them than two immortals with mortal hearts? Perhaps this is why the World chose both of us. In return, you'll have power, freedom, and your family."

I move my queen to capture the bishop he's so fond of, adding it to the little pile of black players against the side of the board.

The aftermath of the last war shaped my entire life. Nothing comes without a cost. "And what of the fallout, Draven? The body counts? A road to peace bathed in blood? What happens if you lose?"

"We won't. Not together." His head tilts, his eyes tingeing red at the challenge in mine. "I've been learning about you, Wraith. You don't get to act like you're holy. Not with me."

I color, and I draw back my clenched fists.

"I didn't kill good people." I feel sick. He doesn't know . . . he couldn't know how much blood has filled the pages of my past. I was mostly sent to spy, but a few of those missions went sideways, leaving me with a body to bury, or scars, or haunting nightmares.

"Killing is killing. Only gods and saints act as if there's a difference." His long fingers twist, his king stealing my queen. I stare in surprise, unsure how I missed it. How did I not even realize I was so close to his king? So caught in taking that bishop, I forgot the endgame. But he never did. He places her on his side of the board, a little trophy. "But don't worry, love, we keep our conquests to this side of the Wall, tow the seraphs and elves into line with those Arcadian Artifacts no one will dare challenge. Gain loyalty from the druids with our fated status and our unparalleled Arcana. We avoid war altogether, seizing power without a drop of bloodshed. Except, perhaps, King Altair's." His eyes darken. "As long as that Wall stays where it is, the mortals have no dangerous magic or beasties to fear."

"Just you."

"Just *us*," he corrects.

My cheeks still burn. "What would your father do if he found us out?" I need to know the worst of it. This deal could be my family's salvation and get us both what we desire. But if I don't know the dangers, then I cannot plan countermoves against them. This plan is pointless if we both end up dead because of it.

"My father's vision for Sedah lacks ambition. But he is protective of his power. He would force me to take on a more intensive obedience spell." He shifts as if each fiber of fabric has become a razor. His look curls to a snarl, like a wolf backed into a corner. "If I refused, he'd torture me, or lock me away until I broke or could be replaced. He might force you to take my place under penalty of death, or likely the death of someone you love. Which is why we cannot be caught. Outside of this room, he has more eyes and ears than blades of grass in a field."

Gone is the weakness I glimpsed. Instead, his face becomes a mask of steel, unbending and immaculate. I clear my throat, yet my voice still comes out strained. "There's a slight problem with this deal. We can barely stand each other."

He scoffs, a smirk lighting his features with amusement.

"I think we can learn to tolerate each other to get what we want." Draven's gaze is unbreaking, and his eyes slide down my body, appraising me. It feels intentional. He knows exactly what it stirs in me. "We can make the others believe it. Fated do not bond instantly. It takes time. Every passerby is our audience, every courtier our judge. If they think they've witnessed us falling for each other, then we can write any story we want. I can protect you and teach you to protect yourself. It will explain why we'll spend so much time together, while we search for the Arcadian Artifacts—and your family—right under the others' noses."

"You really want to do this?" I point between us.

His full lips coil in the corners, reminding me of a jackal before it snarls.

"Yes." He really looks me over now, as if he's measuring all my scars, weighing my worth against his own, testing if I'm the real thing or fool's gold. "Unless, of course, you have some other pressing proposal? Childish dreams of romance with maybe one of your little study pals?"

For a moment my thoughts stray to Wynter, his soft smiles and pretty silver eyes. I wonder if he'll think I stood him up at the ball, or if he'll have heard the rumors of our abrupt departure. He is both gentle and kind. But it doesn't matter, and the more quickly I strike that idea from my mind, the sooner I can move on. Between him and Draven I don't even know who I'd choose if I had the choice.

I'd just want someone who'd choose me back, I suppose.

"No," I say decisively, folding my hands together on the table. "But I'd still like to know what that would look like for us. A story we tell others? Or one we tell ourselves?"

He blinks a bit, the colors in his eyes shifting in an almost dizzying way. I suppose I'll learn the language there one day. They finally settle on indigo as he swallows, shifting in his chair, leaning against one side, supporting his head with his hand.

"I need you to play your role as my partner, at least right now. But . . . when the dust settles . . ." Draven runs a thumb along his fingers, his wings pulling tighter around his shoulders. "I won't ever force you to remain at my side. When our deal is done . . . it'll be in your hands."

I nod. "My family returned and power of my own. So long as I pretend to be your bride and mate and help you seize your throne." Anxiety twinges in my gut. It could be years before we track those weapons down. Does my family have that long?

I lean back in my armchair, really taking him in, but . . . for all his games and arrogance . . . this seems genuine. And if there's one thing I can trust, it's his ambition. "We'll need to start right away," I say.

His eyes spark.

"But how do we know we won't betray the other?" Trust isn't given, it's earned. Built. And it takes more than a pretty face and seductive words to gain mine.

"We'll need a vow that can't be broken." He stands and I copy him. He moves like a dark god, limned with dominance, reeking of potential. Beside him, I feel like nothing but a changeling human, with a hope of being his equal in power and no clear evidence it'll ever come to pass.

I crush the doubt beneath a heel. After all, I was once a girl crying in the snow with nothing. Then I became the Wraith of Westfall. A World-chosen changeling.

I don't know what destiny has in store, but I have to believe it's building to something.

He closes the distance strung between us. "If you do this . . . you need to understand the level of commitment it will take to make it convincing. Whether you're in a classroom, or ballroom, the Oval or Hearth, you will have to act as if this is real, at all times. There can be no romances, no girl talks, no dalliances, no confidants. Even if it comes to us sitting on the throne, the people can only ever see what you and I create. It's you and me against the world. Our fates will be bound, truly fated or not."

Standing before him is like standing on the edge of a ravine, a bottomless chasm with no ending. But it doesn't feel like a choice.

What better path to my family, to vengeance, is there, when this could be a path to more . . . to justice? He's offering me a chance to seize power, to have control over my life for the first time. *I'd* get to choose my fate, the sides I want to play, the people I want as my allies.

His goals would accomplish mine, too.

"I can do that."

"Convince me."

I'm startled by his arrogance, by his unwillingness to leap blindly, like I must.

"I came here with one last hope. You have the sway and titles to make it a reality." I look him dead in the eyes. "But I won't live a life as a trophy. I will hold power of my own, you will make sure of it, and it *must* mean something. No lies between us. I need to be able to bring them here, it's not enough just to find them."

"You'd force them to come here? Even if they were . . . happy wherever they are?"

The idea has never occurred to me—except for . . . well, when I saw my father whole and healthy at the seraph princess's side. The thought sets my blood to boiling, the rancor burning like acid in my throat. "None of them are happy while we're all separated. Not after what's been done to us."

He tilts his head, his tongue tracing his teeth as if he isn't sure he believes that. My veins pulse with liquid-hot rage, but suddenly he speaks. "I can assure you that all your demands will be met. So long as you uphold your end as my partner and confidant." A wicked grin slashes across his face. "Should you fall for me and choose to stay at the end of our arrangement, I can promise you even more."

I roll my eyes. I'm sure he's just fucking with me; he seems to enjoy the way my face heats against my will, flames licking my cheeks any time he suggests there could be more between us. It was fun when it didn't feel so real, but right now his wanton looks are my biggest threat. Falling for him would be reckless, a distraction in the face of all this, and I hate how easily he pulls me into him.

"Are you sure *you're* able to make this kind of commitment? You don't seem like the type to keep his cock in his pants. I'm worried you'll screw this up more than I will."

He puts a hand to his chest in mock offense. "I always keep my promises, Rune. Especially when they're tied up in unbreakable magical bonds."

A tension laces through me. "You'd give up any chance of romance?" He doesn't seem worried about it. I press on, "Sex?"

"You're that certain my charm will never work on you?"

I lift an eyebrow at the idiot, crossing my arms, and he swallows, glancing off.

"Second thoughts?" I prompt, forcing a saccharine smile in place.

The devilish lift of his lips sends a heat barreling through me. "Well . . . at one point, Rune, you'll need to release some tension. I'm patient." That same self-assured grin is back in place. "So, no. No second thoughts. I think you'll break before I do."

He can't be the one to hold that power between us, so I snatch it back.

"You're awfully arrogant. I remember what you said about me in this dress."

His eyes catch fire.

I wonder if his spite would outlast his desire. I toy with the neckline of my dress. "What exactly did you find so distracting about it?"

He steps toward me until we're nearly chest to chest and barely have breathing room between us. Then in one slow movement, he leans into the nape of my neck, his whisper a prayer for only my ears. "Everything about you is distracting, Rune Ryker."

I roll my eyes, tucking my hair out of my face as a fever washes over me. I remind myself of all his promises, ignoring the call of temptation. He lifts his gloved hand to his mouth, pulling it off with his teeth, and the action sets my skin afire.

Maybe I *will* break first after all.

"So . . . partners?" Draven holds out his bare hand for me to take, letting it hang in the air. Three stars are tattooed in the tender space between his thumb and forefinger, and more of the heavy linework I saw on his father curves and juts across the rest of his hand—the outline of the World card imprinted there for all to see. My heart races in my chest as I wait for some unseen trap to spring, or someone to interrupt this moment, warning me to stop.

But it's just him and me.

I clasp his arm and feel his thumb trace across the fabric of my inner elbow. "What are those three stars for?"

"That's my business." The rebuttal is sharp. He clearly didn't intend to sound defensive.

"Is this really how you're going to start this? You'd break the pact before we even begin."

He huffs out a sigh. "One for each member of my family. Happy?"

I read him over, and though he holds my gaze, part of me wonders if he means the one surrounding him or wherever it was he came before. If he even remembers. More mysteries for me to uncover later, especially if we're bound in truth.

"Yes. No lies between partners." I squeeze his arm harder, the muscle beneath the jacket steadying. My loyalty will come wrapped in golden dressings, my devotion to him second only to my family. Hells, equal to them, as I can't save them without him. Our fates will be bound from here on out. I can swear that. I will swear that.

The smile lurking at the edges of his mouth rises, like a wolf cornering a sheep.

"Then it's a deal. So long as you hold up your end, I'll keep mine."

At these words, a magic splices through my veins, magnetizing my arm to his. I can't draw away. My mouth goes slick, my insides are like trapped lightning. The World card at my hip rises out of the pack of cards. His draws out, too. If I wasn't so close, I wouldn't notice the strain in his clenched jaw, or the swallow that bobs in his throat, his forearm tendons flexing as the two cards float above our joined arms. They twist in unison until they've made full circles, a rainbow of light flaring out of each before they glow gold. My forearm burns as if it's been set on fire, until finally our Arcana cards drop to our feet.

I'm flooded with relief as we break apart and take a step back from him, shaking my arm out, the muscles locked up. We both scoop up our cards, and the desire to just sit on the ground is nearly overwhelming. I force myself to stand.

"What . . . was that?"

"An Immortal Pact." He rubs his forearm as if he's been burned by an oven. My own stings. It must be bleeding. I roll my sleeve up and blanch at a dark symbol branded there, a raven mid-flight, the lines sharp and flawless. He grimaces when he sees it but doesn't reveal his own. Maybe it matches mine, or maybe it somehow represents me. I'm too distracted by the pain to find out.

"You could've warned me," I grumble, running a thumb over the marking, but it doesn't seep blood or fade away. It's just there, already healed, yet beneath the surface it feels fresh as a new bruise.

"It's been a very long time since I've made one." I hate how hungrily he observes me. Then as he blinks, the starvation wipes away, a passivity sweeping over him as he requests, "Tell me a lie. Anything. I want to be sure it works."

"Fine . . . um." I struggle to come up with anything creative, but I'm suddenly bone-tired and just want to go to sleep. I can say I'm left-handed, that should work. "I'm l— I'm lllll— I'm right-handed." My tongue trips and half my words are slurred, but I can't lie. A little slice of panic slips under my skin, not as hard as when I swore loyalty to the king, but still . . . it's uncomfortable.

Draven smirks. "And do you find me attractive, Rune?"

I glower at him, furious. His smile broadens the longer I hesitate, but I realize I don't have to *answer* him. I just cannot lie to him. I grin as I realize my out and his eyes watch my mouth as if he wishes to draw out the words.

"What's next?" I ask instead, and he huffs, as if I'm no fun.

"We focus on researching the Arcadian Artifacts. You also need to study harder than your peers, especially with the Arcana that will most help you in a fight if we ever get into a situation like that again." He runs a hand through his long hair, shoulders hunched, eyes barely staying open. "With your focus on the High Priestess, you've started falling behind everywhere else. And you still need to keep working on your mental wards."

"How do you know I'm falling behind?" My gaze narrows and he opens his mouth, eyes suddenly skittish. He flashes me a surprisingly humble grin.

"Color me curious." He shrugs, and my heart pounds, noting a hint of flush at his cheeks. It clears, his movements controlled yet vulpine again. "We'll need to make our infatuation appear gradual but believable. Otherwise, there's little chance of fooling the others. But we need to focus on fostering your power, too. People won't just believe you're a force to be reckoned with, we need to show them."

"Right. Thanks, by the way, for not accidentally slipping a compliment into all that." I cross my arms. "I'd hate to think you thought highly of me."

"I do think highly of you, and not just because you hate it," he says silkily.

"Do you think everyone knows what happened here tonight?" I swallow down my nerves, not wanting to let him know how agitated his attention made me tonight, though I suspect he noticed.

"I'm sure the Court is thriving off rumors right now." Draven unbuttons his collar, my eyes dragging to the movement. "Tomorrow everyone will know I've announced you as my fated mate. Hollow Fest is coming up in a few weeks, but after the festivities my father wants to send me to the elven kingdom of Alfheim, to obtain some dark crystal, zenith, along our border."

I raise a questioning brow.

"Zenith is an invaluable resource, it's what powers our lights, our energy, and typically it's been found only in our kingdom. Only druids can move it, and make it usable through our unique magic. That should've been enough to convince the elves to let us take it but the lines on the maps have moved over the centuries. They've argued that because it's within their borders that it's up for debate, which is why a member of the royal family is required to recover it, to maintain our delicate alliance." He rakes me over. "But if I bring you along, it makes a statement."

"Right." I nod, but my heart is jolting. My brother was taken to those lands, expansive though they are. My mother likely transferred there. "Are children that were Selected more likely to have been given to lords and ladies in their courts?"

"That's the case in Sedah, but with elves . . ." He shrugs. There is a tightness to the movements, a distaste to the frown he wears. "I can only assume it's the same. Why?"

"My twin brother was chosen by them at the second Selection." My hands clench together, thumbs twirling about themselves.

"That was, what? Fourteen years ago? Would you recognize him if you saw him?"

"I'm not sure." I sigh. "I have to believe I would."

"Even if he was raised in Court, it's doubtful he was raised near the palace. King Eldarion refused to raise an heir from the Selections. Eventually he held a trial to find one. Changelings competed."

I cross my arms and find myself glancing to the map he has on his walls. I hesitate but can't help myself from asking, "Where would the elves put mortal prisoners? The ones taken from the prison you told me about—Destarion."

Draven follows my gaze and clears his throat. "I've seen them at their Court as . . . playthings. Elves tend to treat prisoners and some of their Selected as more sport or entertainment than a solution for the Curse." A hint of pity enters his gaze. "Rune, you should know . . . the chances of your mother—"

"I just have to know for sure." I can't help the brittleness in my voice.

I'm surprised when Draven's hand reaches for my shoulder, as if scooping shattered glass. Even more surprised by the look of tenderness in his eyes. "I will find out for certain. And if something happened . . . I'll make sure whoever is responsible pays with their miserable lives."

15

Giving a Damn

Tell them you couldn't leave them; people always
want to hear that. Tell them of your potential, without speaking of the prophecy. Tell them you left
early because it was too hard to let go otherwise.
Tell them whatever they want to hear. Tell them . . .

—Draven's long list of excuses

D RAVEN WAS GONE before I was up this morning, but
he'd left me a note telling me exactly what to say to anyone
asking about last night. I curl it into my palm when I get to
the sign-off—*XO Your Fated Mate*. It pulls a rise out of me no
matter how much I try to convince myself otherwise, the prick
prince of darkness and his coy fucking smiles. I crave a distraction from the way he has my toes curling every time I think of
those eyes on me. Before we went to the ball, I would've taken
him into my bed that night, just to feel something with someone
annoyingly attractive. But with the deal, everything is messy. If I
want him, it feels like more than a vow but a real commitment,
and if I deny him, it chafes against me.

But I don't know if he's manipulating me, or what he really
wants.

And I sure as shit don't know what I want from him.

Rumors of my and Draven's sudden engagement spread through the Forge like hot ash on a high wind. Whispers follow me as I rush to meet my friends for breakfast, and when I find them in the Atrium, Ember gives me such a long, teary hug it earns some questioning glances from the others. I guess she's glad I stayed.

"Is it true Draven's claiming you're his fated mate?" Amaya bursts out, brows disappearing into her bangs.

Draven wanted to check the temperature of the rumor mill about us being fated, but it seems everyone's heard some version of it. He and I planned how to respond late into the night, but somehow, I thought it'd be easier to reply to.

Ember swats her shoulder and Amaya shrugs. "What, he even broke off his engagement. Everyone is talking about it."

"Yes, it was a surprise for me, too." I rub my neck, trying not to fidget further.

"A lot of fated mating bonds don't take at first," Wynter says, giving me an out. But I find my hackles rising a bit. "Some get rejected. You . . . do get a say in it if he wasn't clear about that."

"I know that." Maybe I should've been gentler with that pronouncement, because I didn't know it. I add, "Thank you, though, for looking out for me."

"Of course. I know you can handle yourself." Wynter swallows, chewing his cheek. "Out of curiosity, how did he know for sure?"

Our status is now public knowledge, but the prophecy is one Draven cautioned to keep quiet. We can't be certain how others might react to it. So I lie, "We both felt it."

Morgan's eyes narrow, as if in disbelief. I take note of the reaction—he seems almost angry.

"I knew you liked him!" Amaya grins, then musses my hair and says, "Does this mean I'll have to get a new sparring partner? I don't want to piss off the prince by throttling his bride-to-be. But it'll be hard to replace someone who always makes me look so good."

"Har har." My words are sarcastic, but the smile is genuine.

Felix gives me a gentle hug, and it fills me with the same feeling of calm I haven't experienced since hugging my brother. I want to cling tighter. He breaks off, grinning wildly, and says, "Congratulations, I'm really excited for you. Are you happy?"

I haven't asked myself that in so long it catches me off guard. "Of course."

Shit, I don't even believe myself.

"Are you okay?" Ember hangs back with me as the bell rings and the others move toward our first class. She looks concerned. "You seemed so eager to go with your dad."

"I almost left, but there were no guarantees we'd even be in the same part of Nevaeh had I gone, and with this thing with Draven . . . I didn't want to leave without figuring it out," I tell her, the lies tasting dirty in my mouth. I add with a bit of emotion, "And, I knew I'd miss you too damn much." I bump her shoulder, surprised by how true my words ring.

"Well, I selfishly hoped you'd stay." Ember gives me a tight squeeze. "But I want to hear more about everything later."

"Okay," I grin, but inside I'm panicking—I don't want to lie to her more.

"Like what the *hells* is a fated mate?" She grimaces and I'm glad that I'm not the only one learning everything from scratch.

"And why is the blushing bride-to-be wearing such an impenetrable mental shield? Hiding something, Rune?" Kasper hisses, and I glower at him as he lopes off after the others, still scrutinizing me over his shoulder. I hate that he's a High Priestess Arcana, that even among my friends I have to be on edge.

I feel a cold hand at my elbow. It's Morgan, pulling me back from the others. He lowers his voice. "So . . . you and Draven. I'm guessing you're going to accept the bond? Quite a bit of money there."

My jaw hangs open at his degrading tone. There's something possessive in his eye. As though he's annoyed about the nature of me and Draven's arrangement. The next lie has been written, but I find myself giving it with a lot more ease, as it's true. "Draven and I have a lot more in common than I thought. His net worth has little to do with how he values me."

"I didn't take you for someone who buys into all this immortals' crap. They say you're meant to be, and you just accept it?" Morgan scoffs. "I guess I just thought you were smarter than that."

"You'd rather I consider him for money than love?" I'm surprised how his words chafe me. Maybe it's the vow I've made with Draven, or maybe it's the fact that last night he saved my life. Not that I can tell anyone that. Or maybe it's just that Morgan is acting like an asshole.

"Let's not pretend to be things we aren't." Morgan looks me up and down, a cruel glimmer to his eyes. "He's a rich prince and you're a Wraith. I assumed maybe you were getting close to him to find out what the hells he's up to all day every day. But at least money made sense."

"Draven's . . . not what he seems."

I turn to go but Morgan's hand grips my arm, almost painfully. I yank my elbow out of his grasp, and he holds his hands up. An apology, if not in words.

"You can't trust him just because he's pretty. I've seen the way he looks at you," Morgan hisses. "It's not puppy love. It's like he's plotting how best to use you."

Maybe, but at least Draven doesn't grab me like I'm some insolent child.

"I can take care of myself." I keep my voice level.

Ahead of us Wynter turns back, watching Morgan like a hawk, his brows sternly drawn together. Morgan folds his arms across his chest, anger waffling into something meeker.

"I've watched him cross the Oval with his guards, disappearing into the darkness before the sun rises. I don't trust him, or whatever he's up to. You shouldn't either." Morgan stalks after the others.

I hesitate. Most of Morgan's words I can dismiss. But Draven is gone before me each morning. He's usually back to the Hearth later, too. I see him occasionally, across the room during sparring, but not every day and not nearly as much as I should when we share a house. He's a prince, so I never questioned his constant absence.

But . . . what *does* Draven do all day?

THERE'S NO SPARRING tonight thankfully, and I've spent the day preoccupied with what my new partner in this world might be hiding. But Draven's not at the Hearth at the end of the day to question. Sitting around alone in the big empty house has me bored and antsy, so at the last minute I decide to take up the others on their usual after-hours studying. I'm still struggling to draw the World card, or access its powers, a tightness growing in my chest with each failure. I need to learn everything I can to protect myself and prepare for anything thrown at me.

The memory of King Silas calling me a waste leaves me bitter. But if there's one thing that sets me apart even more than my Arcana . . . it's the level of vindictiveness I'm capable of.

Wynter meets us all outside Judgment's Hearth, which is just next door to mine. We learned in Professor Vexus's class that some of the most accomplished Judgment wielders can use the reverse form of its power to speak to the dead or use them as an army. I've only seen Draven powerful enough to coax the dead to speak, when Mira killed that changeling. But I saw his father use it to command the living just last night. For an Arcana concentrated in controlling the living and the dead, it's not surprising how eerie the Hearth feels. The pitch-black halls, the marble-tiled floor patterned between ivory and onyx, the dark coffered ceiling. A large ambiguous stone figure stands in the entry hall, shoulders balancing a set of scales that gently move up and down. As I draw closer, looking beneath its hooded cloak, I see a skeletal face snarls back at me, frozen in fury.

Wynter walks right past it, as if he's already grown bored of the interactive sculpture. He gestures for us to join him beyond it, his hand caressing my upper back for the briefest moment as he guides me into a large, comfortable sitting area.

That light touch shouldn't send so much warmth through me, but it does, and my attention flickers back to him. Those silver eyes meet mine, so opposite of Draven in their openness, their humility. They flicker to my lips for the briefest moment. I have to look away as the weight of my deal with Draven hits me. These lingering glances, and the potential here, are not an option anymore.

Carved skeletal hands hold zenith in their sconces, the little dark crystals carrying collections of electricity, tiny versions of the great columns in the court that pulsed like trapped lightning.

I never realized they were the source of energy that kept the castle lit or our cold box frozen. I can't help but admire the gilt accented throughout the space either. It's all surprisingly cozy.

Wynter slides the doors closed behind him once everyone settles on the expansive couch. He drops into the space beside me, his knee brushing against mine. I notice Cleona sits close to Amaya, unsure around our group. The two of them have been spending more and more time together, but I think it's her first time at one of these sessions, too.

Ember grins at me, her notebooks brimming with pretty adornments, everything color coded and organized. "So, midway exams are coming up the last day of Tenth Month. Last week we went over how Minor Arcana can affect each of our Major Arcanas. What else might be on the exams?"

"Professor Fenrys said not to stress over remembering every card in the deck as much as just the suites and their structures." Felix runs a hand through his hair, his lips pulling tight in a grimace. "But Professor Anstead seems like she wants us to know most of the cards' interpretive meanings for readings."

"Ugh, I don't want to think about it." Amaya leans forward, grabbing Ember's notebook and holding it out of reach. "Let's do something fun."

Wynter grins and I force my eyes off his full lips.

Morgan struts in, his gaze flickering between me and Wynter. He ignores the open spots and nudges his knees between ours until he's made himself a space. He leans back, his arm resting behind me, and I lean closer to Felix.

"Rune, your elbow is in my spleen." Felix squirms and I mutter a hasty apology, everyone shuffling to make space. I clench my jaw as Morgan insists on still sitting close to me, and on his other side Wynter leans in.

"You okay? You seem tense." He pointedly glowers at Morgan.

"Fine." I grit my teeth, mentally calculating if it would be poor manners to knock out Morgan under a friend's roof. Probably not my best chance at getting invited back.

"*I* could use a drink," Morgan suggests, giving Wynter a calculated grin. What is his problem? He announces to the room, "Let's do draw-offs!"

There's a resounding "Yes!" and Ember throws her hands up in defeat. Wynter rolls his eyes and gets up to grab drinks, Morgan and Amaya joining him.

"I should help." Felix is suddenly on his feet.

"No—not you," Kasper groans, standing less enthusiastically. He grumbles on his way out, "I don't feel like cleaning up glass this session."

"What's draw-offs?" I ask Ember.

"A drinking game. Amaya taught us."

"First, we take a shot, then all try to draw our Major Arcana," Amaya explains. "Whoever does it quickest doesn't have to take a shot next round. Whoever's slowest has to drink a mug of spirits. Usually someone gets sick, but we've all gotten better at drawing."

"Oh." Dread rises in me. I'm definitely going to be getting sick. I clear my throat. "Maybe I'll watch for a round."

I never drank much back home. I used to capitalize on *others'* inebriation to gather information. Still, if I leave now, it feels like defeat.

"Nonsense, she'll play." Morgan returns and sets a shot glass in front of me, sits, and loops an arm guardedly around my shoulders. I cringe.

When Wynter returns a moment later, setting far too many spirits on the coffee table, his silver eyes flicker between us, concern pinching his brow. Kasper returns with a bottle of something clear, tinged green, and lifts it up to a sound of groans.

"What? Wormwood's good for your gut." Kasper gives a devilish smile. "Maybe you slowpokes," he points at Felix, Ember, and me, "will be a bit quicker to draw your cards if you don't want to have to drink the green smog."

He pours a very full cup and then sets the bottle down beside it.

"You don't have to drink." Ember leans in at my side.

I consider that, but I've never really let myself have much fun, and never been presented with the opportunity. This pact I've made with Draven will soon likely change what I'm allowed to do. So, for tonight, at least, I just want to feel free to have fun with the friends I've chosen.

"I'll be fine, thanks though."

TWO HOURS LATER and I'm definitely *not* fine. I'm seeing stars and the phrase *I'm too drunk* seems to be the only thought I can really hold on to. I've lost three rounds but at least the game helped me successfully draw the World far faster than before. I've focused on pulling Strength after, using it to create a bit more resilience to the alcohol. I swear Wynter lost the last two rounds on purpose, just to spare me. Morgan moves closer and closer the more spirits I've downed, even trying to set me in his lap. I hate the way he's been pawing at me tonight.

"Why don't we play a new game?" Morgan side-eyes me, lifting a glass. "What about Candor or Cup? You can tell the truth to a question or take a drink instead."

Looks like I'm about to spill the truth or dinner.

"What did everyone do before coming here?" Felix asks, starting with something easy.

"I worked in a flower shop," Ember says.

"I actually took a year off to travel," Amaya shrugs.

"Me too!" Cleona smiles bright, the two sharing a grin.

"I was a guardian at one of Lord Azazel's temples," Wynter says. I didn't take him for the holy type.

Before I can ask more, I notice Kasper drinks, the question passing over him. A lordling's son who went running for the immortals. I guess he doesn't want the others to know. It makes me wonder why someone with money and power leaves for the unknown.

"I was part of the Ten Spires Clan in Valhan. I moved to Westfall just a month before the Selection. Just my luck." Morgan's bold statement distracts me. The Ten Spires is a collection of mercenaries, smugglers, petty thieves, and other undesirables. There's a stronghold in every territory, and I was familiar with most members in Westfall. He could be harmless, or deadly, living among their ranks. Suddenly his behavior and the fact this drinking game was his idea makes me very suspicious. He wanted me to know this. What's his endgame?

The rounds continue, easy enough at first. What Arcana would you choose if you could switch? What do you hope for your familiar to be once you reach third year? Would you rather have horns or wings after the Descent at the end of year?

But then Morgan turns to me, a glint breaking through the drunken haze in his eyes. "Do you find Prince Draven attractive?" Frustration wriggles in my gut.

"Who doesn't?" Ember says blithely, giggling. I bite down a grin. Draven is objectively, undeniably, and unfortunately very attractive. But I don't feel like telling anybody that, and with the fated matehood status lingering over us, and our vow, I'd need to be truthful and I'm not ready yet.

"I hope that's not the question for all of us this round." Kasper pinches the bridge of his nose.

"Fine, let me rephrase." Morgan sets down his drink and leans too close. "If you could sleep with anyone at the Forge, who would it be?"

Wynter saves me. "I don't think there's enough alcohol on the table for this question." He stands up and I abruptly follow, as does half the room. "Rune, can I get you some water?"

Thank the gods. "Yes."

On my feet I'm twice as sick. Ember looks as green as I feel, stumbling out of the room, and I help her to the bathroom, waiting outside it. Wynter sidles up to me as I guard the door, handing me a glass of water, and points to my boots. "Those are really well crafted."

"Oh, thanks." I don't expect the emotion that comes with talking about the boots my mother made, the emerald velvet sidings soft, the gold glint of thread outlining the sun and moon picking up every trace of zenith-powered light, so I cut myself off. My head is spinning. "I should head out. Will Ember be okay?"

"Cleona said she'd help her. Their Hearths are near each other. I'm happy to walk you back," Wynter offers.

"Oh, I'm fine," I lie, because I'm a gods damned liar who can't stand to accept help. I straighten up, suppressing a hiccup, and he runs a hand through his dark hair, following me cautiously to the threshold. Some of the others wander past us, branching off into the night. I'm happy I don't see Morgan. Either he's still here, or he's already on his way back to his Hearth next door. Either way, I can avoid him.

"He and Kasper left." Wynter lingers at my side, seemingly reading my thoughts.

"He was quite drunk." I fold my arms, wishing the air was cooler. I'm flushed from drinking. If the world could stop spinning, that'd help.

"We're all drunk. I'm suspecting he's just a creep." Wynter gnaws his lip as I stagger, my nodding taking me off-balance again. "Wraiths don't drink much, do they?"

"Wraiths crash parties but don't get invited."

He laughs quietly, leaning casually against the door, the full moon's light gracing the fine details of his face.

My brows furrow. "How are you not as drunk as the rest of us?"

"I have a high tolerance. Plus, I switched my bottle out for water over an hour ago." He releases a small chuckle.

Why didn't I think of that?

Wynter laughs at my flabbergasted expression, the sweet sound carrying off on the chilly breeze.

"Sorry I left the ball early." I don't know what makes me say it. He glances off, his hands in his pockets.

"It's okay. Maybe we will catch that dance another time." He swallows when I don't commit, and the moon glances off his silver eyes as he shoots a look toward my Hearth. "You and Prince Draven seem . . . a strong match."

What do I do here? I shrug, attempting nonchalance, and struggle for the right lie, mind filled with images of the dark prince, those sultry lips, that aggravatingly coy smirk. "Well . . . I mean . . . we're still figuring it out—"

"It's okay." He smiles, yet there's no crinkle to his eyes, no joy. "I can see how you feel about him written all over your face. No need to explain it to me."

But I want to. Some stupid part of me longs to leave this door open. But . . . that's not the deal I made. "You could invite him, next time, if you'd like to?"

The idea of Draven hanging out with my friends feels odd, like bringing a dragon home for dinner. His presence is so big.

I brace myself against the wall, using it for support. I hiccup. "Maybe he'll want to come next time. I'll ask, if he's home."

Wynter grimaces as he hangs back, like not escorting me fights against his better judgment. "Well, it's not far, so if you're sure you don't need me, I'll head in. Try to get some sleep."

I give him a sloppy salute and make my way down the steps. I lope off, everything hazy, and round a large maple tree before realizing nothing is familiar. I've seen this tree, but not in this direction.

Concealed beneath its shadows, Morgan and Kasper heatedly whisper to each other. If I hide now, I'll make even more noise, though I sway on the spot. I bend down, holding my laces, keeping as still as possible, despite my vision rocking, head swaying.

"It's not that I don't agree with the sentiment, but the planning is idiotic at best," Kasper hisses. "I already spent a night in the damn Boiler. I don't want any part of it."

I forgot he and Morgan spent a night in the sweltering detention hall for being too close when that assassination attempt against Draven went down. They've never brought it up, at least not with me.

"We could use you," Morgan growls.

"And Rune? You think that's wise?" Kasper's voice drops on my name. I strain to hear, my body swaying in the wind.

"She's the key—" But Morgan stops himself as I tip over, catching myself on a branch. A rookie mistake but I'm too gone to have prevented it. They both turn to me.

"Hellooooo, boys." I stand and hitch a smile to my lips and point to the tree. "Did this move?"

"You're going the wrong way. Turn around." Kasper speeds off down the Oval toward his own Hearth, jogging a bit to catch up with the others. Felix and Amaya have their arms linked and are singing some bawdy song far down the walkway. Across the Oval, Cleona escorts Ember back to the Star.

"I don't think you were going the wrong way." Morgan watches me, his body still in the dark beneath this tree. "My Hearth is right here."

It suddenly occurs to me how far everyone else is from us.

"I need to get to sleep," I say quickly, but he strides over and scoops his arm beneath mine anyway. He tugs me back, but I push toward the World. I need home. Well, not home . . . but my *Hearth*. Morgan relents, heading with me in the right direction, but his grip is still too firm. I try to pull my arm loose and again the pervasive thought of *I'm too drunk* unhelpfully enters my mind.

I'm seeing double of him. He twinkles in and out of focus. I both don't like and don't trust the lava-cursed boy anymore. What was he stopped from saying just now? *She's the key*—to what exactly?

My hand moves toward my tarot box, wondering if I can draw my cards, but nothing arises. His hand curls over mine possessively.

"You sure you wouldn't rather come back to the Moon's Hearth? I can take better care of you there," he offers. I'd rather do most anything than go home with him.

If I were sober, I'd have him lying flat on his ass in a few swift moves, but with this much alcohol, I'm not as sure of myself. What was he in the Ten Spires Clan? A thief? Muscle? Something worse?

"I didn't know you and Kasper were close." My observation is too heavy-handed. It's clear by the narrowing of his dark brows as he looks down at me.

"We have similar feelings about the immortals." His hand curls to a fist. "I think you'd understand that."

"Well, you're one of them now." It makes me sound like Draven.

"You know, you could use that pretty face of yours, and the prince's thirst for you, to our advantage. Manipulate him to release some of us from this place—imagine having this power in the mortal realm. We'd be gods." He grins at the thought, though the idea falls flat with me.

Alarm gnaws at my gut, thinking about how to get out of this.

"It's the least they could do, for taking us away. The arrogance of the Selection. Give us these powers and then expect us to play good little servants—"

"I'm glad I was Selected," I say, tingeing my voice with ice.

Morgan's expression pinches, like he's disappointed. "Still, we should stick together." He pulls me so tightly against him it hurts, his nose nuzzling my neck. "Come back to my room with me."

I pull away. "I'm pretty sure my mate would notice if I didn't return." My heart is pounding hard enough that my head clears. Some men really don't like hearing the word *no*. And I want to remind him someone more powerful than me will notice my absence.

"*Him*." Morgan's tone sours steeply. As we reach the steps to my Hearth, he glares as if it holds a monster in the darkness of its halls. "You never answered my question. If you could sleep with anyone here, who would you choose?"

I yank my hand from his, glad to be in the shadow of my building now. I don't like the possessive way he's watching me, as though I belong to him. The campus is too dark. The house behind me quiet. *Where are you, Draven?*

"Answer the question, Rune."

"Not you," I spit. He lunges for the tarot cards on my belt, and I manage to summon the World and Strength, leaning out of reach as he swipes at the wind an inch from my throat. I sweep under his open arm and throw him over my shoulder, his weight shockingly light with magic running through my muscles. He slams to the ground in a heap. The Strength Arcana helps me, but I'm sloppier than usual. I barely disentangle before I heave up my drinks on all fours. He crawls over to me, hand clawing up my cards, and he curses at the burn of the two in use.

Adrenaline hits—I need to get away—and I leave the cards, rushing toward the stairs, scrambling toward my Hearth.

Rune? I swear Draven's voice has dropped into my mind, like he heard me. Is that panic in his voice or my heart halfway in my throat?

"You little bitch—" Morgan grabs for my ankle, and I kick him in the side of the face, staggering and running up the steps. I need to put a lock between me and him. I lunge for the door handle. Before I can reach, it swings wide and Draven's standing there. I duck under the prince's arm and then turn back to the threat. Morgan's hand rests against the door just above Draven's, his body still going through the motions of boxing me in. Morgan straightens in surprise.

Draven merely lifts his chin and stares down at him, looking him over slowly from head to toe.

"Can I help you?" Draven drawls.

Morgan takes a full step back, his hand releasing the door though I see some gouges across the wooden surface. My hair stands on end, my breaths not catching, as though my lungs are made of mesh. I bristle when I notice my cards in Morgan's clutches.

"Rune and I were just having a conversation—" Morgan starts.

"I think running away implies it's over, don't you?" Draven snaps his fingers and the World and the Emperor rise into his hand in an instant, their golden light blinding as he summons my tarot deck straight out of Morgan's grasp. "This doesn't belong to you."

Morgan chuffs as Draven hands it back to me. "Look, you got it all wrong—"

"I think I have it exactly right."

Morgan scoffs at our positioning and I think he's about to apologize, but then he deflects to something I've heard before. "Sorry, I guess I'm a little drunk." His shoulders shrug casually, an invitation for Draven to relate as though this was some moment of weakness. Some male way of being.

"You say that as if it's any excuse."

Draven takes a step forward and Morgan retreats. Shadows explode behind Draven's back, framing his wings, blotting out the full moon until the night presses in from all sides. A kingdom of darkness spreads across the front steps, seeping like tipped ink into the Oval. As the Death Arcana he's casting expands, the color of the world begins to change, to that grayscale hue between spaces, and my heart jolts.

Draven's voice descends a few octaves, no longer his own. "You are a poor *excuse* for a man."

"Wait, please!" Morgan's shriek cuts against the night. I race forward, my figure slicing through the darkness like a knife, my feet swift, my legs surprisingly sturdy considering all I've drank. When I reach Draven's side, his eyes glow like the pits of hells, crimson fire consuming everything as he looks down on Morgan crawling away.

Try not to stick your hand into a dragon's mouth . . .

Damning his warnings and my common sense I slide my hand along Draven's wrist ever so gently, careful not to touch his cards whirring with enchantments. His attention shoots to me. The magic fetters out, like water thrown over a fire. The darkness blows out into ash, clearing on the breeze. Draven's brow rises a bit at the touch of my hand against his bare wrist. I don't remove it. I want to make sure he's still in control. He glares down Morgan.

"Come near her again and it'll be the last thing you ever do. Now get out of my sight." Draven waits until Morgan scrambles to his feet and runs across the lawns, sprinting toward the Moon's Hearth.

I shadow Draven, the two of us standing in heated silence. I try to prepare myself for whatever he's about to say, but it's impossible to guess. Finally, I look up into his face, his eyes the faultless dark of gathering dusk.

"Thank you," I manage.

"For what?" He shrugs, eyes locking with mine, a little smirk gathering in the corner of his lips. I smile, relieved at his casualness. His tone is playful, but I'm not sure if he's kidding as he adds, "I just did that for me. I love watching people squirm. Don't go thinking I'm some knight in shining armor, Rune. You'll be disappointed."

"Oh, I wouldn't dare," I tell him with a small, uncertain laugh, crossing my arms, swaying slightly. The adrenaline chased off my drunkenness but hasn't left behind sobriety. As the fear seeps out of me, my gut starts churning again. He offers his hand. I don't bat it away, allowing him to help me inside.

He stumbles slightly at the threshold.

"Are you all right?" The sudden possibility of him burning out hits me low in the gut.

"I'd have to push a lot harder than that." He side-eyes me, clearly having read my thoughts, my mental shield suffering with so much alcohol. "Magic usage is like building a muscle. I've been lucky to have the greatest trainers the realm can afford. I'll be fine by tomorrow."

I stop short when I realize our Hearth is crowded with five or six people, all druids of upper years, all with wings. We've never had anyone over before. Not that we're a *we*, exactly. I don't know why the sudden appearance of his friends has made me nervous. Draven ignores them all, leading me pointedly to my room, again stopping at the threshold, and I'm embarrassed there was an audience.

I stumble inside without him, my vision blurring, the drinks threatening to rise. Draven leans against the doorframe, keeping the door slightly ajar between us. His cunning gaze flits to every shadowed corner.

"I'm canceling your classes tomorrow." He's finally focused on me again. My nausea reaches another high, yet I manage to give him an incredulous look. He rolls his eyes, smirking in that seductive way of his. "Don't get insulted, I know you can handle yourself. If you really want to go, then feel free. But if you want to know where *I* go every morning, then tomorrow, I'll take you. Hopefully you get the alcohol out of your system before that, one way or another."

I hesitate, pretty sure it's about to come out the same way it went in.

"What about . . . Morgan?" I shift on my feet.

"He'll pay for what he's done." Draven's gaze is so severe there's no escaping it. I notice his friends go quiet, and his wings arc higher, the light from the living space all but blotted out. I hate the way Morgan made me feel. Shame and rage in equal measure heat my cheeks.

It's only then I realize my whole body is trembling.

I don't want to sit in the silence of this dark empty room. Lying in that large bed with my serrated thoughts sounds like a nightmare. As I look up into Draven's beautiful face, I nearly plead with him to stay, just until the sun rises. I want him to talk to me until the night bleeds, for his snarky, bratty company to distract me from this horrible night. It's not that I need a guard as much as I really don't want to be alone right now. It took until now to realize how much I trust him. The intensity of his gaze sharpens. Is it stupid for me to want him to dismiss his friends?

"Draven, are we continuing?" An alluring feminine voice calls to his back and he rolls his eyes at her voice, still facing me.

"I'll see you in the morning," I tell Draven quickly, not letting myself entertain that weakness a moment longer. He straightens up, backing out of the doorway, hands in his pockets.

I shut the door and hear his friends' voices rise in the living room as I collapse face down into bed. It sounds like they're teasing him, but I hear only his response clearly: "Meeting's over. Get out."

16

Shadow

The Four of Swords represents rest, refuge, and retreat. It may appear as a way of telling ourselves it's time to breathe.

I FALL ASLEEP NEARLY the moment my head hits the pillow. Most of the night passes in a blur of deep sleep and breaks where I huddle over the toilet. The third time it happens there's a bucket sitting by it with a note that reads, *Take it to your room so I don't have to hear you vomiting all night.* Annoyed, but simultaneously grateful, I bring it back to bed with me and am glad when I don't need it.

When I wake up, sunshine blares through my curtains like streams of heavenly fire, my head pounding. I drag myself to the shower, and as I reenter my room, drying off, a gentle knock comes from outside my door. I stumble over to it, finding Draven standing at the threshold, a mug in his hands. He gives it to me and, grateful for caffeine, I take a huge gulp. Then heave when I realize it's not coffee. I think it had a loose egg yolk somewhere in it.

"Swallow it," he orders, and I choke it down. At my outrage he gives me a broad shit-eating smile. "Hangover cure."

"I wanted coffee." I hand it back, sputtering. He walks to the kitchen. I hesitantly follow, glancing around as if his friends will still be lurking out here. But the living room looks like it always does, though it's odd observing it in what appears to be midmorning. I'm usually gone from dawn to dusk.

"They didn't stay overnight." He moves to the sink, filling the mug. He sets it between us on the peninsula countertop. "Hot or cold?"

"Water?"

"It's about to be coffee."

He doesn't even blink and I wonder if he's ever made any on his own before. The privileged prick just waits for my answer, fingers drumming on the counter.

"This 'privileged prick' is about to do a third nice thing for you within twenty-four hours. I like to think I'm being rather generous with you, love."

"Cold. I think I'll barf if it's hot." I try in vain to lift my mental wards.

He swipes his hand over the rim of the cup, the World card and the Magician floating out of his deck, and the water turns dark. He hands the mug to me. It's sweet, flavored with caramel. I gulp it down gladly.

"Wow this is . . ."

"Delicious?" His eyes are trained on my mouth, his mouth coiling into a shit-eating grin.

"Pretty good, coming from you," I correct. Don't need him getting too full of himself, but he only chuckles. I furrow my brow. "I didn't realize the Magician could transfigure food, too. And are you telling me you can make whatever foods you want but still complained that I ate that imported aioli?"

"That aioli is something I cannot bribe the creator into revealing the ingredients of."

Draven leans against the counter as he watches me drink. My gaze travels the length of him. With all the curtains drawn he's in his human form. His muscle definition is visible beneath his plain dark shirt, waist tight, arms and chest strong. There's something appealing about his rolled sleeves and the clear pleasure he got in making me something. He scratches his cheek, the bones so lovely and defined.

"Plus, I doubt I could recreate it even with the ingredients. So, for now, I'd rather send her heaps of gold, even if I have to share it with you."

"Well, good thing you have buckets of money then." I don't feel a modicum of guilt over his mighty sacrifice.

"So . . . last night . . ." Draven's eyes flick to me, flashing an orange that only grows deeper.

"I don't want to talk about that." I'll do anything to not talk about it, honestly.

He shifts on his feet, and I can tell he's stuck between pushing it or relenting but doesn't look away.

I heave a sigh, my tattoo prickling. Maybe it'll be better to get this out. "Morgan wanted to get to you, so he thought he could do it by seducing and controlling me. Didn't seem to like that I wasn't interested. I don't know the full extent of what's going on with him. But he was bragging about being in the Ten Spires Clan."

Draven listens raptly, bending a metal spoon in half as I quickly reel off Morgan's moves and motivations. He deeply exhales, forcing calm, his eyes glancing off. "They've had some links with a new mortal rebellion."

"Guess being fated mates with the heir of Sedah comes with a few new targets on my back." I take another big gulp, considering that.

Draven's gaze burns and he runs a tongue along his canines, shoulders bunching. "I should've expected opportunists. You'll have guards from now on."

"I don't need them. If I'd have been sober, I wouldn't have needed anything."

"Don't you dare blame yourself."

I swallow, my mouth incredibly dry. "He was trying to get Kasper in on it, I think. Whatever his plan might be to get to you. I dunno, it's a blur now."

"Is Kasper that blond prick in your group?" Draven narrows his eyes.

I nearly laugh. "That's an apt description. How do you know him?"

"He's challenged me in sparring about seven times, the only first-year to do so. He's yet to land a hit. It's like he's a glutton for punishment or something." Draven's shrug is incredibly indifferent. "It's always the same. He talks a lot of shit and then goes down fast. I don't gather he's been in that many fights before."

"And you have?" I smirk, and he matches my look. My heart hammers, chest flushing.

I make a mental note to watch out for Kasper. Is he trying to learn from the best? Or just get a punch in? I remember him saying he agreed with Morgan's sentiment, his silence about his past during the drinking game. Maybe he's just looking to start a fight. I wonder how often Draven gets that. Kasper's a High Priestess Arcana, so I doubt I can try reading his mind. My gaze falls on the clock above the sink, which reads ten fifteen. My heart drops into my stomach.

"My gods, is it that late?"

Relief hits me as his eyes slowly shift back to indigo.

"Yes." A devilish smile plays over his face. "My instructors will be furious with you."

"Your what?" I continue gulping my coffee. Between it and whatever magic was in the hangover cure, I'm already feeling better.

"Let's go. I want you to see what all the fuss is about." Draven fills up his own mug, changing it to something dark and foamy. He walks toward the door, and I follow him, slipping my boots on. He takes a step out into the overly bright autumn day, and I squint against all that light.

I wait for the signature sound of a portal, the rushing sound of dragon wings.

But there's nothing. Draven merely stands there with his coffee.

"What, no dark rides through the void?" What a surprising letdown.

"Technically that 'void' is the knife's edge between the worlds of the living and dead. But I think it's better if you walk. That way you'll know the way if I'm not around." He takes off to our left. I stumble after him, slurping down my coffee. He tracks down a path between the World and Sun Hearths, headed toward the sleeping volcano. He holds out a hand and I pass my empty cup over. The tattoo flashes across the back of his hand and both mugs disappear as if they were never there—but I swear I hear the echo of a clatter, like they just landed in the sink back at our Hearth's kitchen.

"So, you have private classes?" The mystery seems relatively obvious now.

"Yes. Can't have the crown prince failing in front of the entire Forge." Draven's eyes narrow to the horizon, as if he can see the king watching him from here. "Half the week I train with my class, but ever since secondary school I spend the rest of the time with private instructors. Even days I'm with the other second-years, I start with my trainers here."

This path is so peaceful next to the bustle of the rest of the Forge, the only sounds birds, a few buzzing insects, and the crunch of our feet on the gravel. His tongue traces a canine and a little thrill races through my veins. I wish he wouldn't do that. Yet my gaze betrays me, drinking in his lush lower lip, his skin so annoyingly flawless. My eyes travel those defined shoulders, that tight waist, the plump curve of his backside. I nearly trip when he speaks.

"What?" His gaze alights, an excitement obvious there, his shirt tightening with his muscles as his chest swells, a coy smirk lifting his mouth.

"Nothing . . . just," I hesitate before adding, "your father seems threatened by you, but he still pushes for your extra training?" Draven looks me over in that unbreaking stare, with only pure interest, nothing dismissive in it. Like he truly values my viewpoint.

"Well, he's equally concerned I might embarrass his legacy unless I represented the best of Sedah. He can't be seen expecting anything less than excellent. Even if he doesn't seem to trust me."

"Given your plans, I guess he shouldn't."

He grins at me and I squint through the brightness, but his height and wings block the sun, one feathered limb arching over my head like an umbrella.

"Are these just for show?" I have a sudden urge to run my finger down one, see what it does to him. Are they sensitive?

"Are you asking if I can fly?"

"Well, can you? Or do we really have to hike the rest of the way?"

"Would you like to find out?" His brow arcs up and his answering grin is a taunt.

"I've never backed down from an honest challenge, so if you're trying to intimidate meeeeeeeeeeee—"

My words cut off as I'm swept off my feet, Draven holding me tightly between his arms, as if I weigh nothing. He bounds forward, I grasp my hands around his neck, tucking my face in as his wings flap wide, and suddenly, we're airborne.

His wings catch and buffet us, first rushing us in one direction and then another before we stabilize. The air gusts across my face, and my eyes are still firmly closed.

"You have to look if you want to see where we're going, otherwise I might as well have transported us there!" he calls over the roar of the wind.

I force my eyes open and blink against the gale. The fear eases away as I look out upon the vast Forge, nestled against the mountains, castle walls, and the volcano. Exhilaration fills me to the brim instead, nearly making me laugh out loud in astonishment. I've never been so high up in the air and it's absolutely amazing. Freeing beyond measure, though when the wind buffets us, a swoop races through my gut and I grasp hold of Draven more tightly, catching the smirk on his lips as I cling to him. We follow a trail that wends forty feet below us down a small decline where there's a large building I haven't seen before, nestled between the Forge and the volcano. Draven and I leave shadows across the wild golden fields that blanket the ridge leading down to it, the space less manicured than the rest of the Forge.

He moves us with such flowing ease we might as well be streaking through water. Hesitantly I move one trembling hand from around his neck, holding tight with my other.

I let one arm open wide, hand spreading until the air is slipping through my fingers. It feels as though I can grasp hold of the wind and make it submit. I'm surprised when a small laugh escapes my chest, a burden releasing its binding on my ribs. My attention shifts from my outstretched hand to two hawks flying just beyond it. Something shifts in Draven's chest, and I find him chuckling, his smile so bright I swear it could warm even the cold recess where my heart once ticked.

"What?" I shout over the wind, though a grin tugs at my lips. I can't stop myself from taking in his dark hair flying like a banner, the defined shape of his jaw, the stark drop of his cheekbones, and the wild lavender in those eyes. His smirk softens, some of the rowdiness edging away.

"I've never seen you smile before. Not really." His gaze flicks to my mouth.

"Did you think I'd be afraid?" I grin in challenge and his own smile brightens. A heat strikes between my legs. "Go faster!"

The mischievousness returns to his expression in full force, pupils widening, grin so broad it leaves crinkles in his narrow cheeks and the corners of his eyes. He clenches me more snugly against his chest, and we burst ahead, his wings working in quickening tandem. He dips us down, banking hard to the right. My hand no longer lazily glides through the wind like a buffeting sail. Instead, I'm clasping tight to him again, a little thrill-loving sound escaping my throat as he spirals us into a corkscrew dive, spinning us closer and closer to the ground before rocketing back up, racing the sun.

As we reach the height of this magnificent arc he hollers, "Hold on!"

My smile drops along with my stomach and suddenly I'm trying to climb him like a cat as we plummet straight toward the ground. His laughter in my ear is infectious. Even though I'm nearly certain he has a death wish, I stop fighting the fear, letting my hands drift skyward. His eyes widen, he grips me harder, and then he spins through the air, barrel-rolling us until up is down again and again.

My hair is in my face and mouth. Still, all I can do is laugh about it. He darts us down along the volcanic river, the heat diminished but still roasting this close, before pushing up, summiting the hill. His wings rush forward to slow us, as the building's rotunda comes into view. Draven's feet skid across the space in front of it, and he finally settles my quaking legs to the ground.

I collapse to my backside in a fit of laughter as he stands over me, hands on his knees, panting. He shakes his head, a grin still on his lips, looking at me as if he's never seen anything quite like me. Standing straight again, he arches his back, his wings drooping to the black sand.

"I haven't gone that fast in a while, my shoulders hurt." His hand is against his chest, steadying his heart. "I cannot believe you liked that."

"Gods, it's the most fun I've . . ." I trail off. I wasn't about to say "in years." I was about to say "*ever.*" I turn tack, not wanting to put too much into that fever-pitched moment, or into him. "It was so freeing." I heave out a breath, putting my hand flat over my brows to block the sunlight reflecting off those oil-spill downy wings. "I can't wait to have my own."

His smile falters a bit. "Not everyone gets wings, but I'll be surprised if you don't."

I admire the way his shine in darkest teals and deepest purples depending on how the sun hits them. "I'll hate it if I don't."

His wings pull tight, no longer drooping, and I wonder what it feels like to have extra limbs like that. Ones you weren't born with. "Well . . . if you don't, we'll just have to get you a pet wyvern."

I grimace. "Not the same."

His head tilts, his grin like a wildcat's. "Or you can always ride me."

My cheeks heat. "Judging by how out of breath you are, I don't think you could handle me."

His pupils blow out, and he gives a hard smile at the challenge. "Oh, Rune, there's nothing I can't handle."

Heat ignites between us, as unbearably scorching as if the volcano suddenly erupted once more. But this burning is just us.

"Finally, he deigns to show his fucking face." A winged druid approaches us, making me jump. He's at least fifteen years our senior, with coal-dark eyes and warm brown skin. His arms are crossed in front of his muscled chest, and he's glaring daggers at Draven. "You're five hours late, but at least you've got your flight training done. Time for sparring, and I've had hours to brood on it."

He looks to me, expression pinched as if he's waiting for me to explain myself.

"This is Rune." Draven buffers between our staring contest. "She's the—"

"Other World Arcana," the druid fills in. "I know, you won't shut up about her." The druid grins in satisfaction when he notices how Draven can no longer seem to meet my eye, clearing his throat and running his hand through his hair instead. The man introduces himself. "I'm Kenzo, not Ken, and only my two-year-old nephew gets to call me Zo. I'm responsible for teaching this idiot how to fight and win. His father pays me well for it."

"And I supplement that payment, both because he tolerates my tardiness, and so he doesn't report anything too damning." Draven grins at me, and I roll my eyes at him.

"Come on, you two." Kenzo doesn't deny it and walks back toward the open space with the glass rotunda above it.

It leads to a beautiful sparring courtyard, tropical plants fixed around the edges and lining the pathways, the stain of the glass above dappling the floor with diamond patterns of color. Kenzo moves to a cylindrical container where different wooden and metal weapons are stored. He grabs a solid steel bow staff and gestures for Draven to grab a sword. I park on a ledge of a planter, happy to watch for now. Anything to keep my mind off last night.

As soon as Draven has his hands on two swords, they break into training, the fight soon a frenzied battle. Kenzo doesn't hold back one bit, all bulk and strength next to Draven's fleet agility. Their fighting styles are entirely different, yet they're both able to keep the other on their toes, staff clinking against the blunt swords. It strikes me how much Draven holds back in the sparring gym, keeping his full abilities a secret. Draven flips forward, his wings balancing him as he kicks out, slamming into Kenzo's chest and knocking the large druid back. He follows up with a double-bladed strike, slamming into the staff with a resounding clang, but then Kenzo buffets him back with the bow, butting the end of it into Draven's jaw.

Draven staggers back, blood pouring out of his mouth. I go on edge as he puts the back of his hand against it. A second later he spits a tooth into his palm.

I jump to my feet, but Kenzo looks entirely unruffled. Draven just puts the tooth back to wherever it was cracked and summons the World card and the Empress, healing himself, the blood dissipating.

"Now I'm pissed." Draven points a sword at Kenzo, who only smiles.

"Finally, you're catching up."

· · ·

DRAVEN'S SHIRTLESS, sweat gilding his skin and outlining every cut of muscle, the vascularity in his forearms standing out sharp against the tendons of his flesh. Throughout the day he's sustained a black eye, broken ribs, and more split lips than I can count, but none of it has stopped him. A quick remedy from the Empress gets him up and going again each time, and he rarely pauses even for that unless something is seriously broken.

As Kenzo breaks for water, Draven points to the cards at my hip, his lip bloodied again.

"Practice time."

"I thought my classes were canceled?"

"You need a one-to-one approach. Draw the Empress."

His command pulls some strings within me, but I don't think they're driven by the vow. I *want* to learn from him, even though the thought stirs something confusing in me. My last personal teacher was as harsh as he was cruel, but as I meet Draven's violet eyes I relax. Draven is far from the Lord of Westfall.

He pads his lip. "You're healing me from here on out, Wraith. Unless you like me better bloodied?"

"Don't ask questions you don't want the answers to," I tell him, and he laughs before wincing, more blood dribbling down his chin.

I summon the World, then the Empress, its glow pure as starlight. My hand hesitates before reaching for his face and a smirk draws those lips like a thread is woven through one end. Surer of myself, I grip his chin with my spare hand. "What now?"

"Imagine the wound knitting back together, sealing as if it never existed, your power flowing from you to your cards to me." He watches me closely, barely breathing, prone beneath my power. "Just picture what I looked like before."

"You're going to trust your face to my memory?"

"It's not like you've never looked at my mouth before."

I startle, hating how quickly he can rile me, yet his grin is genuine again, transforming his face from beauty to godly. Fuck him. I tighten my hold on his jaw and he chuckles as I urge my power through the cards, like a flood through a pinhole. I'm frustrated when his lip heals only slightly, enough to stop the blood but not to smooth his skin like glass again.

"You even heal angrily." His hand covers mine, his power coming up, brushing my own. "It requires something softer."

Healing is a gift you give yourself. I breathe into him, "I'm not soft."

"But you are compassionate, loving, even kind." He holds my hand to prevent me from pulling away, his tongue dabbing the split. He gives me a wry look. "Maybe not to me, but I've seen it."

My chest crushes inward, and nothing but him exists in this moment.

"Rune's turn." Kenzo's annoyed eye roll tells me he interrupted on purpose, and we split apart.

Draven's shoulders tense, wings popping out in some kind of instinctual protection, but Kenzo just tuts at him.

"You want her to be your equal? Then do not stand in her way."

Draven backs off, moving to where I've been sitting, giving me an encouraging nod as we pass each other.

Kenzo wipes the sweat from his forehead with a rag. "My father trained King Silas to fight. I've been training Draven since this wolf was only a pup." He lowers his voice for just me. "I've never known him to let anyone in. He must think you're very special. Be worthy of his faith in you."

He returns his metal staff to the rack and grabs a wooden one instead. I move to seize the practice swords Draven used, but Kenzo clacks me on the knuckle. My jaw hardens.

"Baby warrior gets baby swords." He gestures to the wooden swords with wrapped handles.

I grit my teeth but obey, grabbing them out of the rack and following Kenzo into the ring. I'm very aware of my body and Draven's watchful eyes.

"Show me what you know."

I spent years training as a Wraith, but the main traits of a spy are to be quiet, clever, and watchful. I could throw knives and hit a target ten yards away on a moonless night, but the only swords I've ever held have been ceremonial. I lift the right one and swing, then try the other only to find his staff sharply meeting it, and the wooden sword spins out of my hand.

"Weak wrists mean we start with one." He begins to pace, walking a slow circle around me.

Knives were always my weapon of choice, typically easier to get a hand on, easier to conceal. Occasionally a recurve bow for anything requiring a greater distance. I grip my remaining sword with both hands.

"Align your knuckles. There, much better." He clacks his staff against it, and though it dips, I don't drop it. "Better. Now keep your knees slightly bent. Legs apart so you can't be pushed over. What are you, some dainty maid in waiting or a lioness? Better."

I wait for him, watching out of the corner of my eye anytime he paces around my back, ready for any sudden movements. He smirks at my unwavering observation.

"I see you're new to the sword but not the fight. So, Rune, show me—" But he doesn't get the next words out, moving to strike when he was almost out of sight. I spin and block him, my wooden blade bouncing back because I swung too hard, not used to the weight yet. He moves so quickly for someone that large, but I'm used to bigger opponents. After all, I was rarely sent to spy on women. I block him once, twice, but then he strikes with the bottom of the staff, and I can't move quick enough, so he takes me out at the knee.

"Good, get up. We go again."

17

---- ⁂ ----

The Devil's
in the Details

The Devil card represents illusion, materialism, and
lust for our darkest vices.

"THERE YOU ARE. I think you've had enough time with
Kenzo . . . today." Professor Vexus stops short when he
notices me, drenched, winded, and bruised. His head swivels
between Draven and me, waiting for an explanation. There's a
narrowed confusion in his gaze, as if he's unsure what to make
of anything.

"You'll have an extra student today." Draven takes a long
draft from a waterskin. He and I have both been performing
drills with Kenzo for the past half an hour, and we're slick with
sweat. Draven moves across to me, drawing several Arcana that
I'm too exhausted to notice, and after a moment my bruises
fade, my sweat giving way to clear skin, hair shining again as if
I've spent hours styling it. He gives himself the same effect, don-
ning his shirt and jacket once more, and I carry mine, following
Professor Vexus.

"This is . . . irregular, Draven." Professor Vexus glares at me over his shoulder. His classes have been informative but awkward. I didn't fail to notice after Mira's punishment that he was absent for nearly the same length of time his daughter was.

"If you want me to keep my word, then you'll accept it." Draven glances at me only briefly, a reassuring smile fixed in place. Professor Vexus grits his jaw but leads us out of the rotunda and into a small lecture hall, where a few other druids already sit around the room.

They stand when Draven enters the classroom. I jolt when I spot Wynter among them. What is he doing here? What are any of them doing here?

"As I explained to you before, you have been selected to train with Prince Draven . . . and apparently a guest. My Arcana is the Hierophant, like many professors here, focusing on memory walking, the ability to revisit memories and share them with others."

Professor Vexus draws his Arcana, and a golden collection of memories from Draven's previous trainings are projected across the space. Professor Vexus has displayed a little of this magic in our regular classes, and this is his Arcana at the height of its power.

"I also have the ability to alter memories when the card is reversed, which is why you have not heard of these private classes before." The visions adjust, showcasing some of these same students in this room at a different time. He meets the eye of every student drawn here, and I watch each of them understand what he's saying at the same time I do. "At the end of session your memories will be wiped to protect the heir of our kingdom's progress or lack thereof, by order of the king. You will have memories only of whatever classes you were pulled from, the lectures shared with me by your professors. Do you understand?"

Everyone nods, though Wynter's more reserved about it than the others.

"How do you choose who is pulled for these classes?" I ask Draven.

"It's random. Mostly. Unless I see someone particularly impressive that I'd like to train with."

"I haven't been impressive enough?" I lean closer to him, my shoulder bumping his elbow. He opens his mouth, breaking into a smile as he realizes there's no good reply to that.

"Third-year Sun Arcana, step forward," Professor Vexus orders, and the only girl in the group, a broad-shouldered vixen with sun-loved skin steps ahead. She has the Sun Arcana tattooed on the back of her right hand and she smiles at Draven like she would've accepted any excuse to punch him in the face. Usually I'd agree with her, though I'm starting to become a bit partial to him. Vexus adds, "This room has been warded by our strongest Emperor Arcana to not take damage, but the same cannot be said for you. We also have a healer on standby but the worse the injury, the longer the healing time."

The Empress Arcana sits in the corner with her head in a book.

"Well, I hope watching my ass get handed to me all morning cheered you up." Draven's voice is quiet, meant for just me, his breath caressing my ear. He gently puts his hand against my upper back to lead me out of the way. I step aside but nod, biting my lip to withhold my grin, as he faces off with the Sun Arcana.

She barely waits for me to move before she summons her card, golden plasma pulling from thin air, wrapping her hands with molten fire. Draven is unintimidated, making everyone wait as he rolls up his sleeves, taking all the time in the world. Professor Vexus leans against the wall outside the center circle, pinching the bridge of his nose as if teaching these lessons is a personal torture. Draven finally flicks his hand above his stack of cards at his hip, drawing out the World, then the Sun. The same kind of fiery magma appears in his hands, burning white instead of gold.

"Good," Professor Vexus tells him. "Now, without killing each other, I need you to focus on fighting with the goal of helping the prince get a better understanding of how this Arcana works in practice—"

I don't think she heard the *not killing* part. She steps forward, punching outward, and a blast of molten fire blares so hard into the wall behind him it leaves a crater. A moment later the hole fixes itself by magic, but Draven is still looking between her and the shot he barely ducked. He grits his teeth, fists coming up defensively, and soon he's shooting Sun power right back. She has far more experience though and channels it into a whip of liquid fire, flicking it to snap right by his head.

"Wait, show me how you did that," he demands.

She stops, put out, but explains how she strings out the magma in her hands.

"Rune," Wynter whispers.

I move over to him as he glances worriedly at Draven before turning to me.

"Did you get home all right? I . . . saw Morgan running from your Hearth across the lawns last night. He was missing at breakfast. No one's seen him since last night."

"I'm . . . okay." What a lie. I fidget on the spot, resisting the urge to bolt. I hesitate, wondering if I should lay it out for him. But what if he doesn't believe me, or believes Morgan? And if he tells the group . . . worrying about others leaving me is a burden

I haven't carried in a very long time and the thought takes me off guard. "I don't really want to get into it."

"All right." Wynter looks me over, checking for bruises, but everything on the outside has been healed. He meets my wayward gaze. "As long as you're okay. That's all that matters."

A sense of relief presses through me. Maybe it was stupid to assume he wouldn't believe me. I try to think of what I can say, his attention wholly on me, but—

"Rune." Draven's gaze snaps from me to Wynter, lingering on his face a moment, scrutinizing it as if he's piecing apart a machine he doesn't understand. His look softens as it returns to me. Existence narrows to the two of us. "I want you to try this."

As I return to his side he walks me through the power, his magic pressing through the World, through the Sun until his other hand glows with holy, blinding plasma. He repeats the steps with me, his eyes narrowing as my magic sputters in response. A migraine forms, burning behind my eyes. Finally, the skin on my other hand smokes, the power sparking for a moment before I jolt and the flash of lit sulfur snuffs out.

"Damn it—"

"No, that was good. You're releasing it." His gaze consumes me, as he watches my mouth a heartbeat too long. He releases his stare, straightening up, and orders, "First-year, your turn."

Wynter startles, walking ahead as the Sun Arcana moves over to Professor Vexus. The professor's long-fingered hands hover on either side of her head, glowing, and her gaze turns distant. Then Vexus explains something to her. She leaves, a serene but withdrawn look in her eyes. I glare suspiciously at Vexus, worried whether I'd ever know if he did something like that to me.

Not if you keep up your wards. Draven's voice pools inside my mind like a coiled snake. Startled, I focus on that mental firewall, shoving him right back out, but he retreats with ease, as if he's letting me do it.

"I don't know what I could teach you," Wynter admits as he steps up to Draven. There's no aggression in his shoulders or stance, his expression passive.

Draven holds his arms out to either side and says, "Humor me then. Try to control me."

After a moment's hesitation Wynter draws his Arcana, a green light blaring in his eyes as he faces off with Draven. The prince waits and Wynter's Arcana lunges forward, snaking around Draven's feet, then climbs up his body. I'm not sure what he's attempting to make Draven do, but I wait, breath held, as he keeps trying. Wynter has the second most powerful Arcana, Judgment, and he can already do so much with it, whereas I'm struggling for the most meager showing of power. A ghostly wail begins to grow beneath whatever pressure Wynter applies, but it stems from the magic, not Draven. All at once Draven's wings buffet upward, as if he's casting the spell off. He lifts his hand and Wynter drops immediately to his knees, bowing low, as if an invisible puppeteer has pressed a giant hand against his spine, shoving him as far as he can naturally bend.

I shoot a warning glance at Draven, but then the haunting glow is gone. Draven releases Wynter, his voice dismissive as he says, "Thank you. You can go."

Wynter looks to me only once, a fearful flutter in his gaze, before he moves to Professor Vexus. I swallow, uncertain, as I take his place in front of Draven. I open my mental shield just a fraction, an eyehole in a doorway. *Did you bring him here just to ridicule him?*

I brought him here to make sure he and the rest of your male friends remember where to keep their hands next time. Draven rolls his shoulders.

I thought they're not supposed to remember these lessons.

He'll remember only that he fears me. Draven summons the World, then Judgment, that glimmer of green light haunting his eyes, like a ghostly candle at the end of a long, dark hall. "Summon your gift."

My magic pulls at the World, then Judgment follows, floating out of its box, hovering one over the other in front of my raised palm. This card feels different than the others, darker, more sinister. A weight of cruel intention.

His brows twitch together, eyes hardening at my struggle. "I need to use it on you, to teach it to you." He waits and hesitantly I nod.

Then I feel it, the invasion of his magic wrapping around my limbs. A panic incomparable to anything else overtakes me as he moves me a step toward him before releasing me. I gasp out, hating the violation in that card, the sinister potential of it.

"There's a reason this card sits one below the World." He nods, as if he's familiar with the chills that now wash across my limbs.

The echo of a complete loss of autonomy shivers through my entire being. Did his father ever use it on him? It was only a moment, but my "fight-or-flight" instincts are hissing for me to run.

He grasps my wrist, not painfully, but firmly. "Make me let you go."

I should hate the way his hand envelops my wrist, but somehow, I think he's the only person I can tolerate touching me right now. His breaths quicken as if he can sense that shift in me. The acknowledgment of ruthless desire. I gather the magic within me, a deep breath with it, releasing both as I concentrate my magic through each card. But the longer it takes, the more my combat training tells me to just use my body to break his grip.

"You're holding yourself back." His eyes are piercing. "Why?"

"My training says to punch you."

"It's more than that." There's a challenge in his voice. Antagonism dances with yearning, some piece of me dislodging, magic churning, and his hand peels away from my skin. "That's it."

His words paint a flush across my chest, and he smiles down at me. The power dripped from me, but I don't understand why it's so difficult to channel. It seems almost effortless when he uses it.

Draven lures over the last druid, a second-year, and the guy steps into the ring without hesitation. I don't know his Arcana, and Draven rubs his chin a moment. I swear the World tattoo across the back of his hand glows red before he stands up straighter.

"The Devil." Draven says it like an accusation. His hand rests against my upper back, and chills race over me as he tells the second-year, "Go ahead, cast an illusion. Over both of us."

The Devil Arcana glowers, as if annoyed to be bossed about, but he obeys the order. The room around us shifts, objects winking out of existence and being replaced in the same moment with new furniture. Draven and I soon stand in a swanky room, reminiscent of the druid court. Music blares around us from a loud band settled at one end, a busy bar at the other, and filling in all available space are other druids, dancing and swaying to the euphoric rhythm.

"Where did he go?" I ask Draven as druids pass between us. He merely observes the space, where little imperfections create cracks in the illusion. The lyrics to the song are gibberish, the faces of many of the druids shift between one moment and the next as if the Devil Arcana cannot imagine them in the full range of movement, and the stale scent of the classroom lingers.

I pass a thought to Draven. *Nothing is quite right here.*

It's impressive but the closer I look, the more things seem wrong.

The Devil's in the details, he tells me, passing through the throng of wildly dancing druids without worry. He doesn't even weave through the crowd, shoulders back and undaunted, and soon I realize if I don't move, they merely pass through me like phantoms. It rankles my instincts, but I fight it, following him through the illusion. He sidles to the bar, something we're much closer to than the stage, and gazes up and down it. Passing a cocky grin my way, Draven nods his head to the bartender. He looks like the Devil Arcana and yet not. His nose has a slight crook, and his hair is longer but its coloring is unnatural, like a bad dye job. His new beard is barely attached to his face. A poor disguise.

My mental shields open a small amount, just enough for me to whisper to Draven on the other side of it. *Not very creative.*

Did he seem bright to you? Draven hisses right back. *I'd like for you to have the honors.*

I can barely draw my cards and you want me to dispel this? I wouldn't know where to start. I shift uneasily on my feet, crossing my arms. All day my power has been like pulling teeth, slippery and elusive as an eel in a hollow cove.

"Watch what I do." Slowly he draws the World, waiting for me to do the same, then the Devil. This takes me quite a bit longer, a sweat breaking against my temple, headache pounding like a drum—but then I have it, floating in front of me, as a circle of magic dances in the air. The second-year glances at us a bit anxiously, making a large show of cleaning a glass in his hands, but the way he handles it I can tell it's weightless, like a poor mime, the illusion only going so far.

Draven tells me, "The magic of the World rests within you. Even without making the Descent at the end of term, where it'll be bound to you." He flashes his tattoo of the World, and I don't look forward to whatever that process will be. I'm thankful I have eight months before I need to worry.

He goes on, "The World enters your very soul every time you handle your cards. That building feeling in your chest looking for an escape is your power. You're scared of releasing it, of unraveling control, but allowing it to flow out of you is what will put you *in* control." He lightly brushes my hand. "Point the flat of your palm at him and fire your magic through it. Like light hitting a prism, it'll flare through the World and then the Devil and turn his own spell back on him, shattering the illusion."

All this time I thought the pressure in my chest was just anxiety. I take a deep breath, my attention moving inward, focusing on the feeling I had thought was stress and frustration. Closing my eyes, I drop my mental shields, and then Draven is there, not controlling me, but guiding me to let the swirling tempest release. I stop fighting it, allowing it to rise out of me. Suddenly the magic awakens, he's gone, and it's rushing down my wrist, my blood boiling with it. A gust of heat races down my arm as my power blasts from me.

The Devil Arcana puts his hands up, the bartender façade fading, the fake beard shriveling, his slightly bent nose shaping back to his own, and his brown hair returning to red. The vision dissolves beneath the flow of this power, this unrelenting tide turning it into nothing but fiery ash on the breeze. He's frozen in a flinch but then opens his eyes, surprised.

I turn to Draven, and he watches me like nothing else exists. Finally, his daring smile turns to the second-year.

"You can go now."

THE LAST PRIVATE CLASS of the day is really a short report of recently gathered intelligence given by Professor Fenrys. It's odd being a class of two, yet I find I prefer it. I've finally broken through my Arcana, and though I've still struggled with other cards throughout the day, at least I can access the World when I call it. And in this class Draven asks as many questions as I do, forever curious for more details about the state of the realms.

Fenrys tells us that tensions with the seraphs are the highest they've been since the end of the war. That word of his broken engagement, rumors swirling about a prophecy surrounding me, and his own defiance in announcing me as his fated mate has effectively reached every cranny and cave in all of Arcadia. How his father and King Altair respond to all of it now will be the determining factors to whether another war arises. Yet King Silas still seems to want to avoid outright battle.

At the end Draven thanks her and she gives us both a cheery congrats. We walk out of the small building at last, the sun casting its last rays over the tall grass of the steep hillside. The world is a wash of tangerines and gold, the air pleasantly cool as we traverse the black dirt path to our Hearth.

I don't want to break the steady silence between us: him clearly stewing on his father and the political mess, me lost in how the fear of yesterday washed away to nothing just by spending the day with him, harnessing my power. But . . . maybe it's my turn to thaw a bit of the ground between us.

"Thank you. For today, I mean."

Draven stops walking beside me, as if he ran into an invisible pole. His hand flies to his chest and he staggers exaggeratedly. "By Azazel's scythe, I swear she just uttered actual gratitude."

"Okay." My jaw juts in contempt at his mockery. "No need to go into heart failure. Actually, can you have a heart attack without a heart?"

"You tell me," he fires back, but we're both grinning, eyeing each other. His smile turns more sincere. "You're welcome, Rune." He swallows, eyes flicking ahead. "Can't have you distracted with our second public date coming up."

"I wasn't aware there was one already planned." My grin falters. Of course, today was more about our deal than some softening between us. He needs my power to emerge so we can have each other's backs, and he needs to show everyone we are more than roommates. What better way than stealing me from classes to spend the day cavorting with him? I shouldn't even be distracted by whatever it is I'm feeling for him. My focus should only be on the vengeance we've planned, and on finding my family.

"The Hollow Fest party is the biggest campus event of the year. It's the perfect time to make a statement." He runs a hand through his hair, the light catching it and shining like moonlight across onyx. Eyeing me from the side, his gaze is still firmly violet, a color it's remained most of the day. "Going together will turn every head, just like at Court. With a little more training, I can teach you how to listen to the vapid thoughts of every other student on campus. If we win them over, we can win over the rest of the Court, too."

"Right." This is all part of his plan, his grand deceit. I knew that. I know that. He may have the perspective of a mortal, but he has the self-interest of the immortal he's become.

"What's wrong?" He halts, shoulders hunched, bare tattooed arms in full view, his cloak hanging over one shoulder and wing.

Dark brows furrowing, his gaze pierces so intensely I wonder if he sees right through me. My mental shields are pulled up high, filling my mind with the image of that snowy field.

"It's n—" But I cannot lie, I can't dismiss it as nothing. My tattoo burns as if a hot poker is pressed against it. I swallow and say something true: "I'll get over it."

"You . . ." He chews his lip, as if he's worrying the lower one away, glancing at the countryside instead. "I don't like it when you shut me out like that."

"I thought you wanted me to learn to protect my thoughts? So I wasn't always forcing them onto you." I shrug and his eyes burn magenta now, as if there's a fire growing behind them.

"I fucked up . . ." His head tilts to the side as if he's trying to figure me out. "Does our deal prevent you from going with someone else? What's his name? The Judgment Arcana in your group?" Draven goes still, vulnerable, judging by the way his shoulders hunch, his leg bouncing. He insists, "The one here today. Autumn or—"

"Wynter," I supply, and he nods.

"I don't know him. But he's from Sedah. I should know him." Draven flinches, eyes darting back and forth, as though Wynter is some missing puzzle piece instead of just someone too lowly for Draven to have troubled with before.

"I don't know how I feel about him," I say honestly. Wynter's soft smiles have made my toes curl in my boots. My eyes drop, only to check back to see if Draven still looks my way. His gaze rankles closer to scarlet. I shrug blithely, continuing to be honest. "It doesn't matter, does it?"

Draven's brows stay furrowed, an incredulous smirk cloying at his mouth before giving way. He huffs, crossing his arms. "Did you need time to explore that dalliance before we get to work? I thought you wanted to be partners—"

"I do," I insist.

"This is the cost." He looks around, but we're alone, and he closes the short distance between us. He points toward the school. "Any of them could be enemies. I don't trust some of the people I've known for years. If they have not left a mark on my skin or me on theirs"—he points to the tattoo I've left behind, a lioness or a jaguar maybe, but he flashes it too quick for me to tell—"then they could betray us. I know it seems stupid to you, us pretending to be more, but it's the way I keep the seraph king from sending assassins for your head. The way I keep my father from snuffing you out in the night. I can't give you vengeance if you're dead—"

"I know that," I snap.

"—and you cannot give me a partner in ruling this wicked realm and the others if you're gone or distracted," he finishes as if I did not interrupt him. His shoulders slump, exasperation hitting his face. "Maybe I can be flexible when our footing is more secure, but if you're seen with someone else, it risks everything we're building—"

"I'm not going to go be with him!" I'm tired of talking about it.

"Are you sure? Because—"

"For fuck's sake, Draven!" I force my voice to lower, glancing at the building we left, but we're still alone. My hands fly to his chest, stopping before I shove him or pull him into me. Curling them into fists, I force them back to my side. "I just thought today was . . . maybe about you giving a damn."

I turn on my heel and start to storm off.

"It was!" He shouts the words at my back, but I don't turn around. I make it to the top of the hill as a whooshing sound fills my ears. I look up to see him soaring off the mountainside, flying off in anger. For a moment I'm surprised he didn't just use the Death Arcana to disappear back to the house. Maybe he thought it was where I was going and didn't want more of a fight. Either way I find myself cold, folding my arms over my chest as I make the long walk to a silent and lonely house.

18

—) ✴ (—

Dangerous Dealings

I know she is out there, and you must not underestimate her skill set or her ability to lure others
into a false sense of security. My Blades trained this
Wraith well, and she is both dangerous and cunning.
Find her.

—Recovered letter from the Lord of Westfall

THE WEEKS BEFORE midway exams pass in a blur. Things
with Draven calm, staying polite, formal, but we never seem
to hit the warmth that was budding between us again. He still
pulls me from class at least once a week for private lessons, and
I always find myself learning much more on those days than I
ever do in a large auditorium. He has me focusing primarily on
the High Priestess to protect my mind, the Empress to heal my
body, Strength for defense, the Star for making weapons, and
Judgment to control others. Yet the more I use Arcana, the more
I realize it's not just power associated with the cards, but feeling
and intention. The Star requires hope. The Empress compassionate love.

Probably why those two are so fucking difficult for me.

Draven also leaves me with different ancient tomes and texts every few days, adding our search for clues about the Arcadian Artifacts to my studies and practicing, usually with scribbled notes of what to pay attention to. We've yet to find any new leads. One time he leaves a book conveniently over the top of a darkly romantic story I'd found on my bookshelf with a note that reads, *If you have time for smut, you have time for research*. Which leaves me unable to look him in the eye for a couple of weeks, the romance book soon hidden beneath my pillow. But I smirk to myself when I realize he must've read it to know what it contained.

Morgan was sentenced to the Boiler, and I haven't seen him since. I asked Draven once how long he'd be there and his only reply was, "Until I'm satisfied." A few other changeling students glower at me now, blaming me, not knowing the full details of what Morgan did, but everyone seems to know I'm close to Draven and that's who put him there.

I'm not sorry it's where he wound up.

Ember, Amaya, and Cleona questioned me about Morgan's sudden departure at the next study session, which the boys were conveniently not invited to. I answered honestly, letting them know just how uncomfortable I was, how his temper spiked, and how Draven came to my defense.

They all exchange worried looks as I confess I'm not sure if I overreacted.

"He tried to attack you." Ember doesn't bother to keep the distaste from her expression. She gently puts her hand on my shoulder, the bright lighting of Star's Hearth casting a golden glow over us all.

"He should be thrown out." Amaya folds her arms, a darkness filling those brown eyes. "Arrested."

Cleona, who has been spending more and more time with our group, seemingly looking for any excuse to be around Amaya, shifts her head, her braids moving from her shoulder to her back. "If I'd been there, I would've burned a hole straight through his great stupid head."

Her eyes glow with golden fire, her stack of cards lighting up from where they sit on the coffee table in front of us. The Sun is the third highest Arcana, limning her like a goddess. I can certainly see why Amaya is drawn into her.

"We can just do study sessions with the four of us," Ember offers. "We can toss all the boys out. Whatever you're the most comfortable with."

"I wouldn't want to kick out Wynter and Felix like that." I smile at the support, tucking my white locks back into a messy bun that's still annoyingly chic. I miss my curls. "Kasper though?"

Amaya and Cleona laugh, but Ember's freckles disappear under a flushed smile.

"He's not all terrible . . . is he?" Ember asks.

"Gods, I knew it! You like him!" Cleona accuses, hiding laughter behind her hand.

I remember the conversation I'd overheard between Morgan and Kasper beneath that tree. Draven and I had filed it away, as nothing more has come of it, but the memory rises like bile now. I blurt, "Why?"

"I don't . . . I mean . . ." Ember stutters, and she pulls a face.

A sense of unease knots in my gut but Ember's blush only deepens.

"He's . . . well . . . he can be kind of sweet sometimes." Ember gives a little shrug. "Anyhoo . . . let's get into Minor Arcana!" She pulls out her notebook and though we all groan I can't help but soak in the little sense of comradery among the group of women. Not one blamed me or even questioned my version of events. I force down the emotion that threatens to well up as we start studying the four suites and how their lower and upper cards all connect.

ONE DAY I RETURN to our Hearth at midday, just to grab a pen, my own having died in the last class, and hear someone in my room.

I just saw Draven at the flight training field, practicing maneuvers publicly, far more advanced than the other winged students. He'd caught me watching him, his shirt lost, apparently, his muscled body glimmering with a sweat that I now blame for causing my unquenchable thirst. I can't get that arrogant grin of his out of my head, or those jaw-dropping, core-stirring V-shaped ligaments that line either side of his glorious abs, getting lost below his waistband. The half of his peers that looked to him like a god followed his attention to me before I turned bright red and nearly ran into a lamppost in my escape.

But . . . he was in class, and even with his wings I don't think he beat me back.

So, who is here?

I scoot into the hall bath, leaning back to hide behind the door, watching through the open crack. Magda creeps out from my room. She carries no cleaning supplies, and her hands worry together. If she gets spying crystals each day, as Draven's claimed . . . where does she get them from? It's not like she'd see the king every day, so how does she report in?

I'm due to class, and between ogling Draven and running back for this, I already risk being late. Something so small might not land me in the Boiler, but it will be noticed. I hesitate only a moment longer.

Fuck it, I'm curious.

I slip out after her, losing sight of Magda for only a moment before spotting her again. She's walking quickly toward some buildings tucked far outside the Hearths encircling the Oval. I haven't had a class out that way before, though there's enough buildings on campus I'm sure I won't visit all of them. Despite my training, and this changeling body, I'm still breathless by the time I catch up to her, having to tuck away into alcoves and hide behind bushes as she constantly checks around herself. She's not a particularly good spy and has to know Draven and I find those spying crystals every day. Is she compelled by the king to keep trying anyway?

Magda darts into a small building, shaded by a vast oak tree. Glancing once over her shoulder, she sweeps inside. A moment later I hear a couple of low voices from an open window off the second-floor terrace. My mortal ears never would've picked up their voices, not with the window barely cracked and heavy curtains billowing in front of it.

I grasp a rain pipe, using it to shimmy up to the balcony, moving as quietly as I can toward it.

"He has found every crystal. I cannot verify what they are to each other." Her voice is clipped, yet I can't help wondering if the frustration is about Draven's attention to detail or being tasked to spy on us. "Without proof or a scent of what they may be up to . . . what is this?"

Who is she talking to? A second spy? Someone working for the king? Both?

"King Silas will receive an envoy from Nevaeh by week's end?" she asks, and the crinkle of paper tells me she must be reading this somewhere. "Is he to entertain reinstating Prince Draven's betrothal?"

Whatever muttered response she receives has me creeping closer and her tutting. "Fine, I will let you know if anything changes, though you may have better luck than me."

I hear them both moving, but sticking around for them to leave only opens more opportunities for me to be spotted. Killing my curiosity for the sake of survival, I leap over the balcony's edge, grasping it and dropping down until I'm on the ground.

I need to find Draven.

I WALK THROUGH the entryway of our Hearth a couple of hours later, closing the door behind me, and the sound of heavy furniture moving reaches me. He wasn't at sparring, but he has the power to skip without punishment, and I'm relieved he's here and not off somewhere else. I follow the noise to Draven's room.

Golden magic whooshes past me, the Emperor card pulling spying crystals from all the places she's managed to plant them. It rearranges furniture and books, his room both messy and tidy all at once as things shift about the space. Most of his books have returned to their shelves, and I realize it's been a while since I've peeked inside here.

His back is to me, the color of those wings shifting from blue to purple in the light, and as soon as I clear my throat he glances over his shoulder, eyes orange, glowing as bright as lava pools. They soften back to indigo when he realizes it's me. The simmering anger tones down, but frustration lingers in his tense shoulders, the lines of his clenched jaw, and the silence he emits.

He swallows, turning from me again. "Magda's been busy."

"Yeah, I can see that." I watch his magic pull out more and more crystals from various spaces. "I'm guessing she figured if she put enough in, you'd miss one this time."

"It's almost like she *wants* me to find them." He crushes the last remaining ones with his power, the light bleeding from them before he angrily casts them in the fire. "I can't for the life of me understand it."

"I can. I just followed her." I lean against the doorframe. The way he's looking at me has me shifting my feet. It's not shock or confusion in those eyes, but delight. My chest floods with ridiculous warmth. "She was telling someone, a guard maybe, that she can't find any evidence that we're fated because of all the spying crystals being found. Said she couldn't sense . . . no . . . she couldn't *scent* it either. Whatever that meant. She talked about an envoy from Nevaeh."

The amusement slides off his face like sap. "Did you see who she was speaking to?"

"Unfortunately, no. From their voice it was a male."

"Then it could've been anyone. A guard. One of my friends." Draven walks toward the two-story arched window. I catch a bit of his face, and for a moment he looks like his father, if only in the cold way he surveys things, leaning with his arm against the glass and staring out at the slumbering volcano as if he will personally rouse it. "If Nevaeh is considering sending an envoy, it's to rectify what the two kings could not."

"What does that mean?" My heart races. I think I might be sick.

"It could mean they're reconsidering my marriage arrangement. Which means I would have no basis in which to protect you." Draven folds his arms across his chest, turning to watch me now with eyes that are as midnight blue as the skies outside. "It's not like they'd allow you to be my consort with the prophecy we all saw. Only a future queen gets that kind of protection and power. Hollow Fest and finals are at the end of the week, and then we're supposed to go to Alfheim. Now I'm not so sure I want to leave with them meeting to decide our fate."

"Can we force his hand?"

"My father's?" Draven shakes his head. "Unlikely . . . though maybe . . . no, never mind."

"What?" I prompt, desperate.

"We could try to progress things more quickly. Up our timeline in terms of our 'romance.'" Draven still doesn't look entirely convinced it would work. "The problem with druids and other immortals is our senses are heightened. We can learn to scent when something is real or not."

"What're you . . . oh." My face heats as I realize that the immortals can't smell him on me. Or me on him. "How . . . do you propose we resolve that?"

"Maybe we start sharing a bed." He chuckles when my eyes narrow. "If only in whatever boring way we must. It'll help. With the scenting I mean. Eight hours a night wrapped up in each other, even platonically, could fool my father." His tongue wets his lower lip and my body bursts into flame. Palming the back of his neck he adds, "I'm not a bed hog, if that's what you're worried about."

No, I'm far more nervous about the intimacy of sleeping alongside him. Sex can be a distant thing, carnal, primal. But sharing a bed? Cuddling? It's stupid to be more worried about my feelings than my sovereignty, but here we fucking are.

"Well, I'm a kicker," I say, and he laughs. "Sharing a bed," I muse for a spell, heart fluttering in my chest like a hummingbird's wings. It's a simple solution, if not a troublesome one. "Fine, starting tonight. As long as you behave."

"I won't break until you do." Draven's promise is hissed, like a blade leaving a sheathe.

"Fine." I swallow, but the alternative likely will mean my head. "Mine or yours?"

"Yours. Whoever Magda was with must be close to me, so it'd be best if I was covered in the scent of you."

Why is eye contact so fucking hard right now? I just nod. "See you in a bit, then."

Exiting through the bathroom, I can't help but notice my preparation for sleep is far more layered than usual. Though I curse myself for caring, I still wind up shaving my legs, adding on several lotions I'd usually skip, and waffling between a summer set of silk pajamas and a winter one. In the end, I opt for the narrow straps paired with lace and bottoms with a shorter inseam than I'd ever usually allow anyone to see me in. We can't smell like each other with fabric between us.

I cozy into my massive bed, bringing a book he lent me for research, but my gaze skips across the page like a stone across a lake, barely hitting every word or three. My heart races, the minutes stretching until finally Draven enters. His cotton shirt and loose pants are plain next to his usual clothes, but the top is formfitting enough to outline every curve of muscle. I wonder if this is what a doe feels, when she spots a lone wolf across a clearing in a forest. Is the heady rush of nerves what makes them go still, the way I do now? He stalks across to me, watching me as guardedly as if the roles were reversed, as if he were the stag and I the alpha of the pack.

He slides onto the other side, lifting the comforter and sheet, and that pressure grows unbearable. The enormous mattress doesn't seem wide enough for both of us—

"Did you put on perfume just for me?" His violet eyes greet mine, holding tight, and the edge of a smile lingers at the corners of his lips. There's an invitation laced in the sarcasm. *Come play with me.*

"It's lotion." I look him over, eyes narrowing. "Are you flexing right now?"

"It's cold in here, without the fire."

"I've heard that excuse before."

He rolls his eyes, smirking like a fox. His attention snags on my necklace, usually hidden under my clothes throughout the day. "I've been meaning to return something to you."

He draws up the World, then Death, and all at once my folded clothes from the Selection reappear between us, the figurine of the little broken king on top of them. "I'll admit it wasn't the kind of toy I was hoping to find hidden in your belongings—"

"Give it." I hold my hand out and he offers it over, treating it as if it's made of finest glass, shockingly gentle, eyeing me uncertainly. I covet it a moment, holding it tenderly before placing it on my bedside table. He hasn't looked away and I say quietly, "It belonged to my brother."

"I see."

"How'd you get it back?" It's an easier question to ask than why.

"It required paying off a guard, and making a rather large offering to appease Azazel but . . . since they decided to delay the changeling burnings for Hollow Fest I figured it was worth checking twice."

My guard drops as I try to figure out a way to thank him without getting emotional, but I come up short.

His jaw clenches in the silence, but then he fills it again, leading us back as if commanding our verbal dance, light and airy and ignoring the generous kindness he just showed as if it were nothing. "Gods, I hope you don't snore. I think I'd rather you just knife me in my sleep."

"That's not off the table." I scoff in his direction, relief coursing out of me as his humor relaxes my body, as if I've slunk into a warm bath. His wings are tucked tight around him, and for a moment a feather caresses my arm, my breasts peaking at the soft touch. I find myself not moving, hoping it trails my skin again. "I'm more worried about whatever birdlike diseases you carry."

"Says the thief of sandwiches. Perhaps I should nail down my wallet and tarot cards, too."

"Priss."

"Trash goblin."

I roll my eyes, smiling, and my attention lands on those horns, nearly scraping the headboard as he slides off his shirt, the pants, too, though he keeps the sheet tucked around his waist. What have I gotten myself into? My gaze flicks dismissively over him as I desperately cling to the pretense that there's nothing impressive in the cut of those muscles, the bold ink on his skin, or the addictive scent of him. Those twin serpents that peeked over his collar are wrapped in dark and light around an image of our world on his sternum, but there's so many tattoos, some bleeding into the next, that I don't know if there's enough time to really drink them all in.

The only coherent thought I have is to elevate the tension.

Snark suddenly the essence of my being, I say flatly, "Oh no . . . your clothes disappeared."

He laughs so hard the bed shakes, the sound riling, and some traitorous part of me wants to make him crack up like that for as long as I can. But his eyes darken with need, and if he's acting, then damn him because the growing pressure between my legs isn't.

He says silkily, "I need your scent on my skin. That wasn't happening fully dressed. You're welcome to take off more, too, if you desire." He settles back as I roll my eyes.

Out of curiosity I lift the sheets, peeking beneath, and his eyebrows jump. "Looking for something, love?"

"Just making sure I won't be kicked by some manicured hooves tonight."

He's wearing some short-like underwear, tight enough to draw everything into formfitting, bulging outlines. His legs are muscled, traced with tattoos like the rest of him. I force my gaze to flick away too fast to take in any more details.

"Well, I was right that they're manicured."

"Better than whatever troll toes you call those things." He laughs as I shove him with my hand, dropping the sheet, and he grins like a wildcat. "You sure you weren't checking to see if some *other* part of me was like an animal?"

"How close would I have to get to tell?" I fire back, and his mouth drops a bit, but he scoffs out a laugh. He's not threatened by a good jab, and from the violet in those eyes I think he welcomes it. But to be fair, from what I glimpsed, there's nothing for him to be self-conscious about. I run a hand along those exquisite wings, mostly to push the one off my half of the bed, and he shudders, eyes closing. Draven quickly rolls onto his stomach, his shoulder bumping against mine as his arms curl around a pillow, wings bunched on his back to avoid further touching. There's a flush to his cheeks from that gentle stroke.

"As happy as I am to let you explore your monstrous appetites and find out, I'm not here for a roast, but to create some very believable heat." His gaze caresses my exposed collarbone, flashing to my neck before traveling too far down. "That is going to require that we lay skin to skin."

"I'd rather not be gouged in the eye." Between those horns and the clawed ends of his wings, there's ample opportunity for a maiming just by lying beside him.

He smirks, summoning the Moon, and he alters his appearance once more, no horns, no wings. "What?" His gaze seems to look right through me, and something sparks in my chest.

"It's just . . . I wish I could change form like that." My fingers twist a silken strand of hair, yet it does not hold a curl.

"You can, with practice." His head tilts. "But what would you change? You're already . . ." I suddenly can't look away from him as he struggles to end the sentence but only lands on "normal."

"Romantic. I'm being swept off my feet."

"I thought you weren't in this for desire?"

A gods damned inferno simmers in my chest. I swear to the gods he can sense it, his own flame rising in response, reflective in those ever-changing eyes. "Fine, I was going to say 'beautiful.'"

Yet my tattoo doesn't burn or even itch. He . . . meant that.

"The only way in which you are normal is that you're still mostly mortal."

I hate how hard it's become just to look at him. "The Oath's transformation . . . it took something from me. Something I'm betting you druids don't find so beautiful." I blink back at him as he furrows his brows, gaze lax. Several Sedah-born druids do have texture to their hair, like Cleona, or Kenzo, but mine disappeared, stolen away. I still don't understand why. My eyes roll and I pull forward a lock of straightened hair.

His jaw works before he finds his voice. "Your curls?"

"Yes." My eyes water a bit, so I force them toward the ceiling. "The Oath straightened it. Did what the girls in every northern territory teased that I should do every day, heat a metal comb over a stove so that I might look more like them. But it's part of who I am. My culture. My heritage. I liked how I looked before. It reminded me of my father's people, from the Isle of Riches.

But your father's Oath forced me to become what druids find attractive, I assume."

"The Oath's design is ancient, and the wording in the spell had a lot to do with recasting changelings into Azazel's image, to strip what humans felt tied them to their pasts." He shakes his head, as though he can see where the spellwork sensed my ties, my connections, and went too far.

The pause between us stretches, his gaze dipping over my hair, flitting to my lips. He sits up, summoning the Moon again. "Let me return what was stolen. It's the least I can do."

My eyes widen, but I straighten up with him. "You can fix it? Permanently?"

"I can bring back the curls, but it won't be permanent until the Descent. Then you can make it so. You can change anything, so long as the Gods Below listen."

His hand rises to my hair, gently lifting a white strand, and he curls it around his finger. The Magician card creates a ripple in the air and a rush of sound like waves, and a scent like the ocean mixed with tropical fruits wafts over me for a wild, heady moment. I grip his wrist, clenching my eyes shut tight, spinning in the memories of my father's home, one I'd only lived in as a child. The only place that ever *felt* like home. For a moment, if I really pretend, I'm back on the Isle of Riches, surrounded by my family . . . still whole . . . before we were broken.

"There." He tucks his cards away.

I can feel the curls, spiraling in texture. I pull one down into my line of sight, springing it, and it bounces and coils back into position. My eyes water. Maybe it's stupid but . . .

"Thanks, Draven." I can't find any better words than that.

"You look the way you're meant to." Our gazes cling tightly, and I'm pulled into his orbit, like the earth dancing with the moon, careening through the night skies on a dare.

"Maybe I should darken it. I always hated being moon-cursed. I used to dye it—"

"I love the color." Draven clears his throat. His gaze slinks to a midnight purple as it flits up and down my face. "Not that it matters . . . but . . . I love the snowy highlights . . . the tempestuous deep grays of the lows. You're like a storm cloud." His knuckle caresses a curl, his mouth parting, pupils expanding. "It matches your personality. But if you want to change it . . . it's up to you."

"No one's ever complimented it before," I blurt before I can stop myself.

My cheeks and chest are afire, and when I finally force myself to meet his eyes, they're a lovely, full violet. We're so close, sharing the same space, the same breaths. I want to map his cheeks with my thumb, explore those full lips with mine, and follow the slope of his throat with my tongue.

Finally, he breaks before I do. "We should sleep. It'll be an early morning."

"More pedicures?"

"I'll be off to princely trainings, peasant." Ah, there he is.

"Should I go with you?" I prefer his classes over mine.

"That's a good idea. We need to see if this works, if our scents linger."

He rolls onto his side, facing me, and I realize what he wants. Hesitantly, oh so carefully, I allow myself to lie in his open arms, my back against his front, using one of his arms as my pillow, and his other wraps around my waist. His skin against mine is so warm, an instant calm threatens to lull me. Yet there's still distance between us, as if to get closer would be to risk us breaking our bet. Huffing, I slink my body until it's flush against his.

He purrs, "And here I thought you weren't trying to seduce me, yet you keep being so deliciously wicked."

I glance over my shoulder. Even in the dark of night I can see the hunger in his gaze.

"World chosen or not, keep it in your pants if you want to see the sunrise, Princeling."

My breaths remain tight as he chuckles, his chin resting above my head; those first breaths with my back pressed against his chest are uncomfortable, even though our bodies mold together, as if they're made for each other. Yet I can't relax; my nerves are at the edge of a cliff. I'm afraid one wrong move will put us both past a point of no return.

He hisses, "You are fidgeting like a child stuck in a lecture."

I roll my eyes to the intricate ceilings. "I'm not used to having a stranger in my bed." Not for sleep anyway. I can nearly hear his mind churning out a roasting retort, so I blurt, "Tell me something about yourself." His breaths hitch and I press before he can think too much, "Tell me about when you were Selected."

He's quiet a long moment, and my tattoo itches, but then— "My father was in the uprising." His chest rises and falls as if he trapped all the oxygen in the room inside it, and with the confession comes a release of pressure. "The end of the War meant vengeance against the mortals involved. It was King Altair of the seraphs that suggested turning us all in front of our parents, before executing us as repayment for the Curse. But when I was turned, the World card was drawn to me, right from King Silas's own deck, and he stopped the executions of me and the other children."

The heaviness of his tone puts me on edge. Not because I'm afraid *of* him, but *for* him.

"I'll never forget the look on my father's face when he saw me as a changeling. The disgust there."

The Great War was fifteen years ago, but I know at some point immortals stop aging. Did he fight in the War? I break the sharp silence with a serrated question. "How old were you?"

"Six." His answer stops my heart, squeezing it to pulp. "I won't settle in age for another ten years, at minimum."

My hands tremble, voice quaking as I ask, "And your real father? What happened to him?"

"King Altair executed him. Then King Silas adopted me on the spot. I was the first to be adopted by an immortal king, though not the youngest."

His breaths are jagged in my ear, as though they whisper through shattered glass. I relax my body a bit more snugly against him and his breathing normalizes a bit. My mental shields lower, more parapet than solid wall, and I realize how much of myself I can see in him. The trauma we share might not be a mirror, but two rivers stemming from the same cruel mouth.

"King Silas saved you and raised you. When it comes to the throne—"

"He stood by as they killed my father." His voice is darkness wrapped in fury. "Would've let it happen to me and the others if the World hadn't decided otherwise. Six is old enough to know when you have been wronged. Young enough to grow around that betrayal until it is a part of your very foundation. As I'm sure you know."

"Do you hate him?"

"I hate all of them." He swallows hard. "The immortal royals have caused so much strain on Arcadia and Vexamire both." He shifts and I find myself slinking my body against his. I can feel his heart thudding through his chest. It beats awfully fast, yet as I lean into his strong chest it begins to slow, matching my own. "But I am one of them. I've been given the chance to change things. To save the immortals and mortals from themselves. I can't waste it."

His hand comes around mine, interlacing over the top of it, his fingers weaving between my own. Draven's breaths send shivers across the nape of my neck, my shoulder. His other hand draws the blanket higher, tracing up my thigh and turning my bones molten. "Your turn."

"Ask me something."

"Who is Kiana?" His question stills my heart, but the pressure of his body lining mine stops me from trembling. He pulls back a little, angling his head to check my face. "You don't have to answer. I heard the name in your thoughts when you first arrived, over and over."

"We were together. Before, in Westfall." Breathing the truth into the darkness releases a weight I've been carrying for some time. "She was all I had. She died."

"I'm so sorry." He doesn't ask follow-up questions, not like I would've. He accepts as much truth as I'm willing to give him. His hand squeezes mine tightly. "I wish I knew what it was like to be loved like that."

"You've never been in love?" The revelation surprises me so much I turn, looking him over. He lies in the shadow of moonlight, eyes like mirrors, animalistic. A shiver races over my skin yet I don't withdraw. I want him closer.

"I . . ." His face lifts toward mine, and I'm drawn to those full lips. He's never looked at me so serious before but he just swallows, watching me as if I hold the answers to the universe. "Was it worth it? Opening yourself up like that?"

I haven't had to consider it. But the answer is too clear to deny. "I would do it again. A thousand times over. To feel that once more. Even if just for a moment."

His lips lift in the corners, hope shining through those ever-changing eyes. "Why, Wraith, you may just make a convert of me yet."

19

Hollow Festival

The claim shared between partners is a chafing, addictive bond, hard to disregard. Yet a claim
exchanged between two fated mates becomes
impossible to ignore, the venom exchanged mixing
hormones until it drives even the most chaste into a
frenzy. Once given, it cannot be undone.

—Immortal book *The Taken*

AS THE WEEK LEADING to Hollow Fest and our midsemester exams passes, I find myself overloaded with studying sessions, Draven's extra homework, and practice; each
day more information and mental strain. Instead, I live for the
nights, craving the contact when Draven and I sleep as tightly
as the spines of two books pressed into an overpacked shelf,
with no give between us. Strangely, it's the best sleep I've had in
years, and each night we talk unto exhaustion, his alluring voice
ensnaring me like a siren into the depths of oblivion.

But on the night before our tests, I tuck in, chest inflating,
my anticipation rising for whatever we will uncover about each
other only to find him sitting on the edge of the bed.

"What is it?"

"This isn't working." He heaves a sigh, hand flattened in the space between us as if he wants to be there instead.

My heart drops somewhere into my gut, defenses gather, mental shields refortifying.

"I listened in to Fable and Malik's thoughts—"

"Who?"

"My friends." He swats his hand through the air as if tossing my question to the side. "They're unconvinced. Our scents are mingling but not strongly enough. Not to mention listening in to the student body, professors, guards. There is question, they want to believe it, but they have not accepted we are fated as fact. With Nevaeh sending an envoy and possibly looking to rekindle my betrothal, we have to convince the world we're fated and now. We need more."

My gaze trickles down his body, but it's not the powerful grace lined in him that makes me shrink into the bedcovers. It's the openness in those purple eyes. "Well . . . I suppose there's only one thing left—"

He watches my lips, his own parting before he interrupts. "There's actually one other thing, between sleep and sex. I could . . . claim you."

"Claim me?"

"A simple bite." Those fangs descend and now I do squirm, as if he's transformed into a vampyr before my eyes. He holds up a calming palm. "If I take your blood into my veins . . . and you take mine, it will change our scents from the inside out. It'll be . . . undeniable. It's something all fated mates do eventually."

"Why didn't you suggest it before?"

"It's rather permanent."

And we aren't? But I keep the thought tucked down, lodged like a scrap of paper under the rock of my heart. "And besides the pain . . . is that the only downside?"

"You'll have a scar." He clears his throat, and I wonder if he's noticed the ones that line my back, though the camisole covers the worst of them. "Mostly you might notice some . . . misplaced desires. Some lust that perhaps I don't deserve." His gaze rakes me over but then stays, his body so still, as if he hangs on my answer.

But the feelings that have budded in my chest, vining through my ribs, rooting between my thighs have teased me to a point I'm not sure I'm thinking clearly anymore when it comes to him. The idea of his mouth finally making contact with my neck has me trembling in anticipation, gaze tracking up all those glorious veins across his forearms, lingering on the tightness of his chest muscles. The slope of his own neck so flawless, not a single nick or scar. He's too fucking pretty . . . it seems a shame. Worse, what if all that I've been holding back comes flooding out? What if I give in to this? To him?

"And . . . I have to bite you back?"

"Yes."

"How long?"

"I've never claimed anyone." He shakes his head, eyes darting away. He palms his neck. "It always sounded . . . too intimate. I can't imagine it'll be long, but . . . we will need to leave the marks somewhere visible. To drink from each other." He clears his throat, eyes violet and hooded as he lies alongside me, gaze magnetized to my tender throat. "Are you in?"

"Yes." Why did I have to reply so fast?

He chuckles, and those eyes darken, not just in color but intent. Leaning forward, he pauses before his lips touch my neck, the addictive vetiver and cedarwood scent washing over me. "Any last words?"

I can scarcely breathe, half a smirk on my lips as I snarl with sarcasm, "Bite me."

Palming my neck on one side, his lips suck against the other, and my skin incinerates. There's no pain, just pleasure, and he tenderizes that soft space with his tongue, lashing it against me, the scratch of his clean-shaven face enough to knock my knees apart. I catch sight of his eyes on mine just once, the glimmer of those cruel canines, and then—

My body jerks into his at the impact, my own fangs sliding down in response. He remains latched on to me, and it's not the pain that has me fisting his shirt in my hands tight enough to tear it off. It's the pleasure of the venom he courses through my veins. Some druid damnation, a carnal desire curling inside begging to abandon this game we play.

And all these silly pretenses I hold on to.

Before I know it, he's released me, only for me to sink my teeth into that space between his neck and shoulder. His throat bobs under my tongue, my clamp harder than his ever was, the claim unyielding. He lowers himself closer to me, giving in as I suck onto that tender flesh. My knees bracket around his hips, locking him in place as he makes to withdraw. But I just want another moment. Another eternity.

He goes limp against me, his hair falling over me, chest flat against mine, hand gripping into my hair, winding it between his fingers. I clutch one of his horns to lock his neck to my mouth, the other hand sliding up those downy wings in a purposeful stroke —

"Rune." My name is both a purr and a beg and suddenly I release him. He pushes away from me, breathing as if he's been running for his life.

"Draven?"

"Fuck." He stands and abruptly leaves. A minute later I hear the shower running. At first, I'm unsure if I did something wrong, wadding one of his discarded shirts from this week against my neck. His blood coats my lips but it tastes like that sweet nectar I clung to when I became a changeling. Shockingly *not* disgusting at all, but intoxicating. There's a lowering in his shield, a feeling spiraling from the other side of this link we share, and I summon the World and the High Priestess to get closer to that wall of thorns and iron. His mind echoes the growing pressure between my legs, begging for release. I smirk to myself.

He doesn't come back for the night, as though I will tempt him too greatly. I don't know how to feel about what just happened. I thought I'd be annoyed at the submission, playing along with more of this appeasement for his courts, but instead I find myself wanting him to return through that door, to pin down my hands with one of his and bite me again. Yet that wouldn't be *enough*. I shake my head as if the thoughts will go with it, settling into the lonely bed for the evening when he doesn't reappear. I could go to him, be the one to break but . . . my pride is too damn strong.

But I suppose he is settling for his idle hands . . . and I have mine.

THE MIDSEMESTER TESTS the next day leave me drinking far too much caffeine, and I can't close my eyes without imagining decks of cards popping into my head. Somehow, I survive each handwritten test, multiple choice question, and practical, the last of which I have only Draven and his private lessons to thank for. Not that I would ever give him the satisfaction of telling him that.

After I finish our last test, I linger to await my friends. Amaya and Cleona are the first to join me. Amaya has been beaming about the Hollow Fest party all day, held at Death's Hearth, her black hair chopped short for the occasion, the jagged edges cut with a razor, and like the rest of the Death Arcanas, she's covered in makeup that gives her the appearance of a skeleton.

"I can't wait to see you tonight! Don't forget to wear a mask, and at the thirteenth hour make sure you've found a soul to collect!" She nudges me with her elbow, making a kissy-face, but then her voice drops. "Are you finally going to introduce us to Draven?"

I scratch at my high collar; the bite Draven left is merely a scar thanks to the increased healing speed of this changeling body, but I've felt hot and bothered by the thought of him all day. He's been annoyingly absent, possibly taking his exams in private.

Cleona's eyes glue to my neck and she puts a hand over her mouth, hiding a grin. "Well, if you've claimed each other, you must've accepted the fated mating bond, right?"

Ember approaches us, worry bunched in the arc of her brows. "I went through every test twice but . . . wait . . . what is that?" She takes a deep inhale through her nose, focus flashing to me. "You smell . . . amazing?"

Amaya and Cleona dissolve into laughter, leaving Ember looking confused.

"Um . . . yes, it's true. Draven and I . . . are claimed. I'll bring him tonight." I don't know how long we play this out before it turns to engagements, wedding plans, and so on. The choice to stay at his side or leave him to rule alone feels far from me, especially as we still have not found any of the fabled objects or a sure location for my mother or brother yet.

"Finally!" Ember links her arm through mine, more excited than I've ever seen, bouncing on the balls of her feet.

"Good, you're done, too." Kasper approaches us from behind, doing a double take in my direction, and I swear I feel some claws on my mental shields, before he looks to my neck, rolling his eyes. He's been cold since Morgan's disappearance. Frankly, every time I look at him my fury sparks, knowing he left me with a wolf and seemingly hasn't cared since, blaming me for Morgan's actions. He leads Ember off, the two talking in low, intimate voices.

"We'll see you and your date tonight." Amaya gives me a wink, linking her hand with Cleona's and I nod, heading off to my Hearth.

"Rune!" Wynter hurries after me, chasing me out of the study hall. He swallows, gaze scattering everywhere but my eyes as he catches up to me. His brows furrow, focusing on my hair. "I keep meaning to say that I like what you've done." He gasps for a stronger breath, meeting my eyes finally. "Are you going with anyone tonight?"

The silver in that gaze is so bright, hopeful. Draven's words hit me again, *this is the cost*. Wynter is someone I could be happy with.

But I didn't come here for happiness. I came here for justice. And vengeance.

At Draven's side I'll get both.

But there's more to it than that, and my interest in Wynter has faded under the heat of being with Draven. Even if it's pretend on his part. I lift my chin.

"Yes. I'm going with the prince." Meeting Wynter's gaze feels impossible, but I manage it and watch the sad acceptance pass through his eyes before he hitches a brave smile to his lips.

"Oh, well, I hope you have a good time." I think he means it. He takes a deep breath and I note the flush creep up his face, as if he just smelled the lie we've planted, drinking it up as truth. He nods to me, face heated. "I'll see you both there."

I nod and force myself to leave. Why is there a stone suddenly in my gut? Shoving thoughts of him aside I turn toward my

Hearth, hurrying off, the cool autumn breeze blowing through my curly hair.

As I walk up the steps, Magda's marching out of it, looking irritable. Stepping aside for her to pass, I break her constant muttering with, "I haven't seen you in a while—"

"He is *on* one tonight!" Her hair's frizzled, though I notice she's gripping another spying crystal in her fist. She takes a deep breath as we stand in each other's presence, and I can spot the understanding clicking in her mind. Her lips quirk a bit. "Watch yourself, girl."

I lift my chin, knowing those bite marks are even more visible as I do it, and slip inside. Draven's door is open, and the sounds of him clanging around his room filter out. I move toward the door, leaning against the jamb, watching as he packs a suitcase, his back to me.

He stiffens before I can say a word, turning to me.

"I think Magda got what she was looking for," I say with a grin and he gives me a cocky smile as he takes in my neck, my lips. "Even if she couldn't plant any crystals today. How did your exams go?"

"Fine. Despite someone's distracting thoughts pressing against mine all day." He gives me an arrogant, knowing look as he takes me in. "And you?"

I check my nails, clenching my jaw a little to bite back what being this close to him threatens to unravel in me. "I know how to stay focused." Even if that claim has chafed through me all day. I change subjects, because I'll be damned if I admit to it. "So, Alfheim? What are we being sent there for again?"

"To pick up some dark zenith crystal. They recently discovered it was in a toxic drake's lair." He acts as if it's a boring task but my attention snags, alarm bells ringing.

"A toxic what now?" I can't help but notice he failed to mention *that* part before.

"A drake. Large, dangerous, usually rows of sharp teeth. There're a few kinds; this one is one of the worst of the breeds." He gets lost comparing jackets for a moment, but I'm not sure how he can possibly be thinking about that when my skin prickles, every fable I've ever read about mythic beasts playing out in my head.

My heart slams into my ribs, looking for escape. "You're taking me to fight a dragon?"

Draven scoffs out a dark laugh. "A drake is hardly a dragon. Drakes are maybe a third of the size. This one would've been able to spit toxic gas or acid, but not fire. Bigger than the wyverns you saw when you came in, but they're wingless, and best of all weak against our magic. Formidable, but not nearly as dangerous as a dragon."

I keep staring at him—is he insane? An actual gigantic magical lizard.

He finally notices how still I've gone. "They've assured me the cave is empty, and the drake is dead."

"Consider me reassured." I note the way he huffs a sigh at my sarcasm. "I just don't like the idea of absconding from our safe institution to stick my neck in the lair of a wingless dragon—"

"A *dragon* can burn mountains to molehills. One burned an ocean and all the mer living beneath it, until nothing was left but bones and desert sands." He crosses to me and leans into my space, capturing my eyes as easily as a cat pouncing on a mouse. "A drake isn't anywhere near that level of power, and as I said, it's dead. I would never take you somewhere I can't protect you."

"Anything else I should know?"

"This discovery site is the largest undisturbed collection of unrefined zenith, and from the reported size of it, the amount could power the Forge for several centuries on its own." He points to the lamps and the strange energy within them. "But I'm hopeful it will give us a chance to look for signs of your family and the Arcadian Artifacts."

My heart rate settles at the certainty he displays. He and his father might have a strained relationship, but it seems unlikely that the king would put Draven in actual danger. I'm sure I can miss a few days of classes now that our midsemester tests are finished. I observe that map on his wall, though the markings are gone, as if he erases them each day. I glance at the zenith in the lamp at his desk, my eyes narrowing.

"So, we'll be collecting this?" I ask, the crystal smoothed and polished like stained glass.

"Well, that's refined zenith." He picks a jar off his shelf and shows me a sliver of dark crystal so pigmented it looks like midnight turned solid. "This is what it looks like in its unrefined stage, where it's more powerful and dangerous."

"You know, it looks familiar . . ."

Blinking, I put it together, all the tomes of boring archaeology, myth, and history compounding. "Do you still have that book with the diagrams of the Arcadian Artifacts?"

"Of course." He runs a hand through his hair and tracks over to his desk, leaning against it as he searches a neat stack of books, my eyes dragging across the length of him. His head leans to one side, that claim mark on full display, and I'm certain it's no accident. I can still feel his stubble against my bare neck, chest peaking, and I cross my legs, fingering the bite mark on my neck and wishing I could hide this want better. How can one man be so fucking devastating?

He hands it to me when he finds it. "Why do you ask?"

I flip it open until it lands on the wand. The dark slender Artifact looks chiseled, and I'd assumed its spiraled form was made up of wood before, but seeing the unrefined zenith in front of me, it looks a lot more like stone. Our arms brush and my skin heats. "I think the wand might be made of zenith, judging by the renderings of it, and it says here it has the ability to transport itself . . ."

Draven leans sharply over the book, hand splaying over mine, heat rising in me as his eyes absorb the page. He breathes, "And no one's explored the cave."

"Is there a chance the wand returned to its original source?" I yank my gaze from settling on his full lips and meet his eyes, dancing with anticipation. "Wasn't there some saying about the wand . . . darkness seeks darkness?"

Draven's eyes lighten as though he can't help but let his enthusiasm over the subject shine through. "They call the wand the Darkstone, or Worldwielder, depending on who wrote the history. It has a unique ability to splice open dimensions between realms." Draven's gaze traces over me, lingering on my mouth. He shakes his head, blinking a long moment before his hand grazes the page again, brushing against mine. "Some say a legion of hells' finest could be summoned with it. Or it could open doors between worlds. But . . . it also has the power to hide itself. The legends say it calls to people. That it can move itself to where it needs to be."

"As if it's almost alive."

He nods. "Whatever its power, no one's seen it in eons, but the last sighting of it was at a battle near another huge source of zenith in our kingdom."

"So, you think it could be in that lair?" I meet his gaze, and he bites back a smile, excited at the potential lead.

"I think there's a chance. It's the druid Artifact, but the lines on the maps changed, and this location was once within our borders." Draven shrugs. "The fact that this cavern's so untouched has me wondering if this is where it originated. It's a stretch, but dark power loves company, so maybe without an owner, it returned home, before that drake happened upon it, attracted to the zenith's power. It's the best lead we have. But we can't tell anyone we're searching for it, lest it gets back to the kings."

"What would your father do if he found out that we were searching for it?"

"He's the kind of man who demands respect but gives none. He cares only for how my actions reflect on him. He expects utter gratitude and nothing short of perfection." Draven's finger traces the wand drawing. "But I'm more powerful than he is, and he both desires that power for himself . . . and fears it. If he found out we were searching for a fable, he'd be embarrassed, and if we actually found one . . . he'd feel threatened."

It seems complicated, more like the relationship I had with the Lord of Westfall than my own father, who cares less how powerful I am, or what I can *do* for him. My father only cares if I'm happy and safe. But Thane was like this . . . a man whose power stemmed from making others small.

Draven looks to the map above his desk, admitting that much vulnerability brings a cost, and right now his eyes shy from mine.

I want him to know the only person I will judge is his father. My hand slowly strokes his, and Draven's breaths still as I squeeze tight. The apple in his throat bobs and the restraint between us thins, a thread under the duress of a razor. Damn. The intimacy of it fills the room, and there's nearly no room left to breathe. So, I distract us both.

"Since we'll be there, should we look for the elves' Artifact, too? Hints to the ring?"

Draven blinks, the spell strung between us faltering but not dissipating.

"The ring, Seithr, or Kingmaker, has the power to exert extreme influence over any living being, completely erasing their thoughts and replacing them with its own." Draven's gaze narrows on the map's flags. "It's rumored to be the source of their vast wealth."

He grabs another book and opens to an illustrated page. The ring is extremely detailed, even more so than the one he wears on his right hand, which holds that magical blade of starlight and demon fire. Seithr looks as if a galaxy is trapped within it, a band of the cosmos crowned between the layers of gold.

"I really hope they're real." My finger runs along the drawing.

He chews his lip and I find myself leaning closer, my eyes trailing the slope of his bare throat, the tick of a vein intersecting the bite mark. Gods, I would kill just to touch him.

A spark remains in his gaze as he glances to me, gaze flitting from my eyes to my lips to my throat. "Something about the stories wrapped around these Artifacts . . ." He sighs with his whole chest, staring at the map and the flags inked across it as if they hold all the answers in the universe. "They gave me hope when mine was taken. And that is a dangerous thing to believe in."

It's what the Selection became for me—something to cling to. However horrible, it was a passageway to my family, a star in the endless dark. Something to hold on to . . . like a dragon curled possessively around its treasure—

"Wait."

I rush out of the room, crossing through our shared bathroom, and return a moment later with one of the many anthologies of myths and legends Draven has loaned me in the past few weeks. It was dull to the point of tears, and I mainly kept it to hide the tantalizing romance novel I've been reading, but something about the elves stuck out—an image that reminded me of a dragon guarding its hoard. Flipping through the pages, I can feel Draven half behind me, watching over my shoulder, thrumming with interest. I stop on a page showing a portrait of the elven king.

"Look at his hands."

In the illustration, the king stands at the entrance of a mighty vault of infinite wealth. Though tiny, merely a smudge of emerald and gold, it's unmistakable—one of the fingers of his clasped hands bears a ring that looks an awful lot like Kingmaker. A grin breaks across Draven's face, like clouds parting to reveal the sun. He scoops my face in his hands, a broad grin on his face.

"You are fucking brilliant, Rune."

A giddy smile bubbles out of me as I look up at him, all gorgeous symmetry and angles and strength. Waiting. He's breathing as though he's run a marathon, his eyes darkening, hooded as if he wishes to devour me. My hand fists the front of his shirt and those pupils widen. What is he waiting for?

Is that how you ask nicely? His inner voice is more growl than anything.

My mental wards have disappeared entirely.

Just kiss me, you bastard.

Those lips part in a smile and then he grips me hard, his mouth claiming mine. He tastes like burning hot honey and the heated edges of sex, making my knees weak from want. My entire body tingles, alive for the first time in years. Within just a few movements my mind wipes clean, my lips parting as his tongue sweeps in, warmth flooding from my mouth to the spread of my legs. My grip on his shirt is so tight I'm sure those golden buttons will rip, but neither of us cares as his hands travel from cupping my face to my back, lower and lower. His hips roll against me, thumbs sliding under the space where my pants rest, caressing along my pelvic bones.

Every sweep of his tongue sends a fire raging through my body, a forge suddenly roused, flame as hot as lava. My veins fill with lightning, and my hands grip around that taut waist, hand sliding up his shirt to explore the muscles stacked over his stomach, digging between ribs, driving him into me harder.

As he pants against my mouth, his hands scoop beneath my backside, lifting me as though I weigh nothing, my legs wrapping around him. He swipes the books and a lamp off the desk, letting them careen to the floor, and sets me down in their place, his hips joining firm against my own. My thumb rubs over the button of his pants, pulling it loose, and his breath hitches, the taste of him hypnotic. His hand entwines in my hair on one side, his mouth leaving my lips to suck against my neck, my eyes rolling as he unravels me as easy as loose thread—

"Your Majesty—oh!" Magda halts in the doorframe, a hand flying to her chest. She holds a couple of garment bags in her hands and sputters, "I heard a crash—"

"We're fine here, Magda," I pant, speaking for us, but she waits for his dismissal.

"Just leave the clothes." Draven's deference is at war with his body language, the guttural way his words tear out of him. His eyes haven't left me, threatening to pull me back into this like an undertow.

The way his eyes are lit up, fervor stoked beneath the violet, turning them magenta, a couple of buttons missing from the top of his shirt, baring his muscled chest, has me dizzy with desire . . . I'd willingly let go of any shore, surrender to more of this.

His hips have pinned mine, but from where he stopped kissing, just shy of my peaked breasts, I'm not sure how far it would've gone. There's an awkward clink as Magda leaves the outfits for the party hanging off the door handle. She leaves but we can both hear her lingering outside it.

I burst into embarrassed laughter and Draven joins me, his hand still wrapped in my hair as he chuckles against me, our cheeks pressed together. He goes to pull away, but I keep him close. The laugh dies, devoured by the want in his eyes.

I force myself to focus and whisper into his mind, *When we're in Alfheim, it's not just the ring or the crystal we should be looking for.*

He stands up, releasing me, gaze cooling as if weighing what just happened against our deal. I curse myself, realizing how it looks, like I've seduced him just to push my own agenda, and his voice curls against my thoughts.

I remember our vow, Wraith. I've been looking into leads. We find your family. We find my items. He grins, a wild, wicked thing. *Then we bring this world to heel. Together.*

A FEW HOURS LATER I enter Death's Hearth, coiled around Draven's strong arm. I wear a flowing dress that's more slip than anything, as white as any bride's. My white hair flows down my back, encircled by a woven ivy crown intertwined with crimson and blackened orchids, twigs reaching skyward on either side. My white owl's mask is pulled snug, a complement to Draven's skeletal stag. Draven wears a tight-fitting onyx suit, the accents all in gold, as he's dressed himself like the druid's highest god, Azazel, Lord of Death, and I am his wife, the White Goddess, who through the moon watches over souls through birth, love, and death, her cycling light a representation of her power.

The night is meant to honor Him above all—the temple on campus overwhelmed with gifts, the numerous candles causing it to shine like a beacon—but his wife is adorned with offerings, too, not only to appease Azazel but to ensure she does not end one's cycle short. The night is for celebrating the hollowing of one's soul from its shell, the transformation only the most *elite* druid souls undertake.

It's odd to be here among immortals revering death when mortals cling to life with such terror. Yet immortals can die only by blade or disaster. Neither age nor sickness will ever take them. To them, death is a holy thing, something earned, whereas even the most devout mortals fear it above all else.

"On Hollow Festival, we celebrate the ecstasy of living. As if it's our last night in this world," Draven whispers into my ear, sending chills racing up my spine. I forget how connected druids are said to be to nature—and sex, it seems, is akin to holiness.

We wend our way through the expansive Hearth, at least three to four times bigger than our own, made up of a large living space surrounded by twisting corridors to all the rooms surrounding it like a spiraling labyrinth. White veins slink through the black marble floors like drags of paint, and the walls are a darker obsidian than I've seen anywhere else. It's packed wall to wall with people drowning in drinks and excess, or gyrating together in every pocket, some coupled too close for dancing.

I can't help pressing the thought to him, *Here we go*.

He shakes his head at me, and I know from the lack of answer, verbal or mental, that he's reminding me to be silent. Any High Priestess Arcana could be listening in, possibly spying for his father or others in the Court. Especially those who've already been chosen by backers. We pass a pillar decorated with realistic skulls, living bats clinging to the walls, their moving bodies making the space pulsate. Music plays from a stage along a wall of windows, some brought in via an illusionist from the Devil Arcana. The song is dark and haunting and utterly unlike anything I've heard. The drumbeats keep me rooted as the piano and violin loosen my body.

"This is wild," I tell Draven. The Lord of Westfall was known for lavish parties, but none had magic, and most of the events were stiff, formal affairs, their after-parties a den of sins. The crowd buffets us closer. I clutch his hand in mine; the other one snakes around his arm so we can't be separated. I realize why so many people were out on the lawns, even for a space this size, there's just too much going on, too much heat. It takes me a moment to realize the bats aren't real but made up of shadows. I wonder how much magic must be getting channeled to keep up the décor alone. I can taste it like iron in the air.

A large, winged druid nearly runs me over, but Draven's magic shields me, a shadow more solid than any in this space, and the druid goes sprawling. When he rights himself, the shadows slink into the floor like a fog, and the male braces to yell at me. The moment he notices Draven standing undaunted at my side, Death Arcana still summoned in his hand, he straightens, eyes wide, and walks determinedly in the other direction. A little ring of space expands around us, shadows nipping at the heels of any who get too close. At the corner of the room some guards corner the druid who almost crashed into me.

"Do they ever take a day off?" I ask Draven, watching the guards pull the druid away.

"They're supposed to back off for the evening but . . . even on a night of revelry they won't take a break." Draven shrugs, and with a free hand smoothly tucks a loose strand of my hair behind my pointed ear.

The unexpected touch causes heat to course through my chest and neck, and my body arches into his. My mouth opens a little, and an increasingly familiar sensation tickles my gums: my fangs have extended. That small stroke unraveled me, and I swallow, mortified, even though he can't know—my wards are too on edge to have dropped. Yet the way he looks down at me, smile genuine and ravenous, eyes twinkling in a violet fever, I'm sure he suspects.

"Dance with me?"

The question hangs between us, and it feels as if he's desperate for my answer.

I nod, grinning, and his grin leaves me breathless.

He puts his hand at my waist and pulls me close, and the world narrows to the two of us. The Devil Arcana controlling the music shifts the songs until a satyr is projected, his face not quite human or beast, eyes a haunting white, and he sings a ballad that fills the hall. It's soft and eerie, the melody slow and evocative.

Then Draven pulls me flush to him. I loop my hands around his neck, nearly on tiptoes to do so. When he leans in, it sends chills down my spine, and his whisper coils against my neck.

"Now is the moment we convince them."

Right. The performance. The thrill threatening to shatter through me douses a bit. When my gaze lifts from his muscular shoulder to scour the room, nearly every head is turned our way. He grins. "Let's make it believable. Or like hounds baying on the hunt, they will scent us out, our lies will crack like bones, and they'll devour us both."

20

Death's Hearth

The Two of Cups represents partnership, attraction, and romantic entanglements. When drawn, it can signify shared romantic feelings.

Drink up.

I LET DRAVEN LEAD US around the dance floor, hugging me close, our bodies meeting like seams, his fingertips straying lower. Though others dance around us, his attention never leaves me.

The way his gaze flicks from my eyes to my lips to my chest is a study in seduction. The crowd's stares are a mixture of jealousy and desire. But I find myself falling for the mask of his duplicity. And while my doubt tells me this is fake, I so desperately wish for it to be real. The kiss we shared still rankles through me, my body a live wire of need. When he catches me staring at his mouth, he grins like a fox.

The way he's pooled against me, I'd happily let him spoon-feed me more lies.

One of his hands cradles my face, his thumb tracing my lower lip, and suddenly it feels too fast, even though we've been curling against each other most of this dance. I realize foolishly I don't want him to kiss me here. Not as an act.

"Careful, Princeling," I hiss, and he swallows. "I'd hate to share too much for a perception that we could save for the privacy of our rooms."

He chuckles in my ear and growls back, "Like this?"

Draven sweeps the mask from his face and his mouth clamps around my tender neck, fangs scraping, sucking as though he will drain me, right at that spot he made his claim. My nails dig into his shoulders, likely leaving marks even under his clothing, and a gasp is yanked from my throat, my body arching into him, one hand twining upward, clasping the hair at the nape of his neck. I go limp, toes curling, and though I'm glad it's not as intimate as a kiss, I'm still red-faced at the attention and my inability to hide how good it feels. I clench harder, trying to silently get the message through that if he continues like this, I'll be panting against him.

Yet his tongue lashes against me and my body scalds.

"Bastard," I pant. My fingers run through the downy space where his wings meet his back. They twitch hard, bunching, and his mouth leaves my neck, his cheek pressed against mine as we keep swaying to the slow melody. I can feel his grin, his chuckle deep and addictive. Chills cascade across my skin, my breasts as tender as if he nipped them instead, and I can't seem to close my mouth. My gaze sticks to him as I pull away to look up into his violet, laughing eyes.

"Too fast?" He wears that damn shit-eating grin like a second skin.

Is this part of the claim? It's easier to blame than my own . . . wantonness. His hands still clutch my waist; mine loop around his neck, stringing me tight against him. This silken dress doesn't provide much barrier for what I want from him. And I want it.

I suddenly don't give a thought to the complications it could bury me in or let my hatred of the immortal royals cloud these viscous desires. He's not *really* one of them, he's like me. I only let myself drown in the craving pulsing through me, the one that promises any repercussion would be fully worth it to have him at my mercy.

"I think you need to get me a drink. And I think we need to go somewhere private," I whisper in his pointed ear, "so I can properly punish you."

His eyes widen, and it seems as though I've genuinely caught him by surprise. His pupils grow, his eyes black.

"Your shields are thin, Rune," he breathes into me.

"Can you hear me?" I'm uncertain if I've thought anything that could endanger this.

"Not . . . words," he gasps, as if I've stroked him with my hand. He pulls from me a little, and I want his velvet suit pushed flush against me again, but then his hand is clenching mine tightly, and he walks backward through the crowd, his eyes unable to stop traveling the length of me in my thin, silken gown. He draws me along, and I no longer care if anyone watches. If they're all scenting what we are and will be.

I just want what's next.

Draven leads me into the kitchen, where some druid is mixing drinks behind a long island like a potion master. I set my mask down, as does he, the two of us lingering against the bar, leaning into each other. Some punch bowls look gelatinous, others hiss smoke, while more bubble and spark. The druid behind the counter has a haze in his eyes and hands Draven a tall glass of something purple and smoldering before he can order. A moment later I'm palming a fizzing magenta concoction. I drink it greedily, too thirsty to go slowly.

Draven chuckles at my eagerness, then downs his in a few gulps. He leans close. "Did you want to stay or—"

"RUNE!"

I jump out of my skin as my friends suddenly surround us. I've been so caught up in Draven's body against mine I forgot they'd be here.

Ember glances to Draven twice before dipping into a curtsy. Amaya and Cleona gasp so loudly that I'm betting they started drinking some time ago, and they clumsily follow Ember's lead. Felix and Wynter bow at the waist, but Kasper at the back rolls his eyes as he sips on some drink. Moody asshole. Draven's mouth opens in a half smile, though I can tell he's caught off guard. We somehow didn't plan this part of the scheme through. If our lie doesn't convince them, it'll fail before it begins.

He waves off their formalities, arm slinking around my lower back, and smiles charmingly to each of them. "No need for that. You must all be Rune's friends? She talks nonstop about her favorite study group."

Ember and Amaya preen at that, and I realize stupidly I haven't introduced any of them.

"You all know Prince Draven," I supply, cheeks heating when I notice Wynter's cool gaze on us. My jaw clenches, but Draven and I have our parts to play, and Wynter isn't included in that. Except right now it doesn't feel like an act.

Felix looks to Draven with shining eyes. "I watched you at flight training and you were amazing, Prince Raven . . . I mean Prince Dragon . . . Prince—"

"No need to hurt yourself," Draven grins, but he looks genuinely bemused at the reverence. "I can teach you if you get wings during your Descent. You . . . must be Felix?"

"He knows my name." Felix's face pales and I bite back a grin, Ember and I exchanging half-mortified, half-amused looks as Felix's toothy smile spreads. He sticks his hand out, human manners unforgotten. Cleona casts him an exasperated look—I'm sure it's not proper for druids—but Draven doesn't miss a beat, grasping it right back. Wynter's expression relaxes a fraction, and Amaya smirks, eyes flowing over Draven in appraisal.

"I'm glad to know you." Draven smoothly turns and his eyes alight on Ember, taking in her red hair as a confirmation of sorts. "Ember. Thank you for being such a great friend to Rune." I look to him in surprise and Ember's smile turns soft, like that touched her. "This color dress looks amazing with your hair."

"Thank you. I'm supposed to be a kelpie." Her dress is a gorgeous emerald, and combined with her red and copper hair, she is stunning. Ember swirls the skirts and expands with, "And it has pockets."

"Why doesn't mine have pockets?" I ask Draven. He grins, leaning into the nape of my neck to whisper something, but Kasper interrupts.

"I'm sure your new master will correct the oversight going forward." He takes an angry swill of his drink, and our friends turn on him in matching expressions of outrage.

"What is your problem?" I demand. Kasper has never warmed to me, always remaining negative and standoffish, but this is new. I remember Draven saying how often Kasper steps up to his mat in sparring, and my eyes narrow at the spark of hatred in the silvery blond man's eye. Wynter grips his arm, hissing something in his ear that sounds an awful lot like *would you shut up?*

"What? Is he gonna have me locked up too if I'm not nice to you?" Kasper asks me. He turns with surprising venom to Draven, who merely blinks in cold distaste at being addressed. "Tell me, how long will Morgan be locked away in the Boiler?"

"The chittering ferret must be Kasper." Draven's gaze alights at the disturbed look on Kasper's face, his feet shifty beneath him. Suddenly Draven feels too large for the space, his smirk spelling damnation, his wings spreading, one encircling me, warming my shoulders, a shield made of ligaments and feathers. "Why am I not surprised you'd take the side of a male who tried to disarm and force himself on my fated mate? You did, after all, see how he was acting toward her all evening and still turned your back on them, leaving them alone."

"I didn't know—"

"Yes, you did." Draven's correction strikes Kasper silent.

"That's why Morgan's in the Boiler?" Felix whispers innocently, eyes round, mouth sagging in horrified disbelief.

Wynter's hand cups over his mouth as if he might be sick and he suddenly can't take his eyes off mine.

I probably should've told the guys what happened, too . . . I just didn't want to relive it again, and I'm surprised how much Draven has sorted out since.

"I guess you don't believe in trials here." Kasper crosses his arms. "She might've led him on. That was her job you know. Seduce, lie, spy. Right?"

"Kasper!" Ember clenches her fists, staring at him as if he's a stranger.

"I see those hits from the sparring ring have crushed your critical thinking skills." Draven's shoulders flex back, and it's clear to me he's preparing for a brawl. I'm surprised when instead he aims his next attack with venom. "If you're going to keep disrespecting Rune like that . . . well maybe you *should* join your friend."

"Is that a crime now?" Kasper's cheeks have reddened, and he takes a step back, the room quieting a bit around us, others drawn to Draven and recognizing how degrading his tone has become. Like vipers they hiss among themselves around our little circle.

"It is when her mate sets the laws," Draven growls, glowering as if Kasper is an unfortunate slug on the bottom of his shoe. "Apologize to Rune, and I'll consider forgiving you."

Kasper looks us both over hatefully, but he manages, "I'm sorry."

Draven looks down on him as if he's still considering further punishment. He leans into the space between my neck and ear, his breaths sending goose bumps across my flesh, and he whispers, "Friend or foe, if someone hurts you, they are my enemy." He leaves a kiss against the tender space of my throat and apologizes, "I will try to behave myself better. But I cannot help it when someone is cruel to you." He meets my eye, awaiting my decision.

But I don't want Draven's first interaction with my friends to include punishing one of them, especially considering Ember's feelings for Kasper. I turn to Draven, our lips barely inches apart. "It's okay. Let's just move on."

A few guards push through the crowd, one leaning into Draven's space, whispering to him. I'm caught between my friends, who are watching Draven like some avenging angel, and half listening to the guard explaining there's been some threat apprehended outside the party.

Kasper takes the opportunity to squirm from our presence, moving over to the bar to drink alone.

Draven soon whispers in my ear. "I need to deal with something. But then I'm happy to make up for my outburst with you and your friends. Unless you'd prefer a private apology?" His eyes glow that bright violet that says he's enjoying whatever game we're playing.

"Depending on how quickly you're back, we'll see what we have time for." My teasing lures out a rogue smile.

"In that case, I'll make it very fast." He retreats with his guards, leaving me with my friends.

"Sorry," I announce to them, rubbing one arm with the other, fidgeting a bit. I haven't wanted to talk about Morgan, and seeing Kasper dressed down may have riled me, but I'm not sure if it went too far with them.

But Felix moves to my side, a gentle hand on my shoulder. "There's nothing for you to apologize for. I'm sorry I didn't know about Morgan. I'd heard rumors he'd upset Draven, but nothing about you—"

"It's okay, Felix." He's so sweet, mouth twisted to one side, eyes searching as if replaying that night over. "I'm fine. We handled it."

"Okay." He nods, still worried, but then he looks at Draven's retreating back. "I like him, by the way. I like how he stuck up for you. And *to* Kasper and Morgan. They're both kind of assholes . . ." Felix trails off, and I've never heard him say a word against anyone before.

"I don't usually like males in general," Amaya adds, watching Draven retreat through the crowd. Cleona looks at her a little sharply as her girlfriend grins at all his assets. "But he might be a good one."

"I'm sorry Kasper acted like that. I don't know what's gotten into him." Ember frets and I shake my head. She doesn't need to be apologizing for him, whatever the two of them are becoming. "He's . . . not like that with me. He usually always knows the right thing to say. I wonder what's going on . . ."

"Don't worry about it." Emphatically I add, "Seriously. It's fine."

She leans close. "How's it going with Draven?"

"I . . . like him. A lot." My face heats enough I'm sure they see the blush.

"How's the . . . fated mating going?" Amaya asks in a loud conspiratorial whisper. Cleona shushes her, and Felix and Wynter suddenly find themselves in their own conversation.

"Hopefully we can start on that tonight." I rub my claim mark and the girls all giggle with each other. I'm not used to this, a group of women who both support and encourage, where they ask because they want whatever I may want for myself, not for idle gossip or blackmail. My eyes dart and Amaya puts a drunken hand on my arm.

"Hey, if you want, you can use my room. You remember where it is, right?" Amaya's offer is nearly drowned under the swelling music, and I lean in to hear her. I laugh, nodding, and she gives me a little thumbs-up. She nods her head at Cleona, who bites her lips. "Don't stay too late though. We are gonna need it later."

I grin and Amaya leans into Cleona, whispering mischievous words in her ear. Wynter broods over his drink, and some pretty second-year starts chatting him up. I ignore the tinge of jealousy that sparks at that, throwing my focus back onto Draven, a bit worried at whatever drew him away. It's taking a while and I fidget on the spot.

Felix leans over to Ember, clearing his throat, and asks, "Do you want to dance?"

"Me?" She tries a small smile, but the corners of her lips seem unconvinced as her attention darts toward Kasper, still moodily drinking alone.

What she sees in Kasper is beyond me. I wish she'd forget him. A splinter wedges into my chest over the fact she'd still like him after all that, and I nudge her forward, encouraging her to instead take a chance on someone more worthy. Felix grins and she takes his hand, but she keeps glancing at Kasper even as Felix holds her in his arms.

Before I know it, Draven is back. He gives the others a small nod of his head, slipping his hand into mine, and drags me away. He's moving too quickly through the crowd, druids and change-lings stagger back from his path.

"Slow down," I hiss at his back.

He doesn't seem to hear, tracking to the stairs, and then leads me up them.

I take one more look at my friends. Wynter determinedly ignores us as he is joined by a second pretty girl. Cleona and Amaya lift a glass to me, the latter catcalling us. Felix dances with Ember, his eyes glued to her, and she laughs at something he said. Kasper shifts from watching her, to me, with something strange in his expression, as if he wants to warn me to stop.

Well, fuck him, it's not his business.

Draven hurries up the stairs, and before I can point him to Amaya's room, he's leading me into a different one next to hers. It's blessedly empty.

When I turn to him, he's already on top of me. I back into the wall, my chest tight from the thrill of what comes next, and then his hands cage me against it, his mouth crashing against my neck and I arch my chest into his.

His lips move sloppier now. I blame the drinks for his teeth-dragging scratches. Unlike the claim, it hurts, as if it's unintentional. I lace my hand through his hair, gripping it like before, but he doesn't stop, as if between whatever happened then and now he's forgotten our silent language.

"What did the guards want you for?" My nerves spike, demanding we slow down.

"What's it matter?" His voice is rough, throaty.

Is he upset? Did something happen? His hips pin against mine, but it doesn't drag out the warmth it did before. The fabric only scratches now, not as soft as I remember. I shift under him.

"Talk to me." My hands move to either side of his face, but his grip only pins them back behind my head. The other braces against the wall, nails extending until he's slicing holes into the wallpaper.

"What do you want to hear, little pet?" His hips slam into mine again, and this time it really hurts. My head clacks against the wall and then his lips crash against mine and he tastes . . . like sea salt and vanilla. But not the food, more like I've bitten into a candle. There's something false there. I pull away and his hand grasps my throat, the kiss lengthening, and his hair smells *wrong*. Hot sand, seaweed, and a sweat that's not his.

I know what Prince Draven smells like.

I know what he fucking tastes like.

This is not him.

I buck, kneeing the impostor in the groin, and he drops, but he grabs my tarot pack off the belt at my hip as he does. I wipe his spit from my mouth, my anger roiling in my gut as I glare down at him. Whoever he is, he's so fucking dead.

His skin morphs, rippling until Morgan kneels in front of me. Gaunter and angrier.

What is this? How did he get out?

I go to drop my mental shield, ready to create a little opening to blast my scream of danger down to Draven. He'll tear this piece of garbage apart in an instant, though there might be nothing left of him by the time I am done with him.

But then changelings are closing in—from the bathroom that links to Amaya's room, others coming out of the closet. They're all masked, and since it's a masquerade I'm sure no one even questioned it. The door snaps shut.

I hesitate, heart racing as I scrutinize my attackers. My hands curl to fists. I may not have my cards, but I am going to beat the ever-loving shit out of them.

"Don't even think about it, Rune," Morgan sneers. "We've infiltrated every inch of this party. Ember? Felix? Wynter? They're the first to fall."

"I know about your shields and I'll know if you try to warn the prince." One of the girls taps her temple, slowly, raw anger in her eyes. "If you so much as holler for Draven mentally or verbally, then our people will kill your friends."

"What shields, Fallon?" one of the strangers demands, and my eyes go wide. He's talking to the girl whose boyfriend was killed in sparring. My gaze snaps to her. She's a hollow thin thing now, and with the full mask I didn't recognize her.

"No names, you idiot!"

I think of those girls sidling up to Wynter below and glance to her hand where the High Priestess card glimmers. The pressure of her power crashes against my mental shields, encircling them. Thankfully holding this mental barrier is something I can continue even without my cards.

Morgan gets to his feet now, walking off the limp I put in his step.

"Rune, you're going to stay here, silently, while my friends take care of your little boyfriend next door." He wipes his mouth with the back of his hand.

I notice a little patch along the back of the fingerless glove, a red fist. Draven and I knew that the Ten Spires Clan that Morgan belonged to had links to the uprising, but I didn't think that Morgan of all people was capable of an actual plot. With him in the Boiler, we'd put discussion of him to rest, free to focus on the Artifacts and training, but now . . .

"Arcadia isn't as guarded as they *thought*." Morgan rolls his neck, and I notice how much thinner he is from the last time I saw him. His face more hollowed, burn marks trailing the backs of his arms. He's spent over a month in the Boiler. "The Ten Spires is working with the descendants of the uprising." He flexes that glove for me to see. "And the Ascension has risen right on their doorstep."

"Fifteen years to come up with a better name and they circled back to the Ascension?" Rolling my eyes, I glance to the other room. Draven's not there yet, though I'm betting they're about to lure him in. "What exactly is your plan here? You going to prance in there as me, Morgan? Give him a lap dance and then assassinate him?"

"I won't be doing it, but yes." Morgan nods to a change-ling girl with dark hair and pale skin. She summons the Moon Arcana, transforming into—

"That's the best *me* you have?" I laugh. Her hair is too silver, she's too damn tall, and her legs are sticklike compared to mine.

"You didn't fool me. She certainly won't fool *him*." It's the truth. "You saw his hands on me. You think he'll suddenly for-get what I feel like? Smell like? Taste like? *This* is the best plan you can come up with? Walk away."

Everyone's silent, and I take in the other changelings, and to my surprise a few are full druids. One draws his Devil Arcana. "We can go my way, lure him in with a figment."

His illusion casting is pretty solid, his version of me far more believable than the blood-and-bone replica. But it's not quite right either, and Morgan curses before turning to me, disgust written all over him. The feeling's more than mutual.

"Then I guess you're going in there." He steps so close he's nearly standing on my toes. "You bind him up with your magic that is now linked to mine." He runs his finger along every card in my deck before sticking them back in my holster. They're thoroughly tainted now.

"What are you even thinking? You'll get everyone here killed, and yourself," I hiss, trying to make him see sense. If not for his sake, then for the rest of the changelings here.

They don't want justice. They want punishment. I can't tell these idiots what Draven and I are planning, or his vision for both Arcadia and the mortal realms—not only would it break my pact, but they wouldn't believe me. I try to appeal to their fury, recognizing it as my own when I first arrived. "I get it. I understand what the immortals have done to us. But this isn't the way to fix things. This is going to make things a thousand times worse for mortals and changelings. You kill one of their royals? They will come down on your quaint rebellion like a boot on an anthill."

"The Ascension is bigger than you realize. Overthrowing the immortal royals will create chaos and allow us a chance at ending their reign over us." His breath is rancid against my face. "And we have a place to fall back to. One that will let us bring these changeling powers back over the Wall to help our families!"

I let loose a dark laugh.

"Then they're a bunch of liars, as are you. Druids don't Select anyone with someone to return to." I scoff, grinning with as much spite as I can muster.

Morgan slaps me hard, staggering me into the wall.

I'm barely able to hold myself up, and he reaches for my throat, but I claw his hand away, scratching a gouge across his face. "You touch me again, and I'll tear your gods damned eyes out."

"You go in there and tie him down, or we kill all your little friends," Morgan growls.

"You wouldn't. They're your friends, too." But I don't like the darkness in his eyes, the way he doesn't even blink at the thought.

"No, they're not. They're just tools. Like you are. The Ascension came to free me. And we need a weapon of *vengeance*, and tonight it's going to be you."

21

Nightmares

The Moon card represents the blurred line between reality and illusion—like moonlight reflected on water, where a single stone can make the mirrored image waver. Our perception may be a deception.

THEY SHOVE ME into Amaya's room. Morgan moves back against the wall and the Devil Arcana begins to weave his magic around the space, until they've disappeared. The bedroom is as spare as it seemed the first time I visited, a few weeks ago for a study session. There are little pops of pink accessories, but for the most part it's a black metal-framed bed, a desk, and a wardrobe.

Footsteps sound from the hallway and the next thing I know Draven's passing by the room. I don't make a sound, praying he'll keep walking. But as if he's magnetized to me, he backtracks, pawing the door open. He leans against it, eyeing me up.

"Does this mean we're turning in early, love?"

The way his body is curled into the opening, mask forgotten, the length of him leaning so lazily against it has my body molten, linked to every primal movement of his. The moonlight highlights his tight waist, those broad shoulders, the hollows of his cheekbones.

"Draven . . ." Gods, this would be so hot if I wasn't terrified. I can't do this. Not to him. His grin spreads like flame doused in oil as he drinks me in.

"I love the way you say my name." He leans forward, as though I have him on a fucking string, but he manages to resist fully walking in. Morgan was right. I am the key to getting Draven. And I hate that in this moment. I want to scream at him to run, guilt eating me alive.

Okay, okay, think. Fucking *think*, Rune.

He's hot. He wants me. But he's also smart. Wickedly, deliciously cunning.

I can figure out how to tell him about the danger without saying a word.

I force a calm over my body, meeting his eye as I step back toward the bed.

He pushes off the doorjamb, hands in his pockets as he crosses the distance to me. I'm reminded just how tall he is, my tilted chin barely reaching his collarbone.

Whatever happens in this room, he needs to walk out of it alive.

He tucks a white curl behind my pointed ears, his forehead touching mine, thumb caressing my neck. My heart liquefies in my chest, seeping between my ribs as his tone turns tender.

"We don't have to be anything but what we are here, Rune. I don't want to take anything you aren't willing to give."

"There's nothing to give. I'm already yours." My words have him checking his vow-inked tattoo. But it was the truth.

Draven's mouth edges into a hungry smile, and his power causes the door to snick shut. I step out of my boots and kick them against the wall, hopefully right into Morgan's tiny crotch, but I can't see them hit anything. If they did, the Devil Arcana must cover it and the sound. But it draws Draven's attention to the other open door. Good. He'll have to splice through the illusion to shut it.

Come on. To my disappointment, his shadows curl around the handle, closing it softly without resistance. The Devil Arcana must be good, better than I thought, though there's still a hint of wrong lighting and oddly shaped shadows.

I sit on the bed, leaving a space for Draven to join me.

He does, leaning back, his wings lazily spread, nothing rushed about the way he moves. Not like the sick impersonation Morgan portrayed, shoving and pushing and—

"Rune, you seem nervous." Draven's wing curls around me, so feather-soft, the gentlest nudge. "You know . . . we don't have to—"

"Quiet," I demand, and press my lips to his. No one can know our plans. No one can know this thing between us isn't fully real. At least that it isn't yet.

His eyes close but I keep mine open, checking all the corners before focusing back on his face. His brows stop tensing together, relax, and look nearly blissful. And for just a moment, I let myself enjoy him.

I press my tongue into him more deeply, and he lets me set the pace, responding with relish. He tastes *good*. I move to his neck, climbing into his lap.

"Rune," he moans. His hands travel my thighs; he groans in the back of his throat as he continues caressing bare skin.

It peaks me, and I ball his shirt into my fists. I grasp Draven's hands and he lets me, our fingers interlocking as I press them down against the bed.

I've wanted him since the moment I laid eyes on him, and I've fought it every second since. All I can think to do is buy us more time, until I can figure out what to try next. I'd be lying if I said I wasn't enjoying him, but I hate that there's an audience for this.

Draven growls, "I've been thinking about this every moment since the claim."

"Only since then?" My heart stills.

"Honestly? Since you were on your knees before me at the Selection." One of his hands escapes my grasp, gripping between thigh and backside. I know his thumb will be tracing in wet if it moves any closer.

The temptation to give in overwhelms me as he pleads, "Let me taste you."

"You are," I tell him, sucking those lips against mine, his kiss better than any sex that came before him.

His thumb does move against me at that, firmly splitting me until he reaches my apex, and I gasp against him. Why does this have to be happening now?

"You know what I mean." The violet in his eyes turns magenta, linked with primal desire.

I regretfully pull his hand away, shoving it into the pillow again.

I want to beg him to run, despite the hypnotic movements of his hands, the rhythmic lift of his hips, but that High Priestess Arcana can send the order to strike at any moment.

I have no choice. And knowing that doesn't make it any easier. I release the kiss, filling my mind's eye with all the faces of my friends who will be slaughtered should I mess this up.

I push against his chest, and he gets the message, crawling back toward the headboard.

I need to get his hands tied, but my cards are linked to Morgan now, which means he controls them until they're reset. Morgan's grubby hands leaving stains on everything.

"Me first." I lock my hands against his hard enough he doesn't fight it.

"By all means . . . ruin me, Rune," Draven begs, bedroom eyes watching me.

I mouth his neck and then whisper in his ear, "Do you trust me?"

His eyes open a bit more, doubt swirling in their depths. He grins. "Gods, no."

"Then let me prove myself," I say, eyes lifting to the spot Morgan and his traitors lay in wait. Draven's gaze follows curiously, and I add more loudly, "Feel my desires for yourself." I can't drop my shields, but he said earlier he could sense what I was feeling. Hoping to hells that's true, I let every ounce of fear blaze through me like a tidal wave through a flood bank. Too much to be withheld.

His hands stop roving, gripping my waist harder, eyes darting between mine as though he doesn't understand what he's reading off me. I lean forward and whisper in his ear, "Tie yourself to the headboard." Keeping my hands bracketed around his own, my gaze flicks to where Morgan and his cowards hide again. I feel him trying to get past my mental wards, but I won't let him in, I can't.

A steely suspicion lingers in the dark indigo of his eyes, but we're out of time. This needs to happen before they realize.

I summon the Magician and press my magic into the curtain ties behind the headboard, changing them subtly, just the color of the rope in case Morgan can sense my power being used. I need him to think I'm the one about to bind Draven to this headboard and so I wrap them around Draven's wrists, however loosely. A second later I'm shifting my body to cover Draven's tattoo flashing, his cards on his hip glowing faintly as his magic blazes across the bonds, binding his hands. I stay straddled above him, pushing myself back. "That's a good princeling, let's make sure these bonds are tight, after all . . . the devil's in the details."

His brow rises, and I hope to hells he understands what I'm implying. My gaze flicks meaningfully toward their hiding spots again but his attention stays locked on to me.

I call over my shoulder, "You can come out now, you cravens."

They reveal themselves one at a time, slipping out of the illusion soundlessly, wolves moving in on a helpless kill. Draven's eyes widen, shifting to yellow as he looks from me to them, and I know his trust in me is irrevocably compromised.

I lured him inside, knew they were there the whole time, and said nothing. Guilt gnaws at my bones. I can't meet the fire burning in his gaze, a red glow forming that I hope to never witness again.

"I'm sorry," I say, but then one of them forces me off his lap, the heat in me dissipating. I'm shoved roughly against the wall, out of everyone's way, and they circle him, trapped on that bed.

"He's secure?" Morgan's every syllable holds suspicion.

Draven's eyes lock on to him, turning red, ignoring the rest.

"No one's going anywhere." I demand, "You'll release the others?"

"Yes," Morgan says, distracted by his catch.

"What are you going to do with Draven?" I growl.

"Quiet her," Morgan orders.

One of the unnaturally strong Strength Arcana grabs me and puts a hand over my mouth, and I go silent. The tattoo on my inner forearm burns like fire as my trust with Draven draws taut. My shields open a fraction, my eyes closing as I remove a brick from the wall, sending a fist through the concrete to find Draven on the other side.

Even in my mind he seems muted.

They're leftovers of the uprising, calling themselves the Ascension. They're using my friends as hostages. They said they'd kill them if I didn't do this, or if I opened my shields to warn you. I wait for a reaction, for something snarky, or scathing, but he's silent. Begging, I say, *Please, Draven. I'm so fucking sorry.*

Fallon lurks nearby, like a monster looking for any crack in the foundation, and her attention shoots up at me. My shields reform as she snarls, "Knock that shit off."

"Did she warn anyone?" Morgan asks, suddenly tense.

"No, just pathetic groveling." Fallon crosses her arms, but her powers press around me, viselike, a headache blaring around my temples.

"What do you want?" Draven asks Morgan, distracting them, his voice terribly calm. He never replied to me mind to mind. Maybe he never will again.

"Revenge." Morgan's fangs descend. "Though it doesn't have to be taken on you. It's your father we want to punish. So, who takes our rage is going to be your choice."

"I can't just call him here." Draven shrugs despite the awkwardness of his tied hands. The snark laced in his tone sparks a flame of hope in the darkness clouding my thoughts. "*So, I guess you'll have to do your worst to me, great avenger.*"

Morgan's eyes slit, his face curled into an animalistic snarl as he spews, "You're enough revenge for me. You chose me, and unwittingly sealed your fate. Then I saw how you looked at Rune. It made you so easy to get to. You threw me in the Boiler for six weeks, but our people broke me out tonight. Having Ward threaten your guards drew them all away, and now you're ours."

Draven's cloying sarcasm thickens the air. "Do you want to hear me applaud your cleverness? Afraid you'll have to untie me for that."

"So much condescension. What else should I expect from someone who's so elitist, so entitled?" Rage fuels Morgan's every movement, from his popping veins, to the spittle at the edges of his mouth. "My mother hanged herself when my little sister was Selected to go with the elves. I was left alone to wallow in fucking poverty until the Ten Spires came recruiting. But you gave me purpose when you Selected me, Draven. You stupidly handed me power. The power to kill immortal royalty."

Something about hearing the worst of my wants flung from another's mouth leaves me sick. I want the immortal royals to pay, but not Draven. He wants better. He's one of us.

Morgan holds a knife against Draven's bare throat, and my heart stops.

"You should get in line behind Rune," Draven says from the bed.

Shit.

Morgan casts the words aside, eyes blazing. "You're going to take a hundred blades, like what they gave my father for participating in the uprising. And you're not gonna call out for your guards. Fallon will know if you do. If you call for help, I'll take your punishment out on her instead." Morgan points the dagger at me.

"That's a little tempting considering she got me into this bind." The ghost of a smile hints Draven's full lips. In my mind there's a little warmth emanating from him though, a reassurance. The burning underlayment of my tattoo lessens.

"I don't buy it. Anyone can see how badly you want her." Morgan nods at me and I hate the enjoyment sparking in his eyes as he takes in my fear, then Draven's, breaking through the performance.

"You're right," Draven acknowledges, and my heart cracks open, because I can tell that's true. He looks at me, a promise pressed in that glance, like petals on a page. Then his attention flits to Morgan. "But there's a problem with your plan. My hands are free."

The ropes dissolve. I never tied them with magic. But he did, kept them on to hear whatever he needed to of Morgan's plan. He's been in control this whole time.

I hear him clearly, mind to mind, when he breaks through my shields, *Get down!*

I drop, hands over my head as darkness floods the room, Draven's power blasting through the bedroom like a bomb. When I look up, coughing from the debris and blood, I spot him standing in the center of the room, golden magic glowing around him in an orbit, the World Arcana and what seems like half the Major Arcana drawn, too. I join his side, the two of us standing back-to-back as the Ascendants stagger to their feet.

I can't use my Arcana, as Morgan still has a hold on it, but I don't need magic.

As if reading my mind, Draven pulls twin daggers from the inside of his jacket, placing their familiar weight into my hand. I put one in each, bracing my back against his as the Ascendants rush us from all sides.

I let Draven take my weight as I lean back and kick one rebel in the knee, dislocating it, pushing off Draven's back and thigh as I dodge forward, sliding and slicing another rebel's hamstring. Draven's magic is brutal, shadows flooding every corner, ripping those trying to escape back by their ankles.

I fight my way to Fallon, noticing how she's clutching her temple in the corner, as if she's sending out a silent order. I smash my fist into her skull and she drops to the ground.

Behind me, Draven summons his sword, holding a rebel by the throat.

"We should keep them alive to question them," I shout.

"Fine." His voice is short, and he rolls his eyes as if not killing them is an inconvenience.

He draws Death, opening a portal. He shoves the rebel through it, screaming, and his sword shrinks back into a ring on his finger. I grasp Fallon by the collar and toss her through it, too.

The two of us divide the room, Draven's portals opening for me to kick or push rebels through, the rest of his magic blocking the doors and allowing him to fight whoever's left.

We work completely in sync, silent and rageful.

The brawny Strength Arcana who'd pinned me before comes charging at me like a bull. I flick one of the knives into his thigh, bracing myself with the other. Then he's on me, swinging his fists wildly. I dodge under his arm as he connects with the wall and leaves a sizable hole. He's all muscle, no skill. I strike with my fist, hitting select pressure points that knock his arm out of socket. He wails, his dominant hand suddenly limp before I use my heel to drop him, knocking a knee out of place.

Lightning crackles near me, and I'm distracted by a Tower Arcana, electricity warping around his fist. For all my Wraith skills, I'm nothing next to this. I can't fistfight a thunderstorm.

Draven's voice, dark as midnight, rolls over us. "Oh no you don't."

Draven summons the Sun, a whip of plasma lashing out and grasping the guy's forearm, scalding burns across his flesh, causing him to drop his Tower card, and Draven yanks him and the last remaining Ascendants through a portal. The room is suddenly quiet as we're finally left alone, every portal closing.

He clenches his fist, and I don't know how to begin to apologize. I don't exactly have a lot of experience with it.

He stares at me as if he's waiting for an explanation. I open my mouth—but someone grabs me from behind.

Morgan.

He must've been hiding under the bed like a coward.

Morgan clutches me to him, glowering at Draven as if he's the Prince of Hells. Maybe he is. Draven bears his fangs, but Morgan pulls a knife and holds it against my throat. Draven goes deathly still.

"What did you do with them?" Morgan asks Draven, his hand trembling and I try hard not to flinch against the shaking blade.

"The same thing I'm going to do with you." Draven's eyes dart to me, holding steady, as Morgan grits his teeth.

"You're not taking me anywhere. I'll take this blood traitor to hells with me—" Morgan cuts off as I stab one knife into his forearm, the other into his thigh. He screams, dropping the knife. I grasp his arm and flip him over my body, and he thuds onto the floorboards.

I'm still the fucking Wraith of Westfall.

I doubt he'll ever forget it.

Draven bears down on him and lifts Morgan off the ground by the front of his tunic.

"What was that you said about a hundred knives? About vengeance?" Draven snarls at Morgan, his voice too deep and raw to match the smooth tenor I've grown accustomed to.

"Fuck you and your little whore."

Draven draws the World to the forefront, inverting it, and Morgan squirms harder, crying piteously as the magic blares into him. No . . . out of him. Draven strips Morgan's power from him, stripping the Arcana from his body. Golden dust is seemingly drawn out from his very soul, regurgitating from his throat and dissipating in the air. But Draven doesn't stop, and Morgan begins to crumble, the magic devouring his essence.

I turn away, clenching my eyes shut, my last glimpse of Morgan reminding me of grapes too long off the vine, curdled to dusty brown husks. A mass drops, the resulting vibration in the floorboards too light to match how much Morgan should weigh, but I can tell by the odd grime in the air that it's *him*. My stomach sours, but I force my eyes open.

Starlight trickles off Draven as his power winds down, illuminating him and me. I should be terrified by the sheer might of his power, but instead I'm only scared by how close I came to losing him.

"Draven?" I want him to look at me. I'd prefer the mercy of his fury over the cold unresponsiveness that seeps from him now, staring vaguely forward, not saying anything. I force my throat clear. "Draven? Are you all right?"

He looks toward me, but his eyes don't reach mine, settling at my knees. "Are you hurt?" His voice is awfully quiet.

"No," I breathe. "Are you?"

The door slams open and guards rush the space, swords out, bows drawn, and magic searching every corner.

Draven ignores my question and turns to whoever the leader is and mutters, "There are more in the party near Rune's friends. We need to find out who they are and how many there are. All but one I sent to the Boiler. Take Rune back to our Hearth and guard her—"

I grasp his hand and when he turns to me, I swear I've never seen that kind of hurt before.

"No, I can help." My eyes are steady on his. "We should start with questioning Kasper."

22

Interrogation

The Nine of Wands often represents the last stand, a line drawn in the sands as the weight of trials and tribulations press down. Success must come at a cost, with the scars to prove it.

T HE BOILER IS a small outlying building located close to the volcano. It's a grim, miserable place, swelling with blistering heat, and it's built like a dungeon. The walls are made of granite stone and concrete, lined with chains and cuffs that make my skin crawl. Every cell contains one of tonight's attackers, transported directly here by Draven.

He and I stand in a boxy room connected to a private cell, watching Kasper through a window. He's strapped to a chair, his skin chafing from the steel.

I told Draven all about my suspicions that Kasper wanted to be Selected. How he watched me, nearly regretfully, when Morgan imitated Draven and led me up those stairs. I don't know how much he knew, but I intend to find out.

The raven tattoo against my forearm prickles like acid.

"We need him to admit whatever he knows," Draven states, eyes sweeping over me in a brush of frustration. "We have others to question."

"Could you just use the High Priestess to dig around his head a bit?"

"I tried on the way here, but he has a mental shield in place." Draven's lip curls and he shakes his head. "He's chosen by the High Priestess Arcana, and one of the very first things they learn is mental shielding. He's unusually talented. And even though I have more training, it's not like reading a book. I could push . . . but those obstinate shields might require breaking your friend permanently. And what if he has no involvement?"

He side-eyes me, as if daring me to say it's okay, but I begrudgingly shake my head, thinking of Ember. "Right, well, we can't do that to him."

Draven's arms cross, the angry detachment in his gaze more worrying than the anger that flared before. He clears his throat. "You used to gather intelligence for a living. Any ideas?" He's never looked at me so critically before. My ribs tighten, my stomach growing nauseous. I need to prove myself. I cannot find my family without his trust.

But there's more to it than that.

I *want* him to trust me.

"Can he see us?" I gesture to the window, but Kasper has only glanced at it.

"No, it's been transfigured by a Magician Arcana. It works only one way; the other side appears as just a wall."

"Pull your guards." I shift as he looks to me, eyes narrowing. "You just have to trust me."

He looks me over, smirking slowly. "As far as I can throw you."

Some of the tension eases from my chest, a sieve opening that lets me breathe a little more freely. I nod, and he summons the

High Priestess, and the guards react as one, all of them suddenly exiting, leaving Kasper alone in that chair, more confused than ever.

I pass by Draven, steeling myself before I enter. I fiddle with the handle, jiggling it like it's locked, then slip inside, shutting it swiftly behind me, looking around the room as if afraid of seeing anyone else. When I spot Kasper, I rush ahead to him. "There you are. Thank the gods. Morgan said you'd been grabbed."

"He's . . . he's alive?" Kasper's brow furrows, suspicion raging in his skittish eyes, his scrunched forehead. "You're not a part of the Ascension."

So, he knows the name. Who's involved. I rush my words as I fiddle with the manacles binding his hands behind his back. "Morgan recruited me, and I've been heading the operation since he got locked away. You saw me—I wanted to get Selected for a reason, this is it. I managed to distract the guards, but that won't last long. We need to get you out of here before they come back and execute you."

"They're going to kill me?"

"They found letters, Ascension paraphernalia back in your room. You were sloppy." I bluff and he jerks, looking up at me with a plea in those icy-blue eyes.

"That's not mine. You have to talk to your boyfriend. Convince him I'm not involved—"

"My cover's blown. Draven was just a mark." I swallow, knowing he's currently listening and watching this whole performance. But he'll know why I said it.

"Why are you helping me at all?" Kasper shakes his head, watching me over his shoulder as I pull a thin hairpin from my curls and begin to fiddle with his locks, making a show of it. "I told Morgan no. I told him it was a stupid idea."

"You're not with the Ascension?"

"No."

"But you wanted to be Selected. You hate the immortals. You told Morgan you agreed with the sentiment of this plan." I stop fiddling, like I won't help him if he isn't one of them. His jaw ticks, eyes searching as if he's thinking through his options.

"Look, I'm not here for rebellion. I'm here for . . . someone else." Kasper spits the words and my eyes narrow.

"Who? Draven?" I keep fiddling with his chains, never popping the lock.

"No. I don't give a fuck about him."

"Then who?" I lean forward, still pretending to pick his lock, but he claps his jaw shut. "If you weren't in on this plan, why did you give me that look when I left with Morgan? You thought he might hurt me, and you did nothing. Why didn't you warn me?" The heat of the room is smothering, yet the knowledge of what Morgan did, and what worse he would've done, is what steals my breath.

"I . . . don't know." Kasper hangs his head, suddenly unable to look at me.

"At the Wall, you stood at the front. Near me, like you *wanted* to be Selected. Why? Who are you after?"

"It won't interfere with whatever the Ascension is planning—"

"I'll be the judge of that." I unbind one wrist, but his other one is still manacled. I stop, crossing my arms and leering over him. "Tell me the truth or I'll leave you to get executed."

He turns as white as fresh snow.

"I'm looking for my father." At least he's capable of uttering one truth. Now I have a baseline, though it's hard to see straight beyond my seeping rage.

"Your father? Aren't you the son of . . . a countess? Your father was obnoxiously rich if I remember—"

"Stepfather," he snarls.

I hadn't forgotten, but it's nice to know it's a tender point. The more sensitive the subject, the easier the knife can slice through. "He was rich. It doesn't mean I was."

I grab his palms, flipping them. My own hold scars, nicks, calluses, but his are fresh as a child's. "Your hands beg to differ."

"He let me live there, but when my mom died, I wasn't welcome any longer. My mother had an affair with an immortal," Kasper confesses, tugging at the restraint.

I blink back my shock, eyes glancing at the wall Draven watches from behind. Kasper's hair is very nearly white . . . like mine, but it's so platinum it's more silver. But his relation to immortals is more direct.

"Who is he?" I ask.

"All I know is he was important enough to be in a vanguard of immortals sent to broker peace during the War. She didn't exactly elaborate. Wanted to pass me off as being the Lord of Shadowfell, though he never bought it. I thought . . . maybe he was a druid, she mentioned he had wings."

"You risked being Selected on the off chance you'd find your father?"

"Sound familiar?" Kasper raises a brow.

"My situation is a little different. I knew who my father was—"

"You sure about that?" he snarls. "Your dad seemed pretty cozy with the seraph princess. Heard he's the right hand to the seraph king."

I tilt my head, reading him over. "It's really obvious when you're trying to buy yourself time, you know?"

Kasper startles, shifting uncomfortably.

"And you don't know anything of more value, do you?"

He looks quickly off to his right, as if searching his mind for some answer.

But I already can tell he doesn't have one.

Draven steps inside the cell and Kasper's gaze goes wide, his pupils pinpricks. He looks back and forth between us and breathes, "I wasn't involved with this. I've got nothing to do with her."

"I heard." Draven turns to me. "Do you believe him?"

I sigh but nod reluctantly. Kasper came here for an ulterior motive, the same as me, but it has nothing to do with the Ascension, even though he knew about it. Draven draws forth the World, then summons the Hierophant to the front, walking the memories of this questioning back, erasing them from existence. Afterward he draws the Emperor, and the last cuff releases, allowing Kasper to go free. Draven brings the Hierophant back to the forefront, and tells him commandingly, "You didn't have a good time at the party. You chose to go home early."

"The party wasn't fun. I'm going to go home." Kasper repeats the sentence blankly, as if he's half awake. He stands up and walks out of the room, the same dissociated look haunting his eye.

His departure leaves Draven and I alone.

The tension strung between us is nearly painful. My attention flits to the wall, and I know guards could be behind it. "Was getting him to confess a test for me?"

"Yes and no." Draven shirks his jacket off, displaying all those strong muscles pressing against the fabric of his shirt. He follows my look. "We're alone. I sent them to interrogate the others."

"But you still have questions for me." I sit in the chair Kasper vacated and he rolls his eyes. It burns my skin, uncomfortable though not intolerable. But I might as well be in the right seat if I'm about to be grilled next.

"I did want to see you put your Wraith skills to the test." He clenches his jaw, glancing to the walls as if it's easier than looking at me. "But I want you. You know that. You used it to make a fool of me."

The vulnerability and outrage in his voice has me squirming more than if he held a knife under my fingernails. "It wasn't fake." My voice pitches in a horrid, scratchy way. I force it clear. "Nothing was. Even with assassins surrounding us. I still wanted . . ." but I cannot bring myself to say "you" because although I know it would not break our deal, it would break *me*. Unexpected tears roll down my cheeks. "I never meant to hurt you."

He drags a chair from near the door, sitting on it backward, facing mine, rolling up his sleeves in the broiling heat of the space until I can see the jaguar tattoo representing me, mixed among the other whorls. His gaze never lifts past my collarbone, and whatever else has happened tonight, knowing he cannot look at me is the worst of it.

"You and I are in a perpetual game of truths." He nods to the raven tattoo burned across my forearm. "But trust is still an earned thing. So, tell me, was I just a mark to you, Rune?"

"No." My lower lip trembles and I force it to flatten, like linen beneath an iron.

Draven's gaze finally lifts to mine and sticks, caught in the honeyed promise of a syllable.

"I knew you were powerful but didn't want you for it. Powerful men tend to be cruel. Immortals more so, at least I thought. You teased but never bullied, and I pretended to hate you to hide how badly I wanted you. Anything else blossomed despite all odds, fruit growing from salted earth."

He swallows, but his eyes don't soften. "Why did *you* want to be Selected?"

"To be reunited with my family." A crease forms between my brows. "You know this."

"And you craved vengeance, for yourself and mortals." Draven steeples his fingers together. "But I want to know why you came searching for this now. It's been years since your family was taken. You'd already made a life for yourself. So why did the Wraith of Westfall come seeking her vendetta *this* year?"

"I tried getting Selected the last two years. I was worried if I waited longer, it wouldn't happen." I swipe sweat from my forehead, baking in this heat. My gut seeps in dread as we circle a truth I've avoided. "If there was a year to throw it all on the line, it should be this one."

"You're not being fully honest with me. I looked into you." He swallows, eyes narrowed. Of course he did, he's too clever to not have. "You'd moved on, fought for your new title, a new life. Five years at the Lord of Westfall's side, his star pupil, his protégé rumored to inherit it all one day. But then you burned down his manor, left him a bloodied mess, and ensured you'd be Selected. So why now?"

His gaze is narrowed, but there's a vulnerability in the question that I deduce means he's still wondering if he's been the target of a different game. A pawn on my board.

"When my mother was taken, our house was burned to ash." I let the sweat drip down my back. "I had nothing. No house. No money. Not even a spare set of clothes. Just these boots and what I had on. At first, I begged on street corners for food. Then I stole. I became pretty good at picking locks and pockets. When the Winter Ball arrived, I posed as a servant and slipped into the Lord of Westfall's manor. I made it into his vault, but then a serving girl spotted me. If I'd have killed her . . . my life would've been different, and I would've had the money to start fresh. But . . . I couldn't, and she alerted the guards. The Lord of Westfall found it amusing." Despite the heat, chills run up my arms, my legs, as I remember his dark laughter. "He spun me a choice. To shut me in that vault until my skin rotted away, or to work for him. I chose the path of survival."

"The Lord of Westfall, that's Thane Blackwell, right?"

"Yes." His name sends shivers up my spine. "He used his parties, at first, to send me to a man, to devour his secrets and gather the blackmail like building a nest of thorns, and when the Lord of Westfall was ready he could send one of us to impale them on it. There were a few of us who worked for him like that. His Shrikes. He broke us against each other, and his Blades trained us to fight. But soon the other girls became more family than anything; all of us had come from the same damn places. There was a final test, for a chance to become his Wraith. It was coveted, a Court position, and we'd be spared from the worst aspects of the job. He called the rite the Hunting Grounds. The best entered. Nobody realized the goal was for only one of us to walk out of it. He told me later he designed it all for me, so he could be sure I was everything he'd made me to be. Spies and Shrikes were more common than fleas in a place like Westfall, but only the best could be his Wraith."

Draven's eyes turn a deep, haunting blue, but he stays blessedly silent.

"Working for him is where I met Kiana."

I notice the slight twitch in his brow, recognizing her name from our nights in bed, from the echo of her in my thoughts. He knows this story ends in tragedy, but he doesn't speak, only gives me room to breathe it into the world.

"We survived it all together, and she made it all bearable. We dreamed of escaping, moving to the Isle of Riches. But when the position for Wraith came up, Thane kept insisting I try. He favored me, we all knew it, but I wanted to get away from him, not closer. At the last minute, Kiana entered, so I did, too, think- ing I was protecting her. It came down to the two of us. I refused to kill her." I drop my gaze from his, but it doesn't stop the tears flowing over. "So, she took her own life just to spare mine."

The feelings I've tried to hold back from that day pour out now, and for just a moment I let them consume me, like oil catch- ing fire. I grit my teeth and force out the rest. "I didn't want to spit on her sacrifice. I let him use me. I became his Wraith, noth- ing more than a phantom trapped in my own body doing his bidding. I was a shadow of my former self. He was abusive, con- trolling. He grew obsessed with me." My hands twist in my lap. I take a deep breath, letting the heartbreak rise like a swelling tide and then release, dragging all those heavy emotions with it.

"The master and apprentice relationship grew increasingly twisted. I still don't know if he saw me as his prodigy, adop- tive daughter, or something darker. He was impossible to read, his mood fluctuating in mountains and valleys. But he resented that I blamed him for Kiana's death. I always will. He knew I'd attempt to be chosen in the Selection again and tried to con- vince me to stay by bringing her little sister to his manor. He presented her to me like a pet."

My heart hammers, body trembling as the rage ignites in my chest. The same fury I felt that day when I finally snapped on Thane. My teeth grind together until I finally glance at Draven, his knuckles white as he clenches the back of his chair.

I growl, "I cut open his face like a six-pointed star and left him in a pool of his own blood, burning that gaudy fucking manor to the ground. I smuggled Kiana's sister to Fenn, and when Reapers called for Westfall to be in the Selection, I returned, desperate to be chosen." I meet his indigo eyes, wondering if he'll damn me the moment I'm done talking. "There was nowhere left for me to go. I was willing to burn down the world just to feel warmth again. The only people I had left were over that Wall, and the only way back to them . . . was forward."

Slowly he stands up, and to my shock extends his hand. "Don't surrender that fire just yet." His eyes travel over me. "I'm still owed a partner."

Relief releases in my chest as my palm slides into his and he lifts me to my feet.

"Even if I somehow find my mother and brother and save my father . . . there's nowhere for us to return to. If I go back to the mortal realms, we'd have to leave the continent to escape my bounty." It would likely still follow me. There's no place in that world I'll be safe. My chest tightens as we breathe in each other's air. "I should've told you all of it when we made our pact."

"It's okay. We all have our pasts. You can bring your family here. They'll be safe so long as I hold my crown." There's a softening between us. "I'll never force you to . . . be any of that to me. I'm not Thane. I meant what I promised. At the end of this . . . you can walk away."

"What if I don't want to?" The words fall quickly.

A twinkle sparks to life in his eyes, shifting them magenta. "Then when that day comes . . . stay." He blinks, tucking his dark hair back behind his ear, running a tongue over those canines. He teases, "But as for now, I'm still pretty pissed."

"Then I'll have to figure out how to stop you from hating me tomorrow."

He shakes his head, a begrudging smirk lifting his lips. "You might be the only person in this world I don't hate."

23

Alfheim

The elves burrow their cities beneath the mountains,
lining their subterranean homes with diamonds broken
from the earth at their whim. They are the wealthiest
of the four kingdoms, and by far the most vain.

—A History of Arcadia

THE NEXT MORNING, I wake to Magda sweeping through my room, throwing open the curtains. I sit upright in bed and yank the comforter to my chest, realizing I'm just in a loose shirt of Draven's and my underwear. We weren't yet warm enough with each other to share a bed again, so instead he gave me this, and my bra is discarded over the nearest armchair.

Magda crosses over to it, but I fly out of the bed, grabbing it first, and stuffing it away.

"Please don't feel like you need to do my laundry," I say quickly. "In fact, you don't need to clean my room at all." If she doesn't, maybe Draven will stop finding spying crystals tucked all over it.

"Trust me, girl, I'd rather I didn't have to. But the king insists his son and Draven's 'royal pet' have a tidy home whilst he's away at school." Magda grabs the basket of dirty clothes, looking put out, but I'm too busy feeling scorned by her words to give a damn.

"Is that his name for me, or yours?"

Magda pauses, lifting a suitcase I've never seen onto the velvet padded window seat.

"The king's. The Court's, too." Her tone is softer this time. She looks me over, but there's no anger there, just suspicion. It softens when her eyes track to the bite mark at my neck. "You're a smart girl. I like to think you may have a good heart, too. But what happened last night with those rebels spread through this kingdom like dandelion seeds in a windstorm. I don't know what your true involvement was, but we both know . . . whatever you're up to . . . you're playing with fire."

Draven enters the room.

"Magda, do not threaten Rune." Draven's tone brooks no argument.

She merely looks me over, throwing her nose into the air before departing, and I get a glimpse of activity bustling in our living space. Draven shuts the door, shaking his head, shoulders tense, and though his look is hungry it doesn't seem to stick to me long. He tracks a path around the room as if he's trying to distract himself from my very bare legs and my body wrapped in his discarded shirt.

"What's going on out there?" I move to the closet, grabbing some of my own clothes while he lingers in the bedroom. He's close enough to peek, and I don't bother closing the door, instead turning my back to him. I know he wasn't fully kidding when he said he was still angry. Hells, I deserve it. But it's now my personal mission to soften him up a bit. I'm surprised by how much I miss the ease between us.

"An assassination attempt on the eve of leaving the kingdom tends to have the effect of a lot more guards getting assigned my way," he informs me.

I glance over my shoulder as I drop his shirt to the ground, and his eyes dart away to the window. Grinning, I keep getting dressed, taking my sweet time.

He clears his throat roughly. "It took a lot of convincing last night for King Silas to agree we could still go to Alfheim."

I'm relieved, grateful even. But last night was a blur of regret and shame and I have things to check on before we take off. "I need to be sure my friends are all right."

"I took the liberty of doing so. They're all safe," Draven rattles off very quickly, determinedly looking out of the window, though I keep catching glimpses of indigo, every sneaking glance leaving a damning snag of color behind. "Everyone's memories of the incident have been erased except for staff and guards. A few more arrests were made, and anyone suspected of involvement was transferred out of the Forge to the Destarion for questioning so we can find out more about this Ascension and its ties to the old uprising. This Ten Spires involvement will have Reapers rooting out their nests in the mortal lands."

"Good. I hope they all burn." I finish dressing, struggling to put on a thigh-high harness, a place to store both daggers and my deck of cards. Why are there so many damn loops on this thing?

"Gods, let me do it." The brusqueness of his voice is at odds with the way he drinks me in. I move to stand in front of the window, and he helps me get the belt on at my waist, then kneels swiftly, but there his hands linger on my upper thigh, his movements slow and steady. There's something about seeing him on his knees before me that threatens to break me, and I flex my hand to stop myself from tugging his dark hair.

The seducer is becoming the seduced. I force my eyes to the ceiling.

"Anything I need to know about Alfheim?" I ask.

"I doubt you've gotten any better at curtsying," he snarks.

I flick one of his horns and he jerks his head aside, a grin tugging the corners of his spiteful lips as he swats my hand away.

"I'll take that as confirmation. The elves are cruel, especially toward changelings and mortals. They won't be forgiving, so just avoid eye contact with their king, be as deferential as that wicked mouth allows, and spare yourself dealing with him by leaving him to me."

He secures the thigh holster, but his hands linger. Draven remains kneeling but still won't look at me. "I found intelligence from Destarion that said a woman matching your mother's description was transferred to the palace in Alfheim. And all children from the years of your brother's Selection live with nobility. So, there's a chance, if we play our cards right, we can safely find them and barter for their lives."

My excitement rises without restraint, a dangerous hope filling me at the idea I might see my mother, possibly even my brother on this trip.

"I can fulfill at least a part of my promise and deal, possibly before the day is out."

"Thank you," I say sincerely. I run my finger up his throat, along the scratchy shaven slopes, until it's crooked under his chin and he's forced to look up at me. Despite the sunlight through the window those pupils blare, the color drifting from continents of blue ice toward purple fields of pining. "And if I help you find the wand, or the ring, *and* I play nice for the elven king, then I'll be holding up my end, too, right?"

I cup his angular cheek, and he leans into the touch, lower lip snagging for a moment on the heel of my palm. He clenches those eyes closed. "I prefer you feral, love. But . . . yes. We search for my power, your family, and uphold our deal."

As if that's all this is. Like he's not staring at me like he wants to take me right here.

I think about what he said about when the day comes that our deal is complete. *Stay.*

He tears himself from me. "Keep packing, we'll be gone a few days. I'll meet you in the living room."

I stuff my suitcase quickly and pull my hair back with a pin shaped like a sword and moon. There are guards near the entrance, and Draven's surrounded by a few students, so I hesitantly lope to his side.

Being social isn't my strong suit, and I've only made the friends I have here because Ember chose me, and she's so outgoing that everyone else just flocked to her. But here Draven stands among a group of friends, the same ones I've glimpsed with him at sparring, who were here the night Morgan attacked me.

Yet he's barely spoken of them.

Draven listens to a tall druid with flawlessly smooth dark skin, his short hair in narrow twists that flare forward. He's got bat-like wings, a mixture of strength and softness in their design. His other friends consist of a whippy female with a little crook in her nose, dusky skin covered in just as many tattoos as the rest. Her black hair is tied in a long, sweeping ponytail. She, too, has bat-like wings, but with a slightly different coloring, like red-hued sands.

The third is a slender blond girl, with gorgeous hazel-green eyes and a dagger-sharp smile. She's annoyingly pretty, her smile lingering and broad. She's the only other one without bat wings, hers like a downy barn owl's.

Draven finally notices my approach, and his hand moves against the flat of my back, keeping me close to his side. I slink into him. My mental shields lower enough to brush his, but there's no flex there. Just unyielding steel. Even with friends.

The one talking bumbles to a stop. "But . . . yeah, anyway. We can discuss the best course when we get there."

"Right." Draven then nods to me. "I believe you all know Rune, but you haven't properly met yet."

Their eyes swivel to me as one.

"Rune, the talkative one is Malik, he's our Devil Arcana."

"I specialize in illusions." His grin is dazzling, and as he takes a bow his hand hovers over the tarot deck at his side. Draven's clothes are replaced with blinding pink garments, but the prince barely reacts beyond rolling his eyes.

"Joke's on you. I look amazing in every color." Draven side-eyes him, though the girls giggle and Malik winks at me, dispelling the illusion until my princeling is once again in his usual black on black.

"Zara is my master of secrets, a Hermit Arcana."

So, the gift of invisibility. I wait but the bat-winged girl only stares at us.

"I don't use my Arcana just to show off." Her eyes are like wells, dark and soul enveloping. I can't hold them long. Malik though, all charm and unseriousness, is lured and leans close to her.

"You should, it's fun." His voice is nearly singsong.

"And the blonde who can't get her eyes off your chest is Fable, our Hanged Man Arcana—"

"Hanged Woman." Her correction feels flirtatious, as does the way she bats her hair back, every movement as graceful as a self-satisfied cat's.

"Time control?" I ask. It's not an Arcana I've gotten remotely good at, still focusing primarily on Draven's list, and she nods, a grin lilting her lips as she looks me over.

I straighten under her scrutiny.

Draven clears his throat. "Fable and her brother Scorpius have been with me longest, and usually if there's trouble, it's because one of them started it."

"Firstly, Rune is far too pretty for you," Fable starts, and my face heats at her compliment. "Secondly, I've saved Draven's ass more times than I can count, but he always seems to forget that part." She slides him a sarcastic grin and loops her arm around mine. "If you ever get bored of him and his whole broody prince routine, you just let me know—"

"Okay." Draven scoots her aside with zero apology, his arm pulling me tightly against his side, palm spread over my hip.

I bite back a smirk as Fable chuckles, ribbing him with her elbow. I lean toward him so I can whisper in his ear. "Jealous little thing, aren't you, Draven?"

His gaze ignites, burning magenta, and I grin. There he is.

Malik blatantly points at him, turning to Zara with a look of glee illuminating his entire face. "I told you! I've only seen his eyes do that twice since I've known him, both times because he was pissed, but around Rune they're a damn mood ring—"

"Gods Below," Draven curses, pinching the bridge of his nose.

As Zara and Fable giggle together, another male druid with bat-like wings walks over to us. He's just as tall as Draven, with features as gold as Draven's are dark. He's beautiful, too, as if Draven makes it a mission to collect a powerful and gorgeous entourage, all of them enigmatic in some way or another that makes me feel a bit overshadowed and small.

Draven's tone has a hint of apathy as he hisses at the new-comer, "You're late, Scorpius. Where have you been?"

"Cleaning up your mess," the blond, Scorpius, growls back, tucking back his long hair into a warrior's bun. He's the only one with three pendants on his collar, so he's the oldest of the cohort. "There were a lot of questions in Moon's Hearth." His hazel eyes finally meet mine. "The hells is she doing here?"

"Watch your tongue. And next time when I tell you to be somewhere, be here on time or I'll leave you behind." Draven clenches his jaw, turning his back on the moody blond, but I track Scorpius uncertainly as he shuffles into a different opening in our little circle. The petulant look he gives Draven chafes something in me.

I spent my formative years with him tattling on my every move to my father. Draven's voice spools into my mind. *I sincerely doubt anything's changed.*

Why haven't you left him in stitches? My gaze lifts.

Who says I haven't? Draven's shoulders lift. *But I can't put him in a coffin. Unfortunately, his sister is one of few people I trust.* Draven straightens his formfitting jacket. *He's also a Moon Arcana, capable of shapeshifting into my body double. I don't wholly trust him, but we need him if we're going to search for your family over the border.*

I fold my arms, taking in his group of friends. Scorpius certainly is the most reserved toward me. I doubt Draven would've told them my role but I'm sure they heard about the rebel attack and that I was there, which might be enough for them to dislike me. Melancholy roots its way into my chest. It shouldn't be important, his friends' opinions of me, and yet . . . to my annoyance, I still find myself caught in their stares, a fly in a spiderweb.

Draven addresses his cohort. "While we are over the border, remember that the elves have a power similar to the High Priestess Arcana. They may not be able to read minds, but they often can read emotion, the change in one's energy, or aura, and the more powerful ones can compel you into doing things against your will. So mental shields up, assume we are being spied on the second we step over the border, and—"

"Compartmentalization! We know, Draven." Fable shakes her head, brows disappearing into her perfectly cut bangs. She says out of the side of her mouth, "You'd think we'd never left the Forge."

Draven clears his throat and adds, "Rune is first priority when we cross those borders." No one turns their head at that faster than me. What is he doing?

"You can't be serious?" Scorpius asks, fangs glinting. Although I agree, I really don't like this guy. "It's our job to protect *you*—"

"That's Soto's job." Draven doesn't so much as blink, his hand gripping my side a little tighter. "If Rune were to be hurt or captured, I would willingly start a war, or worse, to get her back. She's my fated mate. She is the priority." He looks at them each in turn, and taken aback, I open my mouth to argue with him, too, but he only holds up a hand to all of us, ignoring his friends' surprised and confused faces. "Do you understand?"

Each of them nods, suddenly serious.

I'm saved from further awkwardness as Commander Soto calls from the entry.

"Prince Draven, if you're ready, we need to go."

"I'm always ready."

Draven grasps my hand tightly and leads me through his friends toward the forefront of armored guards. There must be twenty people gathered here.

Draven pulls a crown from seemingly thin air, wrought from black steel, spiking like knives to the skies. He addresses the others.

"My father would like for me to remind you all that whilst we're beyond our borders we represent Sedah and blah, blah, blah—you all know the drill. We'll enter at the border and from there they'll transport us to their Grand Palace. After that we'll head out to the location of the dark crystal. Zenith is highly volatile, and the den was home to a toxic drake, so it may hold dangerous residues."

Draven opens the doors to the World's Hearth with his power and we walk down the steps where a host of wyverns greet us right there on the Oval. I almost freeze, but Draven's hand is firmly interlaced with mine, and I stumble toward a bright white one, its scales shining like opals in the sun. It's a little larger than a horse and wears a leather saddle that might be pretty if it wasn't attached to a giant alligator with wings.

Draven murmurs, "She's a windborn breed. Fast, but even children can ride her."

"They're welcome to her." I gape at it. "Can't we just portal into their kingdom?"

"And start a war? Why don't I just portal into the elven king's bedchamber while I'm at it?" Draven chuckles at my glower before his grin dips and he turns away quickly again.

He leads me right up to the wyvern's side and she turns to look at me, her crooked mouth nearly a smile. I remind myself she could take off my hand in a bite. Draven strokes her neck, and the space beneath her jaw rattles, her eyes closing in bliss. "There are magical wards to prevent us from just appearing within their castle walls. It's courteous to meet at a preselected safe point."

"I'm not going to have to deal with some boring, polite Draven there, am I?" I curl a bit closer, and he finally drags his eyes to mine. They're half hooded, and a hint of that fire has returned.

"Darling, I haven't behaved a day in my life." Draven opens his mouth to add more, when the sun darkens above us. Clouds gather unnaturally quickly, and our company shifts uncertainly—this isn't expected. Draven's eyes narrow.

Then seraphs descend through the clouds, and my heart hammers in my chest when I spot my father at the lead. I quickly scan the rest of them, but I don't see Altair with them, or Reva.

Commander Soto calls out, "Flank the prince!"

Soto and his men form a seamless line, while Draven pushes me behind him. A twin of him has moved deftly to his side, and I'm shocked at how well Scorpius embodies Draven. If I wasn't already holding him, I wouldn't know which was which.

The seraphs land in front of us. For one tense beat, everything is still.

Then my father lifts his hands. "I've come in peace, as part of the emissary."

Draven shifts and hesitantly steps forward, throwing a dismissive gesture that has the others spreading out, moving to their wyverns. But they remain watchful. Scorpius turns back into his blond self, melding into the crowd.

I stay behind Draven, even though I long to run to my father, who gives his men a similar discharge, though they're more hesitant about leaving his side.

"I was sent to encourage you to go through with the betrothal, or potentially, a different match among Nevaeh's royalty." My father's eyes flicker to our claim marks, his lips pulling down at the corners before he smooths his expression into something both curious and stern. "But I can see that we are beyond that." His eyes flit to Draven again. "Do you mind allowing me to talk to my daughter for a moment, alone?"

Draven leans in close to my ear, arm looping around my waist as he curls me close, voice lowered. "If you need me . . .

for any reason . . ." His eyes widen, thoughts caressing my own, and I nod to him, understanding. He straightens, nods his head in respect to my father, and then walks toward his onyx-scaled mount, securing each strap of its bridle and saddle.

There's a beat—the silence fills with emotion as we look to each other, his eyes watering. I don't know what to do with the other seraphs and druids watching, and Draven quickly barks an order that has the druids making themselves busy. But this is the most alone I've been with my father since I got here, and I don't want to waste it. I rush over to my dad and hug him tightly.

He holds me, as if in this small encirclement of his arms, I don't need to be brave anymore. This little act, this closing of chest against chest, brings me back to being a child, when I didn't need to be brave all the time. He's never pulled away first but instead lets me cling on for as long as I need, as if he had nowhere better to be.

This is the first time we've been able to talk without an audience in seven years. Finally alone, I blurt to my father, "Are you okay?"

He gives a wry chuckle. "You stole my question." He smiles at me, his teeth stark white against his brown skin. "I'm fine. Adjusting to Nevaeh and being away from you all was a torture. But seeing you again . . . I cannot express how much relief it has brought me."

"And Remus? You said you knew he was okay—"

"I've seen him during my time in the immortal realms, and he's safe. But I've been forbidden to talk more about that." My father straightens, pressing a hand against his white, braided tunic as if pushing down the sin of getting close to some barred topic.

My heart cracks open, threatening to bleed me out.

"Please . . . tell me you're safe here. Tell me you're happy."

"I'm okay." It's honest. True. And I don't want him to worry. "I . . . wasn't for a long time. I was unsafe, alone. But . . . I'm good now." Why is this next part so hard to admit? Maybe because I realize I'm not just pacifying my father's worries but saying something that feels a betrayal to admit. "I'm happy here."

"And the prince?" My father kisses my forehead, and his tears flow with earnest. "Is he a good man?"

Draven seems to sense our attention, and his eyes meet mine, the deepest blue I've ever seen. I realize he's scared. Terrified my father will scoop me up and take me away.

I turn to my dad. "Yes he is." I pull away to look into my father's eyes, to find him smiling in a way that is both devastating and filled with pride.

"That's all a father can hope for. Safety. Happiness. A partner who loves you." He kisses my forehead once more, the act held a little longer. Some silly part of me wants to argue that Draven doesn't love me. That we've never said the words. That I fear he may just want me. My mouth fumbles on how to express that, but my father cups my face in his hands. "I could be wrong. But I'm pretty certain he'd toss that crown into the volcano if you told him you wanted a normal life."

I snort. One thing I do know is how much Draven wants his throne. And power. Sighing, I tell my father, "I don't want to live an eternity like this. You on one side and me—"

"You wouldn't be safe there. In Nevaeh." He curses quietly, his halo at his hip glowing red. He flinches—he can't say more. "We'll have to settle for moments pressed between years, but I am always with you." His warm hand squeezes mine. "I'm afraid I need to talk to your betrothed. But we'll see each other again soon."

I nod, hoping it's true, and he walks away from me, turning into the light of the sun as he moves to where Draven adjusts the onyx wyvern's saddle. As my father joins him, Draven straightens up, and of the two, I can see only the prince's face, the solemn look in his expression and the way his lips twitch. He says something emphatic, to which my father just nods. They shake hands.

Then my father is looking at me over his shoulder, giving me one last smile, before he takes to the skies, the other seraphs joining him, flying northwest, toward the Sedah palace.

My breath catches in my throat, but I shove down the emotion and hesitantly approach Draven's side.

"What did he say to you?" I ask.

"He said if you're still the same little fireball he remembered, you'd throttle me just for repeating it."

I let it go for now, returning his wry smile.

Draven leads me back over to that opal-colored wyvern, shooting me an impatient look when I hesitate to get close to it. "Pretend Spirit here is a horse. You must have some experience with those, I assume."

I sigh and swing my leg over, preparing for the wyvern to throw me off, but she just cocks her head back at me with those fiery golden eyes. Draven settles the reins in my lap. I grip more tightly than maybe I should. Each of Spirit's mighty breaths rattle my thighs. Draven grasps a piece of saddle I'm unfamiliar with, a leather belt that will keep me attached to her for flight. He wraps it around my waist, using an intricate buckle to secure me, palm lingering on my knee.

"Let's stay at each other's sides within the elven borders." He looks over his shoulder. Scorpius and Fable are watching our interactions closely. He adds, "We can trust my friends with a lot, but not our vow, and I don't know Soto's men. They don't know we're looking for the Arcadian Artifacts or your family. Keep your shields up and your eyes open."

I nod. A guard brings him the reins of the onyx wyvern, and he mounts it so smoothly it's as if he was born to it.

"Prepare your wyverns," he shouts over his shoulder, and the others corral their beasts to face the same direction as him. "We'll portal closer to the elven borders to shorten our flight."

He channels the Death Arcana, and a large portal opens. Our wyverns slither through it after him, their front wings acting like paws, and beneath me, Spirit jerks forward, rushing onward.

The darkness engulfs us, raging all around us, as if we were dropped into the ocean, and the winds are buffeting harder than usual. I grip the horn of the saddle. The wyvern's movements are confident, as if she knows where we're going better than I do. I brace against the steep force of wind, my cloak threatening to fly off.

And suddenly we're in an unfamiliar wide-open field. The grass is scrubbier, and steep marbled tan and gray mountains cut the sky like teeth ahead. Strange rock spires gather, like the child of a giant stacked them up and forgot about them. My wyvern keeps walking, its strange trot turning to a wending gallop as it lifts its wings, following the others.

It flaps once, twice, then suddenly it leaps upward, and I'm forced to grasp the horn again, wishing I'd secured the saddle myself. It seems too tenuous a thing to be the only separation between living and dying. With every few wingbeats the temperature drops a degree or two, steadily morphing from a muggy heat to a cool breeze, but the sun stays strong on my face as we climb. The wind laces through my hair, and the feeling of freedom traces my veins like a fingertip on a map, sending blessed chills through me. Once we stop climbing, we even out, and I release my grip, balancing my arms out to either side of me. If I never touch ground again, it might be worth it for this.

Draven whips around, long hair flapping behind him as he watches me over his shoulder. His wings are tucked in tight, body leaning forward, half standing like someone would if their horse was in full gallop. I copy his stance and my little opal wyvern sprints ahead, catching up with him.

"Why couldn't *you* just fly us over the border?" I call over the wind, nodding my head toward those tightly tucked wings of his.

"Why ride a horse when you can just run?" He raises a brow, watching me out of the corner of his eye. "No druid has this kind of speed or stamina."

"How disappointing," I throw back.

He blinks, then scoffs, rolling his eyes and grinning broadly. But it worked.

"Don't worry about my virility, Rune. I'm more than capable of ravishing little old you." His eyes finally spark in that bright violet I've been hoping for.

I grin, holding out hope things are returning to normal between us.

He nods to his right, eyes still latched to mine. His wyvern drops off, diving below to the foothills. I release a held breath as mine follows the steep plunge.

Our wyverns branch off into a cyclical dive, and every buffet of her wings has me trapped between terror and thrill. I rise out of my saddle, but the leather strap holds firm. We loop around a circle of uneven cairns. As we inch lower, a delegation of elves standing in the center comes into view.

Draven is the first to land, Commander Soto a moment after, and the rest of us soon follow, my wyvern skidding a bit on impact, more awkward on the ground than in the sky.

Draven easily slides off his mount in one movement, landing quickly on his feet, and approaches the elf at the forefront of their group.

Each one of them is as lithe and lovely as the next. Their hair is longer than Draven's, down to their waists, shimmering veils of silk. They have no wings or antlers, but their ears and fangs are as pointed as the druids'. Their copper armor over emerald cloth strikes me as decorative. Perhaps they do not need much protection. Or maybe they're arrogant.

Beware the elves of earth, whose power seeps in stone, while misfortune brings them mirth, your desires leave you prone. My father's rhyme trickles into my thoughts.

Draven said they can warp wants and influence the mind. Their cool gazes make me uncomfortable.

The emissary in the lead bows in greeting, though the rest do not.

I glower at them. Who the hells do they think they are?

Fable sidles up to me. She lingers, arms crossed, and hisses to me, "Pull up your hood, your hair makes you stick out."

"I could say the same of you." Her hair is so light blond it's nearly silver, and certainly memorably bright. I'm surprised when she chuckles. But we quiet, monitoring the elves and Draven.

"Your Royal Highness, we are pleased to greet you and lead you to the palace." The emissary looks to Draven's chest instead of meeting him in the eye. "However, we are not supposed to bring soldiers into His Majesty's Grand Palace."

"These are my royal and personal guards," Draven says dismissively. "They go where I go."

"Of course, Your Highness." But the emissary swallows, his hands skittish. "May we offer our mounts? They will traverse the area better once we arrive—"

"I've seen your mounts. I'll keep to my own, thank you," Draven says.

"Of course." The emissary moves to one of the jutting cairns, placing a long-fingered hand against its surface.

A blue light skitters across it, casting runes over the stone. A loud churning fills my ears, like heavy rocks scraped against each other. I look down. Runes shimmer at our feet in that same bright blue, and then the stone platform rotates, slowly at first, but then gathers speed. I stagger and bump against Fable. She puts a hand on my shoulder, holding me upright, blue light forming a circle around the dais. The platform drops, sinking below the ground at a steady speed, and the light of the dais grows until it's all I see.

I grit my teeth, nausea churning in my stomach, legs shaking. The spinning slows, lessening into nothing as the blue light shrinks away. We've been transported somewhere entirely different, standing on an outcropping in a large cavern system that spans hundreds of feet above and below us.

Sunlight streaks through the openings, illuminating the stalactites and branching into different cavern systems. Below us is a second world, green and overflowing with great trees connected by vines, and separated from us by misty little clouds. The kingdom of Alfheim is beautiful, singular in its design.

Elves fly on the backs of creatures I've never seen before, spinning through the small spaces between stalactites. A few riderless creatures land on the platform beside our emissaries, and our wyverns hiss.

Whatever these things are, they look like enormous bats, with dark fur and fox-like noses, their ears oversized, wings more heavily veined. They cling low to the ground, and the elves lie flat across their backs, hugging to their fur.

The druids give the creatures a bit of space.

"Draven," I ask quietly, "what *are* those?"

"They're bakka." He lowers his voice. "And frankly a shitty ride."

The emissaries click their tongues, and the creatures take flight. The spinning way the beasts fly must be exactly why Draven denied them, even if the wyverns seem too large to follow through the odd holes chiseled in the rocks and stalactites.

He mutters, "This route is difficult on wyverns. I've made it a few times, but just watch your head, keep low, and let your mount lead."

"Sure."

He reaches down to adjust my buckle, tightening it one-handed with easy dominance. His hand lingers on my waist, gaze dragging down my body, and I swear I can feel its damn path, arousing every inch of me. My lips part and his own turn into a vulpine grin. Prick.

He snaps his reins and his wyvern dives off the outcropping of rock, gliding above the elven cityscape below after the emissaries. I hunch low, following his lead as my wyvern flies through a hole in a low-hanging stalactite, small enough that there's barely room for us to slip through. We bank hard to the right, soaring nearly vertically, but my elbows and knees still graze the rocks.

We pass through a few more tunnels chiseled through the crags. My head spins as we squeeze between other spires at dizzying speed, bruises forming. The light from overhead cuts in and out, as if I'm riding on horseback through the forest.

I gasp as we come into a cavern large enough to fit most of Westfall.

The full sun shines down on the elven capital below through a circular opening above, the largest castle I've ever seen occupying the center like a sundial. There are figures, likely elven kings and queens of old, chiseled along the sides of this enormous space, stretching hundreds of feet skyward.

There's no time to appreciate it as we dive down. We land on the top of a large turret, my legs shaking from the strain of gripping the wyvern.

But it was so exhilarating.

Draven dismounts smoothly and I fumble at my belt. Before I know it, his hands are on my waist and he helps me slide off Spirit's back. I pat her head, running my hand over the soft scales, and the wyvern leans into it, her golden eyes sparkling, a strange purring rumbling through her. Draven's hands haven't moved, and his lips twitch upward.

"See, not so bad."

"She will do until I have wings of my own. Unless your offer still stands?" I smile up at him, and his brows draw together in confusion. I fill in, "You know, to ride you instead?"

Draven chuckles deep, his tongue tracing a sharp canine.

"Why don't you compare the two before you decide." His hissed words raise the goose bumps across my body and I bite back a grin.

"Okay, you two, save the mate stuff for later," Fable chides us. She puts a hand against her stomach and bemoans, "I don't even know how you can be thinking about anything beyond throwing up after that ride."

Scorpius rolls his eyes. "It wasn't that bad, you've always been such a baby—"

"I am not, you little—"

"Quiet or Draven will think we've never been anywhere before." Malik shushes the blonds, smoothly helping Zara down as if that ride didn't bother him in the least.

"I thought it was a blast," Zara says dryly, her hair pulled out of its long braid. She gives me a slight smile, probably rarer than direct sunlight in this place, and I feel a bit of tension ease with it.

We leave our mounts on the tower, and the emissaries take us through several corridors and courtyards until eventually we reach a grand throne room.

"Here is where we will leave you, Prince Draven," the emissary says. "The elven king awaits." He gives a stiff bow and beckons the others after him.

We turn to the chamber and follow Draven inside.

Atop a dais at the back of the hall sit four tall thrones, crafted from white oak. Vines and flowers wrap around them, spreading up the wall so thickly that I cannot tell where they end. Our footfalls echo across the chamber, our eyes sweeping across the walls as we slowly approach. Soto's hand stays on the sword at his hip, his men equally tense. A few uniformed elven advisors linger about the room and elven guards line the hall like statues. Their king is the only royal member in attendance, watching our arrival with unblinking eyes as he stands with preternatural grace on the dais.

The elven king is so beautiful he's almost hard to look at for too long. The symmetry of his face is nearly unnatural, and the sweep of his flawless hair is oddly mesmerizing. He watches us with bored, pale green eyes, all the more piercing against his deep brown hair, and his attention stays on me a moment longer than the others before he addresses Draven.

My heart raggedly paces, and I feel a surge of *want*, of adoration. Draven's eyes cut to mine quickly, and I realize . . . this must be the power of compulsion and manipulation he warned me about. I cannot necessarily trust anything I feel in the elves' presence.

"Prince Draven, welcome to the great halls of Alfheim. You are our treasured guests. Is there anything we can do to bring you more comfort during your stay?"

"I am honored to be here, King Eldarion. My only request is the recovery of zenith crystals, at your leisure," says Draven. His cold formality is so at odds with the version I'm privy to.

"I must confess we've heard rumors even down in our hallowed kingdom of war brewing between the seraphs and druids." King Eldarion's light eyes settle on me once again. "King Altair has said there's a dangerous changeling in your midst, one whose future has foretold our downfall, and yet you keep this Forsaken One as a *pet*? He also claims you've broken your word, and you're no longer betrothed to his daughter. Is this correct?"

Forsaken One? Seems a bit exaggerated.

Draven's body is occultly still. Then he turns to me, his eyes burning like fire opals, holding a hand out for me to join him at the forefront of our group. I link mine to his and stand at his side, curtsying swiftly for the king, my back ramrod straight. Draven's voice is tight as he says, "It's true I've broken the engagement set by my father for someone far superior. But it was never *my* word I was breaking."

The elven king shifts in his throne at that, leaning forward.

Draven gestures to me, his smile charming, though I see the tension in his shoulders, his wings. "But does she seem all that dangerous to you? We are merely two people, brought together by fate. This angered King Altair. But the rumors of her becoming some . . . Forsaken One are nothing more than jealousy over my unwillingness to let her out of my sight. Take the words for what they are—rumors and lies."

Do not make eye contact, Draven's voice unspools into my mind, and I realize how low my guard has dropped in the king's presence, as if whatever power he holds has been quietly smothering my mental wards. He is by far the biggest danger here. I lower my eyes and look at his hands. There are so many rings on his fingers, but I don't recognize the emerald gleam of Seithr, the Kingmaker.

The elven king's attention turns to me.

His voice is sharp as a scythe as he speaks again. "I'm inclined to disbelieve the seraph king's warning, if only because Altair can be so droll, seeing threats in every shadow. But know this . . . if I find that you're lying, or that you or your pet have any inclinations to deceive or threaten me, I will not hesitate to act. King Silas and the others may have convinced themselves that your changeling kind are part of us, worthy of our crowns, but I have not forgotten where you hail from. You were raised as royalty because of the card that chose you, not by skill or blood right. At least my heir fought for the right to bear my titles, but all I see when I look upon you is a rebel scab who got very lucky. Do not test that luck here."

Draven's eyes burn red, the silence unnaturally thick.

"Husband!"

The entire room's attention shifts to the elven queen as she wanders into the hall. Her skin is as dark as his is pale, her face too perfectly proportioned to feel real, eyes wide and doe-like, lips full and pouty. Her braided hair shines, and I envy the perfection in them. She looks absolutely mortified and the king merely shifts in his chair, one leg crossing the other, frowning as he leans heavily against one arm like a sulking teenager.

The queen clears her throat, her voice tense. "Forgive our king, he has been most strained recently due to the toxic drake roaming our hills. Please, you must be weary from all this political talk. I would be more than happy to show you to your rooms before the feast tonight."

Draven gives the king one last heated stare before nodding to the queen. I walk quickly to match the pace of his longer strides. Passing a thought his way, I eye him apprehensively.

What a prick. I pause, stewing on my thoughts, scratching the claim mark on my neck. *Do all the immortal royals know your parents were rebels?*

He was there the day of my Selection. He's been particularly vocal about his disgust of changelings and was the last to choose one as his heir. The prince of Alfheim was forced to fight in a trial for his place, and he's a cruel prick, just like his king. He pauses, fuming, then suddenly adds, *Keep your guard up, Rune. Elves have magic, too, even if it's not as complex as our own.*

I follow his lead, but I feel the elven king's eyes on my back.

24

A Feast for One

The Lovers card represents not only love but duality, choices, lust, and trust.

W E'RE SHOWN A HALLWAY of bedrooms, ending with a beautiful, two-story apartment for Draven, reserved for royal guests. The living room contains a large wall of windows that looks down upon the busy citadel below and gives a view of the cavernous kingdom beyond. Everything is accentuated by organic elements, as though carved from nature—light wooden floors, expansive floor-to-ceiling windows, soft earth-toned fabrics, and rounded walls.

The queen wears a bland but polite smile as Draven's guards move into the room, searching through it, as though looking for hidden traps. Draven keeps his hands in his pockets.

"I apologize again for my husband's tone," the queen says.

Draven just nods, the embodiment of nonchalance, though a hint of crimson touches his eyes. But I can't help but admire her quiet authority and confidence, so in contrast to her husband.

"I'll send attendants before sunset to guide you to the feast. Please make yourselves at home in the meantime."

"Could we receive a map of where the zenith is located?" Draven drawls. "Just in case we decide to leave sooner than expected." The bite in his tone is unmistakable.

I pinch his arm. The king was an ass but it's no excuse for Draven to take it out on her. I've never tolerated punishing women for the behavior of the men around them. She seems to notice my silent reprimand, the tension of her puckered forehead softening as she looks between us.

"I can arrange for you all to collect the zenith tomorrow, instead of in a few days," she allows.

Draven grunts an acknowledgment.

The queen smiles at me and then leaves us.

Scorpius turns to Draven, running a hand through his blond hair, his body wire-tight. He leans forward. "Their king needs to watch his tone."

"You going to teach him?" Fable cleans her nails with a small knife.

"Let me, and I will." Scorpius doesn't take his eyes off Draven.

Zara and Malik are on the other side of the room, whispering in a way that reminds me of an assured cat ignoring an eager puppy.

"You're baited too easily. I'm more interested in what other lies he's gotten so far from the seraphs, not a pissing contest." Draven folds his arms. "He may have insulted changelings and myself, but the last thing we need is an elf-seraph alliance. We need them on our side if Altair decides to start a war, so for now we play nice."

Malik folds his arms across his broad chest and brings up, "Did anyone else catch that the drake sounded like a current problem? Instead of a resolved one?"

"All clear!" Commander Soto declares from upstairs where I glimpse the main bedroom and a bathroom. Soto trots downstairs, his salt-and-pepper hair pulled up in a warrior's knot. "There's one passage down here behind a portrait, but we've closed it off. No other listening spy-ways."

I doubt that, but Draven looks unruffled. I decide to do my own sweep later.

"Thank you, Commander Soto." He dismisses the guards, who stream out of the apartment.

"If we're going to collect the zenith tomorrow, does that mean our timetable is moving up?" Fable looks at her nails, extending before retracting them, the tattoo of the Hanged Man tarot card catching the light across the back of her hand.

"No, and speaking of time." Draven nods to her, some silent signal, and she rolls her shoulders, summoning her Major Arcana card. The room warps a bit and the air ripples. Dust motes are trapped as if in amber glass, a bat paused mid-flight outside our window. "This will allow us to speak a bit more plainly, should any elven ears be lingering outside. To any outsider beyond Fable's grasp, these minutes will turn to a mere second."

"It's incredible." I poke a fly frozen mid-flight and it merely slides to where I've moved it. Fable rubs her temple.

"Less of that please," she says.

"We're here for more than just zenith." Draven says, "Malik, Fable, I need information on two humans, possibly turned changelings, matching these descriptions. If we find them, I want to be alerted immediately." He passes Fable the paper first and she reads it as intently as any bounty hunter. It's my brother's and mother's descriptions, the ones I gave Draven before we left. "I also need to find leverage for securing them. Blackmail of any variety will do." He looks their groups over. "Zara and Scorpius, you're on blackmail duty."

I note he doesn't elaborate on my family's relation to me.

And while their Arcanas—illusions, shapeshifting, invisibility, and the control of time—give them a chance of finding them . . . I'd still prefer if I could search myself.

If they're within these borders, we'll have an idea by dinner. The elven king will have all his eyes on us, Rune. Remember, you're the Forsaken One. His lips quirk.

Draven's hand bumps mine, and then he pulls it close, interlocking our fingers.

What about the Arcadian Artifacts? My eyes settle on his.

The drake's lair can wait. He looks me over, those eyes heating. *You are more important, Rune.*

I DO MY OWN thorough search of the apartment, finding a couple of spy holes in the bedroom and living room, and block them up before returning to the kitchen and finding one more false wall near the peninsula. Draven watches me work, leaning against a counter, his elbows propping him up as he watches me sidelong.

"I'll need to speak to Commander Soto," Draven muses. "That's the third one he missed."

"We can't all have my training," I reply over my shoulder.

The others left hours ago. This has kept me busy, but I hate being idle while they're out there searching for the very thing I was Selected for.

I rifle beneath the stone countertop until I find a small opening that presses inward. The wall beside him cracks open, barely bigger than a pantry. I step inside it, but like the others it's merely a small space for someone to stand and spy from, with no back exits like the ones Soto found. Enough for a person to fit. Or two people.

The door closes behind me, Draven sidling next to me.

"Ugh, imagine standing in something like this all day," he says. The scent of him is overpowering in this tight space. His body presses against mine to fit us both, his hair tickling my face as he adjusts.

"I don't have to imagine it. I've been stuck in worse."

"That's right." Those eyes are on me, and the space feels molded to our bodies now. He leans over me, forearm resting on the wall behind me. "Sometimes I forget just how formidable you are."

"Be glad I'm on your side. I'll keep you safe, Princeling." Our chests are pressing against each other, and he leans down, lips nearly against my neck.

"Rune, you are by far the biggest danger to me." His breaths are heavy, wanton.

All thoughts fly from my head as my hands rake up his sides, feeling the muscles beneath his finely tailored clothes.

He tenses, but doesn't move away. "You could stab me in the back, and I'd probably beg you for more."

"Everyone knows the quickest way to the heart is between these two ribs." I slide my finger between them, and he bites down on his smile. "Why are we stuck in here when we have that big old bed upstairs?"

Draven grabs my hand and leads me out and up to the bedroom. I take in the large bed with a grin, but when I look at Draven, all emotion has been wiped from his face.

Last night's party, the feel of his skin on mine, my forced betrayal, all unfortunately fresh on both our minds.

My eyes travel over him, then the bed. We're barely a step away from each other, when he hisses, "Should I be looking for assassins in the shadows?" He looks down at me, hunger and wariness warring in his eyes.

"You have to know I wouldn't have gone along with that—"

"If your friends weren't at risk," he fills in, bored. Yet he waits, as though he wants more. His jaw flexes, as if he's trying to clamp down the words, but he still says, "Did you actually want me?"

Heat creeps up my chest, burning up my throat until the words crack like a log giving way in a bonfire. "I'm not that good of an actor, Draven. My body wasn't lying."

"So, it's just your body that wants this." He moves closer to me, his hooked finger caressing up my throat, stopping under my chin as he tilts it up, so I look at him. Is that all *he* wants?

The truth is I don't know what I want from him. At first it was the power and protection he's promised. His throne will allow me to find justice, my family. All my desires and motivations wrapped up in him.

But it's more complicated than just that. What I feel for him is beyond what brought me here; it grows every day, feeding on everything he gives. A fire that consumes all, burns for everything.

And I think we both know it.

I don't know what I want from him. I just know I want . . . him.

"Would you be satisfied with so little of me?" I ask, not ready to answer what is building between us. Not ready to let myself be vulnerable or have what little is left of my heart be torn from its strings again. There's a good chance this will end in disaster; believing anything else seems too naive.

But we are bound together, quite literally, by our magic, by the claim, too. Maybe this gambit works only if we both just break our fucking pride and put our fate in the gods' hands?

Draven searches my eyes, his breaths ragged.

"I'd beg on my knees just to get that much of you," he breathes.

This promises annihilation.

"Then beg," I whisper.

Draven's eyes darken and his lips crash against mine. He is demanding, unyielding, unquenchable. Cupping my face in his hands, he walks me back toward the bed, *our* bed, and then his hands travel to my waist, gripping around my sizable backside, and lifts. Something about feeling featherlight in his palms has me slickening, a tingling rising in my chest, peaking my breasts. He flattens me to the mattress, and my hands comb through his hair, stroking the ridges of those horns. What perfect handles. I tug his mouth to my neck and the moment he sucks against it I'm surrendering against him, his fangs scraping my skin in a way that has me writhing. I couldn't hold back now even if I wanted to.

His weight is pleasingly dominating, ungiving as my hips grind against him. He chuckles into my ear, tongue lashing against my neck, fangs leaving traces up the side, as if praying to bite once again, to worship and consume me as sacrament.

"Gods, Rune, are you trying to get me to cum before I even fuck you?"

It's my turn to break, a smile inching up my face. "Don't you fucking dare."

Yet I can feel his thick hardness pressing against the fabric, a promise of what I have to look forward to. His hands entwine in my hair now, tugging back, and my neck arcs against his mouth. My bones go molten, body loosening in the best of ways.

Sucking and teasing, he moves down, stripping off my shirt as he goes. The part of me that cares for him more than I will admit wants to slow down, suddenly self-conscious of my body. Draven fingers the clasp of my bra, right between my breasts. With a movement that speaks of too much experience, he breaks it free, and the insecure part of me grasps hold of my wits again, hands flying to my chest.

He stops immediately.

"What's wrong?" The way his eyes weigh with hunger has my grip relaxing.

"You're just . . ." But words fail me. He looks so tousled, his hair messy, lips swollen from kissing my skin. My cheeks flush and lines of consternation crease his dark brows. "Practiced."

"Dearest . . . are you saying you're inexperienced?"

"I'm no virgin." I toss him a snarky smirk, and he smiles, clearly not one either. "But I'm also not a conquest. So, tell me, Draven . . . what does that make me, to you?"

His gaze is a caress. "It makes you *mine*."

There's a release in me. I let go, surrendering, lifting my head to claim his lips.

His kiss is calmer, drawn out, tasting every inch. Savoring me like the rarest of wine, as if we might be separated for a lifetime. I cling to his shirt with one hand, cupping his face with the other. His mouth moves to my neck again, and it undoes me.

"I want you, Draven." I would burn every wall I've built between us to have him take me. "But worse, I like you."

He finally pulls back and gasps against my lips, "Slowly, then?"

"I want this. Just . . . take your time," I confirm. Judging by the thick bulge that's shifted against my leg, I will need an adjustment period anyway. He kisses me again, longingly, hand flattened against my sternum. I lay my hand over his, and lead it down, down, down between my legs. "Maybe we start with this."

"I thought you'd never ask." He rips down my underwear, but his hand is tender as it palms around me, and he gives an intake of breath, surprised maybe, as he handles the slickness there. He shakes his head slow, biting his lip. "What naughtiness you're tempting me with."

While he's looking at the space his hand explores, I lift my lips to his neck and the groan he gives vibrates against my tongue. He plunges two fingers down, spreading me, pumping. I moan, but keep my mouth sucking on his neck, mapping the scars I left on his flesh when I claimed him. He continues to work his fingers inside, the palm of his hand grinding against my apex— enough that it alone might destroy me. I cup his hand, demanding those fingers travel deeper. They do, smoothly, adoringly.

The teasing motion of his fingers raises my desire higher and higher . . . I'm not sure it's ever gotten like this before with anyone else. No one's ever been so patient, so thorough. I push my hips against his hand over and over, rolling against him with demand. He kisses my neck now, my breasts, all provocatively enough that I don't think I can take much more. I gasp against him, knowing I'm close.

"Open your mind to me," he pleads.

"Are you going to fuck it, too?" It's a joke and it's not, but it takes nothing to lower the shields there, heightened as I am.

"I want to feel this together." He slinks inside my mind, everywhere I think is just him, the arousal it creates nearly unbearable, my skin afire, my thoughts, too. His eyes close, and he strains against me, the clothes separating us so thin, as if all this might undo him, throw out his restraint entirely. But a moment later his eyes flash open, bright magenta, and he says, "I will taste you before this is done."

Then he's moving to the end of the bed, kneeling on the floor, hand pulling out of me only to yank my body closer, the backs of my knees hooked over his shoulders. I told him to beg, and here he is on his knees.

His tongue takes over, splitting me, turning want into need, pulling the threads of this orgasm so insistently I know he won't stop until I'm done. I've never reached a climax like this with anyone. But as I meet his eyes over my heaving chest, I see no trace of judgment there. He will have me satisfied, or not at all.

"Can you breathe?" I pant.

"Who cares? Fucking smother me, Rune," he demands. His fingers return, pumping into a new position that has my toes curling, eyes rolling back as I reach above me, gripping the pillows, the sheets, anything to ground me.

He releases one of my thick thighs and offers his spare hand and mine entwines in it, like a lifeline, hips thrusting against his fingers and face.

Pleasure strikes true. My hips arc into him, hands clawing into his hair, grasping his horns, and holding. His free hand moves from mine to clench my ass, as if he wishes to suffocate himself in me. His tongue never stops flicking, splitting, devouring. Nothing matters in this moment but this, so if riding his face is what it takes, so be it.

My limbs go limp, I'm breathless, wrung out. Draven climbs back onto the bed, drinking me in. He looks . . . happy, even though we are supremely uneven. My hand strokes the outside of his pants, along his sizable length, and he shudders, kissing my neck again, licking where his claim lays buried in finely laced scars, the smell of me all over him.

"My turn," I huff.

"Is it now?" He stops, as there's a knock at the door.

I immediately tense, and he grabs the comforter, piling it in my lap, so I can cover myself. He wipes his face with his hand, making sure I'm ready. He cracks the door open only a few inches, his wings hiking higher to block me. I can barely see the light from the hall, let alone whoever's there.

"What do you want?" he snaps.

"Apparently we're all late." It's Scorpius. "The elven king is throwing a minor tantrum about it."

25

Dinner

The King of Coins in reverse represents a man of materialism, who wallows in his avarice, one who dominates others through exploitation, possessiveness, and worse . . . ruthlessness.

I'M IN A NEW BLACK and gold dress, crimson cape draping over my shoulders, the deep hood covering my hair. Draven sits at my side, his eyes traveling the length of me like nothing between us was ever interrupted. The long table in the dining hall is full of advisors, courtiers, and Draven's cohort, Commander Soto and our guards lining the walls. I scan the table, hoping for a sign of my brother or mother, but there are no young men and even fewer women seated here.

They have news for us. I'll fill you in after dinner when I hear the rest, Draven tells me, mind to mind, his tattoo glowing.

"What a pleasure it is to have you here, rather than your empty seats," the elven king simpers snidely.

Draven doesn't respond.

I look at Draven pointedly, my hand squeezing his knee beneath the table.

He shifts, clearing his throat, and finally turns to the elven king.

"So sorry, I've been distracted. You're right of course. I take the blame." His hand spreads across his chest, yet his other one grasps my thigh beneath the table. "My team is extremely thorough. I made a promise to my father I'd come home breathing."

"You say that as if there are threats around every turn," King Eldarion accuses. "Even in my own house."

"Well, I've been trained to never mistake a serpent for a toad," Draven replies. The linked bridge between us remains open, like a corridor built within my mind.

Are you seriously implying the elven king is a toad at his own table? I ask, pressing the thought his way.

He's more likely a snake, Draven replies.

Whatever happened to not winning a pissing contest? I press. *Even I'm better at diplomacy.*

Love, your expressions have annotations the whole room can read, Draven responds, and I've heard that before, though not so poetically. I resist rolling my eyes and Draven's meticulous voice turns logical. *I can't assume that he's not in some way working with King Altair. Better to prod and see what comes out. The elves are typically neutral in our conflicts, but Altair can be persuasive, and you heard the way Eldarion spoke to me earlier. We need to know where we stand before we can make the next move.*

"And here you claim the seraph king sees boogeymen in the shadows," King Eldarion manages tightly, holding his wineglass out for a servant to fill.

My eyes snag on the golden manacles at her wrists. They're not connected by a chain, but the bruises make their intent clear. Then I notice her round ears.

I barely hear whatever Draven and the king say next, playing at words as if deciding where to slit the next knife. The woman walks around the king and stops at me, filling my goblet with more rich elven wine, my throat dry as I take in the bruises trailing up her sleeves, little brown and purple islands against a peach sea.

"Thank you," I whisper to her when she's done.

She freezes as if I've turned her to stone. Draven's eyes trail from her wrists to her young face, before meeting mine. The woman nods, swallowing in terror, before she turns and fills Draven's glass instead of replying. She likely isn't allowed to speak to anyone seated here.

All around this room, I catch glimpses of the golden manacles. Dotted among the immortals are enslaved humans. I'm sick; a collar is a collar even if it's studded in diamonds.

Remus. I pray that he was made into a changeling, that he's not wearing the same gold chains. Would I even recognize his face if I saw him again? What did they do with the children? And my mother, taken from an immortal prison, for the gods know what. She's in these lands, assuming she survived at all.

I desperately wish Fable and Malik had news to share with me now.

I wish I had decided to say fuck it, scour this place myself, even if it raised questions with the elven king. My appetite disappears, and I find myself drinking the wine too quickly. Here I am in a pretty dress, with the attentions of a mighty prince. But in another Selection . . . this could have been me, forced into servitude. The World seems to have chosen me at random. I'm spoiled in comparison, given great power I didn't even *want* at first. The two of us are headed toward thrones, but it might not come soon enough to help these people.

You're not eating, Draven points out.

Neither are you, I push back, deflecting. My hands shake, and I clasp them together under the table.

Well, I had my fill before dinner, Draven says, eyes dancing.

They invite me to play, but I can't summon the energy to distract myself.

Draven gently puts his silverware down, laying his napkin across his plate. "That was delicious. King Eldarion, did this beast come from one of your famous hunting trips?" he asks, charm suddenly hitched on like a shield, as if he's shapeshifted in front of our eyes.

Eldarion blinks, thrown in surprise, and my brows furrow. *What're you doing?*

Playing to his vanity. Draven squeezes my knee beneath the table.

"Yes, I killed this one myself, it nearly gored several in my party." Eldarion's grin is smug. "He weighed over a ton. A dangerous but beautiful beast."

"That's very impressive," Draven admits, and if I didn't know how good of an actor he was, I'd have believed him, too. He leans closer, nearly conspiratorially. "I can see that you've imported quite a few mortals who've avoided Selection into your realm. I've heard you're personally keeping Destarion's rates quite low." Draven steeples his fingers, elbows on the chair's arms, his eyes a deep, ocean blue. I know I didn't share the thought but Draven's clever enough he must've figured it out.

The king takes this change in topic as some olive branch. He cuts into his meat and says, "You'd be amazed how many capable hands wind up in Destarion. The mortals' cowardice benefits me greatly."

"And are they all house staff? Entertainment?"

"Some are barely worth the food to feed them. They typically go to the mines, or undesirable jobs for as long as their mortal coils will hold. But we make use of the capable . . . every merchant needs hands, every lady a handmaid, though some mortals surprisingly have immense talent." The king shrugs, raising the glass of wine to his lips. "As you know, elves look for the most artistic and beautiful in Selection, but occasionally we find them hiding away."

I hang on his every word, hating him more and more.

"We have a few every season. Years ago we had one . . . she was rather beautiful, a lava-blessed who became rather valuable. As you know, sometimes we find diamonds in the coal."

My mother's bright red hair flashes in my mind.

King Eldarion's smile is sharp. "During her punishment it was revealed that she had a lovely voice, along with some other enticing attributes. An eastern lord needed a siren for his court, so I sent her to him as a gift. It was quite a prosperous exchange—you should've seen the rubies and emeralds he sent in return from his mines."

Rune. RUNE. Draven's voice turns loud in my mind, and I look to him, realizing my eyes are watering. All I can hear is my mother's singing. My father said it was prettier than all the seraphs in Nevaeh combined. But the rest of my mind is screaming.

I make a show of messing with my sleeve, turning my head aside, and let the tears quickly drop as I try to regain some composure. Draven hisses, *Rune, let me help you. The field. Picture the snowy field. The king, he'll be able to tell—*

I slam the small access point down between us, severing the connection. I can't hear anything more. It's taking everything to not lunge across this table and take out King Eldarion's eyes. My hand runs down my steak knife. How stupid, how unbelievably arrogant, to leave this in front of me, and then say something like that.

The king's attention draws to me, and Draven's warning sinks in under his cool gaze. I remember what Draven said about auras, the way elves can read people, their emotions, their intentions.

I think of that cold snowy field, and a chill washes over me as my emotions numb.

Draven forcibly clears his throat, the sound jarring, and it yanks me from the last of my murderous thoughts. "Fascinating. I would love to hear a voice like that. And . . . where is your heir, by the way?" He looks pointedly around the table. "I was hoping to congratulate Prince Ronan on his completion of the Kingbreaker Trials."

Eldarion scoffs dismissively. "He is off at the Ravine, in his second year. Much like you." It must be their version of the Forge. "The last thing that boy needs is more praise."

"Could you regale us with the Trials? I hear every Selected child chosen by elves competed in it? I enjoy a good challenge, as I'm sure you know. It sounds like it was both deadly and amusing." Draven's asking about my brother, likely among those changelings. I wonder who raised Remus, if he competed in the Trials, how far he got. Draven's team must've found out about the Trials, but he's clearly still trying to narrow my brother's placement in it.

Eldarion shrugs, smirking in amusement. "The Kingbreaker Trials were held to see if any of the changeling children from all of our Selections could be worthy of king. To be declared a true elf. It included several deadly rites. My favorite included them scaling a waterfall to collect an object treasured by our people, while sharks stirred below."

There's uncomfortable shifting at our table; the rest of the conversations seem to have died out as attention focuses on the king.

The queen quietly says, "We lost many changelings that day."

"The Master of Games had secured them all to the rock wall with rope, and only my nephew realized he would have to remove it to leap far enough to reach the object." Eldarion's lips twist to the side as he swirls the wine around in his glass. "Rather clever." Though he says it as if his nephew somehow cheated.

"These games sound like fun, to play or bet on," Draven adds, nudging the king along.

"Sounds like I would've been shark meat," Malik says, and an uneasy laugh ripples around the table.

Images of my brother scaling slippery rock, water splattering his face . . . I remind myself he's an adult now, the same age as me, but I keep picturing him as the child we lost.

Whether he competed in the Trials and lost, or won, or was trapped within these halls . . . it's all a fate I'd never have wanted for him.

"The prince wears the item now, a symbol of his victory. It's a beautiful ring," the king says regretfully.

My eyes snap up, but Draven merely tilts his head, appearing captivated though I swear I can feel his thoughts buzzing even if he doesn't show it. Those soon turn silent, as he masters himself.

"Prince Ronan will make a fine heir." The queen seems to note the dismissive look her husband slid Draven at her comments. "He has proven himself, darling, you must admit."

The table politely nods, though no one speaks up with their support.

Draven looks to me meaningfully, but right now I barely care that this ring might be Seithr, the Kingmaker. I want to know if my brother was one of the changelings lost in these horrific games.

"I didn't expect a winner to be quite honest." Eldarion's smugness makes me want to flip this enormous table. "Many did not survive."

My brother could very well be among the dead. I could've missed saving him, by months.

"What about the other changelings who survived but didn't complete the rites? What are their fates?" Draven asks. I notice he's adopted the same dismissive tone Eldarion uses when discussing mortals. A mirror.

"They returned to their host families, or to the Ravine. Unlike the druids, we preferred to keep our lines pure, for as long as possible, so I did not take on a ward myself." Eldarion reaches a hand across the table, to a small planter in front of us and his fingers lift, coaxing, *persuading* the plant to grow. "I wanted nothing to do with the Selection. I desired only an heir of my own. Yet there is no end to the Curse." A second plant stretches, its stems entwining with the one beside it. At last, a flower blooms, and I've never seen a blossom so strained, as if it chokes on the life forced out of it. "So, we are required to join druids and seraphs, sullying our lines for survival. In the end, I'm glad it was Ronan. As my brother's ward, he will carry the ruthlessness of my line."

"He's certainly something." Draven's lashes flutter a moment, like he can't summon an extra fuck to give about the subject of the winner turned prince. He finally manages, "You must have an account of it and all the competitors who entered somewhere? I am always looking for inspiration. A new challenge."

"It was all recorded for history. I'm sure we can find a completed account of it for your entertainment." Eldarion seems eager.

Even drowning in fury, I can't help but admire the way my princeling manipulates a conversation, leading the king along.

"Is unicorn not to your liking?" Eldarion asks me, and I blink, not understanding him until he lifts his fork, raw meat speared to the end, pearlescent in the light.

My stomach turns, outrage mounting.

"I admit it's not for everyone, but these ones are a rare, winged breed. Sweeter than veal, more flavorful than duck. They say the flavor is strongest in the most innocent."

26

Siren

The Ten of Coins represents legacy, honor, and our ancestral values. Its reverse can foretell family conflicts, especially when a choice arises between the burden of expectations clashing with our own fate.

I F I COULD BREATHE FIRE, this palace would be nothing but ashes and rubble. The rest of dinner passes in a blur of me trying to suppress my rage, unable to focus on conversation.

Thankfully, we move on to the party quickly.

"What's mine is yours." King Eldarion leads us to a grand ballroom.

I find the beautiful scene revolting, the elves' dancing grotesque, the ethereal voices blending into a din in my mind while flutes of elven wine are passed around like poison. Mortals are kept on leashes tightly tethered to their immortal masters.

The king smiles and chats away, Draven's charming smile hiding his contempt, and his friends have casually filtered through the party. I want to ask someone what they've found out, but the only one lingering near us is Scorpius, scowling and shadowing Draven.

I tip back another drink, my hand clenching the flute hard enough to fracture glass.

The crowd swells around us, and Draven pulls me against him, swaying with me in his arms, eyes scanning every corner over my shoulder.

"I need out of here," I whisper to Draven. I shut my eyes to block the world out.

"Say no more." His jaw is clenched so tightly his bones flex beneath the skin. His eyes glow scarlet in the shuddering candlelight. Beside him Scorpius overhears, judgment obvious in his eyes. The scream bottled in my chest threatens to erupt.

Draven's tattoo flashes and I notice a slight light near his hip. His eyes close one moment, and the next his friends are all making their way toward us, summoned by the High Priestess card. Malik sidles up to us, Zara so small in his shadow she could nearly fit under one of his wings, and Fable reappears, tossing her hair over a shoulder. When he notices her, he asks, "Can you give us a bit of time?"

"Make it quick." Her hand floats over her deck of cards, coaxing the Hanged Man, a golden web expanding so quickly it surprises me, enveloping the room. Within a moment everything in the dancing hall is frozen in place except for us. Elves and enslaved mortals alike stand still as statues, the notes of music and chatter mere reverberations in the air.

"I can give you two minutes," Fable says, those hazel-green eyes glowing ever so slightly as she holds her card steady, temple beginning to sweat.

"That's more than enough." Draven turns to Malik and Fable. "What did you find?"

Malik raises his eyebrows. "Who are these mortals to you anyway? Do they owe you a debt or something?"

"I gathered the list of the Kingbreaker participants," Fable cuts in, handing Draven a list of names, her temple sweating as she keeps concentrating on her power.

I snatch it from his hand, scanning quickly. There are hundreds, and . . . I don't see Remus's name, but that doesn't mean it wasn't changed at some point.

"I was able to turn an illusion just now for the king," Malik adds quickly, jokes set aside at the serious look on Draven's face. "He thought he was telling an advisor where that enslaved woman he'd mentioned was being kept, reminiscing about his time with her." Malik smiles brightly and I hang on his words. "She's in Illithial. I've heard rumors of the lord there, both good and bad, but nothing about the condition of his mortals."

"What's the importance of this mortal?" Scorpius growls.

"It could be my mother," I reply shortly.

Draven's friends share glances.

"The mortals here are put under binding spells to this realm." Malik spares a sorrowful glance my way. "If she was here, then that means King Eldarion likely was the one who placed it. I don't foresee him releasing that spell for free."

A thunderbolt of frustration slices through me. Why can nothing be simple?

"Eldarion's vices and skeletons seem well-known by his wife, and anyone they could be leveraged against," Scorpius says with a shrug. "His wife doesn't appear to have any dirt."

"But his heir shows some promise in the blackmail department. I'll need more time to verify the rumors," Zara jumps in.

"Right. Well then, we just need to find a cost. Everyone has a price." Draven's tone is matter-of-fact, gaze red as rubies. He turns to Zara and orders, "Find out anything on his heir for us to barter with." He tucks the list of names into his jacket pocket, adding one last task for the others. "And find out what year the other participants of the Kingbreaker Trials were Selected. We need to narrow this list."

The others nod, and Zara hands a rolled parchment to Draven, who pulls it open, looking it over with cunning, cold eyes. "I also made a copy of the map where the zenith is located."

It's both a map of Alfheim and the neighboring immortal realms, the handwriting tightly scrawled, as if it was transcribed in haste.

Draven draws a line with his finger between the capital and a nearby canyon. "So, *this* is where the zenith is?"

Zara nods.

His voice turns inward, caressing my mental shields until they invite him inside. *The vein is ancient, untouched, and near a derelict, deserted forge. We cannot guarantee the Wand would be here, but—*

But there's a chance, I agree. This was our deal, but my mind is too full of everything Malik and Fable just told me.

And the Ring sounds like it could've been the prize for the Kingbreaker Trials. Which means it's with Eldarion's heir, too far and guarded for us to reach right now. But if your brother survived, he likely attends the same school as the prince—he's the right age—so it's possible our search could turn up both. But we can only try for your mother until we narrow the list.

I give him a tight nod.

Draven loses no time turning to Scorpius and demands, "I need you to mimic me. Do whatever you do to make people think I'm more charming than I am. See if you can get me into Eldarion's good graces. Make note of everyone he talks to. Every person he shows remote attraction to."

"Got it." Scorpius transforms into Draven with all the grace Morgan's poor performance lacked. It's as if he's shed his skin completely, wearing Draven's well-earned confidence and charm, even his haughty smile. But his eyes steep in indigo, never changing, unlike the real version.

Draven turns to Malik.

"I know how to earn my keep," Malik says. "I'll report anything I hear and keep an illusion of Rune, Scorpius, and Zara walking around." Malik's Devil Arcana springs forth, and copies of me and the others are drawn out of nothing, moving to replace where we'd all been standing. "I'll add a little flare to cover anyone sensing the magic we're using."

Fireworks burst out of his hand, rising and halting midair when they hit Fable's power.

"Got maybe a minute left, Draven," Fable hisses back at us.

"Come with me." Draven draws me from the grand ballroom.

We move quickly down a side hall, toward a balcony that juts from the castle over the expansive citadel below, nestled within the vast cavern. Moonlight shines down on this part of the city, dappling the buildings and homes below us in swaths of silver blue. Warm candlelight flickers in near every window below us.

"Illithial," I say to Draven immediately. "We need to get to Illithial."

"Patience, Wraith." He summons Death's shadows, and a vortex of night opens, but it's out beyond the open air. He turns to me. "I cannot guarantee the woman Eldarion spoke of is your mother, but I'm willing to risk pissing him off to see." He points to the spiraling black vortex. "Technically this castle is warded, so creating a portal within its walls would leave holes in their defenses that would set off alarms. But just outside its walls…."

"How about we use some stairs, Draven?" I snap, blood rushing out of me at the devastating drop.

"We don't have time. Fable won't be able to pause that ballroom for much longer, and if we get caught leaving . . . well . . .

I'd rather not think about it." Draven steps onto the railing, leaning back to me with his hand out. His lilting voice teases me, the sweep of his eyes sending chills down my spine as he says, "Don't worry. I won't drop you, love."

"Why do you have to say that like you're planning to?" My eyes narrow but he just takes my hesitant hand and pulls me up onto the ledge as if I weigh as much as a paper doll. I wrap my arm around his neck, and he scoops me up. "Listen, Draven, I can't thank you enough—"

His wings flare wide, and he throws us off the ledge, flapping once, twice, until those wings tuck tight, and we go spinning through the open portal. Floating in the open air like that, it must barely evade the magical defenses of the castle. The dark winds scream, like wolves howling in the night, and there's a scent of decay in the air that's new as we fly through it. Then all at once the pressure of the space is gone and we're at a large estate set into a canyon, windows and doors slanted into the side of the face like little scars. I don't know where exactly we are on the map, only that my mother might possibly be inside. I'm so close.

Draven turns to me. "We can't be seen. I need you to summon your Hermit card. I can cloak us with shadows, but it'll help if you have your own protection in case we need to separate. Remember, elves can sense magic. It sort of smells like fire in the air I guess, so although we'll be invisible . . . we aren't undetectable."

"Wouldn't they have sensed all the magic we just used to leave?" I point behind us, where the portal and castle were moments ago.

"Malik's firework display will undoubtedly put on a show to distract everyone to mask our usage. Hopefully they won't even suspect we've gone." Draven nods to my cards, urging me to summon them.

"Right." I've never used the Hermit for my entire body, only enough to make my hand go unseen. Even then I've usually wound up spotting my body the moment it moves, camouflaged but not truly gone, like a chameleon but not glass. "How does it work?"

"Think of every time you were the Wraith of Westfall. The times people would glance right over you. Every time you were too small to be noticed, too insignificant," he instructs, and I summon the Hermit card, sinking into the memories. I need this. I need this to work.

The memories seep like mud, draping to every inch of my mind. My hands begin to warp in the moonlight, the bronze fading, as if I pull the colors of the world into my skin instead.

"You may be mighty, but you must remember just how no one noticed you even when they should've. How your cries went unheard. How your life went unnoticed."

Tears threaten to rise and when I open my eyes, the opaque coloring fades, my body going clear. I look to Draven, but he's gone, too. Then his hand finds mine, holding it tightly, and I can feel his body brushing against mine. He leads me inside.

We open the front doors quietly, slipping within, but we're not alone.

Shit, Draven swears as a mortal woman scurries over. For all his smoothness, he's not used to having to slink in the shadows. I can feel him moving to try to quietly close it, but I pull him away.

With any luck, she'll think it's the wind. I add a warning. *Plus, if our magic is leaving traces, we need to move.*

Draven lets me lead him away from the door and out of her path. She passes us so close I can see every silver hair threaded through her auburn braid. It's not my mom, but my heart sits at the back of my throat all the same. Does my mom wear manacles just like hers?

She reaches the door, looking out into the night. She lingers, confused for a moment. Draven stands deathly still at my side. The servant sniffs the air but then closes the door slowly, watching to see if it'll open again. There's a breeze tonight, and she seems to attribute it to nothing more. She shrugs and walks away.

Draven's hand tugs and I have to be careful not to trip on any of the rugs running the length of the halls.

Where are we going? I ask, my thoughts quiet, heart heavy.

I've never been here. But I've seen enough elven lords' manors to know how they're typically laid out.

I rely more than I thought on seeing my body to hold my balance, and it's strange navigating up the stairs onto a landing.

More mortals bustle up here, moving quickly from room to room. My horror grows with each one I see, the sheer magnitude of humans enslaved to just one house is revolting. It's refocusing all my anger on the immortals, the callousness of their royal courts.

Voices filter down the hall. High-pitched laughter and glasses clinking.

Looks like someone's having a party, Draven comments.

We move forward, and that's when I hear it.

A haunting songstress draws me forward. That voice . . . I'd recognize it anywhere.

"Her voice could pull a man from a safe ship into teeming waters." The memory of my father admiring my mother's skill hits me low, the smile creeping up his face as she sung for a small crowd at some tiny festival in our old village. I blink away the recollection.

We emerge into a large courtyard, where an intimate gathering is underway. But I can't concentrate on the crowd. Draven leads me over to a fire bowl on an empty table, to mask the scent of our magic. He says, *Do you see her? Is she here?*

I need to see the stage. Tension ripples through me.

Subtle shadows part the crowd, and her face comes into sharp relief.

She's lost weight, and her hair is longer, trailing down her back in a crimson flame streaked with silver, striking against her golden skin. Her pointed ears are on display, and she wears so much jewelry.

She's an elf, one they deemed worthy enough to transform, and I'm a druid changeling. Nature doesn't seem to care because my heart still thumps off rhythm when I look up at her . . . that's my mom.

I'm small again, truly invisible.

The weight of our tenuous last years together compounds all at once.

Draven's hand squeezes mine tighter, as if I might slip into the breeze.

The crowd sways, surrendering beneath her voice. My gaze draws to the gold cuffs at her wrists. An elven changeling maybe, but still enslaved. How many nights has she spent stuck singing like a nightingale in a cage? The king said they discovered she had a beautiful voice . . . when she was in that prison. Under torture. My breaths are weighted, anvils attached to each lung. I need to get her out of here. Right now.

The elves clap politely and my mother curtsies gracefully and walks off stage, gliding through the crowd, fielding thanks as a male performer takes over.

She's there. Now's our chance.

Wait—he starts, but I don't care about being careful. I can't risk losing her.

I pull him along, dogging her steps, but I bump straight into someone, too busy staring ahead. The elven woman brushes her blond hair over a shoulder and seems to blame the mortal walking behind them. I watch her slap the innocent human, berating her about the cost of the dress she wears. I drag Draven onward, afraid of getting caught, terrified of losing this chance.

We slide down the hallway she exited through, and I catch sight of her lava-cursed hair down a different corridor. He lingers in the collision of halls, confused, and I pull from him, rushing after her.

Rune? Rune?!

I sprint, not bothering to keep as quiet as I should. I don't know where Draven is, but he's nearby, slamming on my mental wards. But I don't want to listen to how I need to be careful.

My mother walks into a bathroom, and I clamor inside, the door catching my elbow. She turns, confusion lining her face, and I drop my magic, shutting the door behind us.

"Who are you?" she asks, tone hostile and sharp.

"You don't recognize me?"

Her composure cracks like struck glass. Tears shine in her eyes as she searches my face, as if it will reveal everything I've been through without her. Her lower lip trembles. "Rune?"

"Mom." I throw myself into her arms and she clings to me, one hand clasped around my shoulders, the other bracing against the back of my head. Her arms shake as she holds me and I grip right back, tears rising and overflowing, seeping into her silken dress, ruining it.

"What are you doing here? You can't be here." Her voice chokes on grief.

"I'm looking for you." I search her face, but she's staring at my ears. Soon her fingers trace the tips of them, taking in the brightness of my eyes, then the points of my canines. They aren't extended but they're a little sharper than when I was merely human.

"What have they done to you?" She fights the tears, refusing to let them spill over, though she attempts to smile. "My baby."

My hands grasp her roving ones, stopping her. "I'm a druid changeling now." I try to wrestle my own tears back. "But Mom, I'm okay. Are you?" My hands find the cuffs at her wrist.

"I . . . it's better than it was at first," she says.

My fury burns through me, but I fight it back, not letting it control this moment. There's too much else that needs releasing. "The lord here isn't terrible. He has no interest in me beyond my songs."

"I'm here to get you out, Mom. We don't have much time." I look hurriedly over my shoulder. A pressure buffers against my mind. Draven, searching for me. But I don't want this moment interrupted, so I ignore him a little longer.

"I can't. My enslavement binds me to the house. I can't step ten paces from the door even if it burns to the ground. Not without his permission." She strokes my hair back, a brave smile on her face. Her eyes shimmer, tears flickering in the light. "The king would never allow him to let me go. I've seen his court. I know too much and was forbidden to speak about it. You should return to your new kingdom, before they know you're gone."

No. "There has to be a way." I feel foolish standing here. We should be running.

"Rune, my darling, you have to go." How can she be so calm? How can she accept it so easily?

"But Mom, no—there's more . . . I've seen Dad."

She stills. "When did you see your father? Was he placed with the druids after the Selection?" Her hands stop stroking my hair, settling on my face.

"No, he's the advisor to King Altair of the seraphs—"

"He's what?" She sounds angry, not concerned, and her face heats.

"I don't know how it happened. Have you seen Remus? Dad said he's seen him."

"No, I haven't," she breathes, shoulders sagging with relief. She swallows. "I tried to find him but . . . I assumed he was adopted by a family here."

"Draven's searching for records on elven changelings—"

"Draven? As in the Crowned Prince of Sedah? The Blood Prince? The World Chosen? He's helping you?"

What is with immortals and their grandiose titles? "He's . . . we're . . ." Her expression hardens and there's no approval there as I force out, "We're close."

"Gods, Rune." She looks me up and down in disappointment. Her gaze is wild and livid as she hisses, "You cannot trust him."

My fists clench, knuckles whitening, defenses rising.

"He is the only one who's tried to keep me safe since you were taken." She has no idea what I've been through, none. Draven's the only one who has given two shits about me since *before* she was taken, if I'm being honest. The pain of those thoughts chokes me like weeds strangling a rose.

She shakes her head as if she doesn't have time to explain her loathing of a prince she's never met, as if there are more pressing matters. "And you're sure your father is the royal advisor of the seraph king?" She doesn't look impressed, only terrified.

"Yes. He tried to get me back. Convinced King Altair and King Silas to barter but when the seraph king questioned me—"

"Tell me he did not ask about me."

"Actually . . . he did. I told him you were taken by the elves."
I'm lost as she swears, more tears springing to her eyes. *This* is
what she cares about?

"Oh Gods," she breathes, moving from me, pacing in the
small space in front of the sink. "Do they know you're here?"

"No. I mean . . . they could. It's not a secret I'm in Alfheim
with Draven." I'm stunned to silence as she hugs herself, looking to the door as though enemies will burst through at any
moment. "Mom . . . what do I not know?"

"You've led the seraphs to the doorstep." She stares at the
floor, her voice a disconnected thing, as if she doesn't even know
she's speaking. "They cannot find me. It'll put all mortals in
danger. You and your brother won't be safe."

"What're you talking about?" Has she lost her mind? Has
being here broken her?

"Rune, I never wanted you to know this—" She stops as the
door opens by magic.

"There you are." Draven slips into the room, locking it, and
I breathe a sigh of relief. He makes it two steps in before he
stops. His head tilts as he stares at my mother, and then his gaze
flashes from sapphire to red in a dizzying speed. "Well, I didn't
expect to see *your* face again."

She blinks, and her expression changes in an instant. "*You*
are the prince of darkness?" Thrusting me behind her, she
stands tall, hands curled to fists, snarling.

Draven's fangs have descended, wings spreading to the point
he fills all empty space. I haven't seen such hatred from him
since he squared off with King Altair.

Judgment fills her eyes, a sour, scorned thing. She spits at
him, "Your father would be rolling in his grave if he knew this
is what became of you."

"Well, you'd know, you helped put him there."

"What's going on, Mom?" I demand, hating the panic lining my voice.

My mom's gaze snaps back to me before she looks to him again.

"This is your mother?" Draven looks me up and down, as if he didn't see it before, the accusation obvious.

My back slickens with sweat, legs shaking. What am I missing? "How the hells do you two know each other?"

He glares as though I'm fucking with him, then looks at her incredulously. His hand hovers over his cards and my mother flinches.

My heart is hammering in my chest, this moment a horrible, warped version of what I imagined. This must be some kind of mistake . . .

"Wait . . . Kal . . . just hold on—" my mother pleads.

"Who's Kal?" But neither seems to hear me. All right, that's enough. I growl at them, "Will you both just explain what's going on?"

Draven looks to me, nodding in resignation, then draws the Hierophant. Suddenly a past version of my mother stands between us. Her younger self leans down to a small boy with indigo eyes. He's maybe five years old, his dark hair holding a little curl to it, hanging below his rounded ears. The echo of her past self says, "*We'll make sure they pay. The immortals will never again forget who we are, or what we're capable of.*"

"You want to tell her, or should I?" Draven snarls.

My mother holds a finger up to him, as if she can stop all this with that simple gesture.

Anger burns a trail through me at all this waffling. "Tell me. Now."

"Rune, your father and I were part of the uprising." She stares into my eyes. There's no hint of a lie there.

But all I can do is laugh. "No, you weren't." But I don't know what else to add to that soft rebuttal. My parents? They were no one. Merchants and craftspeople, always too poor, barely scraping by. We were nobodies; all we had was each other.

But she just holds my gaze, apology lining her head to toe.

"And how do you know each other?" I glance at the space where those phantom images still stand, frozen in time.

My mother levels a look of fury at Draven now, seeming to draw some satisfaction as she spits back.

"You're looking at Kieran Ceres's youngest son. Though he was called Kallos then."

27

———— ·⊃ ✳ ⊂· ————

Traitors

Decree 6 of the Post Great War: All children of
the uprising leaders shall henceforth be turned
into the first changelings, sworn to loyalty beneath
blood oaths to the immortal kingdoms. May their
bodies provide the fertile soil of the next immortal
dynasties.

RAVEN'S STARE IS SO COLD it's starker than the field
of snow and ice I collapsed in as a girl. I'm strung between
them, pulled between my love and anger for them. They're
both liars.

"You betrayed us," Draven says between gritted teeth, still
baring them.

She takes a deep breath. "I told your father *not* to go on that
mission."

"How do you even remember that time. I don't," I snap at
Draven, trying to wrap my head around any of it. "We were
children." He's only a year older than I am, and I was five when
the War ended.

"I bet she's to blame for that, too." He grinds the words
through his fangs.

I turn on her.

"I . . . had you and your brother's memories altered by a druid sympathetic to our cause," she explains matter-of-factly. As if this is something any loving parent would do to their child.

My eyes bulge, fists trembling at the violation. I think of Professor Vexus using his Hierophant to wipe the minds of all the changelings training with Draven. I never fully realized the horror of losing chunks of your life.

"If we got separated during the Scourge, I wanted you and your brother safe."

"Yet you didn't give a shit about me or mine," Draven snarls.

"So, you're going to betray me now? Have your revenge?" It's the tone she used with me so many times, challenging me to disobey her. Knowing I wouldn't.

She still thinks of him as a child.

He takes a deep breath, but his nails elongate and clench around his arms as he holds himself tightly. He glances at me for a telling moment. "No. Though King Altair will likely find you now that they know which kingdom you're in. If they haven't already."

"We . . . led them to her?" I feel sick to my stomach.

"Altair likely Selected your father because of who he was and what he knew. He would've recognized him. It must be why Altair kept asking you about her." He jerks his head in my mother's direction. "I didn't understand it, why it should matter. Thought it was merely a test on your ability to tell the truth." Draven's wings tighten up against his rigid back, and he stalks a bit farther into the room, wedging himself into a corner.

As the memory of my interrogation slams into me, Altair's determination takes on a new meaning.

The druids took her seven years ago, for avoiding Selection, I had said.

Then Draven had added, *She was sent to the Destarion.*

The prison keeps records of transfers. We both may have led them to her.

"And . . . my father was Selected first . . . we moved afterward. He wouldn't know where she was. Probably thought she was still in the mortal realm." I look to my mom, and she collapses against the wall, clenching her hair.

"I changed our last name from your father's to protect you kids, stopped using my own first name entirely." She heaves a sigh, devastation written in the frown of her lips. "I knew one day this would come."

I want to break. To scream out my heartbreak and frustration. I came here to save her . . . and look what I've done instead.

Draven pinches the bridge of his nose. "All the pointed fucking questions I just asked Eldarion will get back to Altair. He'll know who and where she is in a matter of weeks. I'm sure he has spies here." He clenches his jaw, and his gaze rakes me over. "I don't think there's anything we can do to stop it. I'm sorry, Rune."

"That is not our deal, Draven." I step toe to toe with him, and he straightens up, fists clenched, as he watches her over my shoulder, like a serpent coiled at my back. "She's not safe here. We need to take her tonight. Can't you undo the magic binding her to this place?"

His jaw ticks. "Your mother is the reason the Selection exists. She created the Curse. We can't do anything for her." He flinches, as if it hurts him to tell me.

I look to her, my lower lip quivering.

"Mom?" I want her to tell me it's a lie. To say it's not true.

My mother flinches. "Your father was a general of the rebel leader Kieran Ceres." She takes a deep breath, tears spilling down her face. "And I was his top alchemist. When Ceres got caught, your father fled with you both. I . . . performed my last duty before escaping to join you."

My mother. The soft singer. The garden keeper.

But the impossibility of it begins to fade under other memories. My mother, who always had a medicinal remedy for any neighbor who'd become sick. My mother, who sold tonics in town and cures for animals and crops. Always picking flowers and crushing herbs. If she could perform minor miracles with nonmagical items . . . then what could she have done with actual magic? What horrors could her rage have unleashed when someone so clever was given something so damning? And Kieran Ceres had his magical blood and the ill will and determination to use it.

But that was all before my father was taken; she'd been a shell for long since. I'd remembered only the beauty of her from that time before, the singing, the everyday magic.

"The Curse and the Selection are the only thing that have kept this world in tentative peace since the War." There's no apology in her voice.

"The Selection ruined *our lives*." The force of my voice echoes in the ensuing silence.

Hot tears spring forth, flowing over my cheeks like lava.

Her voice is steady. "If they find me, Rune, they'll try to make me undo it. I'm the only one left alive who knows how that blood magic worked. That knowledge will put all changelings at risk. The rest of the mortals, too. The immortals' vengeance will be a lot worse than the Selection once they no longer need us."

I can't even look at her. "Draven, we need to free her. Protect her," I insist.

His lips are parted in half a snarl, his brows coming together in frustration. "It's not that simple, Rune."

She looks at Draven, a cold acceptance in her eyes, the slump of her shoulders. "If you cannot take me with you, if you cannot barter me, you should kill me."

"Don't you dare ask that of me." He shakes his head, disgusted.

"They could use Rune to get me to undo the Curse." My mother's eyes narrow on him, leaving me out of the conversation entirely. Why is she goading him with this? "And you? You look so much like your father. It's either a miracle or complete ignorance that King Silas hasn't noticed it. But what's to stop me from remarking on it when Altair comes for me?"

"Mom!" I scold, furious.

"They already know." Draven glares outright, eyes flashing red at the threat.

I stare at him in surprise, but it makes sense they'd know, that they tortured Ceres before his death with his son's immortal transformation.

"Do your people?" she fires back.

Draven's fists clench. *That's not common knowledge,* he'd said about his adoption. Let alone his heritage.

My mother turns to me, a challenge in her eyes. "He knows I'm right. I'm a danger to all of you. Save me or end me."

"We'll find a way to get you out of this." I don't know how, though, and I turn back to Draven. He doesn't move, just clenches his jaw, attention fixed on her like a hunter finding his mark. Everything feels tenuous, dangerous as balancing on a spider's silken string over a chasm. I grab his jaw and move his gaze to mine. "Right?"

Draven blinks rapidly, his eyes so dark there's no color at all. Finally, he forces out, "Right."

"Without your father's blood, it might be impossible to undo the Curse anyway. Yours likely wouldn't work now that you're an immortal, and no one ever found your brother, did they?" she whispers.

Draven's eyes scan her, then flit across the wall, as if he's searching his memory. "He's likely dead." A muscle ticks in his jaw. His eyes go to his boots.

Liar.

My mother only looks relieved. "Maybe then we can't undo the Curse. Not without the help of Nox."

"Who is that now?" I ask, exasperated. At their silence I demand, "Any more vital secrets about the world to reveal?"

"She's the druid's reluctant goddess of night, sympathizer to the mortals' uprising." Draven bares his teeth as voices float and drift down the hallway. He moves toward the door, listening.

"She was also Kieran Ceres's lover. And Kallos and Adonis's mother. Didn't you know you were in the presence of a demigod?" My mother's words twist like a knife, and he freezes, jaw clenched.

That . . . makes a lot of sense. Since I first laid eyes on him, he's felt like something other, something preternatural, and his eyes are unlike any immortal's I've seen. Ancient power trapped in a young man's body, sculpted by a god. Or a goddess.

"Oh, for fuck's sake! You're part *god*? What happened to no lies between partners?" My tattoo burns. It wasn't a direct lie, but one of omission. How many more of those lie between us like land mines?

"My mother was an ethereal. Some call them gods, but . . . it doesn't matter." He clears his throat as I shoot him a contemptuous look. "Any power given to me by her is gone or lays dormant and has since I was turned immortal."

I step away, suddenly exhausted by all this, by both of them. The woman I was, standing at the Selection, desperate to choose my fate seems like a fool now, unaware of the journey she was about to embark on. The Wraith of Westfall, hoarding others' secrets, knowing none of her own. The betrayal that seeps into me slowly burns, until it's eating me alive.

"We need to go." Draven's words roll over my thoughts

My mother glowers at Draven. "If you hurt her—"

"You're one to fucking talk," he snarls back.

"She has nothing to do with this." My mom's tone turns pleading. Desperate.

"I would never hurt Rune," Draven swears, his eyes flashing a toxic orange, as if he could incinerate her with a look. "I made a vow. I will find a way to protect you. For her. Nothing more."

She nods to me. "Go with him, Rune. I'll be all right." Even with all my rage I still hesitate, the bonds that tie us strung so tightly they're shredding. "You have no choice. I'm bound here."

Anger boils in me as I look at her. She's the reason that thousands of families have been torn apart. The reason for all of this. The root to the thorns. Between love and fury . . . my anger wins.

I stalk to Draven. He summons the Hermit and it takes nothing for me to do the same. I give my mother one last look as the invisibility washes over me.

Tears line her eyes, and I hate that all I can think is, *How could you?*

Draven leads me back through the house, his hand an insistent pressure. We spool onto the front lawns, the cool air hitting me, but I can't seem to get a solid breath.

Draven draws Death and the shadows blare into us so hard I nearly stagger off my feet. We step into the portal, and once again I have to turn my back on my mother, leaving her behind.

28

The Hollow Canyon

More than any of the Major Arcana, the Star reminds us not to give up. No matter how hopeless the outlook, we must hold strong, for light will always follow the darkness.

W HEN WE REACH OUR QUARTERS, they're empty. No one's back yet. I'm not sure if I'm happy about that or not. I don't know how much of this I want to deal with.

Draven paces away from me, hands on his hips as he stares through the expansive windows at the hollow citadel laid out before us. The moonlight barely touches it now, clouds obscuring the sky beyond the canyon opening above. Instead, the kingdom twinkles with zenith and lantern lights. I stay still, and he doesn't turn around.

He's the son of the uprising leader and a demigod? Why would they let him live?

"I didn't—"

"*Know*. Yeah, you say that a lot." His tone is frostbitten.

"What do you expect from me? An apology? What my mother has done isn't my fault." Anger heats my words. I'm already struggling with the horrific things I've learned. Every mortal enslaved, or beaten, every death tallied, she had her hands in it the same as the immortals she fought against. The immortals Draven's *real* father fought against. "And you *lied* to me."

"I told you my father was a rebel." He clears his throat, unbuttoning the top of his shirt. I kick off my shoes. "I didn't want to risk getting either of us killed with the truth of who he was. Gods Below, I wish your mother was anyone else."

"How are you going to get her out of there?" I demand.

"What makes you think I can?" His wings fold around his shoulders. "We don't have good options here. King Altair is clearly already looking for her. If I show too much interest in freeing her to Eldarion, then we'll be pointing him her way, too. He'll put it together, hand her over to Altair or keep her himself, torture her for a cure. Whoever reverses the Curse will have all the power in the immortal world, as they could lord it over the others, demand fealty or anything they want in return. If Altair gets it first, he would demand we all join his war against the mortals. Eldarion would do so in a heartbeat, as would my father despite his resistance to it so far. Without the Curse, my father could replace me with an heir of his own, all changelings would be at risk, and the mortals would be annihilated should immortals think we don't need them—"

"I'm hearing a lot of excuses," I spit, "but this was our deal. Or did you forget? It doesn't end because you don't *like* her. Use your station to end the binding!"

"She was right in that I have little choice. And we made that deal before I knew who you were, who *she* was. I can't just go and steal her in the night, it could start a war with the elves—"

"You can't take my father back because he's part of Altair's court. Now you can't save my mother because she belongs to some little lord? You're the Blood Prince of Sedah! And apparently the son of the Bastard King of Mortals! A half god!"

"Yes, and you're the daughter of Reina the Ravager!" he snarls back. Draven searches his pockets, finding a tin, and pulls out something to smoke. Fire flashes right out of his hand, the World tattoo alighting for a wild moment. He takes a deep inhale. He rubs his forehead with the heel of his palm, smoke curling around him.

"Draven, I didn't know who my mother was, I thought I was a nobody! That I came from nobodies!" Why can't he see how hard this was for me tonight? Why can't he look past himself?

"You've never been a nobody. Neither have I."

The coldness in his voice makes me hurl my words. "How did you not recognize *my* father? You knew my mother, but if my father was some general—"

"I'd barely been around Riordan; he was off fighting. Your mom was with the families and my father. I didn't even know his *name*." He takes a puff. "But Altair knows who you are. Who your mom was. Depending on what your father's told him."

"Does King Altair know who *you* are?"

"Yes, one of many reasons I didn't want to be engaged to his daughter and stuck in Nevaeh. He loathes my birth father." He runs a hand through his hair. "The royals know where I hail from, but no one else does. It's . . . complicated for me to talk about."

His arms fold, tucking tightly across his chest. "I thought you were in danger because of the prophecy alone, but for Altair it's more than that. You're the daughter of a rebellion leader, the alchemist who developed the Curse alongside my father. If he finds out she's alive, then you're crucial to forcing her into compliance. And not just her." He runs his hands through his hair in frustration.

He can't seem to look at me, my heart is pounding so hard I can barely stand up straight.

"Equal partners, Draven," I remind him. "I'm not your black-mail, not your weakness on a path to power. Partners."

Draven shakes his head, rubbing his temples, lost in his own thoughts. "Altair knows the truth, but no one can know she's alive, or who she is. If it gets out, there's no place safe for you. Your brother might be hunted down, too, as leverage to get her to cure it."

I hate the truth of his words. My frustration spills over. "I guess our deal is at an end then. If you can't bring my family to me or protect us, I'm not throwing myself into danger to help you secure a crown I don't even want—"

"I'm the only chance you have, and I *will* return your family to you. I just need time to think." His arms fold across his chest as if he's not sure whether he wants to plead or argue. "And I still fucking need you, Rune. We made a vow. At the end of this, I want you seated on the throne with me. So, we can see this through. Vengeance for us, justice for everyone. I thought that was your wish?"

What I've learned weighs me down slowly—what he hid, what she did.

"What do you wish for, Draven? Beyond power?"

He blinks at the question. "I told you. I want a partner."

"Why?" I throw up my hands. With his ancestry, it seems whatever life throws at him, a crown awaits at the end of every road. Son of a rebel leader. Son of a goddess. Son of a king.

"I've never had an equal until you walked into my life. Never someone I could trust."

"What about your friends? They practically worship you—"

"My *assigned* friends, you mean. Every person I've known has been cultivated and chosen by my father, or a royal advisor, or some manipulative courtier. Except you." He pauses, swallowing. "I thought you wanted this, too."

"That was before—" But I can't bring myself to finish the sentence. Before what, before I started falling for him? Pathetic. I flinch, changing the subject. "Why should I believe your greed won't lead you to using me to get to the throne and wanting it all to yourself in the end? You see an equal in me? Or equal power to be used?"

He steps back as if I've slapped him. He asks in a pained whisper, "Is it really so hard for you to believe that I don't want to do this alone? That I don't want to be abandoned by yet another person? That I just . . . want . . ." He swallows hard, but confesses, so quiet it's like a prayer hissed at the gallows, "to be loved?"

I don't know what I expected, but it wasn't that, not that kind of vulnerability, nor the truth dropped into the room like a bomb. I'm stunned, silent.

His jaw clenches, nose scrunching like he's suppressing a growl, and I've never seen him fidget so much. "Am I always going to be a monster to you?"

"I didn't say that."

"You didn't have to." He flinches and his voice breaks. "Keep your shields up."

My tattoo burns like I've been branded. Shit. Do I really think of him like that? Like he's just one of them? And who is *them*? The immortals? The rebels? The gods themselves? He's all and none.

"Draven," I say, but he stalks up the stairs instead, spine straight, shutting the door with a snap.

This space seems too large suddenly without Draven here, like dangers could lurk in any shadow. Breathing hard, I cross over to the hidden spying closet, opening it and slipping inside, the walls around me a comfort, like shields at my back. I slump onto the floor, trying to gather my breath. My hands comb through my hair, and the overwhelming emotions of everything that happened come flooding out of me.

I'm glad he's not here to see me break.

I'm dying that he's not here to make it better.

Knowing what my mother's done . . . what does it say about me if I still love her? What's it say if I don't?

And Draven . . . I need to talk to him. I should go up those stairs right now. I need his apology. I need to apologize. Yell. Anything. All of it.

Yet I feel glued to this space, terrified to cross the threshold of that door. Not because he's a monster.

But because I'm afraid *I* am.

THE NEXT DAY the tension strung between Draven and I grows more palpable by the minute. We portal to the zenith site in silence. The others, his friends, guards, and an elven envoy, make small talk around us. I can't bring myself to say anything. I wouldn't even know where to start. There's still too much roiling inside me to sort through.

The zenith is located in a strange box canyon, which rises at least a hundred feet on either side of us in shades of gray, veins of white and cinnamon etched onto either wall. Draven's clearly displeased about the elves escorting us, though at least they brought a pack of horses for us to ride.

"Why are Mom and Dad fighting?" Malik whispers to Fable, as Draven silently helps me up onto an all-black steed, his body pressed behind mine. We sit molded together, but we may as well be miles apart.

He looks as if he didn't sleep, eyes red, dark circles spread beneath them, and his mind remains closed, an impenetrable steel fortress. His friends look equally disheveled but keep checking us, their exhaustion as evident as their worried curiosity.

I hope the zenith's not far. I'm ready to go home.

I find myself revisiting that word, that momentary slip that seemed to speak the truth.

Westfall hasn't been a home for years, but my enemy's land is somehow mine. I want to be at our Hearth. Curl into *our* bed. The thought softens the storm in me.

I still want this. Him.

"Your Highness, it's just up ahead. I must warn you though, this is a dangerous area, and the toxic drake killed many of our soldiers before we felled it." The elven leader, Älvor, looks back at us over his shoulder, his hair a long sweep of platinum gold.

"But you *did* in fact kill the drake, right?" Malik asks, his voice pitched a bit high.

"Of course," Älvor says. "It was quite the battle, I'm told. Still, it left toxic pools behind. Not to mention this place is home to many malevolent creatures. Nixies, trolls, draugrs, and vampyrs. Frigga spiders are known to take over abandoned drake caves, and are larger than your wyverns, so we should move with caution."

I shudder, gagging at the thought of monstrously sized spiders, and have only the barest idea of what the other horrors are that he mentioned. We dismount from our horses as the space grows tighter, moving the rest of the way by foot.

"When exactly did you find this drake's hoard?" I ask Älvor.

Draven perks a bit at my line of questioning, and I notice the elf's eyes skirt away.

"Shortly before sending word to His Majesty, King Silas, of course."

Fable rolls her eyes at my side, looking under her nails. "What a load of shit." She mutters to me, "They probably knew about this vein of zenith for a long time and are just using the supposed dangers to bargain. I bet there's more in the countryside they haven't revealed, just you wait."

Draven tsks at her.

I raise a brow and whisper, "You think she's wrong?"

"I think she's loud." He slows his pace slightly, letting the elves get a bit farther ahead. He addresses our group, "I want you to be ready for anything. I have a bad feeling about all this."

I glance at the expansive rock walls towering alongside us, stretching hundreds of feet high, winding as if a river had once eroded it before drying up and whittling away to sand. A flash of blue light sparks in a little opening in the rock at my side.

I stop, looking again. And I swear whatever it was *pulls back*, disappearing into the crooked opening. When I bend to look inside, there's nothing there.

"What is it?" Malik asks me, the only one to notice I stopped. He's more on edge than the others. I shake my head.

"I don't know. I thought I saw something."

"What did it look like?" His tone isn't mocking, only curious, worried.

"Like a blue flame? I barely saw it." I shrug my shoulders.

"Draven, your girlfriend is scaring Malik," Fable tattles, though she throws me a teasing glance.

I grin, rolling my eyes, but Draven merely grimaces.

"The zenith den is this way," Älvor tells us, rounding a bend ahead, and we follow.

The canyon narrows before opening into a wide space, where glimpses of crystal glint in the light. But a chasm yawns between us and the other side, with only slender fingertips of stone pillars rising from the vast expanse below like life-or-death stepping stones.

Älvor gestures forward, the rest of the elves standing at either side. "This scattered path is why it went undiscovered for so long. One of our explorers spotted the zenith and decided to chance it. It's the only way in."

Zara mutters about the path being a death trap, and I agree.

"It can't be the only way," Commander Soto argues. He nods to one of his soldiers, who summons the Death Arcana, but his shadows sputter, never solidifying. The soldier shakes his head.

"All the zenith is blockading portal magic."

Draven crosses his arms. "We cannot leave this zenith here. Especially if you say there are draugr in the area. Why didn't you insist we bring wyverns or your bakka?"

"I did mention to your commander that the route was . . . difficult." Älvor clenches his hands together.

I've never seen Draven so astounded. The elven envoy has annoyed him into speechlessness.

"I think we're past difficult here." Draven barely keeps his exasperation in check.

"Should we head back?" Commander Soto asks.

"Just . . . give me a minute." Draven looks across the chasm and sighs. "It'll be tight for some of us, but we'll manage . . . everyone without wings, partner up. Rune." He lifts his hand to me, still not meeting my eye, but I grasp it. To the elves he asks, "Do you need assistance?"

"No, but thank you, Your Highness." Älvor leads the elves across the harrowing path, running and jumping with such swift ease you'd think there wasn't a deathly fall beneath them. Draven scoops me into his arms, and my body automatically gravitates toward his.

I push a thought Draven's way. *Draven, can you look at me?* But it just seems to echo back.

His wingspan is large enough that he struggles where others don't in the narrow chasm, but we make it across in strained silence.

When we land on the other side, the ground sifts under his feet. The cavern is covered with moss on the back wall and lifts above our heads like an enormous hollow turtle shell. Little shafts of sunlight pierce through apertures in the cavern roof to illuminate the mounds of zenith. A lurid, toxic odor lingers in the space. Draven sets me down without a word, and the others spread out, investigating the domed space, mindful of every fallen log or overgrown bush.

"All clear," Commander Soto shouts from ahead. Perhaps nothing lives here, but it still smells like a bog, the air ripe with swampy humidity.

"It stinks like Scorpius's sparring bag," Fable comments.

Zara and I both chuckle, though Scorpius shoots his sister a glower.

"How exactly do we move all this out to the pack animals?" Malik asks Draven, looking more skittish than the others.

"Slowly. Zenith can be moved safely, so long as arcane magic is used during the process. But without the ability to portal it, we have to ferry it out of this cavern in chunks." Draven summons the Emperor, and some zenith rises on invisible hands, a glob of acidic-green ooze stringing with it. "We might have to clear this lovely residue away first."

Fable holds out a hand, reversing the time on the crystal so that it reverts to a state before it was soaked in slime. "Well . . . at least this doesn't take much energy."

Scorpius takes it from her, examining it more closely.

"Be careful, if you're touching it and not summoning, it can explode," Malik warns, watching the small crystal in his hand. A little light activates inside, like an illuminated vein.

"Toss it!" Zara orders as Scorpius stares.

Fable curses, grabs it, and throws it into the chasm. A moment later we hear a loud *bang* that makes it certain her brother nearly lost a hand.

"What a fun afternoon we have ahead of us." I turn to Draven and add, "You sure have a way of picking romantic dates."

A rat chooses that moment to squirm out of a pile of rubble and race off, squealing.

"Yes, I'm sure it's disappointing so far, but there's draugr in the area. Maybe I can show you some *real* monsters soon. Ones far worse than me." His tone is flat and his smile sharp. The cavern goes silent.

I close the distance between me and the prince, and lead him away so we're out of earshot. His eyes spark as I turn on him.

"Look, you're mad, I get it. I am too." My eyes narrow on his stupidly perfect face. "You want to win the award for most pissed, be my guest. But I found out a lot of shit I'm going to spend the *rest of my life* unpacking, and you managed to make it about your own insecurities."

His eyes flare, the indigo spoiling toward crimson.

I sigh, hating this. "I'm sorry about my family." I mean it, too, and he crosses his arms, wings enveloping us, blocking the others out. "I don't think you're a monster. Though, sometimes, I think you're an asshole."

"Gods Below, your apologies are breathtaking."

"I don't hear one given, only rejected," I chastise.

He clenches his jaw hard enough the bones strut beneath his cheeks for a moment. "I'm sorry I wasn't more forthcoming. I honestly didn't think it would matter to our pact. I didn't want to burden you with information I don't wish to know about myself. Though I realize it probably gives you some important context about my nature." Spitefully, he adds, "Monster or asshole."

"Definitely the latter," I growl. Softening a bit, I say, "From now on, can we decide together what is or isn't important for me to know?"

"Fine. And I'm sorry for being harsh about your mother. I'm still angry with her. But I meant what I said. I will hold up my end. Will you hold up yours?"

I pause. "Is that all we are for now? Our vows?"

His gaze narrows before breaking away, and he bites his lip hard enough to bleed. "You and I are bound by more than vows and our pasts. More than the claim we marked each other with." He lowers his voice, wings wrapping tighter around us. "We are written into the other's stars, our paths unbreakably intertwined. You have entangled yourself in my soul, your thorns rooting between my ribs, and I cannot breathe without thinking of how sharply I want you. You are my vexation, my obsession, and though I would rather cut out my heart than let you continue to hold this power over me, I will always—"

"Your Highness, we need you to look at this." Commander Soto's call is firm, and Draven cuts off, red-faced.

I'm breathless beneath what he just said.

His wings clip back, and he nods curtly to Soto, moving to go.

I grab his wrist, stopping him. What was he going to say? "You're bleeding." Why didn't I ask what he nearly said?

He licks the split he bit into his lip. Grasping my hand gently, he brings it against his jaw and my thumb traces the cut. "Only you can fix me, Wraith."

"Oh, Princeling, haven't you learned by now? I'm just going to make you so much worse." I wish I could heal him and all the broken parts of myself, but I've never managed to unlock the Empress Arcana. Or give myself the gift and grace of healing. I meet his eyes.

"You are my salvation," he whispers, leaning in and oh so tenderly pressing his lips to the space he laid his claim.

I can't breathe or move, the yearning in my chest keeping me frozen.

"And my damnation."

Draven pulls from my grasp to meet Commander Soto. Emotions battle within me, overwhelming as a tidal wave. No one has ever spoken to me like that, looked at me the way he does, made me *feel* like he does. It's maddening; worse, I can't name it. It edges toward something I got only a brief glimpse of before with Kiana. Overwhelmed, I barely notice when the elves pass us magical gloves that resist the drake's stark acidic remnants. I tug on my pair as I walk to a small corner of this former den.

"If you find anything other than zenith, please report it to me," Draven says to our crew.

I use the Emperor and its power of movement to pick up the black crystal and shove it in a bag. It seems encountering anything living causes it to ignite. The rats set it off occasionally, but the stones stay blessedly dark when it bumps against other crystal, giving me the confidence to keep going.

But despite all the work, I see nothing but more and more unrefined zenith.

Nothing that could resemble a wand.

I overhear Malik arguing with Älvor. "Are you sure it was only thirty feet long? Most grown drakes grow to at least sixty feet."

"Sir, with all due respect, I saw its body with my own eyes. Dead, yes, but thirty feet from snout to tail," Älvor replies.

"It must've been an adolescent, but that doesn't explain how it created a hoard of this level," Malik disputes and Zara shushes him.

"I think he'd know," Scorpius grumbles. "Pipe down, junior dragonologist."

"Actually—" But before Malik can continue, Draven's cohort all echo, "Actually," as if mocking Malik's know-it-all retorts is a common occurrence. Malik only grins good-naturedly and continues, "A drake isn't a dragon because it doesn't have wings, and an adolescent gaining a trove of this size isn't likely—"

"Fourteen elves died that day. I promise you, it was a full-grown drake," Älvor insists, his even tone turning irritable.

Beside me a rat scurries from under a crystal, and Fable jumps, hands fisting in frustration at the popping crack of zenith. I tense up, too, watching it race away, heart pounding.

Fable curses, "For fuck's sake. Leave it to Draven to volunteer us for this fun little assignment."

I give a dry chuckle, bending back down to gather more.

Quietly she says, "You know . . . I've never seen him like this before."

"Covered in goo? Or pissed at me?" I hold up a large foul piece of black crystal, green toxic sludge dripping off it. I summon the Magician, changing grime into water, and it alters the composition. I stuff the crystal in the bag with the rest.

"The goo I've oddly seen." She giggles at some old memory. Her green eyes catch in the ambient light she creates. "I meant . . . happy. I've never seen him happy, not really."

"I don't think I'm to blame for that," I say, thinking of our argument.

"No . . . but maybe to thank." Fable collects the rest of her little pile. She hesitates. "He deserves it. You probably both do." She nods to me before moving a bit farther, to start on a new pile.

I stand there, guiltily thinking about what that means, what that kind of happiness even looks like if my family isn't safe and secure.

A shimmer of blue light distracts me, glowing brighter. No one else is nearby, and before I can call anyone's attention it races away. I follow the strange flame as it hops along, blinking in and out, leading me farther and farther ahead.

The others' voices grow distant, and my steps slow as I chase what must be a will-o'-the-wisp. My father told me stories about them, some in which they were the spirits of the fallen, luring the ignorant toward what killed them, hoping to be avenged. In other tales, they were sprites leading people toward their fate.

The blue flame appears once more in front of a mossy corner of the cavern.

"Well, nowhere left to go." I keep my hand over my cards as I approach and stretch my hand out . . .

But it disappears. Moss rustles in the breeze from where it hangs over a small opening— a hidden passage at the back of the cavern. I pad the moss aside and gasp, everything in me recoiling.

There's a rotting corpse in elven armor behind it, burnt to charcoaled bone.

Something glimmers in its hand, a shard of black zenith unlike any I've seen so far, carved and spindled, wrapped with a sleeve of charred bark. It's refined, but sparkling in a way I've never seen. Pinching the sleeve carefully, I pick it up slowly.

It drags on something within me, a magical charge pulling at my heart. It doesn't look exactly like the image drawn in Draven's book, yet undeniably I know what it is. The Darkstone. Worldwielder. One of the four Arcadian Artifacts, strong enough to give Draven, or whoever holds it, unimaginable power.

He was right. They exist.

I didn't realize a part of me doubted until this moment.

The cards at my hip begin to glow on their own, as if it's calling to them.

The light illuminates the shifting space ahead. My eyes drag up the scaled wall to the ceiling. It shifts, slithers.

And I meet the burning acidic-green eyes of a drake that's very much alive.

29

---- ◗ ✳ ◖ ----

Drake

Beware the Tower card and the destruction it brings,
heralding sudden change and crisis.

S HIT.

I spin around, racing backward, shoving the mossy curtain aside. The light from the hollow's opening is blinding compared to that dark sanctum. I sprint, putting as much distance between me and the beast as I can.

When I stagger into the clearing, my eyes meet Draven's, and his expression cycles from confusion, to desire, to fear.

"DRAKE!" I shout.

As if waiting for an introduction, the beast bursts in, destroying the mossy covering, loping after me, too smooth and fast. I need a weapon, but every time I've tried summoning the Star, which would allow me to forge a blade made of light, I've failed.

It doesn't have wings but is far bigger than the wyverns, at least sixty feet tall. It has scales like the bark of a felled oak tree, overrun with moss and ivy. Plates of chitinous armor flank its chest like an insect. A glowing green sack of acid rests just beneath its chin.

The others scream and scatter. I keep running, but another second and I'll be flattened—the entrance to the cave is too deadly to cross. For those without wings . . . we're trapped.

The drake's browned, sharp teeth open to snap me up. Fable dives into me and we slam to the side, just before I would've been devoured. It turns, bearing down on the others instead. Bewilderment turns to terror as the beast flattens one elf to pulp, biting down on one of Soto's soldiers and snapping him in half, gore spilling at its feet.

Where is Draven?

Fable yanks me upright and snarls, "MOVE!"

She drags me away as the beast whips around, her magic freezing it in place, but from the grit of her teeth and the strained grunt she gives I know it won't hold. The beast is too strong. Two versions of us twinkle to life, the air warping like a mirage around us. I look up—Draven's across the chamber, creating two false versions of us, sending them running the other direction. It pulls the drake's attention just as Fable's magic gives out, her card sparking and sputtering to the ground.

The drake charges after the trick and Fable scoops up her card and zenith. Mine's in the pack over my shoulder and I'm still holding the wand, so I shove it through the deep V-neck of my tunic, tucking it between layers of cloth at my ribs so it won't get lost or touch skin. We run, making for the opposite direction. Fable chances a glance over her shoulder, blond hair flashing in the sunlight, eyes wide, and I know from the vibrations at our feet that the drake has altered course.

"Get down!" Malik hollers as we race past a small hollow of downed, rotten trees. Fable shoves me into one, but there's not room for two. My panic peaks as she leaves me, and through a hole in the trunk I watch her run a few feet more, desperate for cover. Malik protects her with a makeshift shield of oak, a sword in his hand, the illusions of his Devil Arcana making them disappear. Acid sprays from above us. An unlucky elf screams as he gets a face full.

Draven? Where is Draven? I can't find him through the chaos. I need a weapon.

The drake blows a cancerous plume across the space, and like the smoke from a fire, a bog rises. Trapped in this warped tree there's nowhere for me to go. I pull my hood up over my head, rolling my back toward the small opening in the tree, breathing into the crook of my arm to try to filter out the spreading toxins. The drake stalks past, shaking the ground, and the tree's bark flakes into my hair.

There's a huge boom, and I turn just as the drake crashes to the ground, moss and dust billowing. Someone must've attacked it.

Draven runs from it, sprinting my way, and I squint through the haze as he nearly collides into me, both hands grasping my face. "Are you okay?" he asks, and I nod, blinking against the burn. "Follow me!"

He pulls me out and we run—the ground vibrating beneath us, the beast regaining its strength, stumbling to its feet.

We put in some distance between us and the drake, away from the toxic fumes, but we're farther from the exit now. The drake blocks the only way out. Others are screaming, dying, some of Commander Soto's soldiers are fighting it with magic, others with spears and swords, yet beyond them I see elves fleeing, leaving us behind. I can't see Fable, Malik, or Scorpius . . .

Draven holds my shoulders, forcing me to look at him. "Are you hurt?"

"I'm okay." My exposed skin says otherwise. The back of my neck burns, some of my right arm is bright red, but at least nothing is bleeding. He notices, sliding me a stern look, and summons the Empress, beginning to heal me, his hands trembling as he takes in the damage.

"Summon the Star, you need a weapon."

"Yeah, no shit, but it's not that easy." I shake my head. Even Ember hasn't been able to help me learn her Arcana, the gift of light, of armorers and bladesmiths.

He holds both sides of my face, hands in my hair as his brow rests against mine, the two of us taking shaky breaths together. "It just needs hope."

But that's something I don't have to give.

"Draven! Rune!" It's Fable and the others at the edge of the cavern; they're trying to get us to reach them as Soto and his men fire Arcana at the drake to distract it.

Draven nods at them, and then turns to me. "We skirt the edge. There's no winning here. We take whatever zenith we can and flee."

"What about the rest?" I ask.

"I'll blow the place to high hell before we leave."

"What were you going to say back there? Before?"

"You're asking *now*?"

"We're probably about to die, so call me curious," I snark, and he huffs an incredulous sigh as he finishes healing the worst of my burns. He scans the cavern, but the drake is still distracted.

"That I will always be yours. Until the stars burn out. Hatefully and adoringly, my wicked heart is yours alone." He gives an incredulous sigh. "If you want it."

"Why, Draven Vos . . ." I look into his eyes. Chaos reigns in the background. "You're so very dramatic."

"You are impossible, Rune Ryker." He scoffs, but I yank him down to meet my lips. The moment burns between us, brief, but scalding, blinding in the darkness.

A nearby roar shakes us from it.

"Run," he whispers.

I rush around a pile of black crystal and sprint toward the others, Draven right behind me, the sack of zenith I've managed to harvest jangling off my hip. The ground beneath us shifts sharply, and we skid down, feet crunching over something that squelches under my feet. It's the remnants of eggs larger than I am, littering this area. Draven urges me onward, and I don't stop to gawk at the smoking sacks, throwing myself up a wall of bones and tumbling down the other side of it.

The drake rounds the corner, cutting us off from the exit. Draven flicks his arm to the side, that magical sword of his forming from his ring, burning. The drake slams its claw down at him, and Draven cleaves a finger from its deadly paw. The beast rears back, screeching, and Draven summons the Sun, fire burning to life in his open hand . . . illuminating the smaller, lion-sized drake, rising behind him.

"DRAVEN!" I shout, and he turns, eyes widening, fire shooting out at the drake's murderous hatchling. His friends and guards are screaming for us, rushing our way. I throw myself between him and the mother drake.

The sight of Draven in danger forges something powerful and raw within me.

He's helped me finally feel the thing I haven't dared to since I could remember. Hope. In all its messiest impossibilities. He is the light I've searched for. One I refuse to let be stomped out.

The drake's mouth froths with acid that could strip me to bone. I summon the World, with the Star rising in front of it, focusing on a vision for my family, my friends, and for a better future, with him.

Hope that I can heal.

A shield of starlight forms across my left forearm, my right suddenly weighted with a sword glowing with heavenly fire. As the drake bears down on me, it shoots acid, and my shield protects us both.

Draven steadies me from behind, stopping my feet from slipping, and when the beast clenches its stained, blade-sharp teeth on the sides of the shield, threatening to yank it off me, I hear his voice in my mind, *Strike it now!*

I charge forward with that sword, remembering the lesson between him and Kenzo, every emphasis on pivoting my hips to pack a harder blow, and thrust that blade straight into the drake's feral eye. Blood and gore bursts forth, the monster reels, and I release the handle, just as Draven blares his might into the Sun card, channeling his fire, protecting our back as more of the smaller drakes come streaming over the ridge. One slips his defenses and snaps around his leg. I channel all my rage and fear into my cards. The drakes can have their zenith, can have the world, but he is mine.

I drop the Star and summon the Sun, too. My anger scorches through it, my flames dancing with his, exploding through the space around us, encircling us and engulfing both drakes. Fire and starlight explode. I switch back to the mother and even when my arms shake from the effort of holding that fire I don't relent, knowing I'd rather die standing here than let it get any closer to him.

The mother screeches, vibrating the hollow, and drops with a mighty thud, smoking.

"Are you okay?" My eyes rake over him, searching for injuries.

"I will be." Draven's gaze is hungry, like he wants to kiss me right here. But he staggers, the bite on his leg bleeding heavily. I throw his arm over my shoulder, and we hobble toward the exit.

There's more distant screeching as the surviving drakes divert toward the others, scared away from us, and crest the hill behind, snarling and calling to each other in a strange whooping cry.

More surge from all over, a veritable army. Commander Soto and his soldiers take the smaller drakes head-on, but it's deadly. A drake tackles a druid to the ground, jaw clenching around his skull, bursting it like a cherry.

"Retreat!" Draven calls to his friends and Commander Soto. Malik grabs Zara's hand as they run and leap over the chasm from where we came. Scorpius ushers Fable ahead of him, both of them taking wingless soldiers. I watch winged druids dive over the chasm, buffeting to their escape.

Draven picks up a shard of zenith with his bare, un-channeling hand, and it activates, veins glowing and sparking within it. He throws the crystal back into the cavern, landing in a large pile of zenith.

He sweeps me into his arms and I grapple onto him, barely secure, as he dives off the side of the cliff. I watch the drakes rise, blasting acid and smog at us just before the zenith blows, swallowing them in flames.

30

The Crystal Wand

The worst part about all of it is . . . even if she ran a dagger through my gods damned heart, I would likely grasp her hand just to hold it a moment longer.

—Burned page of Draven Vos's personal journal

T HE JOURNEY BACK to Sedah is quick and fraught with tension. Many of Commander Soto's soldiers have been injured or killed, five of the ten-elf envoy died, and Fable's entire left arm is bandaged from acid. Draven's able to heal his leg enough to travel and, to my chagrin, refuses a brace until we've left the elves. We've gathered only maybe a third of the zenith we'd come for, but the wand I've kept hidden is more valuable than all of it combined.

Eldarion seems nearly surprised to see us return, though he quickly pivots to focusing on the tragedy of lives lost, skirting blame for the drakes still occupying the cave, claiming ignorance to the mated pair and their nest of hatchlings. All of us are worse for wear and more than one druid has whispered that it felt like a setup.

Flying on the wyvern is the best part of our return journey, short as it is. When we finally arrive back at the Forge, many are taken to the healing quadrant. But Draven's already seen to my wounds, and soon Commander Soto's approaching him.

"You'll need to be with us when we bring the zenith to the palace. His Majesty will want to hear about this incident from you personally."

"Just . . . give me a moment alone with Rune." Draven leads me toward our Hearth, limping along. He's healed himself enough, but he will need rest.

As we get closer to our house, I notice Ember waiting at the steps.

"Talk with your friend, but then it's my turn."

"Hey, Em—"

I'm cut off as she throws her arms around me, freezing up slightly at the warm affection, before returning it. Draven smiles at her before disappearing inside.

I ask, "Are you okay?"

"Me? Yes, I'm fine, but I haven't seen you since the party!" Ember pulls away and looks me over. "I was pretty worried. I thought maybe you were hurt but then heard you were on a trip with Draven."

I flinch, realizing I probably should've told her. But it's been a long time since I've had anyone worrying about me.

"I brought you something." She pulls a cute little crystal frog from her pocket and it shines in the light as if it's made of starlight. "There was a visiting market of merchants while you were gone. I remember you said there were frogs that would sound like a little symphony when you lived on the Isle of Riches. Kasper spotted it, but it reminded me of you. I was going to save it for your soul-day but . . . I'm terrible at waiting."

"You don't need to get anything just to commemorate me being born." Not sure when my last soul-day party even was, and I was probably pretty little. I amend, "But it's adorable."

I'm surprised Kasper would pick it up. I clench her hand, trying not to think about how close I got to dying on this trip. To losing Draven.

"You okay, Rune?"

I nod, putting on a smile. "Thanks for checking on me." We both look up the steps and I tell her, "I'd better check on Draven before he goes off to the palace."

"Okay, but then I want to hear everything!" She hugs me again, and I let myself enjoy it this time before I rush up the steps and enter our Hearth. I find Draven shaking his head as he throws some spying crystals into the fire.

"I got the last of them, but keep checking while I'm away."

"You won't be gone long, right?"

"You going to miss me, Wraith?" A wry grin cuts his coy mouth.

I lean closer and notice how his lips part with want as I hiss, "What if I am?"

"Then I'm sorry we don't have more time before I have to return to the palace and haul this pitiful amount of zenith we extracted with me."

"It wasn't a total waste."

His brows furrow together before his gaze sharpens. "Have you been holding out on me?"

"Turns out a drake wasn't the only thing in that cave." I reach into my cloak and carefully pull out the wand. Draven's entire face lights up as he takes it in, all its intricate craftsmanship.

"Gods, Rune, you have never been sexier."

My face heats, the tension between us coiling tighter. I try to stay focused and ask, "Do you think the legends are true?"

"When it comes to the Darkstone, there's only one way to find out." He accepts it as I hand it over, and the colors change, like blood poured beneath the dark crystal. He quickly hands it back, as if it's unbearable to touch. "It called to you, so you should keep it here. Hide it. Don't mention it to anyone."

"I won't," I promise.

"I can't believe you kept hold of it while being chased by a drake." He grins at me, impressed.

I lift the wand, letting it catch on the light streaming through the parted curtains.

"Pretty sure it's why the drake tried to eat us all. But . . . I couldn't leave it behind." I tilt my chin up, but he's not watching the wand with wonder, just me.

Soto knocks at the door and I quickly hide the wand as he steps inside. "I'm afraid we need to leave now, Your Highness."

Draven steals another moment, laying his lips against my inner wrist. "I'll be back. Guards have been assigned to watch over the house. But, Rune . . ."

"Tell me when you get back." I give him a wink, and a smile breaks across his face.

But watching him leave with Soto's men hurts. We've just been through a lot, and there's so much entangled and unsaid between us. I wanted more time.

I move the wand to the unused loft of my room and hide it away in a narrow pen box.

There's a strange sense of anticlimax. I hope to hells it was worth it.

A FEW DAYS PASS, all without any sign of Draven.

Meanwhile our training at the Forge continues to get increasingly challenging. Combat moves into using weapons, and we've advanced to a course that uses magic in battle. I have a leg up on both thanks to Draven. My friends and I continue to practice, and I make it a point of working on maintaining that hope I found to create the Star Arcana, forging weapons and shields, but hope is a fickle thing, and without Draven here I falter at it as much as I succeed.

I host my study group for the third day in a row, my Hearth too empty without Draven's snark filling it, and I wish he or his friends were here to field some of my friend's questions about the trip. Instead, I remain vague about the whole experience. Kasper doesn't show, yet again, and though Ember excuses it as some minor argument between them I wonder if he holds some subconscious memory of the interrogation. I grin every time Felix makes her laugh though, which seems to be a lot.

When the others leave for the evening, Ember hangs behind, telling me all about the fight between her and Kasper. It seems to all stem from his unwillingness to open up, refusing to talk about his past. I hesitate on telling her what I've learned, which is very little, and then get caught in the strings of how I would explain knowing any of it. I deflect instead.

"What about Felix? He's so sweet and he clearly likes you."

"What about Wynter?" she asks me back with a knowing smirk, freckles scattered like cinnamon across her nose and cheeks, those emerald eyes mischievous. I heave out a sigh, balancing a starlit dagger on a fingertip.

"Draven's only the second person in my life to make me feel like this." My face heats at the thought of it.

"Tell me about the first." Ember leans in to listen. "Was he cute?"

And I open a sliver of myself, a careful gift. "She was beautiful."

Ember grins, bumping me with her shoulder. "Tell me all about her."

. . .

EMBER AND I TALK into the night about exes, our past, all of it balanced between jokes and laughter. The next morning I'm picking at a pumpkin cream cheese scone as we all sit in the Atrium for breakfast, when Kasper shows up. Ember jumps to her feet and the two whisper for a bit off to the side before rejoining the group. She puts her hand in Kasper's right at the table. Everyone stops. His pale eyes flick over all of us, as if he's waiting for a reprimand, but she showed me no judgment last night, and swallowing my reservations of him, I realize it'd be hypocritical for me to do anything less.

"If you two break up, she keeps the kids," I let him know. Amaya and Cleona laugh, and I notice poor Felix putting on a brave smile. Kasper grins wildly, and I think it's the first time I've seen something other than a snarl on his lips, and the little act changes his whole face.

"I figured." He gives a little shrug, putting an arm around her shoulders, and she beams, mouthing *thank you* to me.

I smile, but something twinges in me. I haven't heard from Draven in days. The group continues to chatter except for Felix, who makes an excuse about forgetting something in his Hearth. I watch him leave, his shoulders slouched, and I wish I had something to say to him.

That's when I see Malik.

It's the first sign of Draven's friends since returning. Hope sparks in me, and I excuse myself to run over to him.

"Malik! Hey, Malik!"

He looks relieved to see me.

"Rune—I was looking for you, actually." He reaches into his bag and crushes a letter into my hand. "Draven gave this to me at the palace, but I haven't seen you. He'll skin me alive if I don't pass it along," he rattles off quickly, as though scared he's going to get in trouble.

"Are you okay?" I ask. "Is Fable?"

"Yeah, we're good. You?" He looks genuinely concerned and I nod, things a little awkward but I'm glad to see him, to see someone else who was there, too.

He smiles, clapping me on the shoulder, and takes off for his classes.

Half of me is furious at Draven taking days to check in, but the winning part has me running back to my Hearth to read Draven's words in private. I plop down at my desk and flatten the letter. An odd little pen rolls out of it onto the desk.

Wraith,

I'm sorry I disappeared. My father doesn't want me to return to the Forge for the rest of the semester. He's certain the drake being alive was no accident, that they killed a younger male drake but knew a female remained. He's paranoid that King Eldarion and King Altair may have joined forces in secret, both of them hating mortals and changelings, and that Eldarion aimed to be rid of you on Altair's behalf, or me, or both of us to weaken Sedah. While I think Altair would prefer for us to join him too, he may have decided it's easier to carve a path through us instead.

My father thinks that the Ascension's assassination attempt could even be related, after all, no mortals are supposed to be able to get over the Wall, or even pass messages. Not without inside help, and the changelings involved never left the Forge.

My father fears someone's been planted on the grounds. To disrupt things from within.

Maybe he's right. The evidence certainly supports it, and though he tends to err on the side of caution his suspicions have an uncanny knack of ringing true.

Watch your back. I've ordered my friends to do the same.

You can write to me with this pen, it's a twinsoul to the one I have. I'll receive your message instantly. Just put it down when you're done. You'll see.

—Draven

I look at the pen, then grab some paper.

Does this thing actually work?

—the Wraith you decided to ghost

I set it down, waiting, and a strike of pleasure courses through me as it lifts and writes a reply, as if it's been possessed.

Speak for yourself. What took you so long?

—the Princeling you've been ignoring

I laugh, surprised at the relief it brings. A weight seems to unclench itself from around my ribs, dissolving. I chew my thumbnail. Things between us were left so messy.

Malik just gave me this ten minutes ago, I'll have you know.

No sooner have I set the pen down than it flies right back to the page.

I will personally send him to the Boiler for that.

I reply with, *It's the first time I've seen any of them since Alfheim. Have you gotten any more updates?*

It takes a moment, as though he's thinking. But then Draven writes, *Everyone that made it home is breathing, most just stuck in the healer's ward. I shouldn't have brought any of you on that mission . . . I'm sorry we found that drake.*

The vision of its serrated teeth, the stench of the acid, still grip me in the night.

He holds the pen a bit longer than needed, like he's considering more, but finally sets it down and I pick it up. *I'm sorry too, though the you-know-what was a nice reward. Only three more to go.*

I drop the pen and it lifts, held over the paper a moment.

What would I do without you?

I grin, chewing the pen a moment. I force myself to keep going, *And you? Any more progress for your partner?*

There's a pause and then, *I'm working on it.* The pen taps against the page in a little dance. *But I'm using every available channel. I swear to you.*

I believe you. My leg bounces, nerves firing like fireworks in my chest. *Especially if you want me to return the favor you gave me in Alfheim.* I twirl the pen in my hand. *Though I guess if you're not returning there's no good time for you to put me on my knees.*

For a long moment the pen doesn't move. Shit. Was that too much?

You dare tempt me with this now? I'm supposed to be in an advisory meeting in five minutes.

Boo-hoo, sounds like your problem.

How would you like to spend Winter Solstice at the palace with me? That's four weeks away.

I grin, chewing my lip. *So long as you make the wait worth it.*

His pause feels intentional, a temptation to bait me, hanging on his words. *The things I am going to do to you. I'll make certain it's well worth it.* The pen nearly juts through the paper. *And burn this letter, don't leave it for Magda.*

ELEVENTH MONTH BLEEDS away as I settle into a new normal. Eat, magic, write Draven, sleep, and repeat. I find myself relishing the nights spent writing him. There's teasing and banter, and other more important updates. Draven has been hard at work living up to his promises, and each new piece of intel fills me with hope. He's narrowed down the list of potential candidates that could be my brother, and Zara might have some intel we can use as blackmail for my mother's freedom.

The latest news comes on a quiet night with no lead-up, no warning. I'm falling asleep reading about complex divination draws, and their varying accuracies, when the pen lifts.

I think I know where Oathbreaker is.

A jolt goes through my chest.

I wait for more, but the pen stays stubbornly still.

So dramatic, I write. *Consider me intrigued. You going to elaborate?*

I can nearly feel his hand cradling over mine as he yanks the pen back. *Brat.*

We made a vow, out with it, I remind him and yet the pen is slow, hesitant.

It's something your mother said. About my father's blood. It could be a trick of the zenith light on my deck, but I swear the pen trembles. Draven continues, *I started thinking back and my father was from an ancient royal line. He was also the first mortal leader to be able to get a small group of immortals to join him. But how could they have broken their oaths? How could a sympathetic druid have wiped your memories?*

You think he had the Cup?

It may have been passed down to him. I need you to go into my room and check a book. It's emerald, with gold foil along its spine. It's titled The Rise and Fall of Mortal Kings. *There's a bookmark.*

I cross the hall to his room. It lacks all warmth without him here. But it smells like him, and I eye a waffle-knit blanket on his bed, making a note to steal it later. I set down the pen and paper and grab the rolling ladder, looking for the tome. Finally, I find it and take it to the table by his fireplace.

The book is worn, and the page in question has a drawing of a tomb, a statue of a man on his knees with arrows in his back, leaning against a marble sword. Beneath him is a small bowl, for candles or coins. It's titled *The Last Resting Place of Kieran Ceres, the Traitor King.*

Traitor. The immortals would see him as such, but with what I know now about the Curse . . . he and my mother betrayed mortals, too.

I hesitantly take up my pen and a spare piece of paper.

I have the book.

Can you . . . draw at all?

My brows come together. *Surprisingly, they didn't teach it in Wraith school.*

All right, smartass, just try to draw the collection bowl.

Hesitantly I sketch it. It's oddly shaped, narrower than most bowls, with ancient carvings on the side.

Oh dear gods. There's a pause, then he picks up the pen, and I sit impatiently as he draws a clean-lined, finessed sketch, his movements easy, as opposed to my scribbling.

Why didn't you just do that in the first place? I ask.

It's the same, right?

I look at the drawing of Oathbreaker, comparing it to the bowl at his father's grave site. Not a bowl, but a cup, half buried. The images . . . are very similar.

I think so. Draven . . . if you're wrong . . .

I'm not. The ink bleeds against the page, like he forgot to pick up the pen. *I'll be out of touch a few days looking into this. But . . . Rune. I need you to know. It's been fucking misery being stuck here without you.*

I don't know what to say, so I write the only true words I know. *I've missed you too.*

IT TAKES A FEW worrisome nights to hear back.

I got it. His letters aren't as neatly written as usual. They're shaky. He just had to defile his father's grave, to pull the Arcadian Artifact from marble and concrete. I can't imagine his headspace.

Are you all right?

There's a pause. *I will be. I don't want to think about it.*

My thumb runs the length of the pen, wishing it was his hand instead. That I could have been there with him.

With this, we can make things right. Unshackle our bonds. Maybe it's a small comfort. But we won't be forced to keep our loyalties to his father. *With the wand we can summon an army.*

He replies with, *You don't know how sexy you are when you think like a queen.*

A heat pulsates between my legs and my mind flashes to our time in that apartment, as it so often does.

And yet you plan to keep leaving me here until the Winter Solstice. Maybe that wand will get the action I promised you instead. I don't know what makes me write it, but the pen doesn't even reach the table before he's replying.

Are you truly going to torment me like this?

P.S. it'd likely split you in half.

Coyly I reply, *At least something would . . .*

There's a lengthy pause then, *Damn you, Rune.*

As the pause elongates I wonder if he's sitting there, likely in his private room, perhaps sliding his hand down his open pants, gripping himself, waiting agonizingly for a reply. I let the pause turn lengthy, then pick up the pen again and write, *The things I could be doing to you right now . . . but you're trapped in a palace instead. It's too bad. We could've destroyed some sheets. Maybe broken a bed frame.*

The pen seems to jut into the paper when he writes back, *We won't be truly even until you're on your knees for me. Mouth open like a good girl.*

"Prick," I say aloud, hating that this has backfired, riling me. I detest that he isn't here, and for a moment wonder if he might not just find some relief with someone else. Before I can stop myself, I write:

I hope you're not tempted to break our bet first—but the pen moves while it's still in my hand, and I nearly feel his grip ghosting over mine.

I only want your lips wrapped around all of me.

I blush, embarrassed but grateful.

He continues, *I'm more worried about you fucking that wand. Or worse that guy from Judgment who can't keep his eyes off you.*

I'm surprised, realizing he's jealous of Wynter still, who has been nothing but polite to me since our return.

Draven continues, *I'm glad you have friends. Tell me I have nothing to worry about and I'll stop daydreaming about shoving him off a cliff.*

I laugh. Wynter is a beautiful man, druid, whatever, but perhaps too pure, like fresh snow. Draven's like fire, a chaotic mess that burns a path wherever it pleases. My hands are too dirty for the first.

I don't want anybody else. Just your cock in—but I stop writing as ink spills over the page from his side. The words I'd planned to write dissolve under the mess, and I burst into laughter at the hasty scribble on the only clean corner of the sheet.

My brother just walked in and scared the ever-loving shit out of me. To be continued?

I shove the paper to the side and write on a fresh page, *Sure Draven, sure. Tomorrow? (Also, hi Ansel, if you are really there)*

He says he can't wait to see you at Solstice. Also, Ansel is making you a gift and it's hideous. For his sake, please pretend to love it. Let's continue this discussion tomorrow after your classes.

I take the destroyed page to the fireplace as per usual, smiling and laughing a bit to myself as I let it catch, curling to nothing, only ink remaining on my hands.

SEVERAL MORE WEEKS pass and before I know it, the end of the semester has arrived. Draven and I have been passing increasingly thirstier notes, some downright outrageous, getting bolder with each pen stroke. Finally, the day before finals I write, *So, are you planning to return for my soul-day, or do I have to wait till Solstice to see you?*

I've never mentioned its arrival to him, but some part of me has squirmed the closer it's gotten. My soul-day is often overlooked by the Winter Solstice, and it hasn't been something I've celebrated since my family's separation. I'll be twenty-one this year, and a large part of me is surprised I survived this long.

Draven writes back, *Wait . . . when is your soul-day?*

The 15th of Twelfth Month. Some fated mate. We've never used the term on our own, just when convincing everyone else. I let the words hang there, heart pounding.

Had I known your soul-day was this soon I could've showered you with gifts leading up to the day, Draven writes. *Or spent it worshipping you in private. I guess I'll just have to redouble the effort in what I was putting together for you for Solstice. Unfortunately, it'll be late. I won't be allowed to leave in time for your soul-day. But I cannot wait to see your face again. I think I've mildly annoyed every person I know with my inability to think of anything else.*

You can thank these notes for making me fail all my private classes tomorrow.

Better smarten up, I write back. *I won't suffer a partner with failing grades.*

Good luck on your finals Rune. I bet my grades are still higher.

That's the asshole I love . . . I . . . no. Wait. No. Fuck. My elation sours, mind slipping on the truth. I put my face in my hands and groan. I'm too fucking happy he'll be returning to me.

I've known how I've really felt since that day in the drake cavern, when I nearly lost him. These ridiculous feelings flooding my veins were so much stronger than my fear.

I'm hopelessly fucked, I realize, and I think I have been for a long time.

31

·—⟩ ✳ ⟨·—

Soul-Day

I didn't think I could love again after Kiana. I didn't think it was built in me to do it anymore. That my heart was a broken cup, and love would slip through every crack. I tried everything to deny it. To deny you. But I can't anymore.

—Rune Ryker's unsent letter to Draven Vos

I RUB MY HAND as I take a short break between answering questions on my Minor Arcana exam. *What kind of person does the Knight of Swords represent?* Someone associated with the mind and communication, who rarely sugarcoats things and may represent a rival. *What is the meaning of the Ten of Cups when applied to a person in a reading?* Unconditional love. *How would the Eight of Wands enhance the Chariot?* The card of movement would allow the Chariot to travel even faster.

I'm not sure if the written or practicals are more difficult. While everyone else just has to summon their own Major Arcana, its inverse, and pair them with a few of the Minor Arcana to show their progress, mine is more complicated. I have to summon the World *and* the other Major Arcana, too.

Professor Vexus oversees my practicals, and he seems to have some kind of personal vendetta.

"Now the Star card," he orders, having already requested the High Priestess, the Hermit, Strength, and the Devil at record speed. Sweat beads my temple but I summon the World, then the Star right after it. My fingers interlace, the cards floating between them, and when I pull my hands apart, there's a golden dagger of starlight. He takes it in his hand, flicking it across his palms, looking unimpressed.

"Now the Empress." He watches me through narrowed eyes as I hesitate. I can barely heal a paper cut.

"What do I need to heal?" I shift in my seat but as he opens his mouth, looking around for something, Kenzo appears, clapping him on the shoulder.

"Rune is late for sparring. We have our own exams to run."

"She will have to be late. I am not satisfied she's displayed enough—"

"You have passed every other student here after four moves. I hate to think you held bias against a student just because you don't like her fated prince." Kenzo looks down on Professor Vexus until he grits his jaw, clearing his throat.

I notice Professor Fenrys and Professor Atum watching us nearby, their line of students already done.

Vexus clears his throat. "All of us love His Royal Highness. Professor Anstead, wouldn't you agree it's fair to have Rune perform much more than the average student, considering the gift she's been given?" But if he thought appealing to the next strictest professor would help, I can tell by the way the corners of Vexus's lips draw downward he already knows he's wrong.

"She's displayed total competence in everything you've asked, which shows her acumen is stronger than most students in our populace. You're free to go, Rune, great effort today."

Kenzo doesn't exactly take it easy on me either, claiming he doesn't want me thinking I'll be getting any "special treatment." He runs all of us through a gauntlet of drills and fight techniques, allowing us to only receive five unblocked strikes or kicks before we're considered a failing grade. I come out of it with three, nearly four.

I wake the next morning sore and exhausted. I hope it was enough, but I'll have to wait to find out for sure. The results will come in the days before Solstice. At least I have a couple of weeks of no academic work or training. Draven should arrive in a few days at least, planning to bring me to Court with him for the holidays.

And it's my soul-day.

A knock sounds at the door. I hope it's Ember; she's been teasing me about the soul-day present she, Amaya, and Cleona picked out. Something raunchy or embarrassing, I suspect. I look at the little crystal frog on my bedside table that she's already gotten for me. I told her it's more than enough, but she isn't very easily deterred. Felix claims to have made me a present from the moonshine he's been creating, which is likely to make me sick. The day of finals, Wynter gave me a simple leather-bound notebook, a moon and stars across its emerald surface, the edges gold foil.

I open the door, and standing on the steps—

"Draven!" I throw myself into his arms as he stands with a bouquet of black and crimson roses in his hand. He staggers, nearly going down, but his wings buffer out, grounding his feet. He laughs at my enthusiasm, wearing a wildly bright grin as he grips onto me, fingertips clenching into my backside, settling me down onto the icy steps.

I didn't realize snow was something that ever happened here, and a few flakes drift down around us as we stand in each other's warmth. "I thought you weren't going to make it—"

"Come now, I couldn't leave you on the day that celebrates your soul entering this world," he says, still grinning, teeth bright and flawless, eyes luminous violet.

I stretch onto my tiptoes, my mouth locking against his, and he scoops his hand against my jaw to keep me there. Euphoria collides with desire and a calm only he can give. His tongue sweeps mine, my lips massaging his, and I lose myself for a minute.

When I finally stop, he whispers against me, "Gods, I have fucking missed you."

"Well, don't waste any time." I grab him by the front of his jacket and pull him inside. His gaze blackens, following obediently.

"I know I've teased that you have some things to make up for, but as it's your soul-day, I am looking forward to spoiling you thoroughly," Draven promises, chucking down an overnight bag. His hand is on the door, ready to snap it closed behind us, when I hear my name being called.

"RUNE! Happy soul-day!"

Draven hesitates, watching my expression for permission to shut the door in their faces, but I'm sure I heard Ember and peek back to find my friends flagging me down. I wave them over, and Draven groans a little.

"If we're forced to postpone this, then I may as well call my friends over, too. Fable and Malik have been pestering me for days about getting their presents to you."

I can't keep the smile off my face, and he takes my hand in his, squeezing. "But this means your present from me is delayed. I don't want to make them all look bad."

. . .

THE DAY BLEEDS away under a hail of laughter. Draven has food delivered and we play little party games. I open my presents in front of the fireplace. At one point a Solstice tree is brought in by a few servants, the pine nearly too enormous for the space, though Draven insists the place is too dreary without one. We light it with little magically linked strings of zenith lights.

I'm surprised how well Draven and his friends mesh in with me and mine. Malik and Wynter hit it off; the two both like some game I've never heard of. Felix chats up Zara, and I think he's the only one I've seen who can make her smile. Fable and Scorpius arrive a bit later, and she clings to me and Draven while her brother maintains his coldness toward me.

Ember fidgets by the tree, and I make my way to her. The others are spread out, half gathered in the living space, the rest drinking in the kitchen with Draven, who loudly charms the room. I stop at Ember's side, looking the tree up and down, and realize Kasper's missing.

"I haven't had a Solstice tree up in a long time. It's nice to see." Her voice leaves a tinny note behind, like the plink of a piano off tune. She swallows. "Kasper and I got in another fight. Not sure he'll make it tonight."

Some part of me is relieved, but her eyes are lined with tears, and it makes my fists clench up. Do I hug her? Tell her what I truly think about Kasper? "Do you want to talk about it?"

"I . . . it was just weird." Her hands rub together, brows pulled tight, lips curved down. "He kept talking about how much he hates Sedah. That we shouldn't make the Descent at the end of next term. Said our magic was . . . sinful."

"What?" That's an odd choice of words.

"Said he wished we could be Selected by a different immortal group. I told him I love being in Sedah, and he said that was my problem. I finally broke and told him to fuck off and he said you were a bad influence on me." She shakes her head and now my hackles are up.

"Maybe he's the bad influence." I shake my head, unable to help myself. "If he thinks he'd survive the elves or seraphs, he's an idiot."

"I told him if he felt that way, not to come. He didn't."

"Hmm." I hesitate a moment but then say, "Did he ever tell you he wanted to be Selected?"

"Really? No." She folds her arms across her chest. "How do you know that?"

Because Draven and I fooled him into confessing it. "He mentioned it at the Selection. We were standing right next to each other."

"Hey, you two." Felix sidles up to us, a sparkling glass in his hands. He presses his lips together, noticing Ember touching the little lights within the tree. "Everything all right?"

I don't say anything, waiting, and Ember finally manages, "Yeah. I was just telling Rune . . . Kasper's probably not coming tonight."

"Oh?" Felix bites back a smile and I nearly chuckle at his poor attempt to cover it up. He rubs the front of the Fool, the card sparking in his hand, before he blurts, "Anyone would be lucky to come to a party with you, Ember."

"Why are you always so sweet to me?" Ember's smile is sad, and Felix runs a hand through his thick hair, a softness in his gaze that makes him all the more handsome, the twinkling zenith lights flickering over a face full of wonder.

I suddenly wish I was anywhere else. This feels private.

"You're the kindest person I know." He moves closer to her, and I take a quiet step away from them. "You deserve everything you've ever wanted."

I'm nearly blushing for her as I make a hasty excuse and walk away. I look around the room, smiling to myself, appreciative of this little community of friends I've grown. A garden out of dirt and rock.

A gentle hand wraps around my shoulder and I look up into starving, violet eyes. Draven smiles down at me, kissing my cheek, and whispers, "I love our friends, but if I have to wait one more second to give you your presents, I'm going to portal them all into a volcano."

"I heard that." Fable rolls her eyes, sitting on the back of the sofa like a cat.

Draven walks me toward my room, a few *ooooooooh*s trailing after us. He chucks a pillow at Malik, who dodges, and it hits Cleona and Amaya, who are too busy kissing to have noticed it. Fable gestures around the room and declares, "I think that's all of our cues to leave."

Everyone gets up except Ember and Felix, still happily chatting by the Solstice tree, and Scorpius who is brooding over his drink by the fireplace, glancing at me as if I can't be trusted alone with the prince. Not exactly sure why he bothered to come, but I'm too excited about whatever Draven has planned to care.

Draven snicks the door closed, muttering, "I'm sure the last ones will take the hint."

He uses his magic to clip the windows in the room closed and disappears through the bathroom into his room, returning a moment later with boxes in varying sizes, laying them on the comforter.

"There are three gifts, though there would've been more if you'd given me some time to prepare," Draven scolds. "One is a question, one is information, and one is what you truly desire."

"Do I have to open them in that order?" I sit on the bed, pursing my lips.

He shakes his head, grinning.

"Okay, information sounds the most boring," I say, "so let's get that one out of the way."

"It's not boring, or it wouldn't be a present, Wraith. Here." He hands me a box wrapped neatly in gold foil. I pull the top off and find two letters inside.

I furrow my brow, but Draven just rolls his wrist, encouraging me along.

The first letter reads:

> It cannot be said with certainty, but each child of that Selection became a changeling, then elf. None were traded, and none have died. Every name's been altered but a few match the description. I've compiled a short list.

What follows are five names of young elven men and their locations. I glance up at him, holding my breath.

"One of these names is your brother's," Draven explains.

I crawl across to him, wrapping him in my arms. The smile spreading across his face like wildfire presses against my cheek. "And you thought it'd be boring."

"Thank you," I whisper, then I kiss him, deeply, slowly.

When we break apart, he whispers against my lips, "I've convinced my father to allow you to come with me and a delegation to the forest of Eidolon next year under the guise of looking for my familiar. The forest shares a border with Alfheim, and if we go during Autumn Equinox, we can stay near Spirecrest where the courtiers and royals celebrate. I know it's not as soon as you want, but we can find him then."

My eyes well, and I cling to the letter, but he pulls back. "There's more, though I don't know how you'll feel about it." He lifts the second letter.

Prince Draven,

The woman will be safely released to you in two days' time, sold at the agreed-upon price. I will remember the ways in which you went about setting the terms. An oath of discretion will be required at the exchange point.

—King Eldarion

"I received this just this morning. Eldarion's chosen heir, Prince Ronan, has a few secrets he wishes to keep from the public. There was no real way of doing this without turning some heads but . . . druids *do* need sirens for their courts, too." Draven smirks, but it falters. "My father doesn't know your mother's relation to you, or who she was in the uprising, but it's imperative that Altair doesn't learn this. Given what he already knows from the Autumn Equinox, he'd be able to put it together, and harboring her at the palace could be considered an act of war."

"But Eldarion . . . do you think there's a chance he'll tell Altair, given your father's suspicions about them joining sides?" The paper is trembling in my hands.

"Luckily, I doubt Eldarion will want to share the story of how I coerced him. She's been escorted to the palace." He continues. "I wasn't sure you'd want to see her, but she has her own quarters, her own servants."

She's safe. Good. But I don't know if I can ever forgive her, and I doubt Draven can. Hopefully moving her now will have her out of harm's way should Altair come looking in Alfheim. "I'm not ready to see her yet. But, Draven . . . thank you for saving my mother."

He risked so much. I was right to trust him. "Of course." Draven lifts the other two boxes up to me, one black, the other white. "The desire and the choice, respectively."

"Let's go with desire after that." I release a short laugh to dispel the tension. I open the black box and wrapped in onyx silk is an ancient grail. It's heavy, runes cast against its iron siding. My eyes go wide. "Is this what I think it is?"

It must be *the* cup. The spell cleaver. The mortals' Oathbreaker.

"I haven't tested it," Draven admits. "But . . . if it is . . ."

"We're free," I whisper, and he nods. Free of our bonds to King Silas. And I can free my family from theirs. I realize that we're halfway to completing our deal, and I don't want those vows to end.

"Thank you for getting this . . . it must have been horrible."

"I hadn't ever been to his grave before. It had quite the nasty enchantment on it." Draven's voice is quiet, raw, and pained. He shakes his head, thumb running along the lip of Oathbreaker. "A vivid reminder of my worst memories. But . . ." He swallows, teeth gritted. "I broke it. I doubt many other druids could've. I replaced it with a replica, so hopefully if anyone knows what it was, its absence goes unnoticed."

I want to say more, but he hitches on a brave smile and nods to the last gift in his hands, the smallest of the three, wrapped in paper as white as dove feathers. I reach for it and tenderly he releases it.

"I . . . really need you to open that one."

I unravel the bow, finding a beautiful crystal and diamond bracelet cuff inside. It's gorgeous, like pooled starlight, and I've never seen anything with such shine and beauty. I go to slip it on, but his hand stops me.

"This one's a question. A promise but a choice. A real one." His gaze travels from it to me, eyes shifting to a purple I've never seen before. The kind that heralds the early night sky and kisses goodbye the sun. He takes a shaky breath, and I notice his hands are trembling.

Draven clears his throat forcefully. "The one hundred days we've shared has convinced me that I could spend a hundred years at your side and still not have enough of you. You are everything I've always desired and never have let myself dare for. Beautiful, smart, full of conviction." He inches his sleeve up, and I see a cuff wrapped around his left wrist, more masculine than mine, but sealed with the same crystal. "I know mortals exchange rings . . . but I want a life with you here, on the thrones we're owed. This world is better with you in it. It deserves a leader like you, someone fiercely passionate. It's why the World chose you, why the Fates chose you. If you take me, I swear I'll spend a thousand years being worthy of you. Your trust. Your love." He reaches out, his hand cupping my cheek, fingers braced in my hair. "I wanted to hate you, but you've ruined any chance of that. I don't just want a partner bound to me, equal to me. I want one who loves me like I love you, Rune."

I can't breathe. All I know is what he's said is earth-shattering and true.

"How?" My eyes dart, thoughts bundled in the messy roads that lead to this moment. "Can we really move past everything?"

"Our pasts don't define our future. We're both a bit too sharply edged for things to have been absolutely perfect." He leans in close, waiting as I hold on to that bracelet wrapped in promises. "But I prefer thorns and steel to roses and gold."

"So do I, Princeling." My hopeless heart stutters to life, burning away the fears, the doubts, the instinct to stay alone, to stay safe, reigniting my soul. "And whether I spend my life hating to love you, or loving to hate you, I would never choose another. They couldn't even come close."

"Stay with me. Let's rule this wicked world together. Let's better it." He leans his forehead against mine. "I don't care if we're fated for each other or not, we will write our destiny together. I love you, Rune."

"I love you, Draven." I thought saying those words aloud would be the hardest thing I've ever said, but they flow easily, like a melody, strung in syllables my heart has hummed for some time. "I think I have for a while."

"Until fate has her say, and time washes away the name on my grave . . . you are mine." He kisses me hard, claiming me with his mouth, and I pull him into me by his shirt. Let us be damned by our ambition, our vengeance, even our love.

We will rise or fall together.

Suddenly he bites my lip and I pull back as he hunches, groaning.

"Draven?" I ask, panic tinging my voice. "Draven, what's wrong?"

He pulls out a dagger lodged between his ribs, dripping fresh blood. Draven's eyes flutter as he looks to the red spreading across his shirt, speechless, face turning white. Rage rocks me as I watch that blade lift to his throat next, my eyes bulging, body edged as I jump, an assassin standing there.

Kasper.

32

Knight of Swords

The Knight of Swords represents lightning-fast changes and conflict, and his words are both cutting and blunt. In the reverse, he is ruthlessly single-minded, hasty, and obsessed with his own cruel form of justice.

DRAVEN'S BLOOD STAINS Kasper's wrist and sleeve. My hand strikes to my side, summoning the World in an instant, but the knife inches closer to Draven's throat, drawing a bead of crimson.

He warns me, "Don't even *think* about it."

I stop. Draven spits through his teeth, "Well, there's stupid, and then there's whatever the fuck you're doing, Kasper."

"You're one to talk. You didn't even feel me take your cards until I'd already stabbed you." Kasper's spare hand holds the deck.

Draven's lip curls, fangs bared, the claw at the top of his wing angling as if he's about to try to rip out Kasper's eye.

Kasper turns his attention to me. "Now, don't think you can draw before I can cut. Not even the Hanged Man would save him if you so much as flinch. Drop the deck."

"End him, Rune," Draven orders, but I hesitate.

I've gotten faster, better, but even so, it still takes a couple of seconds to draw another card. Kasper would spill his blood all over this bedspread before then.

Damn him.

Furious, I drop the World card, removing my entire deck, and I toss it into the center of the bed where it bounces, landing on the floor and scattering.

Despair crosses Draven's eyes.

"She's smarter than you," Kasper hisses to Draven.

I glare at Kasper, hatred pouring out of me, but he merely gestures around the room, his blade still pressed to Draven's throat. "Now you and Draven have been up to a lot in the shadows. Not surprising for you, Rune, but a little for the prince who stands to gain everything by just waiting for his throne. But I guess I shouldn't be surprised, for the son of the rebel king."

"What do you want, Kasper?" I snarl.

"Your mother. The Darkstone. And you." Kasper gives a cruel grin at the boxes of unwrapped gifts. "Your mother will undo the Curse. The Darkstone will grant any who hold it unfathomable power. And you will provide a great hostage for not only your mother but your boyfriend, too."

"Not if he dies, I won't."

"He'll be fine, as long as you move quick and don't fight me," Kasper warns.

"How the hells did you know about any of this?" I demand.

He just nods to the little frog at my bedside.

"It's a spying crystal. Ember mentioned you liked frogs, and she didn't ask questions. I had to improvise when you kept throwing Magda's away." Kasper sneers down at Draven when he flinches, looking up at him with death in those changing eyes. "Oh, that's right, you thought Magda worked for your father. She wasn't the best of spies, yet you never seemed to find that suspicious. No, she did exactly what I wanted, had you looking over your shoulder at dear old Dad instead of your true enemy."

"Who do you work for then? The Ascension?" Draven snarls but Kasper only laughs.

"No. I was sent by someone far more powerful to gather intel, my father. He will claim me at the end of the year." He shakes his head. "I knew what the Ascension were up to, but I was only ordered to keep an eye on you, nothing more. But after you were asking about an enslaved woman in Alfheim, my orders changed." His lip curls and it strikes me all at once who he looks like. Who his father is.

"You're the bastard son of the seraph king?" I ask Kasper, and Draven blows out a disparaging laugh.

"Last year the seraphs Selected in Shadowfell. He knew exactly who I was." Kasper swallows down rage. His jaw clenches, hand trembling as he holds that knife against Draven. "My mom had just died, I had *nothing*. He gave me this mission, to prove myself to him. And I'd rather die, and kill the two of you, than fail."

"We'll cooperate." I try to keep my tone level. "Just think this through—"

He ignores me and rolls on, hissing in my prince's ear, "King Altair knows you value the lives of those precious mortals . . . too much. Now that we know you're collecting the Arcadian Artifacts behind your father's back, we see what you're really trying to do. Rule all the realms. My father wants the same, but keeping mortals alive . . . less so. And Sedah is *standing in the way*."

"Kasper, *you're* a mortal. I stood on the same side of the Wall as you," I growl at him.

"*I* am the son of a seraph *king*," he spits, his face practically purple. "*I* am more than a mere mortal, and they're going to *pay* for what they did. That wand will help Altair ensure their destruction. And Rune's mother, the Curse Maker, is our greatest bargaining chip to guarantee the other immortals bend the knee. Which is why you're coming with me." Kasper nods at the crystal frog and I realize they must be actively listening on the other side. "My father is on his way right now to collect her at the palace. It's my job to get you and the wand."

"Why does he even need it?"

"Probably to keep it from you two." He glowers at Draven and me. "Get moving."

"You really think you're going to make it out of here? Past everyone?" I demand. I'm not even sure anyone's still here. If they are, then I could raise my voice and they'd come running, but not before Kasper kills Draven.

"You're going to help me." He holds the knife flush against Draven's seething neck as he snarls to him. "*You* broke your oath to the seraphs, scorned Princess Reva, and made your own father an accessory to treason by harboring Reina the Ravager in your halls. We have every right to take her, even if it means breaking down your front doors." Kasper keeps Draven pulled tight against his chest. "And Rune is not a citizen of Sedah until she undergoes the Descent, nor is she actually your fated mate, is she?" His eyes flash to me. "Get me the wand. Or I kill him."

"You hurt him, and you're dead. That's a promise."

Draven keeps a hand pressed tight around the wound in his side, but the blood pools between each finger. I don't know how much time I have before he bleeds out.

"Just bring it to me," Kasper demands. "And don't go trying to alert anyone mentally or otherwise. I swear if anyone comes through that door, I'll cut him to the bone."

I race to the loft, grasping the box at the back of a bookshelf. I open it, the zenith wand glinting in the soft lights. With my cards scattered below, I can't try to fool him with a replica. I force myself not to scream.

I return with the box, and Kasper's eyes light up. "Good, now let's go."

"Leave Draven." I raise my hands up. "He's not going to make it past the Forge. He's bleeding too much." His usually golden skin has tinged closer to gray and I'm sick with fear. If he dies . . . I will dig my thumbs into Kasper's fucking eyes and tear him apart. There would be no place safe for him in this world. "You need me to convince my mom, right? And if you want me to also be a bartering chip to Draven, then you need him alive. But you *don't* need to take him. So, leave him."

Kasper nudges the bloody pool gathering at his feet, trailing down Draven's side. He grunts, "Fine. But you come with me, now."

"Rune." Draven's eyes flutter, the color flaring, settling in a wavering yellow green.

No goodbyes. Warn everyone. Keep Oathbreaker safe. Raise your army to fight him. You survive. Then find me. I push the thoughts to him, our shields between each other nonexistent. A roar fills my head at the pain he's in, the fury and fear building within him that I will leave with Kasper. That I'll do anything, to save him.

"Come on then, wand first." Kasper holds his hand out to me, eyes on the Darkstone gripped in my hand. His fingertips grasp the box, Draven still pressed against his body.

"Altair is never going to accept you." Draven laughs, words fumbling in a way that has my heart racing. He never stutters a word, hasn't once tripped over a syllable since I've known him. "Did your father even tell you the value of that wand? The sheer power? I doubt he'd trust you with all that. You could bow to nobody. Why be loyal to some asshole who never even wanted you?"

"I'm his son," Kasper whispers so softly it's like a confession at an altar, like something so sinful the gods would not bear to hear of it.

"His *bastard* son, you mean." Draven grins at the tremble in Kasper's jaw. Why is he goading this prick?

Kasper growls, "And you are just the rebel king's son. Prince of nothing."

"Still worth ten thousand of you," Draven mocks, and Kasper's jaw clenches.

I shoot him a warning look.

But he only smirks, looking over his shoulder at Kasper. "Even though Altair hates me . . . killing the son of his harshest rival and greatest potential ally seems like a good way to unite the druids against him. I bet you weren't even supposed to injure me, but you got jumpy, sloppy, didn't you, Kasper?" He parcels Kasper with that heated glare, and the tension in the room strings taut. "In fact, if Altair wants Rune to force me into compliance as well as her mother . . . then I'd need to be alive for that. I'd bet that Kasper here isn't allowed to kill me. This is a bluff."

Draven snarls and I glimpse the ring on his finger glowing. When my eyes snap back, Kasper knows something's wrong and the panic is written all over his face. Draven's right, Kasper's probably not supposed to kill him, but I can see something my prince doesn't, the wild look of a man who will do anything to survive who is now backed into a corner. *WAIT.* Draven strikes out with his hidden sword, just as Kasper startles hard, hand jolting, slitting Draven's throat, blood spilling all over the floor.

"NO!" I scream.

The box spins out across the floor as Kasper's fingertips are sliced from his hand, cauterized by Draven's sword, and I lunge forward, catching Draven as he collapses. Kasper screeches in pain, clutching his hand. He dives for the wand, scooping it up along with his fingertips, shoving it all back into the box.

HELP! The scream rents from my mind like a beacon and the door flies open.

"Rune, what's going on—" Felix stumbles in, Ember and Scorpius behind him.

"Get the guards!" I shout at Ember who freezes up, terrified.

No sooner does Scorpius glance between Draven and the blood running along Kasper's arm than he rushes forward, tackling him, the cards forgotten.

Felix summons the Fool, for fearlessness, and his spine straightens as he joins Scorpius in trying to detain Kasper.

Everything's a blur. All I see is Draven's blood. Too much blood.

I drag Draven toward my tarot cards as he clutches his neck, gasping.

"It's going to be okay, Draven." Raw panic coats my voice and I force it back, needing for him to stay as calm as possible. "You're not leaving me right after a proposal, right?"

His eyes finally focus, brows lifting ever so slightly, and I can hear his voice in my mind, though it sounds quiet, exhausted. *You're not . . . making jokes right now . . . are you?*

Whatever keeps you with me.

With shaking hands, I summon the World and then the Empress. Fuck. I've never healed more than a split lip, and his throat's open nearly ear to ear.

Breathe, Rune. He needs you. It's not my voice that comes to me in this dark hour, but my father's. My heart rate slows enough to think and I flick the Four of Swords to the forefront, remembering that it aids healing. I've never used three at once before, but I'd rather drain every ounce of energy I have than let him die.

The cards begin to work to heal him, but it's slow, and I don't know if it'll save him.

Across the room, Kasper punches Felix hard enough to lay him out on the ground, finally snapping Ember out of her frozen trance and she crouches over him, protecting him, tears running down her face. Kasper uses his High Priestess card, always dodging Scorpius's blows, one step constantly ahead.

I keep channeling into my cards, desperate as Draven's skin slowly begins to stitch back together. His eyes blink heavily, and I growl at him, "Draven, don't you dare die on me."

Rune . . . I . . . I love . . .

"Then *stay*." I don't care if he doesn't think he has a choice, if the magic isn't enough. I've seen what a strong will can do, and I demand all of it in this moment. His eyes water, his air scarce, but he fights to hold on.

Kasper strikes Scorpius with his knife, leaving a jagged slash across his face, nearly taking out an eye. A hidden blade shoots out of Scorpius's cuff, but Kasper deflects it, headbutting him, the two slamming into a bookshelf and toppling it over the door. Kasper raises the knife . . .

And Ember leaps forward from where she was helping Felix get to his feet, grabbing Kasper's arm to stop the killing blow. He shoves back, not even looking at who has him, and throws her up against the wall with visceral strength. His knife comes arching down.

Felix shoves her out of harm's way. The knife plunges into his sternum instead of hers. A gasp bursts out of me. Felix chokes, grasping the blade handle as Kasper takes a step back, hands shaking.

Ember screams, and it rends through the space, vibrating the walls, trembling the very floor.

"Ember . . ." Kasper breathes as she clutches Felix. He didn't realize it was her, but I don't fucking care. His hands shake, so much blood coating them. Skittishly he takes in all of us, eyes landing on me.

My glare is a promise. I will fucking kill him for this.

Kasper swallows, eyes fluttering, and he rushes to a window, forcing his way out, and flees into the night. Scorpius looks half-conscious, splayed on the floor, Felix is bleeding out, Ember trying to save him.

I keep channeling, Draven's suffocated breaths piercing me, his head on my knees, his hands on his throat. Felix staggers, colliding to the ground, Ember wrapped around him.

I can't save them both.

We need help.

Draven's eyes flutter. I feel the flicker of his presence within my mind, guiding me, showing me where to mend as I push that magic into pressing the skin back together, forcing it to fuse, to stitch. *You even heal angry.* Draven's voice is a wisp in my mind.

It reminds me of what he said, all those weeks ago with Kenzo's training. *It requires something softer.*

Show me, I beg him. His presence grows stronger within me, a guiding light to lead me where to go, how to heal him. My desperation to save him, my desire to be with him every day of my cursed life, all flood into him, and the bleeding slows.

And I realize it needed deep, compassionate love.

His skin's pale under all that red, but he takes a reedy gasp as I finish.

"I'm . . . going . . . to . . . parcel . . . that . . . fucker . . . out," Draven pants. There's a crimson scar across his throat now, as if it happened ten years ago, the skin not sewn perfectly. His side is still pumping blood and I shove my palm against it, letting that love pour through channeling the Empress, darning skin like two pieces of stubborn cloth, sewing my name into his. No sooner has the first, deepest layer of skin healed over when he places a hand on mine. "Help . . . Felix."

I scramble across the floor to Felix's side, his breaths violent, hacking, body convulsing. The dagger sticks straight into his sternum. If I try to remove it, he'll die. If I don't, he'll die. I turn to Ember. "I don't know what to do. I don't know how to help him."

"Please, please." Ember sobs, holding his shoulders.

There's so much blood all over me. Draven's. Felix's.

"I'm so cold. Why am I . . . so cold?" Felix grips my hand, but I try anyway, summoning the same Arcana cards I used on Draven.

"If I pull the knife slowly, maybe I can try to heal right behind it." I sound frantic, but I'll do whatever it takes. I clench the knife, but he cries out so hard I release it. I turn to Ember, who looks stricken. "Be ready to cauterize it. Maybe it'll stop the bleeding."

I force the healing toward him, sinking into his chest, but I'm exhausted from healing Draven, and it's not as strong. I'm so fucking livid, hopeless, lost.

I choke on a sob. Feeling down deep within Felix, my magic can tell that the knife has bent on bone, pierced his heart. I don't know how to mend a vital organ. It's not just skin or a vein, it's too complex. He's too far gone. Blood keeps pouring out of new places despite the Empress's magic. I don't know if I'm saving him or killing him faster.

Felix reaches out, a finger tracing Ember's cheek. The Four of Swords burns, collapsing to the floor, the imagery burning out like it's been pulled from a forge. Felix chokes. I push more of myself into the World and the Empress, but the latter card begins to burn along its foil, too. It's not working. Blood dribbles against his lips, and his round eyes shimmer with tears. He tries to grab the knife, but his grip is too weak. His eyes flick to mine, blinking off-kilter. "I'm not ready to go . . . please . . . I'm not ready . . ."

"Stay with me," Ember begs, squeezing him tighter.

All at once his eyes fade, pupils dilating, the life draining so quickly, like a waterskin with the bottom slashed out. It's all just gone. The Empress flashes, burning, and drops to the ground, leaving me shaking.

The door blasts open. Cleona, Amaya, and Wynter stand in the fiery entry. Cleona must have used her Sun card to blow open the door. Books burn in piles around her as the rest of our group finally burst through.

"We were all just chatting outside and saw Kasper run by covered in blood—" She breaks off when she sees Felix.

"Is he . . . ?" Amaya can't seem to say it.

"Kasper," I answer.

Wynter's face curls into rage. "Why would he do this?!"

"He stole something dangerous and plans to give it to the seraph king. He's his bastard son," I explain.

Cleona and Amaya comfort Ember, who is sobbing so hard I don't know what to do for her. Fable runs to her brother, and Zara and Malik check in with Draven, the blood still wet on his torn shirt and jacket, staining his skin.

"He tried to take me, too, to use me as a hostage, but Draven stopped him, nearly dying in the process." I rise shakily. "Draven's cards have been handled, but we can still stop Kasper."

"I'm on it." I've never seen Wynter so angry before. He rushes out and I hear the front door nearly fly off the hinges.

The others look to me. Ember still clutches Felix's limp body, whispering to him as though he will wake up, but his eyes are so hauntingly blank.

I tell them all, "The rest of you go after him, but be careul— Kasper's dangerous. I'll be right behind you."

The others run after Kasper and Wynter, though Ember stays with Felix.

Draven's hand braces against his throat, the other one rubbing his freshly healed side. I scoop my cards, calling them to me until I have them all.

Draven staggers toward the door. "You can't seriously be considering going after him."

I snap, "You need to see a real healer."

Draven shakes in anger.

I'm strung between staying here with him and comforting Ember, or chasing down Kasper, but the seraph prince is going after my mom. I have to try to stop him, stop Altair. I whisper to Draven, "Make sure Ember's okay, explain what's going on, it's the best you can do with that much blood loss and no magic."

"Don't let him get away." Draven's voice is horribly hoarse but improving.

I nod. My legs aren't long, but I sprint after the others, flying out of our Hearth, running harder than I've ever managed before, a gazelle bounding through the plains as if chased by a lion. Yet right now, I'm the one that's hunting.

Summoning the Chariot, I increase my speed. Before I know it, I'm catching up to the others and then surpassing them as we race toward the center of the Oval. Kasper's light hair catches the moonlight with two others—someone I don't recognize, and Magda.

Scorpius, Wynter, and Malik scream profanities and threats at them. A black void opens ahead at the dead center of campus— whoever else is with them must be a Death Arcana. He must be there to transport them to the Sedah Royal Palace. Kasper turns and sees us gaining on him. He grabs Magda and throws her, screaming, into Wynter, buying himself enough time to slip through the wobbling portal.

Scorpius tackles the Death Arcana to the ground a second after, and the portal shuts. The yelp the stranger gives is nothing next to the cracking sound of his body hitting the stones. I release the Chariot, wildly out of breath, a stitch firmly pressing against my side. I look down at Magda, but she's bleeding, Wynter holding on to her so she can't run.

"Where did you send them?! Where?!" Scorpius slams the man's head back into the stone and he's whimpering, begging.

"The palace! I'm sorry! He paid me to meet him here at this time with her, that's all I know!" the young man cries, and it seems clear to me that's the truth of it. Scorpius flings his arm straight out, parallel above the stranger's body, and that blade shoots out some hidden spot in his sleeve.

"No!" Malik wrestles him off. "We need someone to send us through too!"

"Like we're going to trust him?!" Scorpius spits.

I turn to Magda, who watches the scene unfold with a coldness I've not witnessed. "Why were you helping him?" I can't understand it but she just sneers.

"Torn from my life to serve the immortals for eternity? Gods only know why they chose me at my age. I have to spend the rest of my days scrubbing my tormentors' floors? Doing their laundry?" Her lips peel back over her snarl. "That stupid boy said he'd let me go home, got me in contact with the Ascension. I thought . . ."

Ember has caught up to us, and my heart pounds as I spot Draven trailing behind her, staggering, still horribly pale. My prince couldn't sit this one out. Typical.

"They get away?" he croaks.

"Yes." I want him to rest but the determination boiling in his gaze is undeniable.

"We're going, now. I need to warn the king. Get your mother out of there." Draven rubs at his throat. He turns to the others, taking stock. "Zara, go tell Commander Soto what happened. We're under attack. Take her and that Death Arcana with you."

"Be a man. Kill me now," Magda growls at him.

"I stopped being just a man a long time ago." His expression holds an immortal's cold fury. Draven announces, "Amaya can open the portal."

"Uh . . . I can?" Amaya glances uncertainly my way.

"Can you do it?" I ask.

"I'll try." She sighs, determination setting her shoulders.

"Be careful," Zara insists, taking one last look at us. She binds the stranger's wrists, keeping Magda close as she moves them both farther into the Forge.

Amaya channels Death. The portal is wobbly, but after a moment it rights itself. She shoots me a proud grin.

Draven's hand lifts, the tattoo on the back glowing as he checks it. He nods to Scorpius, Malik, and Fable. "Ready?"

"What's waiting for us?" Malik asks.

"He said the seraphs would be invading the palace. Prepare yourselves for a fight," Draven tells them, and everyone exchanges a dark look.

Draven's eyes snag on mine briefly before he rushes through with his friends.

I turn to mine. Wynter looks lost to his grief, furious tears drawing paths through the blood down his face. Amaya is being held by Cleona, but she looks to me with determination in her gaze, holding that portal strong. Ember stands like a shade of her former self, no light limned in her at all as she stares into that dark portal.

"You don't have to—" I start.

"I'm with you," Wynter insists. "He killed Felix." He says it simply, like there is no other option. And I realize he's right.

"For Felix," Cleona and Amaya say.

I nod at them and turn to Ember last.

"Not all changelings are traitors." Her eyes spark with fire.

We turn and march through the darkness, and I pray to the gods and stars to keep us all breathing until morning.

33

They Hold No Power over Me

The World card signifies an ending of the Fool's journey. She may be afraid to close the book, to see the end through, but only by completing the cycle, and overcoming fear, may the journey end.

W E EXIT AT the front lawns of the palace. It's an area I've never seen, having only been to Court at the Autumn Equinox, the one night the castle went unwarded. Kasper is sprinting in the opposite direction across the lawn, where it stretches into the dark forests in the distance.

"Where is he going?" Amaya asks.

"He's probably signaling to his allies," I reply, and turn to Draven. "The seraphs will be here soon."

"We need to rouse the castle," Draven croaks.

The others shoot a questioning look my way. "My mom is . . . important," I tell them. I glance to Draven and he gives me a careful nod. "King Altair thinks there's a possibility she could put an end to the Curse and he's here to take her hostage." Our friends break out into murmurs, all of them confused.

"Why would he think that?" Scorpius asks.

"What's it matter?" Wynter challenges him. He points after Kasper, still sprinting away from us. "We need to kill him and protect Rune's mom."

"It's just a surprise to us," Fable says, glancing between me and Draven.

"We don't have time to explain all this." Draven growls, "Listen to Rune."

I roll my shoulders and meet the others' eyes. "This goes beyond Kasper. The seraphs want war with the mortals, and they will go through Sedah to make that happen. If they get their hands on a cure for the Curse, they'll force Sedah into joining their war against the mortals to gain access. It's a lose-lose scenario. Sedah may not have always been our home, but it is now. We need to hold the line until backup arrives."

"We'll follow your lead, Rune." Malik nods to me. He puts his fist over his heart, and one by one, to my stunned surprise, the others follow suit. I take a deep, steadying breath.

"We keep our highest Arcana users at the front, phalanx our formation, and let the lower Arcanas stay in the wings." I turn to Ember, and gone is the far-off look in her eyes, but instead a steadfast resolution lines her very bones. "We need weapons. A lot of them."

"On it." Ember summons the Star and begins to work, crafting swords and daggers and starlit bows.

I turn to Draven as the others gather around her, making requests.

"Someone needs to warn King Silas and move your family and my mother to safety. You're in no position to fight."

His brows draw in, but with his cards tainted and his blood loss, he has no choice. He argues, "Altair wants you. You should come with me."

"I need to help them stall until Zara gets Commander Soto's soldiers." I don't drop his gaze, I cannot for a second let him think I'm afraid of this. That I doubt myself. "There's no time to argue. We'll fight. You get our families to safety."

Finally, he nods, submitting, though there's fire in his gaze. He turns to Fable. "Listen to her. If the tide turns, you get her out."

She nods to him, a solemn look in her eyes that tells me she will obey that order even if I beg her not to.

I grasp Draven by the shirt, kissing him, and he holds on to me like I'm the only anchor in a storm. His soft lips cling to me, tongue parting me as his hands grasp me, cradling my face against his. I don't know if I'm coming back from this. I don't know if the seraphs will siege the castle while he's inside. If my mother will be taken. I don't know what comes next, and I can feel his uncertainty, too, both of us reluctant to separate.

I break first and turn my back on him before I can hesitate a moment longer.

I focus ahead, taking stock of my friends and his, and the mixed Arcana between us. Death, Judgment, the Devil, the Hanged Man, the Sun, the Moon, the Star, and me. The World.

Lightning slams into the lawns ahead of us, almost blinding, and we turn to see a squadron of seraphs in its wake, King Altair at the lead. Kasper runs into the safety of their numbers. A warning bell sounds within the castle and guards appear along the walls, many rushing to defend it, or filtering onto the lawns behind us.

But I can tell by the sheer number of winged seraphs that even with a few more guards, we're not enough. Half of us are first-years, but what choice do we have?

I repeat the mantra my mother taught me, so long as I do not fear them, they hold no power over me.

I summon the World as we march across the sloping lawn to greet them. We spread out in a phalanx, something we've just learned in sparring.

Scorpius at my side mutters, "That's two of your friends who've turned coat."

I shoot a look at him. Really? Now?

He takes my measure in a glance. "If you're one of them, if you've set us up or hurt Draven, I'll kill you myself."

He morphs his body into Draven's, but his cold eyes give away the cheap imitation.

"Lay off," Wynter growls, fangs descending, stalking at my other side. He's the next most powerful with Judgment. He gives me a bit more confidence as the distance between us and the seraphs narrows. We're close enough now to clearly see their faces.

King Altair is at the front of their group, and beside him . . . my father. My heart plummets. His hands shake holding that sword of light, gold eyes shining with tears. Will he kill me if it comes to it?

With his vow, would he have a choice?

Altair's men funnel Kasper to the back, protecting him. Princess Reva's with them, and she observes Kasper as he is, a snake in the grass. Is he now heir to Nevaeh's throne, displacing her? She grasps hold of him, a wave of light blaring down over them, and the two disappear, her shepherding him home.

I wanted to kill him. My fists clench and then I draw on Judgment, and the rest of my group summon their cards up, too.

"Rune Ryker, I'm not surprised to see you here. I suppose I should be thanking you for this." King Altair holds up the Darkstone. "Did you go to Alfheim just to look for it?"

The others in my group check with me, but I stay silent. The vow I made to Draven burns through me, but I wouldn't have risen to Altair's bait anyway. There's no way I'm letting him know what we're up to.

He observes me, the blinding white of his halo floating across his temple like a crown, reflecting off that perfect blond hair. He lifts his chin. "You're going to come with me, as is your mother. I know she's here."

He takes in the battle stances of each person around me. Whether they're fighting for me, or Draven, or because oaths demand it, I don't know, but I'm glad they're here.

I can't help looking to my father. Tears streak my face, but I lift my chin. Just like he taught me to. "Tough luck, Your Majesty. We aren't going anywhere with you," I tell him. The wind whips around me, the steadfast light of the stars and the full moon lighting up the night. The magic burns off our groups; our cards casting a kaleidoscope of colors, the seraphs as white and blinding as lit sulfur.

King Altair takes the first step and we burst like oil thrown in a fire.

Wynter and I cast Judgment across several seraphs, and I bend their will to mine. My magic isn't perfect, but it's enough to be deadly. I cut down a seraph with one of my knives, razor edge slicing through his soft, unprotected neck, then use Judgment to force two more to impale each other on their blades.

I've lost sight of my father and King Altair in the fray. Cleona rushes by me, using a bow that Ember crafted to fire off arrows of fire, knocking seraphs from the sky. Amaya slices through the crowd below, disappearing and popping out of shadows across the battlefield. She comes in for killing blows, and anytime someone gets too close to Cleona, she's there to take them by surprise.

Another seraph rushes me, and I meet him head-on, bolting under his swinging sword and plunging my dagger into his right shoulder blade. He goes to retaliate, throwing a hidden dagger at me with his left hand, but it stops midair. Nearby, Fable summons the Hanged Man and suspends time. I smash my boot into the seraph's skull, knocking him out cold. Ember moves past me, following Fable into the heat of battle.

I search across the battle. Wherever Altair is, my father will be, too. I need to kill the seraph king if I can, or at least stall him. Maybe then I can put a stop to this whole fight.

I nearly collide into someone before realizing it's me, the illusion sluicing right through me, and spot Malik casting doubles of us across the scene to confuse the seraphs. Draven's suddenly at my side, and for a moment my heart leaps. Then I notice his cold eyes, the lack of a scar at his throat.

"We won't be able to hold much longer. We need to distract Altair before he reaches the royal family." Scorpius searches the crowd too nervously to be convincing as Draven. "There he is."

I spot the seraph king across the melee. His gaze locks on mine, and he grips that heavenly sword, marching straight at me. I swallow my fear and refocus Judgment, aiming it all his way and he falters a step. For a moment I think it's working, that I'm bending his will beneath mine, slowing him down, but then Fable steps into my view, wings shifting on her back, hand trembling as she presses the Hanged Man to stop the seraph king from advancing on me, commanding time itself.

I push harder to try to tear through Altair's mind, but his will is walled away under pure steel. Nothing is breaking through.

I switch to channeling the Star, light burning beneath my skin as the card forges a sword made of light. Every instinct of survival within me hones its sharp edges, fire licking up the blade. Sweat beads my brow, but I'm not done—I draw the Sun, the next highest Arcana beside Judgment and the World.

My spare hand brims with lava, cracking across my skin. I likely look like a demon. I'm surely as angry as one. I don't know how long I can maintain this, so I charge Altair just as Fable drops to a knee, forced to release him, Scorpius running to her side, still using the Moon Arcana to impersonate Draven.

Altair's sword meets mine with such ease I immediately realize I've made a huge fucking mistake. Yet my blade holds. We break apart and Scorpius steps in, his hits stronger than mine, like a rabid bear, all brute strength with no grace. They exchange more blows, and I angle to find a way to attack without hitting Scorpius.

Suddenly Altair slams his sword against Scorpius and punches him across the face. The card at the druid's waist blinks out and the king grasps Scorpius by the chin.

"I know how your prince fights. You will never be him—"

I grab Altair's wrist with my blinding-hot hand. He drops Scorpius, who lies gasping for air, and swings his sword to meet mine. I barely block in time and he bends his full weight and strength against his steel. My feet slide back along the gravel path until I drop the Sun Arcana, forced to hold my sword with both hands.

Neither blade nor bone snap.

"You cannot win against me." Altair grits his teeth, pressing his blade down harder against mine. "You will surrender. Then your mother is going to reverse this blight and your prince and his father are going to join our cause." He takes one step forward, then another, my feet sliding with ease. If I meet a single stone, I'm done for.

"You're not exactly convincing," I growl, spotting the crystal wand sticking out of a leather sheath at his waist.

"I think you'll soon see reason." He shoves hard, and I topple back, spinning. One knee scrapes the dirt before I'm up, retreating, the air parting as he swipes his sword where my neck was just moments before. He strikes so hard he's likely to lift me from the ground. Each blow jolts up my arm, wearing me down.

"We wouldn't have found her without you. The information you gave me, and then the curious interest the prince of Sedah took in an elven changeling . . . yes, I have my spies, Rune, even in elven courts. Even in druid ones. But I should thank *you* for leading me straight to her."

My arms shake, blocking his next blow. My knees threaten to give out beneath the burden of it.

I'm losing. There's no winning this.

My father battles his way through the illusions toward us, stopping just behind his king. I summon the High Priestess as I keep fighting, dropping my shields only enough to spear a thought toward my father. *Dad, please help me.*

His voice returns clear as day. The familiarity of it has me nearly breaking, *Just keep him distracted, Ruru.*

I jolt at the nickname. Ruru . . . that's what my brother called me before he was taken. I haven't thought of it in years.

Hope burns through me like a torch flaring to life inside my chest. I keep my chin up, then dodge another blow backward, spinning out of Altair's strike range. He slows.

"Whoa, wait." I put my hands up slowly.

His eyes narrow, and he lifts his sword unhurriedly, tapping it hard enough beneath my chin that my jaw clatters shut, leaving me clenching my teeth. I need to buy as much time as I can get.

"I knew you'd see sense." His smile is a daggered thing, holding the arrogance of a life lived without hearing *no*.

"If I take you to my mother, you have to spare her, and Draven."

"I don't *have* to do anything, but as I said, I need your mother," King Altair growls. "Your smug little master though? Draven. Him, I'll kill for fun if Silas does not submit."

My father makes his move, darting forward, aiming his blade at King Altair's throat. Before it can draw blood, he halts, as if invisible bonds freeze him in place. The seraph king's eyes glow gold. He doesn't hesitate, thrusting his sword through my father's gut, running him through.

My sword drops from my hand. Time stills. Sound silences. All I see is blood blooming across my father's tunic, the whites of his eyes growing in shock. He's gasping at the air, as if the wind's been knocked out of him.

Then a rage I've never known scorches through me. I grasp the crystal wand from Altair's waist and jerk it upright, striking it through the king's left eye. Blood gushes out as it splices inward, coating my arm. He throws me back, staggering.

A hair-raising scream unleashes from him. He slowly jerks the wand from his eye, hand trembling as it teeters in his palm. His fist strangles the Darkstone, though it doesn't shatter, despite its fragile appearance. I run to my father who pants on the ground, hands shaking, pressed against the blood loss in his gut. Altair looks to me once, ruined eye bleeding, the span of it black as if the zenith has *infected* him. Then he shuts it tight, baring his teeth at me. He flicks my father's blood off his sword and takes two steps toward us.

I throw myself over my father's body, covering him.

But then Altair stops, staring at something behind me.

A wyvern soars overhead, and I duck my head against my father's chest as it collides into King Altair, forcing him back. A portaled darkness widens on the lawns, and Commander Soto flies through. The druid army and more wyverns come through behind him, forcing the seraphs to retreat. I exchange one more look with Altair before he lifts his sword to the sky, blinding-white light blaring all around him. Then the remaining seraphs vanish, abandoning the fight, taking Darkstone with them.

I barely care. I turn to my father and demand the Empress to rise from my deck to heal him. Blood taints his lips, and he cups my cheek as I force my energy to rally, my other hand pressed hard against the bleeding, but there's so much of it. My power presses against his wound, but nothing seems to change. Tears roll down my cheeks, a darkness gnawing at the back of my mind that I ignore.

"Dad, stay with me," I insist, the skin unwilling to knit, like paper beneath water.

"Baby girl," he breathes.

I'm forced to look into his dark golden eyes, warm as a hearth. They were the first eyes I ever saw, and as I blink away my blinding tears, I can't shake away the thought that mine will be the last he ever sees.

"I'm so sorry."

"You didn't have a choice," I sob, my jaw trembling. "Just don't leave me. I can't say goodbye. Don't make me. Hold on. P-Please. I came all this way. We're so close to being a family again . . ."

"You can't do anything, honey. Our vows will make sure of that." He coughs blood, but I refuse to accept it. The image of that fucking cup returns to me, laying forgotten on my bedsheets back at the Forge. He says, "Druid magic cannot save a seraph."

But he can't be right. I search for help, but everyone is too far from us, and my gaze won't stray from his long. He wears the smile he wore on his happiest days, and there's no fear there. If anything . . . he looks more at peace than I've seen him, his warm hand still resting against my cheek. I clench my eyes shut, forcing more magic through anyway. I'll bleed myself dry if it stops this. Except it doesn't matter how much magic I pour through, it's like it falls into a void. Exhaustion weighs heavily, and my skin smokes from the effort. I'll burn myself to cinders if that's what it takes.

Then I hit a barrier.

I open my eyes, and his other hand rests across my cards. *No.* I realize he did it intentionally, to prevent me burning out in order to save him. But that would've been my choice, *mine.* Why did he take that from me?

"No. No, Dad. What . . . what did you do?"

"You are what I'm proudest of," he says.

I lean my cheek into his hand, teeth gritted as I sob openly now, shoulders racking against the heartache.

"I love you . . . Ruru."

His hand drops, eyes fluttering before shifting to the night sky above.

Starlight guides him into the afterlife's endless seas.

Silence cleaves a void in the world. Like an arrow piercing straight through a target, there's a gap left in its absence. His eyes don't move to mine, and it doesn't matter that he cannot hear it, my voice still shreds under my grief as I cling to the stranger's clothes my father's wrapped in. I run my trembling hands through the feathers braced against his back, but they begin to disappear, and his body entropies into what it was when he was taken.

A changeling is not a true immortal.

And all mortals must die.

Suddenly others surround us. An Empress Arcana bearing the royal sigils kneels, but it's too late. All they can do is close my father's eyes for the last time. Arms wrap around me, and I cannot pull away. I'm turned and clenched against Draven's chest.

I shake. And scream. Then I break.

Epilogue

T HE DRUIDS DO NOT mourn in black, that is left for honor and national pride. Instead, they grieve in red, a stark reminder of the preciousness of life. There are not many of us to send my father into the after, or Felix, and I'm the only member of my family in attendance.

The seraphs hunted down my mother's quarters, stealing her away while the rest of us were distracted, killing the more than twenty guards Draven assigned to her. He's apologized profusely for not putting more with her, for letting Kasper get the better of him, for the Forge and the palace being attacked to start with.

There are whispers of more traitors in our midst, and of Nevaeh's gathering army. War is nearly inevitable now. The druids have accused the seraphs of attacking on sovereign soil, while the seraphs accused us of harboring a criminal of war. Though I'm unsure when the fighting will break out, there's one thing for certain. If my mother creates a cure to the Curse, Altair will use it as leverage until the elves and druids join his cause to destroy all mortals.

And it's my fault for leading him to her.

My fault my father's dead.

Draven's hand brushes mine as some stranger reads from the mortal *Book of Sorrows*, a chapter about what comes after life in *The Given*, a religious tome of gods, monsters, and how the world was formed. It's barely been a day since the fight, and a public mourning already happened for the other fallen, Felix included, on the lawns of the palace. But for my father, Draven allowed only our friends to mourn with me under the arches of the palace walls. The immortals have a different book of prayers for their beliefs, *The Taken*, read from at the larger funeral service today, and there's a pointedness to Draven's insistence on this one. Tears pour down my cheeks, sticking to the streams of agony they've been tracking all day, gathering under my chin to drip onto my mourning gown.

Carefully, my hand links in his as the words wash over me, like I'm a stone in a riverbed, worn away by the current of grief. There are no sharp edges to me now. Draven grasps my hand right back, squeezing tight.

The pyre is attended to, and though the flames engulf my father's forever sleeping body, the warmth never reaches me. I shiver instead. Draven's hand grips stronger.

AFTER THE FUNERAL, we return to a Hearth still bearing the scars of all that happened. The Solstice tree droops, wrapping paper litters the floor, and drink cups sit stale. I head to my room, burned-up books and broken shelves littering the floor. Draven's blood and Felix's are still smeared across the ground, Kasper's footprints visible in the viscous fluid, like a brand. I knew there was something off with him, didn't trust him, and yet I shoved it aside, ignored it, writing him off as just someone else angry about the immortals. Someone like me.

The difference between us is that he never fell in love with one.

"Let's grab what we need. Then we'll move to the palace." Draven lingers in the doorway.

"What about next semester?" I ask.

"We'll come back. With a lot more wards and guards in place." He clenches his jaw, taking in the space, judging every shadow, every dark corner.

"Can you tell me . . . what did my father say to you that day, before we left for Alfheim?"

Draven straightens, those ever-changing irises bleeding to gray. "He said, 'Take care of her.' He seemed to know you'd resent anyone thinking you needed that. He mentioned you'd be strong until you broke, and that he hoped there'd be a time in your life you didn't need to be so brave anymore. I vowed to do everything in my power." He thumbs the bright red scar slashing across his throat. Draven blames himself for the attack, but I couldn't keep him safe either. The wound hasn't faded—he hasn't had it healed by someone who knows what they're doing. Unlike me. I feel so fractured . . . broken.

Failure.

"You're not a failure," he tells me sternly.

I can't bring myself to care about dropping the shields guarding my mind. What's left to take anyway? I sweep to the bed, sitting on the side away from his old blood, facing the endless books across the shelves, their spines glinting at me in foil letters. All that knowledge I never learned.

Draven sits beside me, hand grasping mine, squeezing when there's no response. "We'll kill Altair, and Kasper, too. There's no death too cruel for what they've done to you."

"How?" I ask, desperate to hold anything to keep my head above the endless tide.

"The way we planned." He searches my face. "We will train. Grow stronger. Become unstoppable. Find the other Arcadian Artifacts. We will never let them see weakness in us again."

"What if I'm not strong enough?" Since I lost my father, my mind has sunk to a darker, tired place.

"You are. And we will burn Nevaeh to the ground if that's what it takes. It won't bring your father back, or undo what's been done. But if bloodshed is the only path to peace . . . to stopping the madness . . . then that's what we do. Gain power to deliver peace."

His hand moves behind me, and he pulls that chalice from the pile of sheets.

"If you want it," he amends. He offers it to me. "You can break your bonds to me, to my father, to being an immortal. With this . . . you can free anyone. Build an army, or save yourself and your loved ones. We can run together . . . if you don't want to fight. If you don't want me after all this . . . you can go. I'll make sure you're safe."

I hold it in my hands, thumbs rubbing the filigree, then look behind myself, to the forgotten box, the engagement bracelet. I pick it up, too, vulnerability appearing along Draven's features, pressed in the upturned arc of his brows, the tightness of his lips, a frown tugging down like anchors. "You're not breaking our vow . . . are you?"

Slowly his lips lift at the corners.

"Not unless you do," he says, some of the playfulness sparking in his dark blue eyes, like sunlight spreading across the waters.

I've lost everything time and time again. But I've never let it stop me, never fallen down so hard I've not been able to get back up. *You are what I'm proudest of.* I would be worthy of that. I'd rescue my mom, find my brother, and take the immortal thrones with Draven at my side and stop this war, save the mortals. For him I would do it. For them. For me.

"We take everything from Altair, like he did to me. We take it all." I slip the bracelet on, where it tightens against my wrist by some magic I don't understand. It's an unbreakable bond . . . like ours. I lift my eyes to Draven's, resolve hardening. "We take our thrones and we destroy anyone who stands in our way."

The dangerous grin across his lips spreads, eyes brightening, like a spark lighting a keg.

"Partners," he agrees.

"Till death," I add.

"Deal." Draven grins wickedly. He pours a bottle of sparkling wine into the chalice, his eyes soft as he tilts it back, downing every drop.

He fills it again and offers it to me, a tension filling the room, as if destiny herself leans in to listen.

I drink.

THE END

Acknowledgments

MY FIRST ACKNOWLEDGMENT goes to YOU the reader. In a sea of amazing stories, you picked up mine. You've supported me and my dreams and a team of people who've believed in me more than I ever have believed in myself. I wrote this book to see a character who looks like me and loves like me get to be the main character in the kinds of stories I grew up adoring and the kinds that helped me discover myself as I came into my own. I hope for some of you, this book helps you feel as seen as it has for me.

The next acknowledgment goes to the love of my life, Ryan, my husband. You bring me laughter, pep talks, and the biggest gift of all, time. You've never stopped believing in me for a second. I honestly don't know if I'd have made it this far without you holding me up, supporting me so that I could pursue this, being an amazing dad and partner in the process. Thank you for making me feel both loved and seen. I love you more than anything.

To my agent, Patrice Caldwell, thank you for believing in this book, for seeing the vision for it and immediately running with it, bringing it to life and holding my hand through everything. You are one of the most badass people I've met, and I'm so grateful every day you chose me. Thank you also to Trinica Sampson-Vera for your guidance, Joanna Volpe for your wonderful encouragement, and the entire New Leaf Literary and the Caldwell Agency teams.

To my publisher Zando and imprint Slowburn for placing so much faith in this romantasy novel, I am so grateful and proud to work with you to bring this book to life. To my editor Nicole Otto for your belief in me. You've made this book SHINE and worked so incredibly hard to take the skeletal draft you first saw and build it up one muscle at a time. Special thank-you to my copy editor Mikayla Butchart for flagging all those raised eyebrows. To Brynne for sliding into my DMs and making me feel so welcome at a publisher full of hugely talented folks. And a special thanks to Sierra Stovall, Hayley Wagreich, Julia McGarry, and the phenomenal Zando and Slowburn teams for your hard work and dedication to this novel.

Thank you to Emily Dodge, my amazing critique partner, who has made me a better writer. I'm here because of your constant encouragement and Zoom calls to talk out magic systems, craft, and plot holes. To Mary Chidiac, thank you so much for kicking your feet with me, keeping me positive, and being my most enthusiastic cheerleader. To Buzz and Jazz, my furry writing companions, I owe you everything but mostly cookies.

To the Writing Community; I've met so many amazing uplifting people. Dana, my witchy sister who always has my back; Berkeley, my debut year sibling who is going big places; Zilla for your amazing advice; Lily X for your encouragement; as well as all my fellow debuts for laughing and crying with me through this wild ride.

To the authors who've broken glass ceilings and taken the time to offer a helping hand for those following in their footsteps— thank you. I particularly want to thank those who took the time to read my novel and offer their enthusiasm and support. Particularly Emily Varga, Cecy Robson, Alexandra Kennington,

Kalie Cassidy, and every author who took the time to offer their kind words and blurbs, which are so helpful for debut authors like myself. Thank you so much to every author and industry person who has lifted me up.

I also want to thank my family and friends who've supported me through all of this and who believed in me. My girl Araceli who would've loved this book, I miss you. A special thanks to my in-laws Dave and Sheree and Grandma Mary, along with the whole family for being so incredibly supportive. To my mom, who has championed me and this dream longest; my brothers, Chris, Ricky, and Sam, for making me funny; my second-mom, Cindy; my nephews, Jeff and Tim; my sisters, Mariko and Lisa; my prima favorita, Dani; my cousin Raven (I can't wait for her to read this); and to all my aunties/tías, uncles/tíos, and cousins/primos in our massive family tree, I love you all to the moon and back.

One reason I wrote this book is because I lost my father, Carlos, at a young age and lived in the shadow of his greatness. Admiring someone who accomplished their dreams and was bigger than life itself led me to loving the fantastical, where heroes could literally be giants. Someone very special to me, my Uncle Sonny, filled his shoes in every way that mattered, and when he died shortly before I started working on this book, I realized how both lucky and heartbreaking it was to have loved and lost not one but two fathers. Rune's pain of losing her dad reflects my loss of both these great men. They taught me to be proud of myself. To believe in myself and shoot for the stars. I know they'd be proud of me, too.

Lastly, I want to thank my son, Oliver, for being my light in the dark, my forever reminder the world is kind and beautiful, and the reason I keep going each day. You have changed my whole world, kiddo. You are so special. I love you.

About the Author

JACLYN RODRIGUEZ is a biracial author of Puerto Rican heritage and has been madly in love with fantasy since before she could walk, forever drawn to magic and the impossible. If there are high stakes and intricate world-building, she's in, and she adores a strong romantic subplot, the more complicated the better. She spends her non-writing time practicing archery and deconstructing her favorite TV shows and films. She currently lives in Tucson, Arizona, with her husband, son, and two quirky dogs. She can be found online at jaclynrodriguezbooks .com. *A Vow in Vengeance* is her debut.

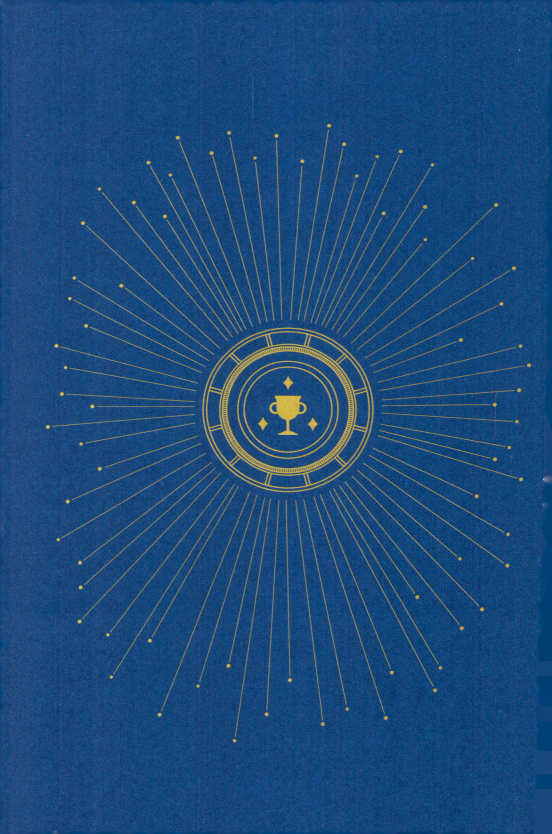